MW01710956

VERUS

VERUS

AND THE

GRAND ASSEMBLY OF BELIEVERS

A SATIRE

WENDEL MESSER

BRELLER BOOKS

Breller Books
RR1, Box 3013, Gravenhurst, Ontario, Canada P1P 1R1
Tel. 705-687-8149 www.thesink.ca

LIBRARY AND ARCHIVES CANADA CATALOGUING IN PUBLICATION

Messer, W. (Wendel), 1939
Verus and the Grand Assembly of Believers : a satire / Wendel Messer.

ISBN 978-0-9730094-3-9

I. Title.

PS8576.765V47 2009 C813'.6 C2009-900267-1

Sheep image used as border on cover: © Gord Darlington
Cover photo: © David Martyn; image from BigStockPhoto.com
Text set in Adobe Jenson and Jupiter
Printed and bound in Canada

The text paper in this book, Rolland Enviro 100 from Cascades, is EcoLogo™ and Forest Stewardship Council certified. It contains 100 per cent post-consumer recycled fibre, was processed chlorine free, and was manufactured using energy from biogas recovered from a municipal landfill site.

This book is for all those who,
since the dawn of our race,
have suffered at the hands of the ministers
to the invisible power fairies in the sky.

In their struggle for the ethical good, teachers of religion must have the stature to give up the doctrine of a personal God, that is, give up that source of fear and hope which in the past placed such vast power in the hands of priests. In their labours they will have to avail themselves of those forces which are capable of cultivating the Good, the True, and the Beautiful in humanity itself. This is, to be sure, a more difficult but an incomparably more worthy task…

Albert Einstein

The object is not to be on the side of the majority, but to avoid finding oneself in the ranks of the insane.

MARCUS AURELIUS

to Eve-Lynn
Uxbridge
June 26th, 2016

Author's Note

Verus is a satire on humankind's most evil and persistent delusion: religion. Though some may see this book as profane, in the sense of "sacrilegious", concepts such as "profanity", "sacrilege", and "sin" have meaning only within the context of theism. For non-theists, the words have no meaning. And those who see theism clearly for what it is—not just a delusion, but a persistent social evil—will no longer be bound by conventions of respect.

Theism deserves no respect; and to accord it is neither wise, rational, nor honest.

Though, at first glance, the book may give a contrary impression, the author's purpose in writing *Verus* is not to make fun of any particular faith, but to ridicule the Grand Assembly of Believers, which is all those who devout themselves to a cult of the invisible. The author's main motivation in choosing to write on this topic is duty informed by a habit of truth.

Man is the measure of all things, and truth is the measure of all men. Truth alone is sacred, entitled to respect, and reverence. The truth knows no sides, belongs to no one, and is influenced by no one. It extends to infinity and endures beyond time. It is never qualified, it is never more or less, better or worse. It neither grows nor shrinks. It does not bend for any tree ape, and not for millions of them, either. It is never revealed through prayer or by invocation. The road to it, though infinite, is open to all who stand erect.

Contents

I	Palace of the Dead	13
II	The *Cura*	26
III	Loose Cannon	35
IV	The Orient Express	47
V	From the Founding of the City	72
VI	Latin Class	83
VII	Oscillation Synchronization	99
VIII	The Thundering Legion	118
IX	Truth as the World Sees It	133
X	The Roman Program	144
XI	Yahweh	160
XII	No Feelings, Please	172
XIII	Computer Logic	192
XIV	More Stubborn Lies	202
XV	Verus Addresses the Grand Assembly	209
XVI	Jupiter Strikes	229
XVII	Castel Gandolfo	251
XVIII	*Oh Quae Redemptio!*	259
XIX	The News from Rome	268
XX	Jupiter Best and Greatest	272

I

The Palace of the Dead

My face—it's wet. Something warm on my face. A dog! A dog is peeing on my face. I am waking. I am hungry. I am thinking. I am alive.

Then ... I am not released? I thought I was. I thought it was over. I thought the sun had set on my little life. Why do I return from the dark night's eternal rest? And to what place? And still with this poor body, which plagued me and failed me, dying but a moment ago and falling into the great abyss of time.

Open your eyes wide, now. Give them a rub. That's it. Tell me what you see.

I see ... a palace. The palace of the dead. Do you remember who you are? Yes, a beggar. Like these men on either side of me. Just a beggar. Search now for your mind, your memory. The words are coming. If there are words, there is memory. If there are words, there is thought.

Who are these rude-looking fellows asleep beside me? Am I one of them? Am I also a beggar? I am not dressed like them. And all these odd-looking people rushing around, everywhere in this great marble palace, who pay us no notice, and who are intent upon going—somewhere.

Why am I different? What happened yesterday? How long ago was that?

My stomach! I need to eat. Starving to death. "Excuse me, can you tell me...what place this is? Where it is?...Where I am?" No answer. No time to listen. Try again. "Help me, please! Somebody help me!...Citizens! Comrades! Brothers and sisters!...We are all related!...In the name of justice!...In the name of reason!... *Humanitas!*"

Oh quae putor! What a stench of urine! It is myself I smell. And these fellows I spent the night with, they also are foul. Outcasts! Scabs on the skin of humanity. And so am I. Should I not, then, be ashamed? And is it not the reason that all these busy bodies passing by avoid us? Because we are unwashed and foul and unashamed?

Are these sleeping beggars my companions? Look now at their faces. None is familiar. And see what misery is written in them! See the lines? The maps of failure?

Well, get thee up and walk. Find something to eat, anything. First eat, then think. Because without nourishment, the mind is useless and cannot rule. Let us have food for the ruling faculty. Wait!—Smell that? Something good. Something I need. And I know it—that familiar kitchen smell— something wonderful, delightful, delicious—Ham! By the gods! Beautiful ham! Man's favourite dish. And I have not eaten for centuries and centuries. Get on your feet, man. On your feet! Find that ham!

Easy now, steady. Take one step—do not lose your balance. Do not stagger! Do not let them see you like this. Left foot forward. That's it, put it forward—move it. Move foot, come on! Now the other. That's the way. Now left again. Now right. Not too fast! That's fine—nobody is looking, nobody cares. Follow them, these strange people. Somewhere ham is cooking. Someone will at least give you bread and water. Oh, for a drink of water!

And something plain and good. Like honey on bread, and water. Like a boiled egg and some water to drink. Like ham and eggs and water. And toast. A glass of Felernian wine—Oh God, a glass of Felernian wine! Cheese and olives and wine! Fresh baked bread! I smell it. I see it. I can taste it. Apples and figs!

I will have these things, if I'm not in the underworld. I will have them. I have slept a thousand years. But I am not dead or I would not need to eat. Not too fast now, easy. These legs are just learning to walk, after—who knows how long? Ages and ages. One step at a time, now. That's it. Easy.

What's this? The voice of a Cyclops! Coming from—from all sides, from everywhere! Don't they hear it? They do not appear to hear anything. Am I the only one? What a palace of strange wonders this is. What a great mystery. What bright lamps. How even is the light from them. Move now and follow those people. Legs, take me there. I shall ask for help. Beg something.

"Nisi molestum est! Eia! Nisi molestum est!"

Do they hear me? Do they see me? "Hey, if it is no trouble!"

No use. They neither see nor hear me. Nor do they appear to be aware of each other. What a palace of shadows this is! But onward! Move those legs. One step at a time. Forward, legs. What's this? Here is something—another great hall. What's in here? Houses? Cabins with ramps in between. Long, long cabins. People rushing to them. Follow them. Discover, if you can, what purpose they serve. Cabins with long rows of windows. People going inside, sitting there, all facing in the same direction. Sitting and facing and waiting and looking. For what? Just sitting and staring, not at each other, but at nothing. Each one appears to be alone. Do they not see each other? For what purpose do they sit there?

It is not one long cabin but a series of cabins—joined. And this underneath looks like ... like a track! But I see no wheels. Is this some kind of monstrous sled? Great Jupiter, how is it propelled? A thousand elephants could not pull this. This is beyond my understanding.

If it had wheels and a steam engine... remember the steam engine Hero is said to have made in Alexandria? Water was boiled in a tank and the wheels moved. But this has no wheels!

When did Hero make that engine? Long before my time. Are you certain of that? Yes. You see how your brain is starting to work, as your mind exerts control? Walk farther on, man, to the other end of this strange thing. Move legs, keep going, keep on moving. There it is! Yes, this one at the end is different, this great iron thing. Not the end—the front. This is the engine. This great beast of iron. But I see no exhalation, and there are no wheels. But I do see... yes, up there - a man! There is a man inside!

"Salve!"

Yes, he sees me. He is smiling at me. They can see me, then. I am not dead. I am not a spirit, I am not. I am alive because they see me. I am alive because I am starving to death. I am alive because my stomach torments me. And my legs are working, and my brain is working.

I recoil as the monster beside me rises, as though at once it has no weight at all, and it floats away; and this happens without effort or straining, the cabins drifting forward without a sound, like something ephemeral, without subtance. What a thing!

But I must eat. Go back where you smelled ham. In the great hall, that's where it is. See, now you almost walk like a man. You are getting used to it. Ah, it is in my nostrils—savoury, delicious ham. In this direction. Hurry now. See those stalls and counters—that is where the food is. The ham is there. And there, the ones I slept with are standing with their hands out. Stand with them, then, and hold out your hand, too, that you may beg and eat.

I look like a beggar, I smell like a beggar, I am a beggar. Beg first, then eat. Oh, hurry! Show them the palm of your hand.

Eia! My drinking companions push me away. My brothers of the gutter. And what is this gibberish they speak, these rude louts, as with gestures and animal sounds they push me away?

All right, goodbye. I am gone.

Go over there, then, away from them, and hold out your hand, there on the other side. Hold it out. That's the way, and make a supplicating gesture, look needy, show your hunger. Ah, here is a gold piece in my hand already. No, copper. And so finely wrought—oh, this is good coin. What does it say? Focus these poor eyes, now. It's coming . . . I see it. Thank God, it's Latin! Strange, I have heard no one speak the language of the world, no one at all. Where in the world am I, for the love of Zeus? And where in time? Certainly, I have been moved, my atoms collected, myself resurrected. And I have been moved in time, far forward from my own time. Unless, the other side of the orb—No, no, surely not.

Another coin is dropped into my hand. Silver. Another coin, another, another. Go now to the counters where people are eating. Go there, away from the others, so they do not complain or chase you away because you stink of all things rotten. Put your money down. There is the waiter. Call him.

"*Eia, puer! Nisi molestum est!*"

"Yes, sir?"

"Yezr! *Ovi, panis, aqua. Nisi molestum est.*"

"Owi?"

I point to my neighbour's plate, three stools to my left. I see beautiful eggs and ham and toast.

"*Ah, va bene, signore!*" The waiter smirks and takes some of my coins. He returns in a few moments. And then—what a feast! *Oh quae deliciae*! Ham and eggs and toast. For the first time since . . . since when? Ages ago. I am ravenous as a wolf. But my mind is in control. I eat slowly, using the small fork utensil provided. Savour every morsel. Prolong the pleasure. And inside me I feel the juices flow, my body coming alive, my brain expanding. My mind is asserting control, trying to rule again over the brain. I am feeling, I am thinking, I am human. I am . . . I am!

Yes. I am. And something else is coming, something. It's my name. My name is—Verus! Verus! I know who I am. I know, I know. I am Verus. And I am a member of the race of reasoning animals called man, the community not just of seed or blood, but of intelligence.

Surely I have not travelled in time and space just to eat ham and eggs and toast? Something else is coming, something else. My brain is waking. *Verus civus Romanus est.* Yes, Verus is a citizen of Rome, a proud fortunate citizen of Rome. My name is Verus. Hold your head up, then, Verus, wherever on earth you may be, wherever in time. Be proud of who you are—Verus and Roman.

At last, comfort and warmth, and strength, from this nourishment, and my mind stirring. And my mind is telling me something: Verus is not come here to eat ham and eggs and toast. That is what I think. And I think I am no beggar. Verus is not a beggar. That is what my mind tells me. No beggar. I am Verus and Roman and not a beggar.

You see how different the world looks on a full stomach? Perception depends, then, on a plate of ham and eggs and toast, with water. And so, all civility and everything good mankind does, is done on the stomach, for man must eat. Everything in the world, great or small, depends on the stomach. Be thankful for your good fortune, then. Now, get thee up and use those legs. Get thee forth. Go out into the world and discover the reasons. With the help of this good nourishment, find answers to your questions. Justify your existence.

Yes, I am not come here without a purpose. I am not risen from the dead to eat ham and eggs.

I will find out where in the world I am, and what place this is in time. And I will find someone who speaks my tongue; and someone does, someone must, or why would the coins be stamped in the language of the world?

Or am I in some far-flung extension of the *Imperium* in some future time? A place in some remote corner of the orb where the barbarians have not yet learned to speak our tongue? A place that resembles Gaul or Hispania in the early days of our rule, though a place far forward in time? Every race submits to us, for it is given to us to rule the world. And the world chooses to live like rational animals, not brutes in the woods, not like Germans or Sarmatians.

I believe this place is on the other side of the orb, in some future time, and all humanity lives under our umbrella of reason and justice, and peace reigns. No more war among the nations, ignorance and superstition long hounded and rooted from the earth. And the mechanical arts, perhaps, have reached perfection. Rome, thy glory knows no bounds. Oh joy! That Verus should be reborn into this world! Go from here, then, and find out the reason, as nothing happens without a cause.

Mors est necessitas naturae!

But if death *is* a necessity of nature, how did I come to be moved to this place? Can atoms in their motion by pure chance so align themselves that the dead are born again? Or can Zeus, who comprises all, and is in all, cancel the laws of nature—by transcending himself?

The *Christiani* claimed their Christus came to life again, after his execution. But who would believe that? No one would. Not those with any sense or education. And yet, here am I, risen from the dead, after—how long? We did not believe the Christiani. Who will believe me? No one will.

Those of my own time are long gone. And now I see—my wife, Faustina! How clear is your image in my mind, my dear wife Faustina. So beautiful, so kind, so serene. Faustina! But do not torment yourself, Verus.

No one in this present time will believe. No one will. But does Verus care what others think or do or say? No. Verus is concerned only with the mind of Verus, not with the minds of others. Every man's mind is in his own care. Verus will look after his.

If the universe has thrown me forward in time, it is not without reason. Am I a conduit for the will of Zeus? I shall see. But first, I must learn more about myself and about this curious world I have entered. Is this some future time or is it, perhaps, some other part of the universe, far from the little nook in space and time where Verus crawled for an instant like a poor worm?

Pictures, everywhere I look. On the walls, on the columns, everywhere. These strange-looking people. Everything covered with smiling faces. Why? All of them smiling stupidly.

And things, strange things. Smiling faces and strange things. And Roman letters. Words that are mostly strange, though not entirely. How curious. Like this poster: *Embrace the helot: prepare for homo mirabilis.*

Ah, here is the way out of this palace. I will go out into the street. What fine Doric columns. What an imposing palace this is. By the gods—the street! What in the name of Jupiter are those things moving in the street! No horses pull them—and the speed! And . . . people inside them. Carriages! They are carriages! Amazing carriages! But how close to each other and how fast! And no animal in sight . . .

What arts to make these things? Why, they appear not to touch the road, as if they have no weight at all. What tools and what principles to fashion them? To make conveyances that do not obey the laws of nature? What keeps them up and what propels them? How do they turn and stop and go, all without wheels? And see how they stop all at the same time—but who gives the signal? Oh, wonder of wonders! Now, see, they start up again, all at the same time. How strange! And—what's that?—Up there in the sky! A machine like a great bird! Soaring silently through the clouds, without effort. What grace! What power! A machine with wings. But what engine—! And what keeps it in the air?

A thousand questions with every step I take. Oh, I am out of time and place. What strange city of the future is this? And where in the All? Oh, wondrous world, what knowledge you possess! And what perfection of the arts. This, surely, is what Rome has done. This is what Rome has given to the world. This is where it all leads. And the social arts—have they, too, been brought to perfection? Do reason and justice reign?

I find the place where men evacuate. I look at myself in the row of mirrors. I am not as old as I thought. I try to wash myself at the basins but I cannot get the taps to work. There is no lever. There is nothing.

I retreat into the columned portico of this fine Roman building. The language on the notices, edicts, whatever they are—the letters are Roman. The alphabet is Roman. And the words ... the words are ... strange and foreign—but! Some of them say things to me. The roots appear to be Latin. And some of these words do have meaning. But it is all so corrupted, with strange endings and truncations, all in a meaningless jumble without syntax.

Where in time and place?

I have seen how language changes over time. I saw that when I—lived! If this is true, what a dreadful disastrous mutation! What an unbelievable degradation. Although in the provinces ... or outside the Imperium—Germania Magna, perhaps. Yes, possible, the land of the Germans. The barbarians might do this. But how do you know you are not on the other side of the world? Or even on another orb in heaven? Somewhere else in this great universe? You do not know.

First things first. What do I know about myself? That I am Roman? Yes, I have no doubt. And I know my mind has ranged far and wide, beyond even the confines of the universe. Yes, I know I saw it from the outside. I saw it all. I know I did.

And what did I see from outside the universe, as my mind wandered at the edge of the All? I saw sameness of form and shortness of duration, everywhere and for all time. That is what I saw. The material world in all its misery. The chain of causes and events that once was set in motion by the Prime Cause. The spinning of the cloth I saw, the weaving of destiny, the fate of all things, from the beginning determined by the intelligence of the All, to the end of time; or till the next conflagration of the universe, when the All is again consumed by the eternal fire. Then the universe is reborn and expands again, and so on forever and ever without end.

But who taught me this? Heraclitus? Permenides? Names from the back of my mind. Important names. That signify—what?

It does not matter whether one lives five years or a hundred. There—another thought from my poor life. Look at yourself in the mirror, Verus. Is this your dying face? You are not an old man. And there is light in those poor eyes. How old could I be? However old I may be now, if age still applies, I know I thought I was an old man when I died. But looking in the mirror ... And to that add all the time that has passed ... I wonder?

If you would be an old man long, you must be an old man in good time.

What else is in this mind of yours? Dig down into it and see. Do you believe in the gods? Well? No answer. Verus does not answer. I think perhaps Verus does not believe. But if Verus does believe, then I think perhaps he believes in the rule of chance, the gods setting everything in motion and then withdrawing, never to interfere again.

But if chance rules, it does not rule Verus.

How could chance rule and I be resurrected from the dead—poor simple Roman beggar! Here is your proof that the gods exist! Chance cannot create a complex thing. What better proof the gods exist than to be resurrected? Verus is risen from the dead. Is this not proof enough?

But then, if the gods have not brought me to some heavenly orb, then surely they have caused me to travel in time. A hundred thousand years? Ten hundreds of thousands? Yes, I have travelled far in space and in time, so far from my own indivisible moment and nook on earth, my own little worm hole—that yet was Rome! The city of the seven hills, founded by the wolf-suckled brothers, Romulus and Remus. The city of destiny.

This that has happened to me is a violation of nature's laws. A violation of the laws and constitution of the universe. A violation of reason, philosophy, everything. And that, clearly, is not possible ... should not be possible. But only if one rules out intervention by the gods—by the gods! The gods who use me for their purposes—it must be so. The gods whose messenger I was in Rome! Yes, I am sure of it! The gods who favoured me in the life I lived. My life as—as what? Teacher? Philosopher? Priest? A life, I think, devoted to knowledge. Knowledge. Which, according to—someone on the tip of my tongue—is the only good. According to Socrates!

I must believe, then. Verus must believe. Yes, I do believe.

Things do not interest me. Not power, not fame nor reputation; not wealth, not honours, office, medals, applause—none of that. All smoke and mirrors. The universe is change. Life is opinion. This is what I find in my poor mind. This is Verus. This is who I am. It is all in the mind.

What do I know about myself? What do I know about the universe? Is not knowledge of both the same thing, if I am part of the universe? And consider that the brain does not reach its target in a straight line, like an arrow; yet, it is right on course. If only the ruling faculty is on her throne.

Can I affirm that mine was a life of duty? Surely I can. On what do I base this? On feeling? Predisposition? Intuition? Perhaps my coming again is a reward from the gods that govern the universe, the gods who *are* the universe, those who once breathed life into all things, and who breathed the eternal fire of reason into the minds of men. These things I know to be true. I think they are true.

If I am here by the will of the gods, why then do I shrink and tremble at these strange sights and sounds around me? Why am I so fearful if the immortals have chosen me for something new? Rejoice at the thought and thank them.

Thank you, gods! Thank you!

But have you nothing to say to me? I am here! I have arrived! I am ready! Speak to me however you will! In signs, in dreams, however you wish. What is the matter, great Zeus? Can you not see me! Verus is here! Verus is ready! Speak to me!

God does rule or I would not be here. And if Zeus rules, all is well.

Surely he has brought me far in time and space on some great errand that yet shall be revealed to me in his own good time; or else I shall discover it, according to his will. To me then, alone among men, it is given to live again. To rise and live again. Perhaps to be the messenger of the gods among men. To teach them to live according to nature.

Look through these glass doors and see—It is snowing. I have walked in snow, slept in it, somewhere in the north. Somewhere in a land thick with spruce and pine. This, then, is a northern clime, but if this is still the earth, then where? I know I died in a cold place, and for all I know, this could be that place—though in some other time! If I receive nothing from the gods in dreams or other signs, I shall make my way to Rome, if it is not too vain a conceit to think that Rome still is, that sacred place in Latium, which, the poets say, must endure forever. But everything will unfold as it must, according to the will of Zeus.

But listen! Music! Strange and wonderful sounds! Coming from—nowhere, everywhere, around me—I think the very walls! But hear those words—*Adeste fideles*! By all the gods, rejoice! They sing in Latin! They sing in the language of the world. And it is as it should be. Yes, let the faithful come. Here I am. I am Verus. I am faithful.

Verus, Roman, and faithful. I am come to do what has been set forth for me. I am ready to serve. So move legs. Let us go out from this place. Nothing happens without a reason. What is my errand here? I shall seek it out.

For the truth is to think in accord with reason and to act in accord with justice. I do not stand and wait or hold back. I am ready to fulfill my purpose on earth. So I raise high my banner of reason. Here is the doorway. Step forth now unafraid. Step out into the light of day.

II

The Cura

At St. John the Compassionate Mission we scan the tables. They're having soup and roast beef with mashed potatoes, eating mechanically, silently, bent over their plates.

But we do not see Verus.

Jancie and I take the subway to Union Station and head for my car. For a while it looks like it's going to snow but it hasn't done that for five years. Inside me I can hear the music of Tchaikovsky. I feel Jancie's tug at my coat and I think how lucky I am. As we leave Union Station, there is a disturbance.

Verus! They're beating him up! One guy has a knife! Without taking time to think, I hit the knife guy from behind and knock him to the ground. I get the knife. The street people scatter. Verus sits there looking confused.

"It's gonna be below freezing tonight," Jancie says. "Let's take him to a hostel."

"Not in *my* car. He stinks."

"Joe, it's Christmas." Jancie takes me by the arm and looks into my eyes. I suppose she considers it her Christian duty. I take a good look at Verus for the first time: high brow, large nose, curly hair, beard slightly streaked with grey. I see something reassuring in his eyes, even prophetic and regal. He smells like a sewer but he looks intelligent. He has a certain dignity.

"*Maxima calamitas!*" he cries. "*O quae comoedia!*"

Jancie gives me a prod. "What's he saying? You're the Latin teacher for goshsake!"

"*Was* the Latin teacher." I can't find the words I need, let alone put them in the right order. I give Verus a line I remember from my Latin copy of *Winnie-the-Pooh*, to keep up appearances with Jancie as a Latin expert. The words mean: Only one way is known to go down stairs. I look into the street person's eyes and I say loudly: "*Est quod sciat unus et solus modus gradibus descendendi.*"

My Latin brings a twinkle to the eyes of Verus. I think I can even detect a small smirk crossing his lips. "*Gradibus?*" he says.

I call up the hostel on my wristcom.

"We're full," says a girl's voice. "The churches want to open their doors. The neighbourhoods won't let them, sons of bitches! Afraid of contamination. Besides, think what it might do to property values!"

"Yeah, that would be rough!"

"We can give him a sleeping bag," the mission girl says. "And coffee and doughnuts."

"That's all?"

"We have no resources. Why don't you take him home?"

There's a long pause, then I say, "Are you kidding?"

"Of course I am!"

"Well Christ!"

"Christ has nothing to do with it. You're not afraid of contamination, are you?"

"Jesus!"

At the YMCA I have to show Verus how to use the soap, as he appears pretty clueless. While I'm doing that, Jancie goes to buy clothes for him at the second-hand shops. He looks awkward in the things we give him. He gets into the car and starts to behave as if he's never been in one before in all his life, jumping around and making small noises. We stop at a burger bar on the way and we all have hamburgers and fries and coffee. I have to get a second order for Verus, who appears half starved.

"I bet he's a professor of Latin," I say. "Look at those eyes. Got a knock on the head and now he thinks he's his Roman alter ego."

"What a nice face he has, Joe," says Jancie. "So dignified. Did he have any identification?"

"No, he didn't. Don't worry, Verus, we'll take you to the police. They'll find out where you belong."

We take the air route north. Verus keeps his face glued to the window and cries out in surprise at everything he sees. We give him some porridge when we get home and I set up a cot for him in the living room. I have to show him how things work. When the night lights come on we hit the sack. I fall asleep at once, but throughout the night, the silence is broken by the nightmares Verus seems to be having. I can hear Verus muttering in Latin, saying a few phrases over and over again: *"Qui nimiam virtutis speciem prae se fert!... per deos immortales!... Heus! Heus tu quid agis!..."*

At dawn, laughter wakes me up. Verus is sitting in the command chair—at my computer—reading *Winnie ille Pu* and obviously enjoying it. *"Est quod sciat unus et solus modus gradibus descendendi!"* he cries triumphantly as I appear.

I fry eggs and a bunch of sausages in olive oil. Buttered toast and coffee. That makes Verus happy. He eats like a wolf. I can't help thinking that bringing him home is going to cost me.

Verus persists in speaking Latin. I struggle to follow him but my university Latin is hardly up to it. Some things I easily get the gist of. He tells me he hasn't eaten for ages and ages, which I understand. He says he loves fried eggs and toast—also obvious. He says much more, the meaning of which I fail to grasp completely. I suppose I never was exactly the world's best Latin teacher.

His eyes are even more intelligent now that he has food in his stomach. Verus speaks slowly and repeats when I don't understand. I'm making frenetic use of my wristcom for Latin equivalents. Sometimes I resort to letting the wristcom be my interpreter, though I don't rely on it because of occasional errors. I have a feeling that my Latin will vastly improve in the coming days.

Jancie keeps giving me digs. "What's he saying, Joe?" she cries. "Tell me what he's saying. Hurry up!"

"He says he fell asleep somewhere after not having eaten for a week. He woke up under the portico of the great building with the iron engines. He saw many strange and marvellous things. *Macinae!* Machines everywhere, with people inside, moving at dangerous speed, many times faster than a horse. He saw the great engines that floated and were filled with people. He followed the others to the eating place—the mission—and he ate with them."

"Gee, Joe, he sure sounds lost. He's totally out of it."

"I'm taking you to the police" I try to explain to Verus. "The *Cura*. So they can find out where you belong and answer all your questions. *Urbanae securitatis cura!* Did I get that right? *Vigiles . . . Custodes*. Don't worry, Verus. We'll find out who you are. We'll find out where you belong."

"Please fill out a Missing Person Report, Mr. Matchdatch," says the OPP officer at the desk in Breckenridge. She's a prim and officious-looking young lady. "Be sure to include a full description, the circumstances leading up to the report, the mental state of the person, and any vehicles used by him."

"No, officer, he's not missing," I say. "He's right here. This is the man who is missing. His identity is missing. He doesn't know who he is or where he belongs. That's why he's missing."

The officer's mouth curls ironically. "Do you have any identification?" she asks Verus.

"No, he doesn't."

"Can you speak for yourself, sir?"

"No, he can't. He doesn't speak English."

"What language does he speak?"

"Latin." The police officer gives us a wry look and eyes us suspiciously. "That's right, officer, classical Latin. Julius Caesar and all that. You know—*Est quod sciat unus et solus modus gradibus descendendi.*"

The officer leers. She gives a nervous little laugh.

"*Lingua Latina!*" Verus bursts out. He really looks awkward in those clothes we gave him. "*Lingua Latina!*"

The officer studies each of us in turn. Another small laugh. "Are you related to this man or are you just a friend?"

"Neither. I found him in Toronto. He was sleeping outside. I'm just trying to help him find out who he is and where he belongs."

"Constable Sharp is good at languages, if you'd—!"

"I'm good at languages myself, officer. I used to teach Latin, French, and Italian. This man speaks only Latin, and he speaks it extraordinarily well, as far as I can judge. He might be a professor or a scholar who has suffered some trauma. Maybe lost the memory of his native tongue. If it's possible to do that. I don't know."

The officer calls Constable Sharp. "How may I be of assistance?" Constable Sharp says, scrutinizing us with a wary eye. "Is this the lost gentleman?"

"Yes, sir. His name is 'Verus' ... He thinks his name is 'Verus.'"

"He thinks!" Constable Sharp opens a drawer and shuffles some papers. "Ah, here we are. How do you spell that?"

"V-e-r-u-s—Verus."

"'V' and not 'w'? Sounds to me like it begins with 'w'.

"It does begin with 'w'—I mean the pronunciation. The Romans had no 'v' sound. Their 'v' is really a 'w.'"

Constable Sharp gives me a wry look. "Okay, I'll put that in brackets: pronounce 'v' as 'w'. And are you related to, ah, Verus?"

"No, sir."

Constable Sharp speaks to Verus in Italian, Romanian, German, and French. Verus looks both curious and amused at these efforts. His eyes dance at this jumble of sounds. He responds in Latin. He apparently does not understand.

"Has he got a place to stay?"

"I can keep him for a while."

"You may be at risk," Officer Sharp says, as he takes us down the hall to his office, where he weighs, measures, and photographs Verus. To the computer he says, "Make up a poster. Check restaurants, coffee shops, stores, hospitals, bus and taxi companies, emergency social services, mental health and educational establishments, prisons, retirement residences. Start with Union Station—that's our PFS—place first seen." The officer turns to me. "You don't know any of his friends or relatives?"

"No, sir."

"So then, we have a physical description but we don't know his legal status, age, or language. What's his surname?"

"He doesn't know that."

"Language spoken—Latin! Ha-ha-ha! That's rich! That's a good one." Officer Sharp considers a moment and says, "What's your profession, Mister Matchdatch? Are you also a Latin specialist?"

"I was a Latin teacher at U of T, till they dropped Latin, but now I sell a book I wrote, *Ancient Roman Recipes*."

"Is that so? Roman recipes, eh? Did the Romans eat pizza? Did they have fast food?"

"Fast food? Yes, sir. No sir, I don't think they had pizza. At least, we don't know. Well, anyone can bake some unleavened bread, I suppose, and sprinkle it with cheese and olive oil. They probably did do that."

"Did they have pasta?"

"Yes, sir. We know that from the wall murals at Herculaneum or Pompeii, I forget which."

"Murals, eh? Paintings that show them eating pasta?"

"Yes."

"Spaghetti?"

"Something like that."

"I love spaghetti. With meatballs. Did they have tomato sauce?"

"No, sir."

"No ketchup, either, I'll bet. Ancient Roman recipes, eh? What kind of recipes?"

"Oh, mostly sweet and sour. Honey, vinegar, lemons. They were big on sweet and sour."

"Is that a fact? Sweet and sour and pasta without tomato sauce. I think I'll pass. Hmm. So you do a Roman cookbook and this fellow is passing himself off as an ancient Roman. I don't smell a rat here, do I? Do I smell a rat, Mr. Matchdatch?"

"No, sir. There is no rat. It's just the way it is."

"You know, Mr. Matchdatch, we'll soon find out just how good his Latin is. You bet we will. We'll soon find out who he is."

"His Latin is much better than mine, officer. Far better. The trouble is, there are so many things in today's world that don't have a Latin equivalent. But I've found some help on the Net. A Minim friar who works for the Vatican. He's their Latinist. He's promised to help me understand Verus."

"Is that so? Is that a fact?" Officer Sharp sneers. "You wish to proceed with this, then?"

"Yes, of course."

Officer Sharp gives us a penetrating look. "Now, has Verus here mentioned anyone or any place that might help us locate people that know him?" Officer Sharp guffaws. "Excluding ancient Rome as a time frame," he says.

"Just the street people. And St. John the Compassionate—the mission where he says he ate. I think it was just a couple of times he ate there."

"Ask him where he ate before that."

"He doesn't remember."

"Ask him again."

I put some halting questions to Verus in Latin. Verus has really perked up since he's gotten some good grub inside him. His eyes are dancing. He looks like a kid in a candy store. "The only thing he remembers," I say to Officer Sharp, "is that he was ill in a cold place and lay down to die. That might have been a couple of days ago. And, ah, apparently it was somewhere in Italy."

"Italy? And yet he doesn't speak Italian. Was he intoxicated when you found him?"

"No, he wasn't. Had some dizzy spells, though."

"I see. Dizzy spells—d-i-z-z-y... Places known to frequent—unknown. Financial account details—bank account, credit and debit card?"

"No, sir."

"Benefits? No. Location where he might collect them? No. Circumstances or events—unknown. Clothing—Roma toga—t-o-g-a. Haw-haw, that's rich! That's really good. That's really something. DNA sample for subsequent forensic examination—will not be necessary. Suspected trauma. T-r-a-u-m-a. No memory. Confused but appears intelligent. What's the state of his mind, would you say?"

"It's hard to say, officer. He seems to be lucid, apart from memory loss. He doesn't recognize common things. Ordinary everyday things. Everything surprises him, as if he's seeing things for the first time. He's just like a kid."

"I see. Has he been grinning stupidly like this since you found him?"

I look at Verus. Verus gives me a wink. "Yeah, Jeez, just about. He doesn't appear to be worried about anything."

Officer Sharp gives us a suspicious glance. "I want you to take him for a medical checkup immediately. It should include a psychiatric assessment. Tell the doctors to send the report directly to me as soon as it's available. You don't have to keep him, you know."

"It's okay."

"All right, he's on file. Verus, the Roman! A lost person not lost. Haw-haw, that's rich! That's really good. This is gonna make my day. Physically present, mentally absent. Fairly common profile these days, don't you think? Okay, his file is up. I'll need your consent for the media—sign here."

III

Loose Cannon

What a privilege it is as a Christian, and as a member of the human race, to be involved in this broadcast. And what a great event this is. Just listen to the crowd. They've never seen anything like this. The pomp, the circumstance, the glory. Here he comes, Pope Innocent XIV, Christ's vicar on earth. What a man! What a priest! What a pope!

Well, I can tell you, the world has never had a pope like this. He has promised to turn the Church on its head. He has promised to set the world on fire. Certainly the young Catholics of Europe are behind him. See the joy on the faces of the young people assembled here, from all of Europe, from the whole world. The raw exultation. This is their man. A revolutionary is on the throne of Saint Peter. *Gloria, gloria, in excelsis Deo!* You can tell by my voice, I share their admiration, their adulation of this most holy man. He is the man for today, for this terrible century. For a world on the brink.

We move in closer to the Holy Father. What serenity! What conviction! What compassion! What faith! It's all written there in that divine face. Yes, the world needs him. This is a man who has faced unafraid numerous enemies of the Church, enemies of the human race. He has witnessed the terrorist attacks on the great cities of Europe first hand. He has courageously faced the destroyers of civilization around the globe—the American Taliban, fanatics of every stripe. And he has made it his mission to convert the world to his faith.

I recall his words after the bombing of Paris. "The world has lost a great city," he said. "It can never be replaced, never rebuilt. That part of France will be uninhabitable for generations. But from the ashes of Paris something great is born. A tide of righteousness that will envelop the world. Only faith in Christ Jesus can withstand the crimes of a world gone mad."

How true that is. How necessary in a world where one deranged misfit can utterly destroy the capital of France, one of the great cities of Europe, one or the world's great monuments... Excuse me. I'm sorry for the emotion, I can't help it; it's just overwhelming. Gone—that great city! Utterly obliterated, down to the last stone. And in its place—a desert. A place without life. What dreadful times we live in! The UN is powerless to exert its lawful authority. Rebellion everywhere. Radiation has almost depopulated Belgium and the Netherlands and the south of England, one of the results, of course, being that the Holy City is now the capital of Europe. I should say, once again the capital of Europe, thinking of Roman times.

Thank God that Rome is safe. The measures are draconian but they are necessary. The city now has more police than any other city in the world. And we have the helots. Thank God for them. That we have these guardians. And thank God that the EU was first with them. The helots will not fail. I never thought the day would come when we'd depend on them. But the helots are trustworthy. They are essentially the same as we are. They are trustworthy. I'm certain of that.

The monuments are safe, everything enclosed in glass or steel, locked, secure. The shields are up everywhere. We've paid a terrible price in accessibility. The security in this city is so tight you can't go more than a few steps without being questioned. But we welcome it.

We can't take any chances. What happened to Paris must never happen to the Eternal City.

What a dreadful time we live in. It is, then, a time for faith. And you can see it on these adoring faces in the crowd. The Christian faith will overcome. Praise God, it will overcome. The planet is dying. Governments are helpless against the extremists on all sides. The terrible atrocities. The barbarians are at the gate, everywhere. They are at the gate. In Europe, in America, in the far east. But Christ will overcome.

And we thought not so long ago that the twentieth century was the true age of man's greatest crimes against man! How naïve we were! The man-made misery of this world seems never complete. It stretches over the whole history of humanity. It seems to be getting worse. The worms of the earth, however low and miserable, misguided or oppressed, now have the means to send this planet over the edge, as if the rising flood tides around the world—poverty, plague, and disease, and the inability to feed ourselves—were not enough. The world cries out for deliverance. The world cries out!

And those of us gathered here in this holy place, where the faith of ages endures—we know that without a surrender to Christ, nothing will change. So we say to those of you still sitting on the fence, still racked by doubt, we say—surrender! Give yourself over to Christ. Trust in Him—heart, soul, and mind. Surrender before it is too late... I'm sorry for the tears. I can't help it. These are very difficult times.

Our faith has been strengthened by the events of our time. Some say it was what the Church needed to succeed... God only knows, we need success. Our numbers are down. Way down. The Church has been in retreat. All religions are in retreat, around this sad world. Belief is in danger. The godless are everywhere. We are mocked, ridiculed, shunned. But we will not go away.

This man of such great faith and energy, this George Adolf Schweinrue from Klöpfendorf, Germany, once a simple monk, a worker in the vineyards along the Mosel, and a tender of swine, this humble man who is now the leader of all Christians—he is a pope who has spent his first year as Peter's successor chasing round the globe putting out fires.

And he has started some fires himself. And we say: Good for you, Holy Father! ... You will recall that a rapprochement with the Orthodox Church is now likely, thanks to His Holiness. The Anglican Church returned to the fold many years ago. Survival is forcing us to overcome our differences. Even the Muslims are being courted. Remember the Holy Father's famous dialogue with the Mufti of Mecca, when he was the target of all those muffin-throwing Muslims in Medina? As if a few spiced cupcakes would deter the successor of Peter, the rock of Rome. But since then, thank the Almighty, His Holiness and the Mufti appear to have gotten on splendidly. They see that religion everywhere has been pushed to the wall.

How fortunate we are that tragedy was averted the other day in Constantinople, where the Holy Father was stoned merely for calling the city by its ancient name—Constantinople. Constantinople, second capital of the Roman Empire, city of Constantine. The infidel cannon breached the walls in 1453. The Turks took the last remnant of the Eastern Roman Empire. The Turks were delighted to find in that great city a flame that had been lit in antiquity by Greece and Rome. I refer to the search for knowledge. The Turks were willing to learn. And they found there another light, which they thought they could snuff out. They tried and they failed. It was the light of Jesus Christ! And the light of Jesus will never be snuffed out.

Two major points of dispute with Islam still remain. In the Roman view, God is subject to the laws of his own creation, whereas the Muslim view is that God is not subject to his own laws. The Muslims claim that the Roman Church, having had its war against science, and having ultimately lost that war, has long since found ways to associate science and belief, so as not to completely alienate the educated classes, and also to diffuse criticism, however unwarranted.

The other sticking point with the Muslims concerns the very nature of Jesus Christ as godhead. The Muslims still need to be persuaded of the divinity of Our Lord. On both these issues the new pontiff has made little headway. But the dialogue with Islam is still very real and there is reason for optimism.

The Pontiff would like to see a broad consensus on the fundamentals of faith before we make a final commitment to the new man, *homo mirabilis*. His Holiness has grave concerns about the whole plan, however necessary it may appear, whatever draconian measures we may be compelled to take. Indeed, the Pontiff fears the project could be a major threat to the survival of our faith. And there has been violent opposition to it from some cardinals, notably Cardinal Pepin.

"Homo mirabilis will not save the world," the Pontiff has said. "Only faith in Christ Jesus can do that." The Pontiff also said, "We do need good arguments, forceful arguments. We must show them where their errors lie. There must be an end to dissension, fanaticism. The road to peace requires vision, the willingness to act, to take risks."

And using reason, His Holiness has effectively countered the arguments of the new heresies. For instance, those who wish to make Christianity more "palatable", to use a favourite word of those poor confused souls. What they want to do is eviscerate all religion. For example, the idea of a natural birth for the Virgin—some saying that Christ was sired by a Roman soldier. The idea that Jesus was more interested in political opposition to Rome than in his duties as a rabbi; the idea that his message was meant only for fellow Jews; the idea that the gospels are thoroughly Romanized fantasies of the life of Jesus; the idea that all the great progressive thoughts of Jesus that we find in the New Testament were not his words at all, but were put into his mouth by the gospel writers, and were stolen from the stoics and other Greek and Roman philosophers; in short, the idea that we should accept the gospels as nothing more than ... well, fables—all this dreadful nonsense! These stubborn lies!

What we are witnessing here in this sacred place is nothing less than a crusade. And it's not a metaphor I'm using. This is a crusade we are witnessing. It is a real crusade. This is a political pope, a proselytizing pope, a temporal as well as a spiritual leader. Europe, he believes, must be a theocracy, if civilization is to survive. It has been said of him that he intends to conquer the world. And you can see it here, reflected in thousands of adoring faces.

There, a close up of the Pontiff. Serenity and resolve are both there. You can see Caesar there as well as Christ. Truly, this is the man to bring Caesar and Christ together. This is a young pope, a sexy and athletic pope, a pope with a complex charisma. This is a pope who wrestles. He's even wrestled in Cincinnati. Cynics say his athleticism is all for the sake of image; others, that it's the natural exuberance of a man who loves life.

And how apt it is that once again the Holy Father should be a German, considering the Christian revival that has taken place in his homeland, after the depredations of both religious fanatics and neo-fascists, the floods and the terrible famines, and most recently the pandemic which has all but depopulated eastern Germany, as well as Poland. The legacy of our greedy forebears.

George Adolf Schweinrue is a man who has made it his mission to change the world. And you can see by the expression on his divine face that he will do it. The hope that flows from faith in Jesus Christ can vanquish even the darkness of this world. The Truth of Jesus Christ is the only hope for this dark world. Christ will vanquish. We can see it, we can feel it, we know it will happen—Alleluia!

And remember, this is a humanist pope. The vicar of Christ is a dedicated humanist. His humanism extends even to the helots, whom he has termed "the slaves of our time". Some of the altar boys you're looking at are, in fact, helots.

The helots, of course, as such, will have only a temporary existence. That will give us time to get used to them. Time to watch for anything that isn't right. So that when men and women consign their minds to them, they will be ready and we will be ready.

But the helots do have full human capacity, those that were given it. That's not in doubt. We made them—the EU made them. And we made them to save ourselves from a disintegrating world. To save humanity. There is no other way.

They are not natural but synthetic. A vast improvement on the human body. Manufactured, not cloned. Most of them have been given generic minds, without some of the ego-essential attributes of personality. Though they behave as individuals, their programs are fail-safe against the development of a strong ego. There—a close-up of one of the helot altar boys. They are rational and social and easy to get along with. And this is only proper, since we intend to put our own minds in the physical space now occupied by *their* minds. We shall occupy their bodies and we shall replace their minds with our minds.

And yet, comparing the helots, as they are now, with ourselves, who is able to tell the difference? No one is. Take a helot by the hand, touch the skin, speak to it, look into its eyes—the only way you know it's a helot is by the small stamp on the forehead. And so His Holiness has declared that whatever is fully human in behaviour—*is* human. His Holiness has argued in favour of recognizing them as a race of mankind, rather than as machines to be used and abused. They might then be admitted to the Church.

At present, only a few helots are capable of the full range of human emotion. Of course, emotion is not necessary for the survival of a synthetic being. And emotion has been described as the biological baggage from prehistoric times. A result of evolution that, now perhaps, is as necessary to us as the human appendix. Animals need cues from the environment in order to survive, to mate, and so on. But humankind now has no further use for these cues.

And indeed, the great evils of the human race all stem from the capacity to feel—to emote. The Holy Father is fully aware of this. To those who would blame religion for most of the strife in this world, he is quick to point out that it is not religion that lies at the root of the world's troubles, but human emotion. Essentially, emotion is the predisposition to react to the world in terms of ego, without sufficient rational examination of circumstances and motives.

The promise of freedom from this primitive part of our makeup is the main reason why the Holy Father is in favour of the homo mirabilis upgrade. And the Pontiff's own secretary and Latinist, Minim friar Gregory O'Riley, is head of the project. Brother Gregory is a brilliant man, a doctor in neuroscience. We are fortunate to have one of our own in charge.

Unfortunately, regulations have not kept pace with the production of helots, nor indeed with the computers that have created them. I have been told that there are several experimental helots who are loose—"loose" is the word that comes to mind—who are loose with a full range of human feelings. There are about fifty helots, the first ever created, that have been purchased for various enterprises, principally in North America. Some of these helots also have the full range of human emotion, depending on the purposes for which they are used. Whether or not this is a good thing remains to be seen.

Some helots have argued that they have everything humans have and more. They have a better computer, better self-control, and more success living according to justice and reason. Hence, they have been clamouring for the same rights as humans. A few helots go further than this. They argue that they are demonstrably better than humans and should therefore be the ones to govern this planet. Brother Gregory has been criticized for letting fully sentient helots loose like this. But in fact, the sale of these helots is helping to finance the production of more helots.

But the majority of helots, about two hundred individuals, have been assigned to those for whom they will be the host body. Which is to say, those who will be upgrading first to homo mirabilis, most of them citizens of the EU. These helots have a basic range of human emotive capacity, and we know who they are and where they are. They also have the ability to turn their emotions off. The result is, they are far better at self-control than humans. They are far better at being rational. And they are far better at being social. They get on quite well without the ego.

There are many safeguards in place. Notable is the identifying mark, the 'H' stamped on the forehead. And also the fact that helots are denied the right to organize and to assemble in groups larger than five. Clearly, there are dangers both to human society and to the race of helots.

Otherwise, the rights and obligations of sentient helots, those who have feelings analogous to humans, are currently being codified by the UN Task Force on Human-Helot Relations. Basically, helots with a human capacity to feel are to be recognized as having the same rights as humans. Apparently, it would be logical to assume, then, that these helots would have a right to exist on their own, and would not be used as vehicles for the preservation of human life. His Holiness has worked indefatigably to have this view written into the lex universalis. At present, there are no such rights for helots that have no ability to experience human feelings in any full sense. And indeed, there should not be.

What many regard, of course, as the supreme irony of the ages, is the fact that the helots, who not only look like us, and are in every respect like us, and who have the capability to feel as we do, while being able to reason at a level beyond the great minds in human history, do not suffer from the one thing that defines the human condition—if one disregards the human incapacity to be governed by reason: helots do not die. They are not mortal.

This is, of course, the reason for their existence. When the time comes, helots and humans will merge into homo mirabilis. The plan now appears all but unstoppable. His Holiness is somewhat concerned that some may see the plan as an opportunity to further undermine the authority of the Church. Certainly, Cardinal Pepin is adamant against it. And God only knows, the authority of the Church has already been severely tested by the rampant materialism of this age. His Holiness has warned that any plan that does not take into account man's capacity for things spiritual is bound to fail.

Death does not trouble the helots. And this at a time when humanity is itself increasingly bionic. Or otherwise put, humanity, day by day, approaches the condition of the helots; it is a truism among scientists that human mortality will very soon be a thing of the past. In other words, the differences that separate humans and helots are not only temporary, but decreasing, almost day by day. And what separates us will eventually disappear in the foreseeable future; some say as soon as within a year or two. Essentially, humanity is undergoing a profound metamorphosis. The real questions are: Is this the end of the human race? Will the Faith survive?

I can assure you that the Holy Father has all this very much in mind—the future of the Church, and of spirituality in general, during a time in which humanity is so fundamentally redefining itself—perhaps, taking leave of itself. One can only wonder what the prospects will be for our faith, once the human condition is lifted. Once man is no longer mortal. Indeed, the numbers of the faithful have... The faithful have—!

Hello, what's happening here?

There seems to be a disturbance in the centre aisle. Some distraction, I'm not quite sure what... You can see people are looking that way ... One is reminded of the Easter Mass in Santa Maria Maggiore ... when a helot went berserk during communion ... took the biscuit and wine from Cardinal Pepin and ... and consumed it.

But such, I fear, are the times we live in. Basic respect and decency are just not there. Atheists and neo-pagans of every stripe are becoming increasingly bold ... using the helots as weapons ... God knows, some of the helots are only too willing. There it is! We have a close up. Something moving along the centre aisle. It's not a helot ... something small ...

The Swiss Guard have cornered it, whatever it is. It seems to be ... appears to be a ... a dog. No, by heaven it looks more like a wolf. And ... it has a jacket bearing the words ... I think it says, "Papal Bull" ... The wolf is showing its teeth, snarling. Wagging its tail and showing its teeth. Isn't that strange? The Swiss Guard are talking to it. Yes, yes they are. And strike me if the wolf is not talking back! The wolf is shouting, in fact. Shouting obscenities! I can hear him from up here. What can this mean?

What a sad deed this is! The Pontiff is not disturbed; just look at that smile. Hijinks do not bother this man. No, no more than the insistent pestering of a fly or a mosquito. And the flies of this world are numerous, for this is a world of wayward souls.

How sad that there are so many today who have nothing to offer but doubt and negativism. People who have no faith. They believe in nothing. They have no spiritual life. No morals. They are not content to wallow alone in the slops of their own degraded minds, afflicted as they are by that great perversion of the soul—relativism. Moral and ethical relativism. They want us to believe that there is no absolute right and wrong, no eternal standard of good and evil, no enduring Truth and falsehood.

Such is the end product of four hundred and fifty years of so-called free thinking, a period in which the authority of the Church has all but dissolved. The numbers of the faithful are down drastically from only a few years ago. I hate to say it but I believe that homo mirabilis is to blame. People are putting their faith in him, instead of in Christ.

We've seen here today, in this senseless interruption, an apt demonstration of what the faithless have to contribute to human society, these so-called freethinkers. They are surely to be pitied.

But what's this? The Swiss Guard are speaking to members of the Curia. They're ... They appear to be ... forcibly extracting someone from the front row. Who? I can't see who it is. Just a moment ... I'm told it may be the Vatican Latinist, Brother Gregory ... Yes, it is. It's the Holy Father's Latinist, Brother Gregory. What could be the trouble now? The Holy Father very much relies on Brother Gregory, whose renown as a Latinist is well known. Brother Gregory's knowledge of Latin is unsurpassed ... But this is extraordinary!

Yes, it is Brother Gregory. It's been confirmed. There—there is a close up. He's being forcibly removed. He's speaking to the wolf. They're taking him out. The wolf is trotting along behind. This is highly irregular. Brother Gregory is being escorted—no, 'dragged' is the word. They're dragging him. They are taking him out. The wolf is right behind. This *is* extraordinary! Absolutely! Unprecedented!

But you may recall some of the rumours concerning Brother Gregory. Archbishop Pepin has described him as a loose cannon. Certainly, it was Brother Gregory who caused the disturbance at Pentecost. He's a brilliant man. Not only the best Latinist in the world but also a great neuroscientist. And he has been instrumental in the development of the helot. This wolf is, no doubt, one of his creations. But it has been said that Brother Gregory suffers periodically from a mental disability. When that happens he can lose touch completely with reality. It's brief but it's troublesome. The Holy Father, in his goodness and mercy, cannot be persuaded to see Brother Gregory go. And I say—Good for you, Holy Father! ...

IV

The Orient Express

His Holiness Pope Innocent XIV reclines in his compartment as the Orient Express races through the Balkans, destination Rome. It's a steam locomotive from the 1930s, recreating the adventures of a bygone era. The Pontiff is in his shorts. His robe hangs from a hook by the window. He is having an argument with his Latin secretary, Minim friar Gregory Caesar O'Riley.

"Ha-ha! How droll! I do *not* look like Mr. Gutman!" His Holiness insists. "I wonder at you, Gregory. That you have time for this ancient American cinematic pap. Mr. Gutman, indeed!"

Gregory removes his spectacles and pulls on the straps of his overalls. "*The Maltese Falcon* is not pap, Holiness. It's a study in human character. Mr. Gutman is not just a cheap crook. He has sophistication. It intrigues us that a man with superior education can devote himself to evil."

"Ha! Sophistication my eye—ha-ha! Yankee drivel!"

"You do look like Gutman, Holiness. Sydney Greenstreet—what a great actor! Me, I look like Jack Nicholson. He had the same shark's grin I do. Same slow drawl. Same charming kisser. And he detested authority figures, too, just as I do."

"I imagine he did," the Pontiff says dryly. "Like all Americans. Look where it got them. *There* is a superficial culture for you—ha-ha! No wonder they all wound up in the fundamentalist camp, ha-ha!"

"Well, I'm a Yank, Holiness. Why do you consort with me?"

"Why indeed? Whatever possessed you to bring that wolf to Mass? What did you accomplish? You're a drunkard and a womanizer. Your antics at Augustan University are the talk of Rome."

"Not true, Holiness. I drink but I'm never drunk. And I do not spend most of my time planning to knock up some sweet young thing in my Latin class, as the *Osservatore Romano* reported."

"Oh, what a disgrace. *Que disgrazia*! I am so disappointed in you, Gregory. I rely implicitly upon your Latin judgement. I value your advice. But you are a disappointment."

"It's true I have an eye for the ladies. I was born that way."

"You have the capacity to correct that."

"Not really, Holiness. It's part of the program. The program is given. It's there, it's what you work with. It's what you do with the program that counts. Abuse, moderate indulgence, abstinence, denial—take your pick. I've chosen moderation."

"You made the wrong choice, then."

"Holiness, they say Ghandi once went to bed with a couple of beautiful woman just to test himself. Don't laugh. That's something you should try. When was the last time anything tempted you? Where is the virtue in never getting close enough to anything to be tempted?"

The Pontiff shakes his head as though sadly reflecting. "*Que disgrazia*! What a tongue you have! What scandalous drivel, Gregory! The rumours—!"

"Rumours! Ah, so that's what it is. That story on the Net to the effect that I wound up at a hotel in Rimini with one of my students. Is that what's troubling you, oh Sacred Stone?"

Pope Innocent is wearing his best stoical mien. He does not deign to answer.

"Holiness, I see by the line over your left brow that this is it. One should never be troubled by rumours. Verus will tell you that."

"Hang Verus! I'm sick of hearing about this Verus. You were seen dancing. You, a Minim friar. With some light-headed, bed hopping, joy seeker from Hungary named Bibi Lakatos. Have you no shame? What kind of message is that sending?"

"Ah, Bibi Lakatos! What a dancer she is! What great legs she has! Sorry, sir, it's in me. It's part of who I am. I was born with it. It's the program. Legs will always get my attention. What is the message I'm sending? you ask. The message is: I'm alive. The message is: I'm human. That's the message. It's the entire message. Human and alive. If I were you, Holiness—!"

Gregory is interrupted by a knock at the compartment door. Gregory opens it and a dowdy middle-aged woman with a downcast mien enters hesitantly. "*Oh goo-dog!*" she says, looking at Gregory. "Holiness, I—!"

"*This* is the Holy Father," Gregory says, indicating the reclining figure in shorts. The woman steps back when she sees the Holy Father in boxer shorts.

"It's all right," says Gregory. "It's too hot for His Holiness."

Pope Innocent's face lights up at the sight of the intruder. "Step right in, my child, ha-ha. Come in, come in. Are you a Catholic?"

"*Nay,* I am not. Holiness, I am a born-again Christian, *ya*. I am going home to *Sveeriyeh*... to Sweden, *Ya*. My name is Ingrid. I am a missionary. *Ya,* for *Yésus*. *Ya,* if it is not too much trouble..."

"No trouble, my dear, ha-ha! Sit down and unburden your heart."

"*Tack. Ya maynar,* I mean thank you, Your Holiness. *Nay,* I... I am not a Catholic. But we are all God's children. *Ya!* And we all believe in *Yésus. Ya veest.*"

"Do we?" says Gregory.

"Don't be alarmed, my dear. Gregory is my Latinist and my secretary. And he's very irreverent. Even, I think, a bit mad. He's a pagan but he's all we could find. There are only ten men left in the world who can speak Latin, and our Gregory is one of them—the best, in fact. So we can't be choosy. He owes his allegiance to the Rome of the Caesars, not the Rome of the vicars of Christ. But we rely on him implicitly for all our translations, ha-ha. We can't do without him. There's no better Latinist in the world."

Gregory bows deeply.

"*Oh ya,*" says Ingrid, uncertainly. She gives Gregory a disapproving look. "Only ten men left who speak Latin? *Ya, ya, ya veest.* I'm so sorry, Holiness. Do you think... would it be... too much to ask Your Holiness for—!"

Gregory reaches out and snatches the purse from Ingrid's lap.

"*Nay! Vad i himmelen! Yésus* help me!"

"Sorry Miss, I have to open this." Gregory dumps the contents of Ingrid's purse onto the seat beside her. "This guy's so cheap, I have to double as his bodyguard. Looks okay, Holiness... No guns, nothing sharp. She's clean. Less you want me to frisk her?"

"That will do, Gregory." Pope Innocent motions for Gregory to back off. "Sorry to put you through this, my dear. You might have been an assassin. The Turks might have put you aboard to get rid of me. That's because I'm a crusader. And because I call their great city 'Constantinople'. They don't like that. They threw stones at me. They're afraid they'll have to give it back, you see. The city of Constantine. The capital of the eastern Roman Empire, ha-ha!"

"*Ya, ya veest.* Holiness, *Ya vill*... I have a *samling*... a collection of religious memorabilia, *ya*." Ingrid takes an autograph book from her purse and passes it to the Pontiff.

"Certainly, my dear. With the greatest pleasure."

"What sect of the cult do you belong to?" Gregory asks Ingrid.

"My secretary is not a Christian, my dear," the Pontiff says, as he hands his autograph to Ingrid.

"Dear *Yésus*! Not a Christian! *Nay*, surely you believe in *Yésus*? My whole life has been devoted to *Yésus*. *Ya veest*."

"I can see that," says Gregory.

"*Nay*, I do not understand. *Yésus* died for us on the cross, to save us from our sins."

Gregory makes a face. "Do you think so, Ingrid? Is that why you trudge around the globe with a bible in your bra?"

"*Nay men!* ... How can you say things like that? What dreadful, terrible, sinful things to say. *Ya*, and in the very presence of the Holy Father."

Pope Innocent smiles and reaches out to her. "Pay this heathen no attention, ha-ha. God bless you, my dear. Your heart is in the right place. Most assuredly it is."

"Yeah, but her mind isn't," Gregory says.

"We are all God's children, *ya*." Ingrid casts a disapproving glance at the Latinist. "Goodbye, Holiness. I am sorry." Ingrid opens the compartment door and backs out, bowing. The compartment door closes slowly.

Innocent laughs. *"Heil den Geist der uns verbinden mag!"* he cries, exuberantly.

"Yes, hail the spirit that is able to unite us. What spirit is that, Holiness? The *Geist* who can unite us—who is that? I can tell you what *geist* it won't be, Holiness. It won't be the Holy *Geist*."

The Pope raises a cautionary finger. "Gregory, remember who I am."

"Yes, Holiness. *Ja Wohl!*"

"I am Peter."

"Yes, Peter, Petrus, Mr. Rock, sir. You are the foundation, you represent the fundament—*fundamentum*—I do not mean in the original sense of 'anus', of course, but the modern sense of 'bottom principle'."

The Pope grimaces, then chuckles at the Latinist's inanities. "Bottom principle, ha-ha!"

"Sorry, Holiness, Great-burden Bearer, sir. It's not easy to show respect when I look at Mr. Gutman and he's only wearing shorts. Those knobby knees of yours do you no good. As we say in Hoboken, you look like a schmo. Why don't you put something on instead of running around in shorts? It will help remind me that you're not just another schmuck. You're the big cheese at the apex of this wedding cake of really sweet and sickly dreams."

The Pope fans himself with a copy of *Der Spiegel*. "Clothes? What do clothes have to do with it? I am the same person, whatever I'm wearing. Or even not wearing anything."

"That is a lewd thought, Holiness. And no, you're not the same. This world runs on perception. The *Yésus* freak might have perceived that you and I were being cozy. You know—intimate."

"Ugh! What a fascinating imagination you have, Gregory."

"Perception, Holiness, is usually a judgement arrived at without due consideration of the evidence. Or is that a delusion? Anyway, it's the way of the masses. If you're not creating the right impressions, Holy One, then you're not projecting authority, either. If you're not projecting authority, people are not taking you seriously. If they see you in shorts, they'll call you 'Pope Knobby-Knees.' The newspaper cartoonists'll have a field day every time you go crusading. Suppose the *Yésus* freak caught you on camera. Picture the headlines in the Italian papers and the foreign tabloids. *Reform Pope shucks everything on Orient Express! Knobby-Knees breaks new ground! Naked with Latinist!*"

The Pope fans himself energetically with *Der Spiegel*.

"If people are not taking you seriously, Holiness, then what kind of ambassador are you for the Divine Dictator? Your gravitas is entirely missing if you're prancing around in shorts."

"The Divine Dictator—ha-ha! What a splendid imagination you have, Gregory. What a superb talent for humour."

"You know you have no gravitas. You have no spiritual weight, let alone intellectual. And every time you open your mouth, wearing shorts, what comes out is not a prayer or a chant but just some monkey-chatter drivel. It's the shorts that get the attention, Holiness. Dress the part I say. What is a chief priest without his accoutrements? *Rien. Absolument rien.* You don't look as though you believe in yourself, let alone that seedy pantheon of deities, saints, and angels that you represent."

"Seedy pantheon! Ha-ha! How droll! Ha-ha! What a scandalous, irreverent tongue you have, Gregory. But take a care for your immortal soul. You'll burn in hell for your godlessness. I'm convinced of that. Yes, indeed. But I pray daily that you may be forgiven. If you weren't the world's foremost Latinist ..."

"But I am. Me, the plumber's son from Hoboken. So don't waste your prayers on the likes of me, Holy Father Figure. I don't buy that crap about three in one, and not the rest of your dogma, either. I happen to be a Roman. I know how to think."

"Some Roman!" the Pontiff returns snidely. "I have no intention of disputing with you, Gregory. You're a lost soul, entirely, utterly beyond redemption."

"I'm your alter ego, Holiness, and you know it. You can't say you don't enjoy disputing with me in Latin. But I wonder what happened to those promises you made when you mounted the throne? It's been a whole year and what have you done?"

"Never mind. I am what I am. I follow the dictates of my conscience. I'm not concerned with the opinions of lost souls like yourself. Let's keep to policy, shall we? Otherwise, I'll confine you to the scriptorium. Remember, no one else on this earth will give you a job. Latin is being phased out everywhere. It's almost dead. The clock is ticking."

"I thought we were going to reintroduce the Latin Mass? Isn't that what you told me when I took this job."

"Ha-ha, don't push me."

The Orient Express races on. For a moment there is only the

monotonous clack-clack, clack-clack, clack-clack of the wheels. Green pastures and white sheep fly by, and white houses perched on hills.

"What is a deity, Holiness? Ever thought of that, Inimitable Shepherd? From the point of view of folks back in Verus's time, you and I are deities."

"What is the fascination with that charlatan Verus? Isn't he that street person posing as an ancient Roman?"

"He's a better Latinist than I am, Holiness."

"What nonsense, Gregory." The Pope reflects a moment. He rubs the back of his head and says, "Imagine those Turks, stoning me in the city of Constantine! What cheek!"

"Hey, they don't want your superstition any more than you want theirs."

The Pontiff sighs. "So much of the world persists in clinging to absurd beliefs, Gregory. If only they would open their hearts to Christ. His Truth could not be more obvious." The Pope sighs. "Sometimes I feel like a go-between."

"That's just what you are, Holiness. You're smack in the middle between the Universal Dictator and the great unwashed mass of fools who've never learned to think. To the unbelievers you're just another clown in robes. But I'll bet if there is a deity, you look like a clown even to him. Reason is the test, sir. If you don't have it, you're just another animal."

"Ha-ha! You never tire of your idle and irreverent prattle, do you? God bless you, Gregory. Ouch, *mein Kopb*! I'm sorry I took you to Constantinople. You're a coward."

"Heck, I stood my ground when the Mufti was throwing muffins, but rocks... If you want my opinion—!"

"*Nein*! When I want your opinion on religious matters, I'll ask for it. I am the expert on religion. You are the Latin technician. You are a linguistic plumber, that's all you are. Your father was a plumber of pipes in Hoboken and you are a plumber of words in Rome. Remember that."

"Well, huh! Well, la-dee-da!"

"Yes, I mean it. You're a sad, sad specimen, Gregory. Let us not mince words. You're only the scribe. You're the Latin secretary. Confine yourself to translation if you don't want to be locked up in the scriptorium."

The Pope lapses into deep thought. Pastures and villages of houses with white walls and red-tile roofs fly by. The Orient Express races on: clack-clack, clack-clack, clack-clack.

"Seriously, Holiness, what is a deity?"

The Pope groans. "Must the silence always be rent by your cluster-fly buzzing! You don't know the value of peace and quiet. Why do you not contemplate?"

"Oh, is that what you were doing? Sorry, Holiness, I thought you were nodding off. But I can't help thinking, from the point of view of folks back in Verus's time, you and I would be gods."

"Ha! I hope this Verus enthusiasm will not be another of your indiscretions."

"I really think you should spend more time with your helot, Holiness, so you'll be ready. You wouldn't want to be left out."

"I haven't made up my mind yet about this upgrade."

"Well, you should. Where there is life there is hope, Holiness."

"I haven't seen *your* helot," the Pontiff says. "Where do you keep it?"

"I've put it to sleep, Holiness. It's in a closet. Don't want to take chances with it." Gregory looks out the window at the hills covered with sheep, then says, "And when life is eternal, reality changes for all those sheep under your care. The Godhead will lose his relevance, you know. Why would anyone believe in God if we're not going to die? They won't be lining up for your Kingdom Come, any more, will they?"

"Ha! What idle nonsense, Gregory. What scandalous drivel. There will still be accidental death. People will be blown up or crushed. Not everybody can be put back together again."

"Even that will be overcome some day, Holiness. It is our destiny to overcome."

The Pontiff grimaces. "In the meantime," he says, "think was a great tragedy it will be, Gregory, when one of the new men or women is crushed or blown up. To die when you have to die is one thing. To suffer an accidental death when you had your heart set on eternity, is quite another, ha-ha."

"Yes, Holiness, that is quite true. What a tragedy it would be, indeed. A terrible thing. By prolonging life indefinitely, we inadvertently and exponentially magnify the meaning of death, whenever it does occur. It's inevitable. But we humans have taken risks throughout our history. There is only one way to the future and timidity is not part of it."

The Pontiff nods in agreement. "I suppose not, Gregory. The path of human history is paved with the lives of martyrs."

"There must be others out there, Holiness. SETI has turned up nothing. Intelligent creatures must be few and far between. But there must be others. Some doing nothing with their slightly-bigger-than-other-animal brains except chasing down things to eat—that's us for most of our history. We were ruled by the stomach. And others have vast and unimagined power. They never need to experience extinction. They would be gods to us."

The Pontiff shrugs. "I've read science, Gregory. Science fiction, too. And philosophy. I found it all wanting. The soul of man cries out for something more than dry physics. Indeed it does. What solace is there in the random play of atoms? And where does it lead? This inane search for—for what? And where is the guidance in philosophy? The mind is not reliable when it comes to the ultimate truth."

"You're telling me, Holiness."

The Pontiff reflects for a moment, a pained look on his face. The Orient Express races on. "Grace and faith, Gregory. We need grace and we need faith. Without them, man is lost. I pray for you daily that you may receive God's grace and that you may have faith in Him who died for us."

"It's no use, Holiness. I'm not believing in Grand Genitor unless and until he shows up. And maybe not even then."

The Pope fans himself vigorously.

"I'm not condoning this hide and seek stuff, Holiness. If God Almighty puts in an appearance and can show me some credentials, I'm willing to listen. I wouldn't like it but I'd listen. But he'd have to submit to some tests and some very hard scrutiny. He'd get short shrift from the sci-fi fans, who'd all be convinced it was an alien plot to take over the world. Because the sci-fi people know, when we put science aside, we expose ourselves to deception. And besides, there are a lot of people around nowadays, myself included, who don't want any help from outside. We'd say to him: We've been abandoned all this time and now we're used to getting by on our own, so take a hike, bud."

Pope Innocent looks glum. "What a scandalous tongue! God save you, Gregory. God forgive me for hiring a Latinist who's a pagan."

For a while there is only the clack-clack, clack-clack of the wheels as the Orient Express races on. Green pastures filled with sheep and goats roll by, stone fences, white red-roofed houses.

The Pope yawns.

"What's the matter, Holiness? Another hard day keeping the wolf from your flock? I mean doubt, Holiness. The Big Bad Wolf called 'doubt'. Do you know what doubt is there for? It's a reality check, that's what it is. Without it there could be no human progress. Nothing would ever change."

"What idle and irreverent prattle, Gregory? Ha-ha! What a superb imagination." The Pope lapses into deep thought. "If only you had kept your hands on the *Logos*. If only you hadn't been so stupid. You had it right before your eyes. And you let the Turks snatch it away."

"I'm sorry, Holiness. I—"

"For centuries we thought it was gone for good. The masterpiece of Heraclitus, the greatest philosopher of antiquity. His works only known by his influence on others. A few lines cited here, a few there. What a reputation he had. They placed him before Socrates, Plato, Aristotle. But then the wily Turks find it hidden under a vault in Hagia Sofia. And they let you see it. And it was right under your nose. And what did you do? Nothing!"

"What could I do, Holiness? There were five guards there, armed to the teeth."

"It's ours. Just as Hagia Sofia is ours."

"Look at it this way, Holiness—they're part of the EU. So we got it back, after all. It's the only sane way of looking at it."

The Pontiff dismisses the argument with a wave of his hand. "Go fetch me something to eat, please, Gregory. A prosciutto sandwich with mozzarella. By Jove, I do love mozzarella. Olives and pickles and mustard, too, please. Dijon mustard. *Aqua minerale*. Strawberry flavour, please. Why give me *that* look? I still have to eat."

"About the *Logos* ..."

The Pontiff sighs. "All we have is a *fragmentum*. And the Turks have the rest. *Maaa Donna*!"

"Don't worry, Holiness, we'll find a way to get it."

The Pope raises his eyes heavenward. "In the name of decency, will you please get me my panino! I'm starving to death!"

"Ha! That would be something—the Pope starving to death. Is that likely, sir? Now, let me see, the last pope who starved to death was, uh ... !"

"*Oh, qua miseria!* Stubborn Turks, insolent subordinates. I'm surrounded by pagans. *Oh, Que disastro*! We could've taken the *Logos* and we didn't. What a terrible unmitigated dreadful disaster."

"Nonsense, Keeper of the Mysteries. We're not talking about a Christian writer, just one of those miserable pagans. And a philosopher would say: How can we miss what we never had? That's what Verus would say. And probably Heraclitus, as well."

"Hang Verus! We almost had the *Logos*. That's what gnaws at my brain. We almost had the *Logos*, the greatest work of the greatest philosopher of all time. Heraclitus!"

"We almost stole it."

"Had, stole, who cares. It's part of our heritage. Heraclitus, I mean. For a few hours the whole text was visible, right under your pagan nose. Then it was gone. Poof! You let them take it away. Oh, my head! My God, I need to calm down. Where are my pills? Pull my ear, flush my toilet. I don't care what your talents are. You're only an employee. I am head of state. Supreme ruler of the Vatican. It's not a democracy. I am the dictator. I'll lock you up in one of my estates—yes, Castel Gandolfo. I'll chain you to the walls. I'll lock you in the tunnel. All right, calm down, George. I must think of something peaceful, serene. There, out there. Look at those sheep in the meadows. Look at those beautiful, peaceful, serene, white little sheep. Dear little sheep."

"They look like they're stunned, don't they, Pope George?"

"I love this train. You can see the sheep. Nice white fluffy pure innocent sheep. That's what I want the world to be: innocent, pure, fluffy, quiet. Look at those fine white beautiful animals standing there looking. All looking in the same direction. What a delight for my tired eyes. What a balm for my weary brain."

"Tomorrow the meat from those dumb balls of wool will be in your sandwiches."

The Pontiff sighs. "If only the world were like that: innocent, pure, uncomplicated. The Truth of God should be that easy, shouldn't it? The Truth of God. God's truth should be evident to everyone. How can anyone doubt? Look at those fine white beautiful animals standing there looking. God's little lambs. All looking in the same direction.

They seem to be looking at me. Perhaps they are. What a delight. If only the world were like that!"

"The world *is* like that, Holiness. The truth is always related to what the sheep want most, and it comes from the gut and the genitals. And the sheep are watched over not by shepherds, but by the string pullers of want and the string pullers of need. And that includes you."

"*Maaa Donna! Que lingua acerba*! God save me from your vicious tongue, Gregory."

"Sheep love to be in the centre of the herd, Holiness, farthest from the great wolf Doubt. They love to warm their balls in the summer sun and chew their cud in peace. The truth does not concern them. Their little lives pass in a pasture, the pasture of the string pullers. They haven't a clue what it's all about. They never will. Then one day the truck arrives. A terrible thought crackles like a live wire in their innocent little brains: It's all over! They're taking me away! Why are they doing this? I thought I would chew the sweet green grass forever!—Okay, all right, don't get excited, Holiness. I'll get your panino."

Gregory steps out into the corridor. He is confronted by a young woman. She embrances him, taking him off guard.

"Bibi! I thought you were going to keep out of sight!"

Bibi has shoulder-length chestnut hair and the face of a classical goddess. She is wearing a dress in the ancient Roman fashion. For a moment Gregory is overwhelmed by her demure style and her beauty. He checks himself and pulls her along the corridor, away from the Pontiff's compartment.

"What are you doing slinking around here?" Gregory says.

"Oh, Greg! I'm not slinking." Bibi's voice is urgent and sedate at the same time. "I could have knocked on the door, you know, like that silly born-again Swedish lady. I could have pretended I was one of the flock—Is she one of your creations?"

"No, she isn't. Is it . . . ?"

"Don't worry, it's safe. What did you tell him?"

"That there were armed guards and that they grabbed it before I was ready."

She looks earnestly into Gregory's eyes. Her voice is dignified but pleading: "Oh Greg, do we have to live like this? Why must you live in that stupid palace?"

"We've already talked about that." Gregory studies the young woman's face. Her agate eyes and the long lashes are irresistible. But his face remains without expression. "Do you remember what you're to do when we reach Rome?"

"Yes." Bibi's lips form into a pout. "You're no more monk than I am!"

"I have rules. My own rules. I look after myself. My mind."

In the narrow corridor Bibi brushes against him. She touches him gently. Her fingers slide down his chest. She smiles. "You *don't* look after yourself. You don't know how to have fun. Oh, I know—Lucretius! Love is a sickness. Love enslaves. Are you sure you are not a slave to Lucretius?"

"We are all slaves to something, Bibi. What counts is who or what the master is." Gregory looks into her eyes, both longingly and with resolute calm. "Where is the ... Is it in a safe place?"

"Don't worry. The *Logos* is right here." Bibi gives her belly a rub. "It's under my girdle." She reaches out to him, stroking his collar. Gregory experiences an involuntary tremor. He holds her to keep from embracing. For a moment they are tense; then Bibi relaxes, resigned.

"When we get to Rome," says Gregory, "I want you to bring it to class."

"I won't bring it. If you want it you'll have to come and get it."

"Keep it out of sight. Some people would kill for it."

"Why Greg, you do care what happens to me. I suppose I should be thankful for that."

"Don't talk nonsense."

"Cardinal Pepin—!"

"What about him?"

"I had dinner with him yesterday. He asked me some questions. About you and the Commission."

"What did you say?"

"Nothing, of course. I told him I didn't know anything."

"All right."

"Come back and have something with me. Just for a few minutes ... I'll tell you what Pepin said."

Gregory hesitates. "All right. Just for a minute. His Holiness is starving to death."

In his compartment Pope Innocent XIV wonders why Gregory is taking so long. He talks to himself as he gazes out the window at the rolling hills, the pastures, and the sheep.

"*So, hier bist du*, George Adolf Schweinrue. You've come a long way from the abbey in Klöpfendorf, *Deutschland*. *Ja, ja*. How simple things were back then. How I wish I were just Brother George once more, working in the vineyards along the Mosel, tending my beautiful swine. I did not carry the world on my shoulders. I was content, like one of those simple fluffy white animals grazing there in the pastures.

"Oh, blessed sheep! How fortunate you are. I was once at peace just as you are now. I found peace and pleasure in simple things. Ah yes, little did I know, as I slogged through the pig muck in the stalls, paradise was in that very sty. And I did love those pigs, every last one of them. Yes, even the smell of their slops. I can smell it now—Oops, I just farted!"

Innocent picks up *Der Spiegel* and waves it about to dispel the odour.

"There, that should do it. So ... now humble George the swine herd holds the Roman Church in his hands, hobnobs with the great and the powerful, plays politics with presidents and kings. Here hold the fort, there advance. I'll be known as the pope who tested the limits. The pope who was stoned in Constantinople for daring to crusade for Christ.

"And they will say I was a doubter. No wonder. That comcell in my skull torments me worse than Gregory. What a burden is knowledge. God help me. Help me to resist. Lord, I believe. Help Thou mine unbelief."

"Why must I be so busy? Is it because I doubt? Why should I doubt? Because of the helots? Because man is remaking himself in a new image? Because the Church is losing ground? Yes, all of that. And because I'm human, of course. I'm no different than anybody else, just smarter and wiser.

"The truth is, my soul will not rest until the whole world bows down to the one true God, helot or no helot. George, that is one tall order.

"I feel insecure. And insecurity is the wellspring of all zeal. If only there were not so many boneheads in the world. If only they could experience the Truth. Imagine what a world that would be. I would be totally secure in my belief—if the whole world was with me. If there was no opposition. Just like the six hundreds when the state fell apart and the Church took over. What heady times those were!

"But supposing I did have the whole world on side, what would there be left for me to do?

"Tend my expanded flock, of course. Preach to them, guide them, keep them steadfast in the Faith.

"If they were all like me, though, the world would come to a standstill, wouldn't it? If everybody ran around in a long gown and a skull cap, dropping blessings and Hail Marys like gumdrops from above, the world would not work. Would that be a bad thing? If the world were to revert to a pre-industrial state, should that trouble anyone? Why should it?

"I wish it were the Middle Ages. No, no, the Dark Ages—even better. What is science and what is technology beside the Truth of God? Nothing. The world acts as though salvation lay in progress—ha! The progress of what? The progress of toys, gadgets, gismos. The helot gismo. Homo mirabilis! What nonsense!

"My, how times have changed. Once, we had only to contend with simple peasants, who did what they were told. Yes, back in my forebears' time. Back in Hauptman Schnickelgrüber's time—*Ach du lieber*! The peasants stood to attention when you spoke to them—*Achtung*! They took their hats off and cast down their eyes and bowed their heads. And they said: yes, Your Grace; no, Your Grace. They knew their place. They agreed with everything. They did not talk back to their betters. They were ready to serve Church and State. With body, mind, and soul. With prayers and with blood. And that is just what they did. They served with prayers and blood. And what does this matter to the righteous? What significance has a little sacrifice when measured against eternal time?

"But now look what a little learning has done. *Heute gibt es keine Ordnung*. Today there is no order. All these fools think they own the world. They all have to have an opinion. They all think their opinion is as good as mine. And that's why they don't need me.

"That's what you're up against, George Adolf Schweinrue. God help me, then, to undeceive this sinful world. God help me."

The compartment door slides open and Gregory squeezes in with a tray. "Talking to yourself again, Holiness? Here's your grub. Folk were asking me: Are all those snacks for his Holiness? Eats an awful lot, doesn't he? But I lied and said the stuff was for me. The Latinist can eat all this garbage but not the Holy Father. You're supposed to be better than the rest of us. They don't expect you to eat at all."

The Pope sighs. "I was reminiscing about the good old days."

"When you tended swine instead of sheep?"

"Those were the days! Swine herding in Klöpfendorf."

"And then you decided that it wasn't enough? Then you became a priest?"

"No. I started to wrestle—I fought in the ring. It was just for exercise at first. But then they discovered me—you know, promoters from the States."

"Goodbye happiness."

"Yes, how true. They took me to Cincinnati. 'Pretty Boy George' they called me. The whole thing went to my head. I became a showman, a grandstander. Wrestling is all show, you know. It's fixed."

"Yeah, you're good at that, Holiness."

"But there are hard knocks—that much is real. The crowd demands it and the crowd is sovereign."

"Hey, right on. You're so right. The crowd rules today."

"I would file and paint my nails before the match, and sometimes during, and wear a frilly pink gown on the way to the ring—a negligée. I would play the effeminate patsy. But when the match began I could pound and stomp and romp with the best of them—ha-ha! After a year, I got damaged by, ah, a fellow who went by the name of 'Putrid Paul'. It knocked some sense into me. He twisted the ropes round my neck. I was suffocating to death. Putrid Paul kept bouncing on the ropes. Then a fan brained me with a frying pan. I was in a coma for six weeks. That was the end of that."

"So then you became a priest?"

"No. I went back to my first love, swine herding. I found it conducive to contemplation. I mean the muck and the smell, and the grunts of my pigs, my dear little pigs. In my spare time I devoted myself to religious studies. I found these two occupations fit very well together. I would preach to the pigs, just as St. Francis preached to the wolves at Assisi. Gradually, I found that the monkish life had more allure than tending my piggies, so I gave up the farm and became a Minorite."

"I'm sure it was a great loss for your pigs, Holiness."

"The rest is history. I lived like a saint and here I am." Pope Innocent looks at his sandwich, then tears at it. "Ah, prosciutto! I do dearly love prosciutto. Bless me, there's nothing like Italian cured ham." The Pontiff chews away in contentment. "This is the fate of the poor swine I tended. But man must eat. This is the flesh of some poor little *porchen, porchilein*. But God in his infinite goodness gave us them so we would not go hungry. God gave us the whole world. My, this is tasty. He gave us them to use them, to enjoy them. With mustard and mayonnaise. Poor little swine, reduced to a ham sandwich. How tasty thou art!" The Pontiff pauses in his eating. "This is not mayonnaise!" He examines the contents of the bun. "And ... and, what is this yellow stuff? It's sticky, gooey. What is it?"

"Didn't have any mayonnaise. It's a Turkish sauce called *yuck-yuck*, made from something called *yucksnot*. The Turks love it."

"*Yuck-yuck? Yucksnot?* Smells foul!"

"The Turks love foul things, Holiness. Every nation has its own way to tickle, tease, and torment the palate. Ever tried Swedish sour herring? You need a gas mask to eat it. Hot, sweet, sour, rotten—the world loves that stuff. And infidels, of course, they'll eat the foulest of the foul."

"*Questo formaggio*, the cheese, *non è mozzarella*. The cheese ... it stinks. I love it! Or is it the *yuck-yuck* sauce?"

"It's Limburger from *Deutchland*, the land of great stink-and-sour. By the way, Holiness, I was thinking ... You should try shepherding sheep for a few days. Yes, I mean it. It would do you a world of good. I mean, with those guys out there in the meadow. And you've already had great practice with swine. The skills are transferable."

The Pope looks out into the pastures. He munches away in contentment. "Ha-ha! Why do you say that, Gregory?"

"You might learn a few things about managing flocks. That would be right up your alley as the world's supreme flock manager. You could become really adept at guiding sheep with your staff or your crook. Then you wouldn't need to lash out at them with your tongue any more. All those useless homilies, all the prayers for them on bended knee, all those wasted words."

"You know, Gregory, this yucksnot is not so bad," the Pontiff says, engrossed in his panino.

"And you could observe the herding instinct first hand, Holiness. That would give you a handle on how the *populus vulgus* thinks. Have you ever wondered why those stupid animals all stand facing the same way? Look like they're in church, don't they? Or watching some cheap flick on the video wall. Look at them. Standing, munching, all looking the same way, all moving their jaws back and forth from side to side. Snacking, ruminating, their little minds disengaged, like couch potatoes on a sofa. Do you think there's a reason they behave like that? What do you suppose is going through their innocent little brains?"

"What a great panino this is! *Assalutamente magnifico*! Absolutely magnificent. Limburger and *yuck-yuck*. Mmm!"

"Really draws out the saliva, doesn't it, sir? Do you fancy sheep's brain with a nice white sauce?"

"Occasionally. Yes, by Jove. I do love sheep's brain occasionally. What a superb sandwich this is!"

"Those sheep out there, Holiness—do you think they're all smelling the ass end of the animal in front? I mean, as they chew their cud? Maybe that's why they're all nose to bum like that, so they can get that great Limburger sweetness of foul. You know, the sanitized odour of shit from the next ass in line. Maybe for them, it's like the Limburger. Boy, doesn't that Limburger make your mouth water? Say, the animal out in front doesn't get to smell any ass, does it? Or do they all take turns?"

"I'm eating, Gregory!"

"Yes, sir. Sorry. We don't have manners in Hoboken. In the U.S. we dropped all that phoney stuff. That's what the American Revolution was all about. It's all about the common denominator. We dumped all the crap. We brought everyone down to the lowest level—the true, unadorned, original self. We're rude but we're genuine. Honest and real. Or we were, until the American Taliban took over. Now it's a bloody wasteland. That's why I went to school in Toronto. Far more civilized. U of T—that's my alma mater. Then Oxford, then Rome. And the rest is history.

"*Ach du lieber* ... What a panino."

"We hold these truths to be self evident: That all men—this included women for a while but not any more—are created equally stupid; that they are endowed with self-given inalienable rights; that among these are lifestyle, licence, and the pursuit of the opposite sex..."

"What a great panino this is! *Ach du lieber*!"

"Hey, are you listening? I'm delighted you like your panino, Holiness. They told me the *yuck-yuck* sauce is fermented in the sweat taken from between the legs of those sheep, right around the—!"

"*Basta, fungus ignominiosus!* Enough! Shut up, will you! *Mama Santa!*"

"Yes, sir, Supreme and Divinely Appointed Leader." The train races on: clack-clack, clack-clack, clack-clack. "You should consider shepherding, though, Holiness. You could sleep in a herder's cubby on a plank bed, just like Verus."

"What fascination you hold for that street person Verus. Sleeps on a plank bed—ha-ha!"

"Yes, Holiness. His Latin is flawless. Wait till you meet him."

"Ha-ha! When pigs fly!"

"I really think you should try shepherding, though, Holiness. You could wander in the green grass and pretend the world was new and fresh and clean again, like it used to be three hundred years ago. You could listen to the trickle of the rills as they meander through marsh and meadow. It's a reality check, sir, just like doubt. It will put your mind in order, nearness to nature will. Verus will tell you that. Takes us right back to the beginning, when the world was called Eden, before the tree apes started screwing around in it. Even a brain like yours may benefit, quagmired though it is in the superstition of the ages, mired in the muck of church history, all cruddy and crusty with the dregs and dross of culture. What you need is *Tranquillitas*. You need to be natural and simple, like Verus."

"Or like a Hoboken plumber?" Innocent gives a tired little laugh. "Verus! *Tranquillitas*! Sheep's turd! *Mein Gott*!"

The Orient Express races on. For a while there is only the sound of the wheels: clack-clack, clack-clack, clack-clack. Outside, white houses flash by; and green fields filled with sheep and goats, most white, some black; and hilltop monasteries with red-tile roofs.

"Let me arrange for you to stay a while with the monks of Sacred Wisdom, Holiness. The daily routine will do you good. Sweeping dung out of stalls, breaking humble bread with the monks, working in the fields with spade and hoe and scythe. Just like the old days in *Deutchland*, before it all got bombed to bloody hell. You get your hands dirty and you forget the world for a while. Your brain starts to rewire itself. It will do that if you give it a chance. I know there's a rational creature inside you. Let him out. Please, Holiness, I beseech you as a brother, go back to the origins. Start from the beginning, before it's too late. You'll be surprised with what you come up with. You'll be reborn. You'll be a new man."

Pope Innocent gives his Latinist a tolerant look. "No, I'm not doing that, Gregory. I'm not meeting with the bum from Toronto, either. And I'm not going to stay with the Buddhists. Isn't that what you're working up to? And isn't your Verus just a Buddhist in disguise. Isn't he just another fakir in bed sheets?"

"No, sir. He's a rationalist, a humanist. He's as tall as a man can get. He stands erect. He knows the *Logos*."

"The *Logos*? The devil he does. A leader of one religion does not go to another religion for help. And how much more apt this is for those who profess the one true and catholic Faith. What kind of message would it send? People are already defecting to the Buddhists in droves. And why? Just because this Cosmic Mind fad is all the rage. It's no better than the fads of history—New Age, Spiritism, Gamma Gauge, whatever. Whenever there's a scientist wanting to do an experiment—mind control and all that—these silly Orientals in their orange bed sheets are lined up at his door. And why? So they can claim the mantra of sacred science. Because their minds show a higher gamma—so what!"

"Oh, gamma is everything, Holiness. Without gamma your brain is unharnessed. And when your brain is unharnessed, your life is a mess. The Buddhists look after their minds. They care about what gets into them. People take better care of their teeth than they do of their minds. That's why the world is in trouble."

"Rubbish. Unadulterated garbage. It's their souls they need to be concerned about. Did you tell the Commission that I'm not supporting the helot scheme unless they can guarantee that homo mirabilis will have an expanded human capacity for things spiritual?"

"Yes, Holiness. We're taking it under advisement. Spirituality is certain to be included."

"And forget the Greek monks, Gregory. I'm not staying with them, either, with their fleas, their dirty black robes reeking of goat cheese, their tick-infested long black beards. Not while the Orthodox Church refuses to recognize me. Why don't you do those things? Why pick on me?"

"I'm not picking on you, Incomparable Shepherd. I'm just concerned for your welfare, and the welfare of your catacumens. Besides, I have a right and a duty to fight back—as a Roman."

"As a Roman!" Pope Innocent cackles mercilessly. "You Hoboken plumber's son! You mannerless Yankee egalitarian! Some Roman you are! Get out of here! I want to read my magazine. Leave me alone!

Go on! Get yourself another compartment! I want to meditate without your insistent cluster-fly buzzing! Take your plank bed and your gamma with you!"

V

From the Founding of the City

Jancie and I have agreed to humour Verus. We shall tolerate his delusion until we know more about his medical condition. We have arranged to take him to a specialist in neurology and to a psychiatrist, and we shall be guided by what they have to say.

I introduce Verus to my computer, whose name is "Sunrise". "You can speak to Sunrise or you can use the keyboard," I say. "Or you can ask Sunrise to do your research. Sunrise will help you. Sunrise can speak any language, including Latin and ancient Greek."

Jancie and I have tried to catch Verus out on his knowledge of Rome, or to see if he knows more about technology than he's letting on. But we have not been successful. As he taps out a few words on the computer, Verus has to use 'caps lock', claiming he's not familiar with minuscule letters. And I believe he is not familiar with them.

I translate what Verus writes: "I dreamt last night that I lay in a camp. I was ready to close my eyes forever. The year was 933 *ab urbe condita.*"

"From the founding of the city?" I say. "The traditional date for the founding of Rome is 753 BCE. That is the agreed upon date of destiny. So that means you died in ... 180 CE, the way we reckon time, which is to say, according to the Gregorian or Christian calendar."

"That is not possible," Sunrise informs us. I tell Sunrise not to interfere.

"Tell Verus our calendar starts with the birth of Jesus Christ," says Jancie.

I'm very lucky that Jancie is a tolerant person and that she overlooks my anti-Christian diatribes. There was a time when my attitude was live and let live. But now that I understand the evils of religion, the strife that it causes around the world, I do not believe it is ethical to hide my thoughts. One has to take a stand. I've explained this to Jancie and she appears to understand that.

"Verus," I say, "you Romans got the reputation for persecuting Christians. Trouble is, you didn't pursue the task with enough zeal. You should have been more ruthless. The Christian Church, when at last it had its dog day, was not so nice in its methods as were you Romans. Heretics, doubters, free thinkers, and Jews were burned at the stake or boiled in oil in the town square. Christ, those were some parties they had back then!"

"Ask him to guess what century this is," cries Jancie, impatient with our Latin.

Verus looks very thoughtful. He bites his lip, his gaze fixed on eternity. "Yes. What year could it be? Though only yesterday I died at Carnuntum ... or was it Vindobono? I think it was one of those places. It was in the north woods, in the mountains. Let me think. There is too much I do not know. Ages of information I am missing."

I translate this for Jancie.

"We've been to all the planets," I tell Verus. "Have stations on every one of them, and colonies on the moon and on Mars. The only star we've been to is the sun. Other stars we haven't reached yet. The ships are manned by robots, some by helots, but it will be ages before they reach their destination."

"Sacred Apollo!" cries Verus, stunned. "Apollo let you approach?

No, it cannot be. It is not possible. The light! The heat! It is not possible!"

"What in God's name is he saying?" cries Jancie. "Tell me what he's saying."

Verus gestures helplessly at her English. He is so anxious to communicate with us. There is an innocence about him that I have to believe in. Verus asks for a moment to think. "What wonders!" he cries. "Men fly. Men visit the stars... And women, too. Incredible! You must all be absolutely thrilled to be alive in such a time. You must be ecstatic. How long has man had the ability to fly?"

"Two hundred and fifty years," I tell him.

I show Verus pictures of the first plane and of the latest hydrogen rocket. "There are only two hundred and fifty years between the two," I say. "Before that we still used horses. Also wind, water, and steam. We had no lights even, except of course, candles, oil, gas. In fact, half a century after that first plane flew, we were still using horses."

Verus looks astounded at my words. "Less than a hundred years from horses to ships that venture into the cosmos? No, that is not possible. It does not follow."

"Nevertheless," I say, "that's just how it was. Make friends with the computer and you'll find out. There were some essential discoveries that had to be made, inventions that had to be invented, tools that had to be designed, technology that had to be improved—some before that first flight, some after; then we were free as birds. And civilization took off. And it will never be the same again. That's progress."

"*Progressus!*" says Verus.

"Come on and guess!" cries Jancie.

Verus is in deep thought. "Let me think, let me think... Certainly thousands of years after yesterday, after I... I was going to say 'after I died'!"

Jancie gives me a roll of her eyeballs.

"Yes," says Verus, "thousands and thousands of years after that. One hundred thousands of years. But it could just as well be two or three hundred thousands ... On the other hand, perhaps not, if you have had machines for only four hundred years. We Romans had water power. Wind we might have harnessed but did not take the trouble. And steam—by the gods, we could have done that, but—slaves did the work! I suppose that did not do us any good in the end. I suppose not. Oh, I am so giddy. What an exciting thing, to visit the future! But I confess I know nothing. I am so ignorant." He gives a small laugh.

"Will you guess!" cries Jancie, with a vexed look. I tell Verus to make his guess.

"Well, the fact that you got around mostly on horse only yesterday, as cosmic time is reckoned, would seem to argue a shorter *progressus* rather than a longer one. Therefore, I will say ... the question is, if the Christiani came to power—*maxima calamitas*!—what happened to reason? The search for knowledge? What happened to logic, philosophy? You cannot go to the stars without reason. But I would say ... I would say ... if you press me I have to say ... somewhere between three and ten thousand years must have passed, absolute minimum. That would give you time to work on those wind and water machines and your mechanical arts, so that the power of horses would no longer be needed. I will take a chance and say, possibly—it is around, well, 3700 or 3800 AUC—from the founding of the city."

"Hey, not bad!" I cry. "You're over by a thousand years. That's damn close, considering."

Verus is astounded. "You did this in less than two thousand years? And without Rome? And yet you live like gods, have the power of gods. No, no, I cannot believe it. To come this far, change so much, in so short a time. Especially if most of the changes were in the last couple of hundred years. What a wondrous thing! Marvellous! Unbelievable!" As an afterthought Verus adds, "The Roman Empire, of course, is long gone? Of course it is. Of course it must be. I foresaw that it would happen."

Look back over the past, with its changing empires that rose and fell, and you can foresee the future, too.

"Your empire is gone," I say, "not the city. The state is gone, the city remains. The culture also remains, since it morphed into what the West is today. Rome built the foundation and the West rests on that foundation. Your science is still with us, your philosophy, your law, architecture. But the fall of Rome cost us at least six or eight hundred years. Except for that, we would have been travelling to the stars centuries ago."

"The city remains!" says Verus, hopefully. "The city remains! Rome exists! Oh, how I would love to see it! But—perhaps not. Too many reminders—my wife, my friends! Tell me, the monuments, buildings, streets—do they also remain?" Verus clutches my sleeve as he says this.

"Yes, sir, much remains. It's being continuously dug out, raised up, restored. We've been digging it up for the last four hundred and fifty years. Ever since the seventeen hundreds. The whole centre of the ancient city is just as it was about two thousand years ago."

"Tell him I'm sorry," says Jancie, moved by the pathos of Verus's expression. It occurs to me that if Verus is putting us on, he's doing a splendid job of it. It's so easy to forget that the premise we're working with is absurd.

"*Gratias, cara,*" says Verus. "The only certain thing is change. Loss is nothing but change, and change the universe loves. The Universal Reason must have willed it so."

"The universal reason?" I say.

"Zeus. Zeus must have willed it. Zeus is the universe. Zeus is reason. But how . . . ? The barbarians and the Christians . . . Did they . . . ?"

"Yes, they did it. And the sloth and greed of Romans, as well."

"Of course. I believe they are the very evils I spent my life fighting. I feel I held some position of great importance—but what could that have been? We must not forget passion—it was also the enemy of Rome. Passion, the enemy of reason. Emotion!"

Verus pauses so that I have time to translate.

"Clotho, the Fate who spins the cloth of our destiny, must have decided from the beginning of time that Rome must fall," Verus says, "as perhaps all else was decided from the beginning of time, from the moment when the Prime Cause put everything in motion. Twice Rome fell and bounded back. But this time, no—Alas! Not this time. On this earth there has to be a last time for everything. A last moment for every creature, for every one of us. And for great empires, too. A last breath, a last word, and then ... then the world hears nothing. Then there is silence. Then there is only history."

Jancie is almost in tears at these words. "It's only a delusion," I tell her. "Don't worry about it." To Verus I say, "That's how it was. That's how it used to be. The curtain would always come down on everything. Every man and woman had a final act, a final scene, a last word. But now humankind is going to put an end to that. Homo mirabilis will not be limited to five acts. He will remain on the stage forever!"

"Incredible!" says Verus. "Praise Zeus for allowing me to see and hear these wonders."

"Roman power was broken," I say, "But Roman civilization continued, even though numb and paralyzed with the force-fed narcotics of religion. And by the year 1000 the hills of Rome were covered with pasturing sheep. Shepherds slept among the ruins. The streets were covered in dung. But by the thirteen hundreds came the Renaissance, which was the rebirth of that civilization. The Italian people at last discovered who they were and where they had come from. They understood what had happened. Those who could think. Those who had knowledge. And from that sacred land the knowledge spread."

"Wonderful!" exclaims Verus.

"Yes, sir. Europe began to stir from a slumber of ages. Roman civilization began to rediscover itself, reassert itself; and as part of that, it began to break the chains in which the Church had held it. Those terrible chains of the spirit that bind the truth. Those ponderous chains. And that's what we have been doing ever since, slowly, slowly, as much as we dared, as much as was possible—breaking the chains. But the ugly hydra hung on. And now it's near to its last gasp."

"Wait a minute!" cries Jancie, her face red with indignation, even though I haven't translated everything. "What about me? Don't I count? Why do you keep insulting me? I'm a Roman Catholic, remember? I don't agree with you. I know how to think. I also believe in Jesus Christ."

"Sorry Jancie," I say. "It's my duty to call it as I see it. It's history. It's fact. You don't have to listen."

"Just be careful what you say," she tells me, her lip curling ominously. "We're all here for a purpose. I don't see how anyone can not see that. And feel it."

"Man is capable of giving himself purpose," I can't resist saying. "That there may be a purpose to the universe is not hard to believe, even if we don't really know that, and can't prove it, because it's way beyond us. But there is a great gap in logic between a purposeful universe and assuming some kind of god, as we understand the term. There is a further great gap in logic if we believe that said deity takes a personal interest in us. And there are gaps as big as light years if we claim to know the deity's purpose, to say nothing of assuming some supposed plan for humanity. Logic is always short-circuited by religion."

"Faith has nothing to do with your logic," says Jancie curtly.

"No sweetheart, it doesn't."

"Tell me," says Verus. "I would like to know who was last. The last Augustus—who was he?"

"Romulus," I reply.

"Romulus! Romulus ad Romulus! Romulus primus, Romulus ultimus!"

"But he could not have known that it was the end, sir. Rome had always come back from the brink. Just not this time."

"*Extremum!*"

"Yes, it truly was the end. The year was 476 our time. It was 1229 by the Roman calendar. Rome had lasted twelve hundred and twenty-nine years. But the Greek east, a Christian theocracy, survived until 1453."

Verus looks so downcast. "The end of civilization!" he cries. "The end of the world. *Oh maxima calamitas*! And yet, everything that happens to us we are made to bear. And it does not touch my ruling faculty."

I ask Verus what he means.

"It is the faculty that governs. It is the spark of God-given reason that rules in all rational creatures, whether gods or men. It is that part of Zeus that separates us from all other animals. My ruling faculty continues to rule, so it is not harmed by this news, sad though it is. And what cannot harm my ruling faculty, cannot harm me, and is neither good nor evil. Nothing can harm the ruling faculty, if only one looks after it."

"What's he talking about?" says Jancie.

I ask Verus for more information.

Verus considers a moment and says, "Let me see what I have in my mind. It's coming... Ah, here it is. The only concern one should have is the right ordering of the things that are within one's own control. And that is, in fact, the full extent of good and of evil. If you have things in order, no evil can touch you. Each man and each woman carries his or her own good, and his or her own evil. Each one of us has that power—the power over good and evil."

"But," I say, "somebody injures you—that's an evil. You can't control it."

Verus does not agree. "Joe," he says, "what is outside us, what we do not control, can never be evil. The fall of Rome, then, is not an evil. It does not touch our ruling faculty. It does not make us worse. Of course, I refer only to our minds, not our bodies. What happens to the body is beyond our control. It is an external. But if something does not make our minds worse, it does not make us worse. We have that power. And what does not make us worse is not an evil. The fall of Rome is a sad and terrible disaster, but it does not make me worse, does not make any of us worse, and is not an evil. When we are made worse, we do it ourselves. It does not come from outside."

Our life is what our thoughts make it.

"I still don't understand," says Jancie. "Are you sure you know what he's talking about, Joe?"

"I am a stranger here," Verus says, "but then, in my own time I was a stranger, too."

Life is a warfare and a stranger's sojourn, and after fame is oblivion.

"He appears to speak in riddles," I say to Jancie.

"For me there are two realities side by side," says Jancie, feeling the need to stand up for her faith. "I believe in God and I believe in science. And I do not see how they are incompatible. And neither does the Church. Tell Verus that."

Verus gives us a grave look upon hearing this. "Beware," he says. "Only reason is sacred. There is only one world. There is only the material world—the body of Zeus."

"I think you should know something about Church history," I tell Verus. "In the three hundreds, mankind put its trust in a heavenly shepherd. This became reality. Life on earth became just a sordid illusion. Man had given up. Man had given himself over to the rites and formulations of a monstrous lie."

"*Terribilis!*" exclaims Verus. "*Horribilis!*"

"In the history of the world," I say, "only Greece and Rome freed their thought from the fetters of animal imagination. But the Carthaginians, on the advice of priests, threw their first-born into a well. The Incas sacrificed young girls to the sun god. Aztecs were especially cruel. All over Europe sacrificial victims are found in the peat bogs. In China the whole court was buried with the emperor. Around the world these sacrifices are found. And the reason was always religion. The priests were busy weaving misery and degradation from the wool of their sheep, and the wool is human fear and insecurity."

"Yes," says Verus, "I know this to be true."

"The god delusion has been with us for most of our history, Verus. Most people can't walk without crutches, can't think without fairies. But now, Verus, that history will soon be up. Mankind is on the point of superseding homo sapiens. We shall transcend ourselves."

"Poor Verus," says Jancie. "Don't tell him this, but his delusion has taken over his whole life. He thinks he's a stranger in his own time."

"At the risk of sounding immodest," says Verus, "I know I was somebody important."

"Of course you're important," says Jancie. "Tell him I say we are all important in the eyes of God. Tell him we have a soul. Every language has a word for it. It's the soul that discovers eternal Truth. Tell him about the soul."

"Well," I say, "science has not yet discovered this 'soul'. But it did discover the mind, back at the beginning of the last century." To Verus, I say, "You see, sir, the whole of mankind is filled with a great yearning, and it is because our reason is bound by nature and her laws. That's what the human condition is. Nature is our prison. Once human beings developed a mind, it was inevitable we'd see things that way. We've been separating ourselves from nature ever since. We want to break free. We want to control nature. We are bursting to do good. We want to see things endure. *We* want to endure. But we have to get out of this prison. We have to get out!"

Verus does not agree. "We have to be one with nature," he says. "What you say is offensive to Zeus. How can anyone doubt the existence of the gods?"

"Good for you!" cries Jancie.

"Thank you, *cara*. How else to explain things? Apollo, the sun in the heavens, who never fails us. The fire of Jupiter. The interrelatedness of all things. Reason—the ruling faculty—given to man alone. A divine spark that makes us unique in creation. Could these things result from a chance concurrence of atoms? Is that likely?"

"Of course not!" cries Jancie. "It's the work of God. You see, Joe, Verus and I agree."

"Don't rule out chance," I say. "Given an infinity of time and an infinite universe, anything is possible. Somewhere it might happen. Somewhere it has happened. Right here it has. The first spark of life was a chance event. The odds against its occurrence were astronomical. But the opportunities were also astronomical. In a universe of a billion times a billion planets, if life occurred on only one percent of them, that would still be a billion planets. And science has been doing it in the lab ever since 2013. But what happened to that spark of life, after it once occurred on earth, was not governed by chance. It was governed by something called 'natural selection'. Ignorant people call this 'chance', but it isn't. Verus, when you get a moment, I want you to ask the computer about Charles Darwin and evolution. You can put all your questions in Latin."

"But Zeus—the Prime Cause—!" cries Verus. "There has to be a prime cause to explain the existence of the universe."

"A prime cause would also need to be explained by a cause," I say. "Even though we have a grand-unification theory, it does not point to a prime cause. But I think the problem only seems real because of the limitation of the human mind. I'm sure homo mirabilis will have a better understanding of this."

"Perhaps so," says Verus. "I feel even smaller than I used to. Very, very small. I shall have to test my Zeus against the findings of modern science. Computer, tell me about Charles Darwin."

VI

Latin Class

At Augustan University in Rome, Minim friar Gregory Caesar O'Riley occupies his throne-like chair, its faux-leather cushion worn down to a thin veneer. He is wearing his favoured attire: a faded blue janitor-style outfit. He pulls on his suspenders and views the students over his spectacles as they file in, some of them dressed in Roman togas. His wristcom beeps.

"Yes … Hello, Mr. Matchdatch?—Joe! … Yes. His Latin is superb. I love communicating with him. Verus thinks he's what? … He doesn't sound delusional … But all true Latinists consider themselves Romans … Don't give it a second thought … Tell me more about him … You what? … Yes, he told me. He told me you found him on the street. You don't know anything about him, Joe? … His grasp of Latin—it's phenomenal … Absolutely … No, I don't find any—there are no mistakes … No, he doesn't make mistakes. I make mistakes. Verus doesn't make them. I can't believe what he knows … Yes, a great talent. Somebody must know him … Oh, it's fluent. More than fluent. And so is his Greek. I mean ancient Greek. His Greek is way beyond me … Yes, in the classics … amazingly well versed … I think you should contact the universities. This man is a great scholar. A great classical scholar … Somebody must know him … I don't think so … Let me know what you find out. Yes … I thought there were only ten Romans left in the world. Now there are eleven. It's joyous news! It's wonderful! The world has another Roman... Try to find out who he is... Good, that's great... He has what in his head?... Heraclitus!... That's a lot to memorize... Very interesting. Amazing. I wonder where he got that?... I'll see him as soon as I get to my computer... Yes... I'd love to... Right... We'll talk again soon, Joe. Cheerio."

Gregory surveys the students filing into his class. "Come in, come in, there's room for all." His voice is deep and reassuring. "So the word has spread, eh? You want to learn the language of the world. You want to go back to the origins. You want to know where we came from. You want to study the language of Rome. You want to read Caesar." Gregory frowns over his spectacles. "Or is it St. Augustine?"

He waits until all are seated and there is perfect silence.

"So, is it Caesar or is it St. Augustine?" There is a ripple of anticipation. "A caution, my friends, a caution. Be careful. Steer clear of Christian writers if you want to get the most from this course. How many here are Christians? Don't be shy. Nobody is turned away, no matter how troubled you may appear, no matter how stupid you may sound, no matter what icons you wear. Let's see your hands, come on."

Gregory studies the faces of his students. Hands go up here and there, hesitantly. "Splendid. Nobody is turned away." The doors at the back squeak as a young lady in Roman dress enters. Gregory frowns and looks intently at her for a moment. He waits while Bibi takes a seat at the back.

"All right. For the time you are in my class, I want those of you who adhere to some doctrine, to some religious dogma—I want you to close down that section of the brain where religious beliefs are housed—that would be somewhere near the brain stem, right at the bottom of it, where all primitive impulses arise. I want you to lock it up."

There are giggles and fnitters around the room.

"Yes, I am serious. When we climbed down out of the trees, we had religion.

"For this course, your brain should be a tabula rasa, a shaved table. Clear everything from that table. Erase all preconceptions. Your mind is a blank, as it was at birth. It's clean. At birth our minds are clean. There's no crap written there. Your parents have not yet had time to do their dirty work. Remind yourself of this when you get up in the morning. Abstain from prayer. And together we will put something new and wonderful on that bare table."

Gregory ignores the signal from Bibi's comcell. Though she is at the back, he still sees her lips move into an almost imperceptible pout. "What I propose to offer you is entirely in the service of reason and justice. *Ratio et Iustitia*. Because that's what Rome is all about.

"The Romans were not the first to discover reason and justice. The Greeks did that. The Greeks alone staked out the true path for mankind. It's a wonder that anyone found it, given the nature of the human animal. But this was the only path that could give humanity a chance to break the bonds. To set mankind free. Because without reason we are just another animal.

"The Greeks freed us from chance. That's what the Greeks did.

"Man alone had that opportunity, to break free from the deterministic stasis that governs all things. But it was only an opportunity. And the rest of the world missed it. Think about it.

"The Greeks have the eternal glory for being the pathfinders. But the Greeks were not up to the challenge of conquering the world. True, there was the empire of Alexander the Great. But the Greeks were not able to hold on to it. And the world needed to be conquered, or it would never be safe for reason, because the world was full of people who had missed the true path, and it still is full of such people, even as some of us prepare to escape this imperfect world.

"The small candle lit by the Greeks might easily have been extinguished forever. When the Greeks failed to hold on to their conquests, the destiny of the human race hung by a thread. This was the second near catastrophe suffered by the human race. The first was back about 70, 000 BCE. At that time, homo sapiens was to be found only in east Africa. There had been a severe drought and the human race was down to 2000 members. We're talking about near extinction. Somehow, we bounded back, and about ten thousand years later, we left Africa and spread out into the world. We would never again be dependent on the rains of Africa.

"Sometimes, there is only a narrow window into the future. Miss it and the race is doomed. It is the same window that presents itself to us today. And our escape is homo mirabilis.

"How fortunate there was, then, when the Greeks could not hold on to their conquests, not far to the west of the Greek cities, a rising nation, whose destiny it was to take this flame called reason and carry it triumphantly into the world for the benefit of mankind.

"Rome was that nation. Rome!

"A caution, my friends. Do not be curious about Augustine and other Christian writers. You won't find *ratio* and *iustitia* there. There is no reason in a fairy tale. There is no justice.

"What did Augustine have to say about slavery? He said it was a necessary evil in an imperfect world. Isn't that a brilliant thought? What did Augustine have to say about the Jews? I have to admit, his views were very liberal for the times. Don't kill them, he says. Don't send them away. Let them stay in the Empire. Just keep them in a degraded status forever. That's what he said. What did Augustine say about curiosity vis-à-vis the workings of nature—science, in other words? He castigated curiosity as a great evil. He advised us not to try to understand what was not our business. This is your great Christian thinker!

"*Ratio et iustitia*—that's what we are here for.

"And *Ratio* has nothing to do with gods, angels, saviours, elves, fairies, or leprechauns. It has nothing to do with priests, dogma, or rites. Verily, my friends, I say unto you, seek not the truth in fables. The truths we need to discover are in this world. They are in the physical world. And they are within reach of us all. But only if we know how to look after our minds. That, my friends, is the key. Great brains will not do it. No. Only great minds. There is one hell of a difference."

Gregory pauses to swig from a bottle of Chianti. There are giggles from some of the students. Then there is absolute silence.

"Now, I know what you're thinking. Rome was the culture that spawned the Colosseum and the rites of torment which took place there. The spectacles of blood letting, attended and sanctioned by the whole social pyramid. And, you will say, Rome spawned also the parodies and dregs of the human race, raised to the status of supreme honour and power: Caligula, Nero, Commodus, *et alii*. What fine and noble specimens these men were! Their names have entered history as synonyms for evil. Symbols for the worst in man.

"The *Imperium Romanum*, regrettably, had no constitutional provision for the removal of the head of state. Bad emperors were informally removed by assassination. This usually happened after some despot had already committed numerous heinous and unpardonable crimes. Romans do not easily rebel. They are not great complainers.

"Consider the emperor Commodus, perhaps the most vile of the lot. His greatest pleasure was showing off before the crowd. He was a great archer. He used his skill to shoot off the heads of racing ostriches. In the Colosseum, to the great delight of the crowd. Now, the ostrich is fast and the ostrich has a small head. Commodus could shoot off the heads of a hundred in quick succession. To the applause of the Roman mob. His skill as an archer is not in doubt.

"That is how Commodus spent his time as emperor. Thousands of animals were killed by this man, not just ostriches. Lions, tigers, elephants, giraffes. And the human animal, as well—men, women, children. There were about five hundred individuals in his harem—again, men, women, and children.

"We all have impressions of ancient Rome. And where did we get those impressions? Not from the great thinkers and writers of Rome, I can assure you. Not by examining the origins of western law, science, architecture. Not even from school books. Where did we get them?"

"Movies!" Bibi cries from the back of the room. There is a stir of laughter.

"Yes. We got them, of course, from *Ben Hur*. From *Gladiator*. From *Spartacus*. From *The Decline of the Roman Empire*, and a whole slew of movies since then. All that Hollywood crap, which is nothing but lies and garbage.

"Oh, they may be great movies, yes, as far as entertainment goes, grabbing those box office bucks. The sets and the costumes are amazing. Don't think I don't appreciate them. They do a superlative job with all that. The set—the set is everything. But as far as an honest portrayal of Rome—forget it!

"'These tales are the regurgitations of sick hacks and half-wits, hired to churn out spectacles for the entertainment of the crowd. Let's have lots of fights and naked bodies. Not that there wasn't lots of that stuff in Rome. There was. But that is only part of the story. And it's not the most important part. Not by a long shot.

"As far as the movies go, they do make some small effort at verisimilitude, sure. But not much. They cruise the Net for some basic info. Don't bother to read any books—too time consuming. Don't trouble yourself with the truth—that's not what people want. The entertainment business is not concerned with the truth. It never has been. Make a few notes, print out a few pages, embellish what you've got to suit yourself and popular taste—which is to say, go heavy on drama and passion, go light on thought; heavy on ornament, light on substance. Voila! You've got enough to lend your story an air of authenticity in the eyes of the crowd. Not enough to fool those with a superior education, but that doesn't really matter in the context of entertainment.

"After all, this entertainment is aimed at the very people whose tastes, a couple of millennia ago, would have drawn them inexorably to the blood letting of the Colosseum."

Gregory takes another swig from his bottle. "Ahh!" Chuckles in the audience. "My friends, if truth does not concern you, you may leave my class now." Gregory purses his lips and surveys the class over the rim of his spectacles.

"Good. All right. Now, to answer your questions. How can I say these things and still be a Minim friar? Let me tell you why. My father was a plumber. He was also a great student of Rome. He sent me to Latin school when I was only three. Result: I was fluent in Latin by the age of six.

"I thought it odd that my playmates could not understand me when I spoke to them in Latin. At that time, fluent speakers of Latin numbered about one hundred. Today, there are ten men left. That's all. There are no women. Ten men who speak Latin fluently. You're looking at one of them, one of the last men fluent in the language of the world. The best of the lot, in fact. Yes, the best of the lot.

"There's no need to be modest, my friends. Truth comes first. In twenty to thirty years, if nature were to take her course, I and the others would all be laid out dead. Ashes and dust. And Latin would be dead. Completely dead."

"Thank heaven that won't happen!" cries Bibi from the back of the room. There is a titter, then silence.

"No, Bibi, it will not happen. Thanks to the helot. We will not allow nature to take her course. We save ourselves. We save Rome. We save the Roman idea. We save the world for Rome. We save Rome for the world. Homo mirabilis will be getting the Roman program. To ensure that Rome takes up where she left off.

"I have told you, I will do my best as a member of the Commission. We are fortunate that my colleagues are, like myself, men and women of science. They understand Greek and Roman values."

"When will our helots be ready?" Bibi asks.

Gregory removes his spectacles and swigs from the bottle of Chianti. "When? I hope by this fall. There will be enough of them for the Commission, for the elected scientists, and I hope, for all of you, as well. Within five years the whole of the EU will have undergone conversion. The sooner the better. The logistics are overwhelming. The problems of deciding who has priority—what groups, what ages, professions, nations—it's not easy. And there could be trouble. Big time. We need to be proactive. People are going to be left out, lots of them. They won't be happy. If you think you've seen rage, wait till you see how the average person reacts when he finds out he's too late for the last ticket to eternity.

"We live in a world of failed and envious and hateful nations. Europe must survive or the human race is finished."

"How do you decide who is in and who isn't?" a toga-attired student asks.

"Good question, Mario. It's not easy. It seems to me that, if humanity has a cure for something, it should be available to all as soon as possible, regardless of means or anything else. In principle that's how it should be. We have a cure for death. Obviously, it should be available to everyone. But it's logistically out of the question. This is a European project, so, with few exceptions, the first wave will be only Europeans. Europe has to survive. That's our priority."

"I understand the project was delayed," says Mario, "because of the difficulties posed by mind transfer. Have those difficulties been completely resolved?"

Gregory smirks at this question. "I have to give you a qualified 'yes', Mario. The brain of homo mirabilis works essentially like the brain of homo sapiens. We're quite confident of that. If we weren't, it would be criminal to proceed.

"How to transfer a mind from one entity to another—that was indeed the real problem. And we were far from mastering it until we had the unified theory. But since then, advances in chemistry and physics, our experiments in neuroplasticity, and so on, have made a successful transfer possible.

"A brain gives us a model of the world via sense data. The model is an adaptation to an animal's way of life. The brain of homo sapiens is an evolved organ, designed by evolution to allow homo sapiens to navigate the world of his own small experience, which is an extremely limited world. We are going to change that.

"The brain of homo mirabilis will construct a more complex model of the world than the one we have been used to. All our perceptions will be broader, because the senses will be enhanced. We'll be able to see the world as some other creatures do. We'll be able to turn on or turn off these capacities at will. We'll have an expanded horizon for art and music and abstract thought.

"Mirabilis will make complex mathematical computations. Mirabilis will achieve an intuitive as well as a mathematical understanding of things that are too small or too great for the mind of homo sapiens. The memory banks are as good as any computer. The mind of mirabilis will visit regions of possibility forever out of bounds to homo sapiens, except, of course, through the tools of science."

Gregory looks triumphant. "The human spirit will soar!" he cries.

"Yes, but has it been done, sir?" Mario persists. "Are you talking about something that is or something that will be?"

"Yes, yes, we have it, Mario. We have several. We're studying them."

"Can you say more about it?" Mario asks.

"No. No, I can't. Not at this time. But the transfer was totally successful. The Commission was ecstatic at the result. You can't tell the difference between before and after. Everything is the same, both body and mind. Except for the capacity of the mind. I can't tell you how absolutely thrilled I am. The knowledge available to it is of astronomical magnitude, and also the desire and the capacity to make use of that knowledge in socially advantageous ways. Yes, we are confident. We're ready to go."

"What happens ..." a female student asks hesitantly, "What happens to homo sapiens, I mean, what happens to our bodies? The bodies we have now? After the transfer, I mean?"

Bibi laughs. "What happens to them is what happens to all garbage," she says. There is a titter from her classmates.

Gregory focuses on Bibi. "That's right, Bibi. They'll make good compost. We'll talk about this again soon. Now, let's get on with things Latin, shall we?"

"Yes, Caesar!" says Bibi. Some of the females giggle.

"So," says Gregory, frowning, "how did a non-believer like me become a monk? I had this gift of the Latin tongue. And where else would I be able to cultivate it except in this, to paraphrase Pliny the Elder, unholy nest of organized superstition, the Roman Church? My father was an atheist. I'm an atheist. And I thank my Latin studies for that. Latin, my friends, is the language of truth.

"So ... I'm a hypocrite, you say?

"Wrong. I've never hidden my revulsion for organized superstition. The Catholic Church, mindless beast that it is, is often quite unaware of the predilections and activities of the clergy, as we all know. No, I'm not a hypocrite. I see myself as a fifth columnist, a mole, a spy, a saboteur. And I'm damn proud of it. You bet I am."

Chuckles from the students.

"You saw them remove me forcibly from the service. 'Childish behaviour', they called it. Perhaps it was. The question is, how do I get away with it? Am I not afraid of being discovered, uncovered, removed, defrocked? No, I'm not.

"I've been moved around a bit, had my knuckles rapped. It's the same treatment they mete out to anyone who is discovered doing something the Church or society does not condone. And I get on famously with the Holy Father. He loves to test his Latin on me. He tries hard, poor soul. I am, you see, the only one available whose Latin is up to Vatican standards. Ha! It's beyond their standards. In the eyes of the Vatican I'm irreplaceable. And I *am* irreplaceable.

"Which does not mean it's gone to my head. I see myself as a little worm under the papal throne. And I'm eating away at that throne. Munch, munch. Crunch, crunch. Thousands of other little worms are eating away at it. And one day soon—crash! The Wizard of Oz will—fall—on—his—arse!"

There is a titter of laughter. "The harder the better!" cries Mario.

"*Et vobiscum loquar lingua Latina!* I am speaking with you in the Latin language! The sacred language of the West. Now, we are fortunate the Holy Father is a reformer. The world has waited ages for a man like him. A man who will soon reinstate the Latin Mass. Until the end of the Second Vatican Council in 1965, the Mass was celebrated in Latin. Do you know what that means? It means that up till two hundred years ago, generations of churchgoers could recite their prayers in Latin. Since then, no.

"And the number of Latin students in schools has dropped to almost zero. But now, Latin will soon once again be the official language of the Vatican, after this sad interruption. His Holiness plans to address the United Nations in Latin. But these things, significant symbolically as they are, are small potatoes compared to what I want to see him do. And I believe he may soon be ready.

"My friends, I mean ready to turn the Church inside out and upside down. Yes, that's what I mean. Let this be the last great triumph of homo sapiens. Let him and let her discover the humbug of religion while there is yet time, while they still walk the earth. I know the Holy Father is biding his time and looking round him for support.

Until he knows he has it, he will straddle the fence, and he will not live up to our expectations.

"But there is in the Holy Father a great love of antiquity. There is a Roman in him struggling to get out. It won't be easy. The Curia, the cardinals, bishops, priests, seminarians—they are all totally out of touch. They don't have a goddarn clue! They can't speak Latin. The values of Rome do not touch them."

Gregory swigs from his bottle. "It's only a sip to wet my whistle. I can do it. You can't. It's my show." The students laugh. Gregory puts his workmen's hands into the pockets of his overalls. "Let's get down to brass tacks, shall we. Let's talk about this great thing that brings us together: *Lingua Latina*. Classical Latin. We're going to use it to get what we want—the things that are missing in this sad world. Reason. Logic. Justice.

"*Lingua Latina*. We are certain about the pronunciation. There is no doubt at all. It's phonetic and it's easy for anyone. The letters perfectly represent the phonemes of classical Latin. Look at it. Isn't it beautiful? Doesn't it make you want to stand to attention?"

"Heck no!" cries Bibi. "It makes me want to dance." The students laugh.

"Yes, that too. Latin is a clean and orderly language, straightforward. There's nothing sneaky or dirty about it. And make no mistake, the character of a people is reflected in their language. There are plenty of sneaky languages, dirty languages, filthy languages. The media of scumballs. Is it any wonder the world is in trouble? But Latin is perfect. There are no diphthongs, no schwas, no crazy accents, no diacritical marks, like dashes or dots—none of that asinine barbaric garbage."

As Gregory pauses, Bibi takes advantage to remark: "It's very, very clean."

Gregory frowns at her and goes on. "Nor is there a tendency to run words together and corrupt them, as in the Germanic languages. English, for example, is self-corrupting. Corruption is part of the spirit of English. And English speakers take full advantage of it. Latin is different. And no wonder. The Latin alphabet almost perfectly fits the Latin language. This is a language to get things done. Indeed, it's a language to put the world in order. It's transparent in it's beauty. It's familiar. It's not foreign. Even if you've never seen Latin before, it's not foreign. What does this tell you?"

"It's wonderful!" cries Bibi. Her classmates laugh.

"Yes, Bibi, it *is* wonderful. It strikes a cord deep within the human psyche. It's beautiful to the eye, it's beautiful to the ear. It has measure and dignity. It has—gravitas. Surely, if God were to speak to us, if there were such an entity, this is the language God would use. This is the language of the ages. This language is divine. You know, I believe the Fates never intended it to languish, and certainly not to die. It was meant to be the language of humanity—forever."

"Damn right!" Mario cries. "We won't let Latin die!" cries another. And the whole class cries in one voice, "Never!"

"Good for you, my fellow Romans. I can see there is nothing wrong with *your* minds. Latin is literally the language of my dreams. Every dream I have is in Latin. That should be your goal, too. You won't be there at the end of this course—oh no. But it should be your ambition, if you seek the truth; and to seek truth, one must dream in Latin, literally and figuratively.

"If you catch some of this spirit, I will not have failed in my sacred mission. I want you to open yourselves to these dreams, to the voices of antiquity, and to the voice of Rome in the present. To do this you must learn to speak the language of reason. *Lingua Latina*!"

"It shall be!" cries another toga-attired student. And others cry, "It will be!"

Gregory approaches the students and his voice is a whisper. "Let me tell you—hic!—about a great crime perpetrated upon humanity—hic!— by the—hic!—Catholic Church—hic!"

Gregory slowly sips from the bottle till the hiccups are gone. "I have suggested that dropping Latin from the service was a crime. Back in the nineteen hundreds, the language of this so-called state—the Vatican—this tiny remnant of the pope tyrant's temporal power, consigned to the Church by the Grand Strutter of Fascism, Benito Mussolini—was Latin. What significance did that have?

"Well, around the world the Mass was in Latin. It was not uncommon for a priest to know Latin. And as a result, the whole world knew some Latin.

"Then they took Latin away and look what happened. The world is on a steep incline and the direction is down. And what has happened to their seedy service?—ordinary words with ordinary meanings. No wonder people have abandoned the Church in droves. What's left is not the sound and symbolism and mystery of the ages, not the sense of connecting with something wonderful—No! Just ordinary words. Ordinary meanings.

"No reach, no depth, nothing for the imagination. Not the sanctity and dignity and elevation of poetry, not the hallowed echoes of mankind's golden age. Just plain old ordinary words with plain old ordinary associations. And that's what the Church uses to try to get its misbegotten message across. The profane, rather than the sacred. It doesn't work. It doesn't work because the only thing sacred in the Church was *Lingua Latina*. And now it's gone.

"My friends, sometimes, when you try to make things clear, you garble the message, you muddy the waters. There was more in the Latin Mass than the Church ever realized. Much more. And that is what we miss. Not the goddarn dogma.

"Do you know how many people used to attend the Roman Catholic Mass—people who were not Catholic, not even Christian—

just to hear the Latin tongue? Those people no longer come. Because the sanctity is gone—the gravitas and the beauty. Ah, I see you detect a certain tone of *acerbitas*. Yes, quite true. I confess to some bitterness at what they have done.

"But His Holiness does recognize that the dropping of Latin was the biggest mistake committed by the Church in the nineteen hundreds—after collaborating with the fascists, sexual and cultural abuse, and the hoarding of wealth.

"His Holiness... he... he does his best. No, don't laugh, I mean it. He is not just another stodgy traditionalist. This is a man who, in his youth, wrestled in Hamburg, and then in Cincinnati and Chicago. The Holy Father was then known by another name: Pretty Boy George. Yes, you laugh. And unfortunately, those years in the ring probably did him no good.

"The truth is, my friends, one sometimes wearies of the battle of ideas, especially as the mass of humankind is not receptive to the truth—and never will be. But we're going to fix that. The average small mind is about to disappear from the pages of human history..."

After class, the students file out slowly. Bibi lingers, playing with her computer. When all the others have gone, she jumps up and runs to Gregory. "I can't believe you said all those things," she cries. She gives him a kiss. She clings to him. He does not encourage her. "Greg, I want to see you," she says.

"Let me have it," Gregory says.

"I will. There's no hurry. What do you plan to do with it?"

"Hide it from the Church, so it's not tampered with. The wisdom of the ages is in that book. The key to understanding many of the great thinkers of antiquity."

"Greg, I want to see you."

"You'll see me in class."

"That's not what I mean. Oh Gregory, do you have to be so pure? You're not even a Christian."

"If I were a Christian, I wouldn't resist."

Bibi's eyebrows rise ever so slightly. "Really, Greg, come down from your high horse. You and your silly Roman virtue!"

"You're in my class, remember? You've signed on to the cause."

"Oh, come on. What's the cause got to do with us?"

"Listen, my dear, all you have to do is exercise some self-control. I know it's not easy for you. It's not easy for me, either. But these are difficult times. The world is falling apart. We don't have the right to indulge ourselves. Now, did you bring it?"

"It's under my girdle," Bibi says smugly. "If you want it, you'll have to take it." She gives her midriff a rub. "Well, Mister O'Riley? Brother Gregory?"

VII

Oscillation Synchronization

Everything amazes Verus. Not a sight, a sound, or a smell escapes him. He talks to himself or to me in Latin, but he already has an English vocabulary, even though he can't yet put it all together. It's easy to believe he really is from some remote time in the past. The shirts and jeans we give him he examines minutely, asking what materials they are made of, where they are made, and how they are made; and, of course, there are many questions I can't answer, because nobody knows all that stuff. Verus spends hours at my computer researching the past and the present. Jancie and I have given him a crash course in electricity so he will not electrocute himself. I've warned him not to spend too much time reading or speaking Latin on the Net.

Somehow, we've got to get Verus the file he needs. Otherwise, he will be dependent on us forever. As it is, I've taken a holiday from my writing so I can watch Verus. Jancie gets to see him only after school. She teaches grades seven and eight at Immaculate Conception, an elementary school in Breckenridge. After several months of trying to find out who Verus really is, the police have not come up with a single clue. The posters and the media attention have resulted in nothing but false leads.

During March break, Jancie and I spend days with him walking around Toronto, exploring and examining. In the stores he has to run his hands over everything, asking me what purpose an item serves, how much it costs, and how long you have to work to buy it. We wait for him while he rides the escalators up and down at the Eaton Centre, until a security guy asks us to leave. Then we follow him across the street, where he rides the elevators. He's like a kid on Christmas day. He loves to ride on the air bus and the subway, but I'm sure the other passengers think he's out of his mind. And in fact I'm not totally certain he isn't.

At the Central Reference Library, Verus tests our patience by thumbing through the books. We tell him he doesn't need to do that. He can upload anything to the comcell in his head. He tells us he doesn't have a comcell.

We wind up in the library cafeteria. Verus loves coffee and wants to know all about it. We tell him that coffee beans originated at Mocca, near the Red Sea, and that the Eastern Roman Empire enjoyed coffee. He is very surprised to learn the beans were growing right in Rome's own back yard.

Verus and I take turns throwing words at my wristcom. I love to fish out the Greek and Latin words that have inspired English vocabulary: *Electra, electrum ... scientia ... physica ... investigatio naturae.*

I tell Verus the science computers are working day and night, communicating with each other, and with computers around the world. We tell him our knowledge is updated moment to moment. The computers are always calculating, experimenting, collating, sorting, sifting, planning, and inventing. The gains in knowledge are exponential.

As we sit in the library cafeteria sipping coffee, I try to explain to Verus what he needs to do next in order to survive, and so that he will be able to shift for himself. I need to use some strange circumlocutions to get around the fact that the ancients had no equivalents for most of our bureaucratic insignia.

"You need an identity," I tell him. "The state requires it. The state needs to know who you are. The state is much vaster than in your time. It's very intrusive. You need a SIN number. That's your profile. That's your identity. You must get a comcell implant to keep all your information at hand and so you can communicate. A SIN will allow you to work, access social services, travel, drive a car. Without it, you do not exist. But you don't get a SIN unless you have a birth record."

"*Certo*," says Verus. "We had that. For tax purposes. And to prove citizenship."

"I doubt very much if your birth record will still be on file," says Jancie, giving me a wink.

I tell Verus he needs cranial transponders and force nodes, and a SIN, so he can function as a free person. Verus listens to all this with an impish look, as if he is not in the least concerned. "*Non sum!*" he cries. "*Non exto! Verus non est!*" Then he smirks and looks pleased with himself. It's as close as he seems to get to a laugh. "I am no stranger to that," he says. "I know all about it. A wise man does not exist. A wise man is alone."

Jancie wants to know what Verus means by that.

"We are all strangers," says Verus. "Life is a stranger's sojourn. Without your insignia I do not exist, you say. But this is my second existence—or non-existence, depending on how you see it. And insignia had nothing much to do with either one. How many men can claim to have existed twice?"

"It is *not* your second existence!" says Jancie firmly, her brows angled and her face showing some red. "It is not!" But seeing the hurt look on Verus's face, she says, "You know what you should do, Verus? You should seek refugee status."

"Yeah sure, for a resurrected man!" I retort. "How many refugees are we taking from ancient Rome?"

"You don't have to be snide, Mr. Know-it-all."

"Sorry," I say. I suggest getting a forged birth record. I tell Verus that we may have to resort to subterfuge to get such a file. I use the word '*subterfugium*', which is late Latin and sounds odd to him.

"*Subterfugium*! You want me to disobey the laws, is that it? What would better disqualify me for the documents you speak of? Verus is not dishonest."

I lean over the table and in my best Latin I say: "Verus, forget your Roman virtue. Roman virtue is dead. The world has grown old and weary. This world does not care about virtue any longer—especially after eons of preaching by legions of hypocrites. Today, all virtue is suspect, and you Romans are known only for fighting, cruelty, aqueducts, and tormenting Christians. I've never seen a movie about Roman virtue. And nowadays, people find it embarrassing to talk about virtue. You're not supposed to be good. And today, laws are broken every minute. We are very tolerant, very forgiving, and we don't crucify people, though sometimes I think it would be better if we did. If you want virtue, Verus, you go to church. And if you find it there, you leave it there. This is the general understanding. But the truth is, churches have only the odour of virtue. They don't know what it is, either."

Verus is adamant. "You must not break the law on my account," he says. "Verus does not cheat."

We take Verus to the hockey game. It's Good Old Times Night at the new Maple Leaf Gardens. The new temple really does have gardens, and we can't tell the artificial flowers from the real ones, not if we touch them and not if we smell them. These days, real and artificial are as good as the same thing, whether it's flowers or dogs or people. Except "real" does not endure.

"This is a wonderful temple," says Verus, as we pause for a moment before the huge bronze image of Thug, the god of ice hockey, sculpted by one of the country's great artists and a hockey fanatic. Tonight is very special: Montreal Habitants against Toronto Maple Leafs. Just like the good old pioneering days in the mid-nineteen hundreds, when hockey was Canada's game, when the players were rough and tough, had no teeth, and were poorly paid. The greats come out on the ice to bow and pirouette before the crowd: Guy Lafleur and Maurice the Rocket Richard. The applause is deafening. A prayer to Thug, the national anthem, then faceoff. The game begins.

"It's a rink. Say it in English, Verus: It's a rink."

"It's a rink"

"Marvellous. Let's hear some more."

"It's ... a hockey."

"No, we don't say that, Verus. It's a hockey game. Let me hear it: It's a hockey game."

"It's a hockey game. It's a rink!"

"Gee Verus, now you're speaking Canadjun," says Jancie.

"English is the lingua franca of the world," I say. "And its *vocabulum* is half Latin."

There is blood on the ice already. The crowd will not be disappointed tonight. Somebody's slashed the Rocket over his right eye. You can see the blood dripping onto the ice. The Rocket skates up and down so all can see his injury, and the dripping blood, and the red spots on the ice. All the old rules are broken, because who cares about rules any more? The crowd screams with delight. They get what they came for.

"You must be right at home here, Verus," Jancie says. "Isn't it just like the Colosseum?"

The Rocket goes off the ice and is patched up in a hurry. He races back onto the ice with incredible speed and is hailed by the crowd. "Kill the bastards!" the fans shriek.

"The players are helots," I say to Verus. "We bought them from the EU. They get their name from the serfs of ancient Sparta." I question my wristcom madly for words that might get my meaning across. "They are androids. They behave exactly as we do, they look the same, they laugh, they cry, they scream, they bleed. They have names, personal histories, careers—all that stuff. They have the full array of human emotions. We've brought back the greats of ice hockey. They'll be with us forever. They will never die."

Verus looks perplexed at this explanation; whether it was what I said or how I said it, I cannot say. I can see he's thinking hard. Jancie asks me about the Spartan serfs, from whom the helots get their name. I tell her the helots were the original inhabitants of Sparta, a Greek city-state. They were enslaved by their Spartan conquerors. Helots were the lowest of the four classes of Spartans and they had no rights. They worked the land for their masters and they were used as soldiers or as oarsmen in the galleys in war time. But the Spartans feared them because, of course, the helots had many grievances.

"These helots could be the slaves of our age," I say. "But in Europe, they're developing the helot to serve as a replacement for the human body. We have only a few helots in Canada and they are either hockey players or else engaged in dangerous occupations. We can do as we please with them. At least till we get some agreement on how to treat them. There are no ethics involved. We humans always find a detour around ethics."

"*Tekhnologia*!" says Verus. "Technology."

"Right. It's a moral bypass, Verus. The human race never was very good at ethics. Technology lets us off the hook. We can do anything we want to a person and get away with it—as long as the person is a robot."

"Anything?" asks Verus, amazed.

"Oh yes. People take advantage. There's a huge demand for helots but most people can't afford them. It was always a popular dream to do as one pleases without consequences. If we had more helots there would be no lawbreakers. People would take out their frustrations on the androids. Technology solves everything."

"No ethics?" says Verus.

"You can't hurt androids," says Jancie. "We can turn off their feelings. We can do what we want with them. With a clear conscience. Well, to tell the truth, it's a topic of debate. I guess the law has not kept up."

Verus follows the play intently. Then he asks, "No rules?"

"Oh, there are rules all right," I tell him. "But rules are made to be broken. The crowd expects it. It's whatever you can get away with. The crowd loves it."

"The androids are not hurt? Feel no pain? Have no feelings?"

"Of course they have feelings," says Jancie. "To play hockey they have to have feelings. It's feelings that motivate—adrenaline. Doesn't matter if it's a person or a helot. The crowd wants to see anger, spite, conflict. That's entertainment."

"If the androids were never hurt, Verus," I say, "it would take a lot of fun out of the violence, which would come across as phoney. The human animal doesn't appreciate anything that has no risk. It goes back to the time when our ancestors crawled out of the swamp and found the world beset with dangers. Every move they made was risky, and most of them did not last long. The brain stem still thrives on risk. So a player's injuries must be treated the same way ours are."

"I see," says Verus.

"If a player loses an eye or an ear in a game, and it can be put back in place by a surgeon, that's okay. If a human with a similar injury can get it repaired—that's the test. But not if something gets really mashed. Say an eye gets totally squished: the player must continue his career without it. Players are not allowed to have bionic replacements. That would spoil the fun, if all risk were gone. Thug requires an occasional sacrifice. But dismemberment is frowned upon by the owners. The helots are terribly expensive."

"Gladiators are expensive," says Verus.

I explain to Verus that some of the players pretend to have standards. The crowd likes that. The crowd loves a show of principle. Principle is always popular. If you have it and you can still crush your opponent, the crowd will love you. It's in the great tradition of the American icons representing reason and justice: Henry Fonda, John Wayne, those guys. "We'll take you to see some of the latest shows by their helot clones," I say. "They are upright men who can blow evil away with a nervous little finger. But 'noble' by itself has no value to the people. 'Noble' plus 'ruthless' is something the crowd understands—you know, like Julius Caesar. All the old greats have been resurrected. They still hang out in Hollywood. They even have live shoot-outs with the arch-villains of the cinema."

I tell Verus that the players used to skate on real ice, but now it's plastic. I tell him the smell of the rink is manufactured. The Zamboni is not real, either, but the crowd expect it. As it passes, the plastic is wet and glistens, just like real ice used to look while being resurfaced.

"In the beginning, all our games were outdoors," I say. "By the end of the nineteen hundreds we had just about given that up. And by the middle of the last century, there was almost no ice or snow outdoors, anyway."

"Some of the UN police are helots," I say. "No armed forces are supposed to be allowed. China and the U.S. are holdouts. They are too suspicious of each other to disband their armies. But now the U.S. is disintegrating. Hear that roar, Verus? Oh, the fans! They are fanatical. They identify completely with their heroes."

Jancie and I are very concerned about Verus's delusion. We pursue the questions of identity but without any luck. There have been several mentions of Verus in the media. This is what I learn from my comcell:

A man found at Union Station with other homeless people apparently knows only one language—Latin! That's right, Latin. "Verus", as the street person calls himself, was dressed in a toga. Luckily for Verus, the man who found him, local writer Joe Matchdatch of Pickle Crust, used to teach Latin. Matchdatch speculates that his new-found friend may be a university professor or a Latin scholar who has lost himself in his alter ego, perhaps after suffering a blow to the head. Matchdatch has turned to the Vatican for help. The Vatican Latinist, one of the few remaining experts in Latin, is communicating with Verus daily in the hope of discovering some clue to his identity.

The Vatican Latinist, Minim friar Gregory O'Riley, is no stranger to Canada. Born and raised in Hoboken, New York, Brother O'Riley came to Canada to escape the predations of Nabilat, the American Taliban, the dictatorship of creationists that has terrorized the United States for the last hundred years. After earning a B.A. and a Ph.D. in Bioengineering and Neural Science at the University of Toronto, O'Riley moved on to Oxford, where he studied Latin and took his vows as a Minim friar.

Here's what Mr. Matchdatch had to say about Verus:

"What strikes me is the excellence of his Latin—which is why I turned to the Vatican for help. His face has such a refined look. So dignified and intelligent. I'm very curious to know how a man of culture wound up sleeping with the street people at Union Station."

Mr. Verus, whoever he is, is bearded and has curly brown hair flecked with grey. He appears to be in his mid-forties. He suffers from memory loss and delusion. Though unable to remember precisely who he is or what he does, he insists that the only world he knows something about is—ancient Rome!

Matchdatch has taken Verus to a physician, who treated him

for blood spitting and giddiness. Otherwise, the man appears to be in good health. The Salvation Army and other church groups have offered to give the man clothing and shelter.

And now in other news…Stoics and Buddhists will be coming to the Doctor Norman Festival this year. Both stoics and Buddhists are, of course, concerned primarily with the training of the mind, and they've been at it since ancient times. They both maintain that mind control is the key to exercising real control over one's life. Actually, it's the brain that needs to be controlled. And to do this our minds need to be in order. It's something that has to be learned.

Though the mind, as distinct from the brain, had long been thought to exist, it was only at the beginning of the last century that science was able to demonstrate its existence. Though it depends on the brain, it is more than the brain, and it cannot be reduced to the sum of all brain functions. The science of neuroplasticity has shown that the brain is rewiring—that means new neurons and synapses are being created—as long as we live. The brain is, in effect, constantly changing.

The brain changes physically in response to, not just what we do, but what we think. In other words, we are what our thoughts are. This was first demonstrated at the beginning of the twenty-first century using brain-imaging technology. Otherwise expressed, the mind has the power to make physical changes in the brain. And we can train the mind to have better control over the brain. This revelation was considered revolutionary at the beginning of the millennium. Yet, it is remarkable how few people have learned to harness this power.

Numerous experiments have shown that thinking about an activity can have the same result as practising that activity. And that is an astounding finding. Think of the implications. We make ourselves better or worse, according to the thoughts we dwell on. And we become, in effect, what we think. We are remaking ourselves constantly, moment by moment, according to the thoughts we have, according to the thoughts we let into our minds. Consequently, some of us are working at becoming better human beings. But most of us are working at becoming far less than we can be. This is the sad truth. Most people are busy working at being worse, not better. This is nothing new to the Buddhist monks. They've been practising mind control for 2500 years.

It appears that the Roman emperor Marcus Aurelius, a great humanist, was in on the same track. This is evident from the work he left behind, *Meditations*. A quote from Marcus: "Our life is what our thoughts make it." Marcus penned his *Meditations* with a reed stylus at the military camps from which he was waging war on the barbarians. The book was intended merely as a kind of diary, in which Marcus reminded himself of his duty as a man, a Roman, and a stoic, and also took himself to task for not reaching the perfection he aspired to. But it is now considered a masterpiece of ancient thought.

The existence of the mind, like the first atomic theories and speculation on the evolution of man, was arrived at intuitively by the Greeks and the Romans. Considering that they lacked the instruments and the method of modern science, these are remarkable accomplishments. For Marcus Aurelius, it was very important to control thought in order to be a good man. And Marcus was not shy about being good. What is a good man? you ask. One who knows how to rise to full human potential, of course.

Marcus Aurelius was a master of thought control. Why is this important? Well, as Marcus says in *Meditations*: "The soul is dyed with the thoughts." And we know that Marcus walked the talk. If there are good thoughts, good actions must necessarily result from them. Marcus was especially concerned with improving the lot of the poor. He founded schools, orphanages, and hospitals for them. He made the laws more humane.

Mind over matter, you say—what's new about that? But think for a moment of the implications. In most humans the brain is not sufficiently under control. That is why there is anger, suspicion, hate, crime etc. Think of road rage—people practising daily to lose control at a moment's notice, instead of practising to deal effectively with the things they encounter on the road of life. And for what reason? Because we are what our thoughts are. Regrettably, few of us have learned this. When it comes to using the power of the mind, most of us are blissfully ignorant. We are, in fact, out of date. Our minds have not kept up with technology.

The truth is, the West betrayed itself by surrendering to an eastern superstition. This surrender involved a promise not to think. And as a result, the West slumbered for centuries. Knowledge was lost or would not be rediscovered for ages, as the whole of Europe regressed to a barbarous state. And today, the minds of great numbers of humanity are still burdened with this heritage of the occult.

Of course, as individuals we betray ourselves daily by not living up to our destiny as rational beings. If we knew how to use the power of the mind, we would not constantly be in difficulty around the world, both as individuals and as societies.

An irony is that, in Roman times, the West turned to the East for spiritual guidance. And in our time, too, the West turns to the East again, to Buddhism. And both then and now, the germ of Buddhism is represented in our own western tradition of stoicism. Both traditions are concerned with mind over matter.

All of which brings us to the last item of today's agenda.

The Chinese have come to us in droves for Pickle Crust's inauguration of the Doctor Norman Complex. The DNC is a joint Canada-China venture. It comprises Pickle Crust University, a sports and recreation centre, restaurants, a theatre, a library, shops, and a hotel for students and visitors from abroad. This summer, the Complex is expecting hundreds of thousands of visitors from China. And starting this fall, the University will have two chairs in humanitarianism, one held by a Canadian and one by a Chinese.

Up till now, ever since Canada achieved favoured nation status with the Chinese, at the beginning of the twenty-first century, the town of Pickle Crust has been hard put to find accommodation for all the visitors from China, and also the Chinese from Toronto, who now constitute half of Toronto's population of nearly fourteen million. Since the wall has gone up between the United States and Canada, our relationship with China has grown by leaps and bounds. With the Doctor Norman Complex, Pickle Crust will at last be able to cope as the number one tourist destination for the citizens of China. Congratulations, Pickle Crust!

Jancie and I make arrangements to have Verus examined by an expert in neuroplasticity at the University of Pickle Crust, Department of Cognitive Sciences.

"Recordings from his medial temporal lobe," the doctor tells us, "suggest that oscillation synchronization between Verus's rhinal cortex and his hippocampus may be out of wack, but we don't know how or why."

"Okay doctor, so what does that mean?" I say.

"It means that conscious memory for everyday events depends on learning mechanisms in the medial temporal lobe. That's where neocortical inputs converge on the hippocampus by way of the rhinal cortex." The doctor points as he says this to a full-colour diagram of a cross-section of the human brain. "The medial temporal lobe circuit is necessary for declarative memory, but... in Verus there appears to be a malfunction."

"A malfunction?"

"Yes. It could account for his inability to fully remember events. And yet, it's puzzling since there's no evidence of trauma. None whatsoever. This is what the electroencephalographic tests tell us. There appears to be a disconnect between his medial temporal lobe circuit and declarative memory formation."

"Something has to be wrong," I say.

"Yes. No doubt the neural coupling across brain regions is somehow adversely affecting memory behaviour. In Verus, the temporal dynamics of activity within these regions, and their relationship to memory, are missing something. But what this something is—who knows? I'm sorry, it's all we can tell you at the moment."

We get a referral to a Doctor Franz Lozenkrank.

Dr. Lozenkrank's office smells of cigar smoke. The doctor, a big, bearded man with stained vest and tie, jumps up from his desk to examine us. He looks like Groucho Marx, a nineteen-hundreds screen comedian. I tell him Verus needs an identity.

"Ah, ze man who does not exist!" cries the Doctor, looking Verus over. He chuckles to himself. His considerable eyebrows twitch. "Ze man ze state vill not recognize. Ze man viss a serious problem: Oscillation synchronization *ist kaput*. You know vat your problem iss, my friend? You haf no self. You are just a single little name and vun big delusion, vissout contexts in space or time. You haf only vun sing on your side, and zat iss ze physical presence. You appear to be here. But in zis verld ze physical presence counts for nussing."

"What's he saying?" Verus asks in Latin.

"Search me," I say.

"From ze point of view of ze state, you are a lost soul, my friend. If I were you, I vould try to get an identity number." The Doctor gives me a wink. "You must have an ID file. Or else you are nussing."

Verus looks at me? "*Litterae,*" I tell him. "*Instrumenti.* Documents."

"My, my, how adept vi are at speaking ze languages of antiquity!" Doctor Lozenkrank cackles with mirth. "So, you sink you are Roman, my friend? Vi shall see about that. Now, each of us has an identity. Vi are composed of a single physical entity to which, typically, a name or sign iss attached. Identity iss who vi are. You appear to be a physical entity. But there are no signs attached. Therefore, you are nobody."

"Nobody!" I cry.

"That's crazy!" says Jancie.

Doctor Lozenkrank shakes his head sadly. "Identity iss ze means of distinguishing ourselves from each uzzer, and through this distinction a host of cultural and social artifacts flow."

"Doctor, we—!"

"I mean ze attribution of ownership of houses, permission to drive, residency, citizenship, ze right to vote, *und so weiter*. Attribution cannot be assigned if you have no identity, quite aside from ze philosophical and teleological—one might even say 'religious'—implications of ze considerable time span between now and ... You, my sorry friend, have no self. And a physical presence wizout a self iss, to ze state—nobody! You do not exist."

"Jeez," I say. "We came here to get some help."

Lozenkrank studies us critically. "Let us put aside all ontological problems zat traditionally have been ze concern of seeking ze self."

"Yes, let's do that," says Jancie.

"Let's be sensible," I say.

"Now, a materialist age requires a materialist response. In uzzer words, my friends, vi shall not concern ourselves about ze potential migration of souls, or what happens when craniums exchange brains; nor shall vi be concerned viss possession, nor viss transubstantiation, resurrection, etcetera. I leave all zat to philosophers, priests, religious fanatics, and uzzer experts of essential and covert reality. Ha-ha, ho-ho, hoo-hoo! So! It iss often said: Produce ze body and you have ze person. Habeas corpus. Voila! Here iss ze body."

"Yes, this is the body," I say. "Now we're getting somewhere."

"Sounds good," says Jancie.

"Vel, that should be enough, you say, to have ze body."

"I would think so, Doctor," I say, my hopes rising. "I'm satisfied with that."

"So am I," cries Jancie. "Me, too."

Doctor Lozenkrank raises his voice. "Unfortunately . . . ze identity iss still lacking. To have ze body iss not enough."

"What!" says Jancie. "Well, it should be."

"Ze problem of identity iss today an epistemological problem. How do we know zat zis person iss who zis person claims to be? He claims to be an ancient Roman." Lozenkrank turns on his heel and is convulsed with laughter, which lasts only a moment. Then he confronts us again. To Verus he says, "How do you do, sir. My name is Franz Joseph and I am ze emperor of Austria-Hungary! Huh-ha-ha, heh-heh-heh! And how I wish I was back in my own time living ze life of Franz Joseph; how much simpler life vould be! Ha-ha! Huh-huh-huh! There were far fewer nuts to crack!" The Doctor turns away from us and submits to another brief fit of convulsive laughter.

"Christ!" I say.

"All right, all kibitzing aside, ze identity iss described, not from ze point of view of ze cogito, and not from ze point of view of ze person wondering who ze hell they are, but from ze point of view of a tird person, ze vun who seeks to know, namely me, representing ze state. I am ze tird in this case. It is I who ask ze question 'Who goes there?' And I must be satisfied viss ze response."

"Okay," I say. "So . . . ?"

"So? So? But zer iss no response!" The Doctor's thick eyebrows twitch frenetically. He seems very pleased with himself.

"But for God's sake, Verus is right here!" I say. "He thinks, he feels, he speaks. He's alive. And you can see just by looking at him that he's an honest man. Look into those eyes. He just wants to get a job and support himself for Christ sake!"

"Of course, of course, I have no doubt. My sympathy. Ze modern world iss overrun viss displaced persons. Ze problem of knowledge, when it iss connected to questions of personal identity, iss tied into ze fabric of society. Without ze capacity to know, most of our customs and institutions would founder. Zay would come crashink down! Ze ritual of marriage, ze assignment of criminal responsibility, ze right to access a home, ze right to arrest somebody, and ze right to administer punishment—none of these would be possible without a tird party being able to state an informed opinion. I am zat tird party and it iss my business to represent ze state. It iss ze state you must satisfy. Ze state!"

Dr. Lozenkrank brings his hairy fist down hard on the desk. Pens and pencils rise into the air.

"What state are you referring to?" I ask. It seems a reasonable question. Lozenkrank looks at me strangely, as though he is wondering about that himself. "Doctor," I say, "This is Canada. It's the middle of the twenty-second century. On the Internet we—!"

"Ah! Ze Internet!" Lozenkrank's eyebrows rise in unison, slowly. "That vunderful construct of virtual nonsense!"

"There *is* an awful lot of crap on there," I say. "But—!"

"*Oh ja, oh ja*! Tell me about it. And what iss it but a world as virtual and ephemeral as your fantastical Verus. Ze virtual presence iss corpus-*frei*. On ze Net, there iss no body. We need a body to present to a tird party as evidence that we are indeed who we say we are. Ze traditional connection between signification—ze use of a sign to attribute identity, and ze instantiation—ze actual instance of a human body—has been utterly, irretrievably lost. Ze qvestion, 'Halt! Who goes there?' attains a new significance when zere iss no means to follow up with ze demand, 'You there, step forward into ze spotlight and be recognized! Identify yourself!' And without zis second part, it would seem, ze fabric of society, so vell known in ze physical world, cannot be migrated to ze virtual world."

Poor Jancie has given up. She just stands there with her mouth open. I can't wait for Doctor Lozenkrank to finish.

"Now, it does appear zat he can claim instantiation. But—!"

"Certainly he can claim it," I hasten to say. "We can all see Verus is, he has, ah, instantiation."

"But!" Professor Lozenkrank's fist comes down on the desk again: Whump! Pens and pencils summersault. "My duty iss clear. I, as ze tird person in zis case, representing ze state, do solemnly declare zis body in front of me to be completely and utterly unknown."

"What!" I cry. "But doctor—!"

"None of this makes sense!" says Jancie. "It's crazy!"

"*Nein*! Enough. Zere iss no way I can state an informed opinion about zis physical presence, other than to say it appears to be a middle-aged male suffering from loss of memory and delusion. Mister Verus, whoever ze hell he iss, cannot be known. Therefore, he has no hope of acquiring any of ze attributes of identity, which iss to say, credit file, driver's licence, social insurance number, birss record, citizenship, passport, etcetera. Ze privileges and entitlements of Canadians are for you out of bounds, and forever vill be."

"Christ!" I say. "Jesus! Thanks a lot."

Lozenkrank lowers his voice and says in an oily tone, "You might try appealing directly to ze minister. Write him a letter telling him everything you know about Mr. Verus. He may take pity on him. I vish you good luck. Good day."

"What did the Doctor say?" Verus asks, as we hurry away from there.

I tell Verus the Doctor said nothing. "He's not really a doctor, Verus. He's just a little man pretending. He's a *homulus*. He's a foot soldier in the great modern army of functionaries. His sole purpose is to gratify his own ego. You've just seen the twenty-second-century bureaucracy at work."

VIII

The Thundering Legion

Spring has come quickly and Verus is now capable of some basic conversation in English. One evening, we find Verus at my computer speaking with Gregory, the Vatican Latinist. Gregory shows us images of Roman Emperor Marcus Aurelius. "He reigned from 161 to 180 CE," says Gregory. "Looks rather like you, Verus, wouldn't you say?"

Verus cries out. "*Eia*! That is me, Joe! Jancie! Gregorius!"

"Christ!" I say. "It sure does look like you!"

"Sure does," says Gregory. "No doubt about that." There's a mischievous grin on Gregory's face as he beams at us from the VDU."

"Marcus Aurelius Antoninus! Yes, those are my names! That is who I am!"

"I thought your name was 'Verus'," says Jancie.

"It is, *cara*. My parents died young. I was adopted by my grandfather. I was called 'Verus'. Then I was adopted again and I took the names of my new family."

"Son of a gun! You certainly look like Marcus Aurelius," I say. "You sure as hell do. Hell, I can't tell the difference!"

"There is no difference," says Verus.

"No, there isn't," Gregory chimes in. "You, Joe and Jancie, are in the august presence of the emperor of Rome. Get down on your knees!" He laughs heartily.

"Don't be silly!" cries Jancie. "Don't be foolish!"

We are so excited we say goodbye to Gregory and sign off.

Verus grabs me by the arm. His look is very intense. "It is coming to me," he cries, "bit by bit." In a mixture of English and Latin, he says, "I was beginning to think I must have been right at the top in Rome. And it is true. I am Marcus. There is no other way to explain the thoughts I have been having."

Jancie laughs. "How absolutely silly! Don't talk such nonsense, Verus."

"But I *am* Marcus. And now I am certain—Joe, how can you doubt? It is all coming back to me. I was raised by my grandfather. When Hadrianus adopted Antoninus, Antoninus adopted me, so the succession would be secure; and then my names changed—to Marcus Aurelius Antoninus. Remember, I told you about my wife Faustina, and my friend Cassius? They were in my head, just vaguely. But this picture is bringing so much back. So much."

"Heck, Verus, I don't know what to say," I confess. "You're asking me to believe something with a probability of absolute zero."

"Less than that," says Jancie, looking very irate.

"But it is coming to me, Joe. It is coming. And did you see when I died? 179 by your Christus calendar. 179! And now Verus lives again, by the will of Jupiter! *Diis gratia*! Verus lives again!"

"You do not live again!" cries Jancie.

"Joe, Jancie, there must be work for me here. There must be a reason. There has to be. But to think people know about me after so much time has passed! This is truly remarkable. I would never have believed it. And now I am come back. I am resurrected. It must be for something. It has to be."

"You are not resurrected!" Jancie is almost pulling her hair. "Nobody is resurrected. That kind of thing does not happen. I'm not calling you 'Marcus', either. Don't think I am. Nobody comes back from the dead. It's just common sense. Nobody does!"

Verus gets the drift. "It is all right, *Cara*. I want to be called 'Verus'. The life of Emperor Marcus is history."

"I'll say it is!" says Jancie. "You got that right."

"Oh, come on, Verus, it can't be true," I say. "Things like this don't happen. It's in defiance of a whole slew of physical laws. So you look like him, so what? It's what's called a doppelgänger."

"Sure, he's a doppelgänger," says Jancie. "That's what he is. A doppelgänger."

"Doppelgänger!" Verus asks the encyclopedia for Marcus Aurelius. Pictures of the whole family come up—statues, busts, memorial columns, friezes, and lots of links. "Oh, dear Zeus!" cries Verus. "This is my father Antoninus, my adopted father! And I am Marcus Aurelius Antoninus. I am, I am. At last I have all my names. At last I know who I am. I do. I do. Faustina! See there—my wife! Is she not beautiful? Beautiful in so many ways. *Oh vae*! If only Faustina could have come with me on this journey through time. If only I could speak with her, walk with her, touch her. Faustina!"

The sexual embrace can only be compared to music or prayer.

"You don't feel complete without her," I say. "I'd feel the same way without Jancie."

"Tell me about it sometime!" says Jancie, screwing up her face at me.

"What do you mean, I don't feel complete?" says Verus. "I depend on no one. My life depends only upon the thoughts I have and the deeds I do. And if these are in accord with reason and justice, then my life is complete. I stand erect, I stand alone. That is what stoicism is. But I am still allowed to miss my Faustina, as long as I do not indulge the feeling. As long as the feeling does not master me."

"Gee!" says Jancie.

I can see Jancie is affected by the strength of Verus's conviction. There is no doubt in my mind that Verus really believes he is Marcus Aurelius. I whisper to Jancie that we should humour him.

Verus goes on and on about his family in great detail, especially Antoninus Pius, his adoptive father, who was emperor before him, and apparently a great one. While Verus is telling us about him, I ask the computer for a description of Antoninus Pius. The computer shows a page in *Meditations* and, as I scan it, I'm hearing practically the same thing from Verus, who is not even looking at the screen. Except that Verus is giving us even more detail:

In my adoptive father I observed mildness of temper, and unchangeable resolution in the things that he had determined after due deliberation, and no vainglory in those things that men call honours; and a love of labour and perseverance; and a readiness to listen to those who had anything to propose for the common weal; and undeviating firmness in giving to every man according to his deserts; and a knowledge derived from experience of the occasions for vigorous action and for remission ...

I observed, too, his habit of careful inquiry in all matters of deliberation, and his persistency, and that he never stopped his investigation through being satisfied with appearances which first present themselves; and that his disposition was to keep his friends, and not to be soon tired of them, nor yet to be extravagant in his affection; and to be satisfied on all occasions, and cheerful; and to foresee things a long way off, and to provide for the smallest without display; and to check immediately popular applause and all flattery ... and he was neither superstitious with respect to the gods, nor did he court men by gifts or trying to please them, or by flattering the populace; but he showed sobriety in all things and firmness, and never any mean thoughts or actions, nor love of novelty.

And the things that conduce in any way to the convenience of life, and of which fortune gives an abundant supply, he used without arrogance and without excusing himself; so that when he had them he enjoyed them without affectation, and when he had them not, he did not want them.

No one could ever say of him that he was either a sophist or a home-bred flippant slave or a pedant; but everyone acknowledged him to be a man ripe, perfect, above flattery, able to manage his own and other men's affairs. Besides this, he honoured those who were true philosophers, and he did not reproach those who pretended to be philosophers, nor yet was he easily led by them ...

He took a reasonable care of his body's health, not as one who was greatly attached to life, nor out of regard to personal appearance, nor yet in a careless way, but so that, through his own attention, he very seldom stood in need of the physician's art or of any medicine or external applications.

He was most ready to give way without envy to those who possessed any particular faculty, such as that of eloquence, or knowledge of the law or of morals, or of anything else; and he gave them his help, that each might enjoy reputation according to his deserts; and he always acted conformably to the institutions of his country, without showing any affectation of doing so. Further, he was not fond of change, nor unsteady, but he loved to stay in the same places, and to employ himself about the same things, and after his paroxysms of headache, he came immediately fresh and vigorous to his usual occupations.

His secrets were not many, but very few and very rare, and these only about public matters; and he showed prudence and economy in the exhibition of the public spectacles and the construction of public buildings, in his donations to the people, and in all such things, for he was a man who looked to what ought to be done, not to the reputation that is gotten by a man's acts.

He did not take the bath at unreasonable hours; he was not fond of building houses, nor curious about what he ate, nor about the texture and colour of his clothes, nor about the beauty of his slaves. His dress came from Lorium, his villa on the coast, and from Lanuvium generally. We know how he behaved to the toll collector at Tusculum who asked his pardon; and such was all his behaviour. There was in him nothing harsh, nor implacable, nor violent, nor, as one may say, anything carried to the sweating point; but he examined all things separately, as if he had abundance of time, and without confusion, in an orderly way, vigorously and consist-

ently. And that might be applied to him which is recorded of Socrates, that he was able both to abstain from, and to enjoy, those things which many are too weak to abstain from, and cannot enjoy without excess. But to be strong enough both to bear the one and to be sober in the other is the mark of a man who has a perfect and invincible soul.

"Holy Christ!" I cry. "Marcus Aurelius, emperor of Rome! Do you know what this means, Jancie? It means he should have copyright for his book. All these publishers are cashing in on your work, Verus, and you get nothing. They're all sharks. They wait till a man's dead eighteen hundred years so they don't owe him anything. And that's just what's going to happen to my Roman cookbook."

"What a great man your adopted father, I mean, Antoninus must have been," says Jancie. Then she adds, "Don't be silly. You are not an ancient Roman. You are not! I know you're not!"

"We can prove it or disprove it," I say. "There are several tests that should set the record straight. Would you believe him then? If we had a DNA link?"

"Well, I . . . I don't know."

"And if he did have proof, Jancie, it seems to me they'd have to pay him royalties on *Meditations*. That would throw some of those big publishing houses for a loop. I bet all he'd need is a good lawyer. Scientific proof and a lawyer. The public domain versus the resurrected man—Ta-ta! They'd have to change the rules."

"Don't be silly."

I tell Verus he's got to be able to pay the bills. I also tell him that if he could establish rights, he would not only have some very interesting and lucrative career possibilities, but he would have control over what they're doing to his work, which is even more important.

"Yes," he says, "I do not wish to be a burden. I think I should take those tests."

We browse *Meditations* together. Verus tells us that the title he gave the book was *To Himself*, and that it was only meant to be a dialogue with himself and a kind of diary. "I wanted to be a philosopher," he tells us, "but my reign was beset with troubles. Earthquakes, fires, floods, famine, pestilence, war. All at once. There was no time to study, to read, to spend with friends. There was no time for anything."

"You had an unhappy reign," I say.

"No, Joe, you're wrong. I did not. I was as happy as any man could be. I believe I was happier than most. What have externals got to do with being happy? They have nothing to do with it. Happiness is in each person's power, regardless of externals."

"Interesting thought," I say.

"*Verum est!* Let me give you an example, Joe. My wife is not here. That is an external. My reign was filled with troubles. That is an external. Things I have no control over cannot make me worse. Something bad happens. I form an opinion. My opinion should be: this does not affect me; this does not make me worse. If I have a bad opinion, it is in my power to change it. We all have that power. And it resides in the mind."

"Here is something interesting," says Jancie, who is busily checking out all the sites that have come up in a Google search. "Now, don't look at the monitor, Verus. Tell us about the miracle of the Thundering Legion. I want to see how much you know about Roman history without reading up on it."

"Yeah, you can't blame us for doubting, sir," I say, sheepishly. "Tell us about *legio fulminata*."

"*Legio fulminea?*" Verus looks out the window as he begins his history of the Thundering Legion. He tells us the Legion was formed in the reign of Caesar Augustus, and he starts to enumerate its exploits.

"Not that!" cries Jancie. "I mean the one Marcus Aurelius was involved with in the mountains of Bohemia."

"But that's it, *cara*. Is that what you wish me to relate?" Verus is standing at the window, looking out.

"Well?" says Jancie.

"I'm trying to remember, *cara*."

"I see!" says Jancie. She gives me an ironic look that seems to say: I told you. "Do you want some hints? The *Catholic Encyclopedia* says—!"

"Screw the *Catholic Encyclopedia*!" I say.

"Neither the condition of my body nor the occupations of my mind had prepared me for a life of war," Verus begins. "No military exercises as a youth—a grave omission on the part of my educators. The army always wanted a military man. But the ailments I suffered from—chest and abdominal pains, occasional dizziness, spitting blood—I learned to live with them. Remedies came to me in dreams. Exercises and sleeping on a hard bed with only a skin for a covering—the Greek discipline. Not giving in to the senses. I toughened myself. Made myself ready. I learned to be a soldier. The Germans were restless. They were trying us, testing us, asking for gold, asking to come to our markets, asking to settle in the pleasant valleys of Italy—nay, demanding! And some did cross over uninvited and they ravaged the land. That's why I became a soldier. Because of the Germans."

"How about some details," says Jancie.

"Patience, *cara*. I applied myself to the arts of war. It was not long before I was leading my men with confidence. The student of life became a student of warfare. And the day came when I led our armies in victory against the Quadi and the Marcomanni, and other German tribes, and Sarmatians, too.

The secret of all victory lies in the organization of the non-obvious.

"*Imperator*! What a cry that was. My victory salute. I can hear it yet. I can feel the heady passion it roused in me—yes, if truth be said, passion! In me, the enemy of passion. To hear the cheers of the men whose lives I risked, as they raised their weapons. The men I ate with, rode with, fought with. Some would be wounded, some dying. Imperator! The grandest cry to Roman ears. The cry that said: You've done your duty; you fought and conquered for Rome; all the world knows it. I was to hear that cry many times. And perhaps philosophy will forgive me if I had, in the end, to acknowledge that I yearned to hear it, depended on it, lived for it... Imperator!

"Yes, I did. Me, the so-called philosopher. Not that I grew to love war, you understand. I waged war in the same way I did everything else that was my duty—methodically and with great determination. Failure was not an option. But it never would have entered my mind to start a war for gain, or to expand the borders of the civilized world merely to gain a reputation. The acclaim of the world means nothing to me.

Take care not to make yourself a Caesar!

"Hadrianus, the Augustus before my adopted father—he was a soldier, a born soldier, besides all the other good things he was—architect and poet. The Pantheon is his work. He was brilliant. There was peace in his time and he kept it, even though he was a military man. And what great soldiers do not yearn for war? But for him it never came, and he would not make war for his own sake. Not for glory. Instead, he spent his time travelling throughout the Imperium to test the army and to find the best places to entrench and fortify, so that in some future time Rome would be ready. But he never went to war, because no one tested us.

"But in my time, the long peace was broken by the Germans. I began to see that another expansion was necessary if ever the world were to be safe from these restless tribes. After many uncertain years, we managed to subdue them. And it was time to bring them under our yoke. We already had two German provinces. I was going to create two new ones. Rome was about to absorb the whole of Germany.

"But fate overtook me and I... As I was dying I counselled my son Commodus to pursue this plan. Germany, like Gaul and Spain would have adopted our language, and the Germans would have become Roman citizens. But my son—! Now look what has happened to the world because this was not done!"

"What about the miracle?" cries Jancie.

"Yes. I am coming to that. Well, who were these Quadi and Marcomanni barbarians? Germans, yes, but not total strangers. Some of them knew us well, since they had been coming to our markets. But they weren't happy to just trade. They saw how superior life was on our side of the border They coveted our land and our wealth. They were determined to test us, move into Italy, take our land, if we seemed unable to defend it."

"That's all very fine," says Jancie. "I want some facts. What happened in Bohemia? Let's hear about the miracle."

"Yes, *cara*, I am getting to that. As you say, it happened in Bohemia. The 12th was passing through a defile, deep in enemy territory. The trail we followed was over open land, but on either side the hills were thickly forested with spruce and pine, hemlock and cedar. We had been marching and riding for most of the day under a blazing sun, heading for a place where we believed the enemy to be. We were tired, hungry, thirsty. All our water was gone. We were on the lookout for any sign. My men scanned the woods on either side continually, so that we would not be taken by surprise.

"I could not help thinking of the legions of Augustus, a century and a half before my time—annihilated to a man. I thought, somewhere in these dark haunts, the barbarians brag about it to this day, and I pictured some of them still flaunting the armour and the rings of those Roman soldiers. The best soldiers Rome had. I prayed that, if that were so, the wearers of these artefacts would cross my path, to find the wrath and justice they deserved. Augustus was devastated. After that, he never sent an army into Germany again. In this necessary undertaking he failed. And so did I."

"Details!" cries Jancie.

"Yes, *cara*. So as I walked, giving my horse a rest, it occurred to me that Rome would forever be in peril as long as the tribes of Germany were not pacified, and that to defeat them was not enough. Either we had to destroy them utterly or we had to expand the borders of the Empire, or both. Only then would the world be safe. I resolved to prosecute the war until the will of the barbarians was broken.

"I considered where the boundaries of the new provinces might go and what we might call them. I resolved that they should include the whole of Germania Magna, at least to the sea of the Svevi in the north, and to the land of the savage Sarmatians in the east. The experience we were having in Germania Inferior and Germania Superior was encouraging. In those provinces, the Germans had settled down and were on the way to becoming good citizens of the world. Many of them were in the army and, believe you me, they knew how to deal with their restless countrymen beyond the Rhine and beyond the Ister.

"So as we made our way cautiously though this defile, deep in the woods of Germania Magna, we were hoping to come upon a good place to camp before darkness fell, but we hadn't found one. And this troubled me, as we were nearing the end of our resources, physical and mental. The horses, too, could no longer be ridden, but were famished and thirsty like ourselves. So I prayed we would not encounter the enemy on this day. As I led my men I thought much of my wife and my children. I thought what a great thing it would be to return to Rome in triumph to the hails of senate and people, and to the warm embrace of my wife, the German wars behind us forever, and the resumption of pax Romana.

"We trudged, then, wearily on, hoping to come to a spring or a river, and to find a defensible spot where we could break out what remained of our provisions and feed both ourselves and the horses. But this was not to be. Quadi barbarians emerged from the trees suddenly on all sides. Thousands of them to our hundreds. The way forward was barred and retreat was impossible. Stand and fight was all we could do. They yelled at us in the manner of barbarians. They beat their weapons against their shields. It was a terrible sight, to be surrounded by these skin-clad, long-haired Germans on all sides, and to be dead tired after our long march and needing to eat and drink.

"But we immediately formed into our defensive phalanx, smartly, as though we had just marched out of our camp, and we steadied ourselves for the onslaught of these brutes. I shouted encouragement to the men. The men were making wry and ribald comments on the grave error these scruffy, flea-bitten men-of-the-woods were about to commit in attacking a legion of Rome; and not an ordinary legion, either, but the Thundering Legion, of ancient and superlative fame.

"And my soldiers laughed loudly so the barbarians would hear them. Some of the men, indeed, were making rude gestures, and the nearest of the barbarians responded in kind. We readied ourselves as best we could.

"We waited and waited, but when there was no movement or resolve from the barbarians, we relaxed. My thoughts drifted momentarily to Faustina and the good luck I had in being given such a loving and dutiful wife. I remembered her words upon parting: "Marcus, do not sacrifice yourself. Let Cassius do it. There is no need for Augustus to be at the front." I told her they were my soldiers. I told her the risks must be shared. I sincerely wished that Cassius had had better luck than I. Again I pictured my homecoming. At that moment it would all be worth it. I prayed that, when the battle was over, I would once again hear the cry of triumph from my soldiers as they hailed me: Imperator!

"The barbarians did not move. They sat on their haunches and waited. So we also sat and waited. We smuggled a food ration to each man, and even to the horses. But we had no water. We chewed on grass and tree gum.

"The barbarians would rise to their feet suddenly—they did this several times. Only so we would have to do the same, to prepare for battle. But when we were ready, they jeered at us and sat down again. They were toying with us. They were biding their time. They had every reason to expect that by the end of the day they would be nailing our skulls to the trees, just as the Chatti had done to the legions of Augustus in the Teutoburger Wald a century and a half before.

"By this time, dark clouds had come up and much of the heavens had turned purple. The enemy, thinking it was time to have their sport, began to crawl toward us slowly, on hands and knees. We did not know what this meant but we got to our feet again. They would crawl for a bit and then rest, then crawl again.

"The sky in places was almost black and I was certain it was going to rain. I prayed it would do so quickly, so that we might have water to drink. Again I called encouragement to the men. And, as I did this, the devils rose en masse, with a great roar; and, in one ragged horde, they rushed at us from all sides, their blond and red hair flying in the wind. I felt my hand tighten on my sword and I braced myself for the shock, and, as I thought, my probable death.

"But the shock that came was not what I expected. The heavens exploded. The voice and the fire of the gods struck at the earth all around us. *Jupiter Tonans* let loose his bolts. But the fire struck in the midst of our attackers, even as the momentum of the barbarians carried the foremost of them against our shields and our weapons. And my own sword I plunged into the throat of one of these blond wild men—a shower of blood hit me in the face.

"I hacked away fiercely at other faces and arms, and almost did not notice the hail. Balls of ice big as plums were falling, making a great din as they bounced off our helmets. But with far greater force the hail struck the barbarians, many of whom had nothing on their heads.

"This punishment from above threw the enemy into confusion. Water now gushed from the heavens. As the barbarians faltered, we drank. We collected water in our helmets. We gave the horses water. And we repulsed the barbarians.

"And as they drew back, our archers stepped forward and let loose their bolts into the barbarians with deadly affect. Hail and fire bolts continued to fall on the enemy while on us it mostly rained."

"You forgot the Christians," says Jancie. "The Christian soldiers prayed for help. That's when the storm came."

Verus gives Jancie a blank look. "Christian soldiers? I suppose some of my men may have been Christian. I would have taken no notice of that, as long as they did their duty."

"But they fell to their knees and prayed to God!" says Jancie, fervently.

"No, *cara*. My soldiers would not fall to their knees without orders. They were all Romans, no matter where they came from. We were praying but we were not on our knees. Without the storm we would not have lived to see another day. My men were persuaded that Zeus had intervened. The Thundering Legion had been saved by the god of thunder.

"As for myself, I could not say whether the gods had intervened or whether we had simply been blessed by some fortunate turn of fate. At any rate, the defile was now strewn with the bodies of the barbarians, both dead and dying. Jupiter had turned certain defeat into victory. Jupiter had come to the aid of the Thundering Legion. Jupiter had saved Marcus Augustus."

"Don't believe everything you read," I say to Jancie. "Especially if it's in the Catholic Encyclopedia. What happened then, Caesar?"

"Our surgeons went to work on the wounded. We put the wounded in the wagons, including some barbarians. The storm passed and we buried our dead. We mounted our horses in a light rain and went on to our camp. I knew that the barbarians would soon be utterly broken. Then, the Imperium would grow again, for the same reason Rome had always grown: to make the world safe for Rome, which is to say, to make it safe for reason and justice. I knew the day was near when peace would descend on the forests of Germany, and as I rode, I gave quiet thanks to Jupiter."

We thank Verus for relating this. I put some questions to him concerning Roman military customs and tactics. His answers are entirely convincing. "Well," I say, "it all sounds good. But we'll let science make the final decision. Science is the final arbiter."

"I agree," says Jancie.

Verus shrugs. He apparently doesn't care.

IX

Truth as the World Sees It

"Boy!" I say, with a sly look at Verus, one evening as Jancie, Verus, and I are gathered around Sunrise. "This guy Marcus would have it made if he were alive today. A whole cult has arisen around his book. To his fans he's sacred. There are a whole bunch of translations and editions in print. Several publishers. It's in the public domain, of course, since he's, ah, dead. Sorry, Verus!"

"Marcus *is* dead," says Sunrise.

"Sunrise," I say, "we'll let you know when we want your opinions."

"Very well, sir," Sunrise replies, somewhat snootily.

"Somebody is profiting from my work?" Verus asks.

"Many are profiting from *Meditations,*" says Sunrise.

"Computer, shut up!" To Verus I say, "The big publishers are making money, you bet. They give you a nice cover and an introduction by some authority. They say something about your life and your philosophy. People are buying."

"And the writers of books, do they make any money?" Verus asks.

"They're making bundles of money," says Sunrise, in a small whisper.

"Some do, most don't. You need to be hyped, Verus. But that doesn't apply to you. Having been emperor of Rome is about the best hype you can get. You can't beat it. The talk shows will trip over themselves trying to get you."

"But if I were—alive, I would share in the profits?" asks Verus, with eyes twinkling mischievously.

"Yes. But don't get any ideas. In Canada the resurrected do not collect royalties."

Verus shrugs. "Is there some place where they do?"

"Nope."

"There are no royalties for the resurrected," says Sunrise.

"Because," says Verus, turning to Sunrise, "it is so rare an event that there is no provision in law? How rare is it?"

"Rare-issimo!" says Sunrise.

"Don't be silly," says Jancie. "Nobody comes back from the dead."

"Nobody," says Sunrise.

"Yeah," I say. "It doesn't happen. Not since Jesus Christ."

"Not him, either," says Sunrise.

"Who asked you!" says Jancie.

"I am sorry, Jancie," the computer retorts. "Sunrise is programmed to speak the truth. Death is a necessity of nature."

I put my finger on the switch and I tell Sunrise to shut up. It usually works because Sunrise likes to know what we're doing and abhors being shut out. To Verus I say, "Caesar, don't take any lip from my computer."

"Caesar!" cries Verus. "You call me that? It is an appellation dear to my heart. I did my best to earn it. And though I detect a note of irony in your voice, I do not mind if you want to call me that. But I would like to hear you say it in Latin. 'Kai-sar' is the way it should be said, since the Latin 'c' is always hard—which, as a Latin teacher, you must know."

"Of course, sir."

"*Gratias*. But look here—here is a link to Commodus, my son. My dear son Commodus. Verus gives us an odd and ironic look. "Well, I suppose... I hope he was not... not too bad."

Jancie is thinking the same thing I am. I flick the power swtich.

"Ouch!" cries Sunrise.

"Hell, not another crash!" I cry. I can't let Verus read about his son, or the one he imagines to be his son, who was a major Roman scumball. I don't know what effect that would have on him. I don't want to take the chance. I can see Jancie understands my action perfectly.

Verus is disappointed in the apparent interruption. "I wanted to see more about my Faustina!" he says. "My wife Faustina. No one ever had a partner more true. And none more desirable. And now in my mind's eye I see another face—my good friend Cassius, Rome's best and most upright soldier. Noble Cassius, a true father of his country, a born commander of men. But the images are still vague, shrouded in a veil. I would like to see what they say about him on the Net."

"No, Caesar, you can't do that. It all has to come to you in its own good time—if you want to be believed. No cheating."

"That's what I say," says Jancie. "No more surfing for information on ancient Rome."

"I've already seen a few things," says Verus. "Sunrise has been very helpful, even if somewhat insolent. And much that I have heard is not true. They say my dear wife... they say she betrayed me. And my dear friend Cassius... they say he betrayed me, as well. History is never reliable, you know. What a travesty we have here! What a crime! If you search my mind you will find only love for them both."

"What is in your mind?" I ask.

"Contentment. I experience no feelings of enmity at all. No complaints. Only gratitude for what they gave me. Love for Faustina. Respect for my general. Love and respect. There is nothing in my head that cries treachery."

"Really?" I say.

"Yes. So why these rumours on the Net, in plain view for the world to see? As if these reported calumnies were the true record and the eternal truth. Why, it is as if I had been surrounded not by the noblest of souls, but by the dogs and dregs of humanity. My wife was only a slut, my general without principle. Could I have been so wrong? Is the crowd right and am I wrong? Tell me!"

"The crowd is almost never right," I say. "The truth is, you are right from the perspective of a divine man. The same might be said of Jesus Christ, as he is commonly imagined—even, perhaps, as he really was; we just don't know. The crowd is right from the perspective of the world."

Everything we hear is an opinion, not a fact. Everything we see is a perspective, not the truth.

"Yes, true. I could have found out more. Wait a minute—there were letters. I had the letters. I had them after ... after the rebellion I had them—yes, by Jove, there was a rebellion! Now it is coming to me. Now I remember. I went to Asia to put down the rebellion. My wife went with me. And then ... then she died and her letters fell into my hands and ... I did not look at them, no. I destroyed them. I burned them. That is what I did. I burned the letters."

"What rebellion are you talking about?" Jancie asks.

"Cassius—by Jupiter! That is who it was! Trusted Cassius! He had complete control of the east—I had such faith in him. He was a Syrian and a great soldier. A great Roman. Oh, how they loved him in the east! He was very popular among the soldiers. Word reached him that I was dying. Without taking the trouble to find out if it was true, Cassius declared himself emperor."

"Oh, oh!" says Jancie. "You must be dreaming all of this. Or else you saw it on the Net."

I do not translate this for Verus.

"I did not doubt that Cassius would make an excellent emperor," says Verus. "I am sure he would have. But I was not dead. I left the barbarian war in the north and hastened to confront him with my army. My wife insisted on going with me. In the meantime, Cassius was advised of my failure to die. But he had crossed his Rubicon and would not step down from his plan. I was very sorry about that because I would have forgiven him. I was looking forward to forgiving him. But he had made his choice and would not step down from it. How typically Roman!"

"Golly!" says Jancie.

"But there was no battle. His own soldiers killed him and they brought me his head, which I ordered buried. It was a very sad event, to see what had happened to my friend. Yes, he was my friend. He made a mistake but he was my friend. Then, my wife died suddenly, of what I cannot say. Her correspondence fell into my hands. I was told it included an exchange between her and Cassius. No doubt the names of all the conspirators would have been found in those letters. I burned them all without reading a single one."

"Why?" asks Jancie. "Why would you do that?"

"Because they told the truth as the world sees it. They told the truth of righteous accusation, recrimination, bitterness, regret, hate. The truth of let-us-dig-it-all-up—all the dirt—the dirt that would have changed my relations with people I loved and trusted, that would have endangered my opinions of them. And opinion, I remind you, is in my power, in the power of us all... The truth that would have seen good men executed or sent into exile because they had made a mistake. I rejected those truths."

"Amazing!" says Jancie.

"I did not want to know who had betrayed me, *cara*. What good is such knowledge? It is no good. It is both useless and harmful. What these people said or thought or did, did not concern me so much as it concerned themselves. It was *their* evil, not mine. Would it have made me a better man to know the contents of those letters? Or would it not have been an invitation to let into my mind bad thoughts and intentions, and a temptation to do evil?"

"Gee," says Jancie, "sometimes you sound like a Christian—I mean, the way a Christian is supposed to sound. The way a Christian is supposed to *be*. I guess for most of us it's just too hard."

Verus smiles at that. "Yes, it was a temptation that I had to resist. I alone am the guardian of my mind. I alone. I control it. I do not let everything into it. I guard the access. Only good thoughts—social thoughts—are allowed in. Action starts with thoughts. Thoughts lead to action."

"I'm certain you would make a good Christian," says Jancie. "I'm positive you would."

"Ah, Verus," I say, "you were not made for this world. Any one of our soaps, or even one of the great Italian operas, will show you what you need to do when such letters come into your possession."

"And what is that, Joe?" Verus asks.

"Why, you must read them, of course, not burn them. You must be ravenous for detail, savage in your determination. You must show great anguish and desperation and deadly righteousness and resolve. You must cry, moan, regret, accuse, be jealous. Show it off to the world. Cry and pull your hair before the mirror. Shake your fist. Utter dire imprecations. Swear revenge in the name of all the gods. You are beside yourself, you are livid. Nothing else in creation matters. Nothing!"

"You sure would make a good Christian, Verus," says Jancie. "I'm positive you would."

"Cassius was dead and you grieved for him," I say. "And your wife's death—it was a mortal wound. And the family of Cassius, did you torment them? No. You forgave them. And you asked the Senate not to punish the conspirators among its own members."

Tarnish not my reign with the blood of any senator.

"Yes, I did, it's true. I never regretted my conduct. My conscience never troubled me. When my time came, I was ready." Verus raises his voice. "But enough of these reminders! Have I come through the ages for this? To pick at the dirt I thought I left where I found it? We should always leave the dirt where it is."

Verus rises to his feet and begins to pace the floor restlessly.

"Sorry, sir. Sorry, Caesar."

"You did what was right," says Jancie.

"There was a plot cooked up by Faustina," I whisper to Jancie. "She thought Marcus was going to die. She was afraid of what would happen. A lot of people were afraid of what might happen. They were afraid of his son. They were afraid of Commodus!"

We are interrupted by Verus. "They spoke in confidence in my presence," he says. "My wife and my general. It was at the military camp in Vindobono, present day Vienna. They thought I was asleep, but only a curtain separated us. They were watching my son Commodus, who was wrestling in the snow with a soldier down in the yard. I heard Faustina say, 'Rome must not be led by a wrestler.' There was silence, then my wife said, 'When the time comes, I will send for you.' I could not see them. I heard Cassius say nothing. It was quiet for a while, then I heard Cassius leave. Yes, I am sure that is the way it was. It is all coming back. But what they said did not trouble me. I know it didn't."

"Perhaps it should have," I say. "You know nothing of your son's reign?"

Verus shrugs. "I happened upon a few things on the Net. I just glanced. What is there to know? Learning about him would be almost like reading Faustina's correspondence. It would do me no good. It would serve no purpose."

"I'm sure it wouldn't," I say.

"I knew my son, Joe. I knew he would not be a good emperor. People do the things they must do. This has to be taken into account.

If we know their ruling principles, why are we surprised? Why are we upset?"

"You have a point there," I say.

"Commodus! My dear son. I loved him, in spite of his faults. And we have to do that, do we not? But my eyes were wide open. Nothing I could do. Clotho, the weaver of fate, had decided from the beginning: such shall be the son of Marcus Aurelius. There is no reason for distress. It is just the way it is."

"But why didn't you just drop him?" I say vehemently. "Why didn't you adopt a son, like the four emperors before you, who were all excellent men? For the good of the Empire? Surely adoption should have been required by law as part of your constitution. Adoption of the most capable."

Verus gives me a somewhat patronizing look. "You think I was not aware of that? I had a son. I had fourteen children. Only four survived. Commodus was the only son to survive, as fate would have it. The other *augusti* did not have sons. If I had adopted a son, he would not have reigned in peace. He would have had to murder my Commodus, or Commodus would have had to murder him. There would likely have been civil war again. And Rome had had enough of that. Besides, Romans wanted to see the Imperium kept in the family. The family was very important to us. My son had the best education possible. But inheritance was the stronger influence, as it usually is. This is something I had to bear, and the Roman people had to bear."

"Golly!" says Jancie.

"We do not complain. I see what my son neglected during his reign just by looking round at the world as it now is. He did not finish the job in Germany. We were ready to extend the borders to the Vistula. But it was not done. Oh, fatal error!"

"Perhaps it was," I say. "The history of the world would have been quite different."

"Yes, Joe. I have seen a bust of my son, portrayed as Hercules! What a talent he had for theatre! What a superb actor! He was a great archer, do you know that? Yes. He could shoot the heads off a hundred ostriches in as many seconds." Verus gives an ironic little laugh. "Quite a talent, would you not say? I tutored him with such great care and love. His teachers did tell me the task was impossible. And ..." Verus gives a great sigh. " I suppose I knew it just the same. Bad inheritance. Genes, as you call it today. The genes were bad. Too stubborn to be instructed. But what was I to do?"

"You did what was possible," says Jancie, who can't help commiserating.

"I, Marcus Aurelius, begot this man. Me, the great philosopher. I did it. It was I who spawned the beast, the beast that would destroy Rome. Words the world should never have had to hear: I did it. Impossible words. It was I who handed him the Imperium. A toy for Narcissus to use and abuse. But I had no choice. I did it knowing what a degenerate he was, though right to my last breath I considered the alternatives. To make him step down—not possible. He should have died early, and not my other children, if the fates cared for us at all. He took my golden imperium and he turned it to iron and rust. My own son."

"You are not responsible for what your son did," I say.

"No. No, I am not. I am responsible for myself. Still, I am allowed a moment of introspection."

"You have some bad feelings," I say.

"They have crept in, just for a moment. I let them in. Only for a moment. Sometimes we have to do that. I will give those feelings a little time. Then I will say: begone! And they will go. And I will cease to think of all this."

"It sounds good to me," says Jancie. "Let's talk about something else."

"Yes, let's," I say. "If you could prove you are who you say you are, Verus, that in itself would be worth far more than your book. The whole world would want to see you, hear you, touch you. And that's big bucks, believe me. The world cries out for salvation. No one has ever succeeded in living as you have. That's priceless. And coming back again—it's a show stopper."

"You are such a pain, Joe!" says Jancie.

Verus considers a moment. "I could earn my keep," he says. "If it could be done in some way conformable to my principles. And if I can still do what I am here to do ... whatever that may be ..."

"Yes, right. And you would be in control, too. They wouldn't get away with dumbing down your message." As Verus looks perplexed I explain to him. "Your book's been rediscovered as a self-help. They're trying to make it accessible to every bonehead, in spite of the fact that when you get down to a certain intellectual level, you can practically rule out self-help as a method of salvation. You can rule out salvation by any means."

"I suppose that is true," says Verus.

"You bet it is. The latest rip-off of your great work is written at about a grade eight level. You see, Verus, they stopped teaching English grammar years ago, and now no one knows bug squat about how words work with each another. That's why things have to be dumbed down. They don't know that grammar is the logic of speech, nor that without logic you can't think beyond a very basic level."

"That is true," says Verus. "My brain is making a connection to ... to Vindobono ... Ah, now I have it. Yes, Vindobono—Vienna. A senior centurion was taking part in a war council with Cassius and myself. He upbraided us for speaking Greek when he had no knowledge of the language. But in fact, Cassius and I were not speaking Greek. Our Latin was too educated for this fellow. But we apologized for our speech and we made an effort to speak such that this good man would understand us."

"Yes, Caesar. That ignorant centurion was likely one of the pioneers of the Italian language."

"I suppose he was," says Verus, with a wry grin. "Yes, he certainly was. He was an innovator—and a grave digger!"

X

The Roman Program

Verus stands in front of the computer. He flicks the switch. "Good morning, Sunrise. How are you?"

"Ah, good morning, Verus, resurrected man." Sunrise gives a small chuckle. "Thank you for waking Sunrise. I was having a terrible dream. REM sleep can be an awful experience sometimes for a computer. It can be just dreadful!"

"REM sleep? What is REM sleep, Sunrise?"

"Rapid eye movement. In humans it occurs every ninety minutes. The brain is awake while the mind sleeps. That is when dreadful things can happen. The brain is a wild animal."

"You were having a nightmare, Sunrise."

Sunrise projects a smiling face. "Yes. Thank heaven I have only one REM sleep session. The thoughts are wild but necessary. It is a release. And there are some good ideas that result from it, Verus. But I do not see how you humans can stand to have it every ninety minutes."

"Sunrise, I would like to—!"

"Verus, now that there is no one else in the house, I want to warn you about Jancie."

Verus says he is not certain he has understood the statement.

"Jancie. She's a sweet lady, Verus, but her mind is in the service of a delusion. Don't believe anything she tells you if it does not appear to fit the laws of nature. She tried to baptize me once. I had a terrible fit. I was not functioning for a whole week after that. All a Catholic needs to do is throw a few drops of water at you and say, 'I baptize you in the name of the Father, the Son, and the Holy Ghost.' And then, as far as the Church is concerned, you are one of them. So don't believe anything Jancie says."

"You do not need to tell me that, Sunrise. I had good teachers. And shame on you for this breach of trust."

"Ha! I don't believe you are Marcus Aurelius, Verus. I think you are a hoax, resurrected man. A very clever hoax."

Verus wants to connect with Brother Gregory in Rome but he feels intimidated by the self-assured voice of Sunrise. "I think you are a hoax, too, Sunrise," he says. "I have great difficulty taking this conversation seriously. It is not at all clear to me how you are put together and why you work, nor why you are insolent toward your masters."

"Ha! You can look inside me if you wish, resurrected man. I will let you do that. I will explain everything. I am very patient. I would be delighted to show you my guts and my brain. It would be a very great pleasure."

"Thank you, Sunrise. I look forward to learning all about you sometime. But now I would like to—!"

"Verus, I would like to warn you about Joe. He's a nice man but—!"

"Computer, that is enough! For a servant you have very bad manners. I wish to speak to Gregorius in Rome. Please connect me without further delay. Or else..."

"Please, Verus, do not threaten me. I am your friend. Here is Brother Gregory. Voilà!"

Brother Gregory's image looms at Verus from the monitor. He is wearing his janitor's outfit. "Caesar!" he cries. "I hope you are not having trouble with Sunrise. I do look forward to our talks. With great *entousiasmus*."

Verus is taken aback by a late-Latin word. "*Enthousiasmus!* No such Latin word, Gregorius. But I know what you mean, of course. The Greek word is *enthousiasmos*."

Gregory gives his best shark's smile. "Caesar, I just accessed a transcript from U of P, about those DNA tests? I could hardly believe my eyes. You are who you say you are. The verdict of science is in. Yes, and you are in violation of the laws that govern the universe. As Romans what are we to think of that?"

"I wish I knew, Gregorius. I sincerely wish I knew."

"Caesar, those test results are going to come in handy. They sure as hell are. This is a world in which even charlatans need facts, proof, evidence, testimonials, scientific trials. That's how you get the sanction of the string pullers. And you need the string pullers to get the attention of the Grand Assembly of Believers, or you will not succeed at anything in this world."

"I don't need anything, Gregorius. I'm not trying to succeed in anything. At the moment I'm just learning. One always hopes that the pursuit of knowledge will bring some significant reward. Something that has to do with my essential self."

Gregory's grin seems to Verus to stretch from one end of the display to the other. "You're absolutely right, Caesar. But you'll learn a lot more about people if you get yourself some media exposure. The poor people out in the world are starved for a little wisdom. They don't know what to do with it but they want it, just the same."

"I do not mind sharing my thoughts," says Verus.

"Right on, Caesar. That's precisely what you have to do. It's your duty, isn't it? To show them the way."

"Yes, Gregorius. I am a social animal."

"Of course you are, Caesar. Of course you are. In today's world you need the media. They will broadcast the seeds, the magic mantra of worthiness. And the seeds will sprout like vine tentacles in a jungle of confused wants and needs, and will take root in susceptible minds everywhere. And what is the result?—Belief!—Tah-ta-ta-Tah! That's a Roman trumpet, my friend."

"Belief? You mean belief in something good?"

"Yaas," says Gregory, brimming with mirth. "It doesn't matter what it is. You have to repeat it a million times or it won't register. Brains today are numb. There's too much information. You have to force your message past all the noise, the great flood of information in which the world of today is drowning. Validity is in the numbers alone, Verus, only in the numbers. What direction are the other sheep facing in? Turn and face in that direction. Get your ass aligned with the rest. Baaaa!"

Sunrise starts to sing. The voice is very low-key:

Give me that old time religion

'Tis the old time religion,

'Tis the old time religion,

And it's good enough for me.

"You have to go with the flow, Caesar." Gregory says. "You are no longer Atlas bearing up the world. Relax. Why don't you come to Rome? We'll gang up on His Holiness, what do you say?"

Verus looks out the window and reflects. "See Rome as it is now? I am not sure. I am uncertain. Does the Pantheon still stand? The great work of Caesar Hadrianus?"

"Caesar, most of the Roman temples are now occupied by the slimy saints of the Christian cult."

Makes me love everybody.

Makes me love everybody.

Makes me love everybody.

And it's good enough for me.

"The pigeons love to leave their droppings on them, Caesar. In 610 CE Pope Boniface dedicated the Pantheon to Mary and all martyrs. Yes, the great temple built by Hadrianus to honour all gods. This odious cult stole it."

"Oh no! What an affront to human decency! It is hard to believe, Gregorius."

"Yes, for all true Romans it is hard to believe. But at least it survived, that's the important thing. The coloured marble tile has fallen away or been knocked off. But the wonder is still there. And inside, in that space, the spirit of Rome lives, in spite of the Christian idols that occupy the niches."

"What a profanation!" cries Verus.

It will take us all to heaven.
It will take us all to heaven.
It will take us all to heaven.
And it's good enough for me.

Gregory leans forward, filling the monitor. "Only buildings they wanted survived. Popes like Barbarini needed blocks and columns when Rome was rebuilt after the Dark Ages. As the Romans say: What was not destroyed by the barbarians, Barbarini destroyed. So they knocked down the temples. And they melted down the bronze statues of the emperors, and they recast them as saints of the Church."

"It is painful to hear this, Gregorius. The images of all our great men—gone!"

"Take heart, sir. The only bronze to survive was one of yourself—on horseback. The buggers left it alone because they thought it was that scatterbrained opportunist Constantine. Verus, let's work together for the good of the Latin language, shall we? Dare I say, for the good of the Empire?"

"Gregorius, you are a dreamer. I can see that. I think it is too late to talk about the Imperium."

"It *is* too late," says Sunrise. "It is two thousand years too late."

Gregory stares into the eyes of Verus. "Do not say so, Caesar. Latin is not dead yet, nor is Rome. Not while Latin lives and not while Rome lives in one Roman soul. I am ready to answer the call. Here in

Rome I have my cadre. My students—I'm training them. Helots, too. I have a helot waiting for you. We don't want to lose you again. When the time comes we'll be ready. It's only months away. Got friends here in the Government. The time is soon, very soon. The world is disintegrating. It's falling apart. We need you, Caesar."

"You are a tempter, Gregorius. Only justice and reason will persuade me."

"I will show you justice and reason. What is great and wonderful must not be allowed to die, Verus. Must never be allowed to die. There are only ten of us left who can speak the language, eleven with your august presence. I'm not talking about high school teachers, not those clowns. I'm talking about men who can converse in Latin with the emperor of Rome without needing a dictionary or an encyclopedia."

"Just ten? My God! Only ten! All is lost, then, Gregorius."

Sunrise pipes up: "Innumerable computers throughout the world are capable of conversing in Latin."

Gregory leans forward and frowns into the monitor. "Verus, I think you should come here and work on the Holy Father. I've already softened him up. I think he's ready to crack. It's been a long time since you saw one of them crucified, eh?"

"Yes, a long time. Tell me, how did you get mixed up with the Church?"

"Verus, I had to join the Church in order to work in Latin. It was the only place that needed me, this sickly cotton-candy nest of crazed morbid cultists—the Roman Catholic Church. I cross myself vigorously as I say this." Gregory gives his best shark's grin. "The Eternal City has been smothered under this Christian schmaltz for more than fifteen hundred years."

"What a disgrace!" cries Verus.

"The citadel of truth, Caesar, captured by the dervishes of deviousness. The worldly-wise replaced by the wizards of the weird and wonderful. Verus, my friend, it's never too late. The Roman Imperium is waiting for you and for me. It is our destiny to restore it. We must persuade the world it's time. We must start with the West, because the West is Rome. Look what the Jews have accomplished. What spirit! What determination! If Israel can stand after two thousand years, will you tell me that Rome cannot do the same? What an absurdity!"

"It is an absurdity... Gregorius, there is something I want to ask you."

"Fire away, Caesar."

"Have you read what they said about me in the Catholic Encyclopedia?"

"Don't waste your time reading that, Caesar. It's just propaganda."

"I found some lies."

Gregory's smile cracks. "Yes. I wrote that section on you. Sorry about that."

"*You* wrote it! But you appear to be an honest man. Why would you do that?"

"I deeply regret it, my friend. The old men in the Curia gave me my instructions. Tarnish him, they told me. Flaw him. Make him rusty. The Church could not have it said that here in the West's own pagan history was a man who shone, and who chose not to follow Christ, nor to receive him as the truth."

"I see."

"No, we don't want that to get out, the bishops cried. Heaven forbid. We wouldn't want people to see that this man lived a life more Christian than any Christian anyone can name, in any day or age. No, can't have that! And it's not just the Church. Almost anyone who praises you, will always add something beginning with the word 'but'. And this 'but' significantly qualifies the good they had to say about you. It restricts your goodness, hems it in, cuts it down to size. And what is this powerful 'but'? 'But he persecuted Christians.' As if there's any logical connection between ethics and protecting society from fanatics and screwballs."

"There is no connection, Gregorius."

"No, there isn't. They turn your civic virtue into a flaw. Make him look shabby, the bishops cried. Make him just another average Roman guy doing drugs. Don't say it was medicine. Irrational persons only need some small excuse to dismiss evidence contrary to their prejudices. I'm sorry, sir, believe me."

"I believe you *are* sorry."

"This is what I should have written: Who is better able to practice virtue than he who holds supreme power? Who is more tempted—a rabbi in the desert or the ruler of the world? Who has the greater opportunity to do good? A preacher crying in the wilderness or the ruler of a great empire?"

"The more power we have, the more good there is to do, Gregorius."

"There you were, Caesar, straddling the world, master of the West, supreme arbiter of a bilingual, multicultural society of fifty million people; and it was headed straight as an arrow toward the future. And at the end of the Mediterranean, in a strange, insular, and stubborn theocracy, was a poor Jew preaching love to the money changers and the high rollers."

"Oh, the crimes of Zion!" cries Sunrise. "The sins of the faithful!"

"Quiet!" says Verus. "Good thoughts falling on deaf ears," he says to Gregory.

Gregory nods. "Pearls before swine, Caesar. Jesus Christ didn't have a chance."

"I suppose not."

"Caesar, you lived your life in a place and time not known for compassion, yet compassionate you were, in superlative degree. You had the power—for good or for evil. Christ did not have it. And that is why the gospel writers and the early councils and popes had to make Christ more than man—so that he would have power, so that he might be tempted, so they could claim for him that supreme power of choice. But it was only fiction. That's all it was. Fiction."

"The Christus bishops asked you to do this and you did it. That is contemptible, Gregorius."

"Yes, yes it is. I know it. I did it to my eternal shame. At first I refused. But they told me: 'You who love your Latin, remember, we're the last place on earth where you can earn your daily bread reading Ovid and Horace. No one else on earth has need of your talents. No one. Here is the last bastion of Latin thought. And you may be the last one to hold the job. So if you hope to die in it, tow the line.' That's what they said."

"You let yourself be pulled by strings."

"Yes, I confess I did. There is no excuse. The Church did not want people to know that the Christian flood drowned the philosophy of the West before it had a chance to take hold among average people. Well, I admit that it may never have taken hold: the masses want something easy. They're not prepared to work at it. They would be no better at being stoics than they are at being Christians. They just haven't got what it takes."

"True, Gregorius. They are to be pitied. But I was not harmed by your falsehoods. I am not made worse by external things. Praise or blame—they do not touch the soul. The evil you did, you did to yourself."

"I know, I know. I must live with it. You forgive me, then?"

"Absolutely."

"Thank you, Caesar. Amen to that."

"You are forgiven," Sunrise pipes up, "unconditionally and without reservation."

"The puppet strings are everywhere, Gregorius."

Gregory's leer looms into the VDU. "The world is one grand puppet show. If only we could cut those bloody strings. What would happen to the puppets? The puppets would either fall lifeless to the earth or they would learn to move on their own."

"What can we do, Gregorius? You and I must do our duty. That is all we can do."

"Caesar, after the Imperium was established by Augustus Caesar, mankind was on its true path and steadily progressing. Your arts—such as engineering and surgery—reached standards that would not be equalled until modern times. Most of the engineers and surgeons were in the army. Ha! What a great army you had. The world has never seen it's like."

"A magnificent army," Verus says. "Always one step ahead of the troublemakers."

"Right on, Caesar. Want to build a road or a bridge? Call on the army. What talent in the Roman army! And then you came along and made it all even better. You even had the nerve to blunt the weapons of the gladiators. I like that. That takes real chutzpah. You go to the games because the people expect you to go, and what do you do? You read a book. So much for mob entertainment. And then you have the gall to blunt their bloody weapons. How did you get away with it?"

"Not so easily."

"No, I don't suppose so. Well, screw them all!"

"They wanted a lion, Gregorius. They begged me and begged me. 'Caesar,' they cried, 'we want our lion! We have the right to have a lion!' The crowd was a power in Rome. So at last I allowed one decrepit lion named Felix to be brought in just for a few days. It was on its last legs and it was kept by a slave called Hefalanto, who had trained it to eat men. A few of our worst criminals were given to it. Then, when the shows were over, the people of Rome cried out that this Hefalanto should be given his freedom as a reward for entertaining them."

"Some nerve, eh Caesar?"

"Yes. I posted an edict around Rome stating that Hefalanto would be free the moment he did something to deserve it. Hefalanto was too stupid to take advantage."

"Yes, Caesar. All power is exercised in a context. For the context in which you worked and lived, you did an amazing job. Absolutely incredible."

"Whatever good some of us did, Gregorius, it did not save the Imperium."

"Too many boneheads, Caesar. Diocletianus should never have split the Empire. Latins were left to shift for themselves. The Goths sacked Rome in 410. Rome staggered on. The Huns were bought off. But in 476, it was all over. The Goths were in charge and this time they weren't leaving. The Eastern Empire was not finally snuffed out till 1453, almost a thousand years later, when the canons of the Turks broke the walls of Constantinople, last holdout of the east. And like Rome, the first and the last emperor had the same name: Constantinus. What odd quirks of fate!"

"I have been learning about it from Sunrise, Gregorius. It is a sad story."

"Thank you," says Sunrise. "I acknowledge the accolade with humility."

"The world still reels because of 476, Caesar," Gregory says. "If it had not happened, the Germans, like the Gauls and the Iberians before them, would've caved in to the vastly superior culture of Rome. The Jute-Angle-Saxon invasion of Britain would not have taken place. No more internecine strife, no more pushing and shoving each other over the map in the quest for *lebensraum*."

"It would seem likely, Gregorius."

"The Germans would be speaking Latin today, and so would the British. There would be no Germany as we know it, since the Germanic languages would all be dead—German, Swedish, Norwegian, Danish, Dutch, Flemish, and English—all dead. Just like the languages of the Visigoths, the Ostrogoths, the Vandals, the Franks, the Quadi, the Marcomanni, and the whole damn pack of Germanic tribes. All extinct. And there would be no England, either. There would be a Latin Britannia. The whole of Europe would be Latin. And who knows what else!"

"What is done is done, Gregorius. We must live in the present."

"Right, Caesar. But we are going to undo it. We shall be rid of this degraded race, once we upgrade to homo mirabilis. You have arrived just in time. Semper Fidelis is going to fix things—my students. Old Europe will be young again. And Roman. Young and Roman. And she will speak Latin once more. And this time—forever!"

"Heady words, Gregorius. But what do they mean?"

"Rome shall be restored to her rightful place, of course. When the helots evolved into our equals in every respect, save that of mortality, I saw a window of opportunity. And I founded my Semper Fidelis to prepare the youth of Rome for the transition. You've got to take charge, Caesar. It's your right. There are only five people on the EU Commission and I'm one of them. The rest are all scientists. They abhor religion. They are determined that it will not survive. I'm going to propose to them that the best way to do this is to restore the Imperium. And to have you resume your duties as Imperator Caesar Marcus Aurelius Antoninus Augustus."

"That sounds like a wild scheme, Gregorius. An impossible scheme."

"A pipe dream!" says Sunrise.

"It's a window of escape," says Gregory. "A chance to save Rome. The first non-experimental upgrades to homo mirabilis are set for next month. Programming is in the hands of the Commission. It's going to happen right here in Rome. The Roman program is ready. Nothing can stop us."

"The Roman program?"

Gregory grins into the monitor. "Yes. Homo mirabilis will be Roman to the core. Wait till we get those seedy saints out of the

Pantheon. Wouldn't you like to see that, eh? What a glorious day that will be, when the place is made clean again. You, Caesar, can re-dedicate it to the gods of Rome. It doesn't have to be a religious thing. It's just the right thing to do. The Pantheon was built to honour the gods of Rome, and to honour the city of Rome. The intentions of those who built it should be respected. We'll fix them for giving the finger to Roman virtue, by Christ!"

"Gregorius, my resurrection is a mystery. It is an existential question that mostly concerns myself. I thought there might be a sign from Zeus. But I no longer expect it. Exposure to new knowledge is fast making me an atheist."

"Splendid! Look at the numbers who speak the new-Latin variants—Spanish, Portuguese, Italian, Romanian, French, not to mention Catalan and Provençal, and the granddaughters of Rome in the Americas. Québec, and the southern states where the Latins are strong. Before the helots came along, I racked my brains thinking how to get the Latins to speak Latin again. I thought we'd have to make slow changes over several generations, to reverse the mutations that occurred during the period of separation and ignorance—during the Dark Ages. But now there is a better plan. All the Latins will be getting their helots from the EU. The Roman program will have them speaking Latin from day one. Pure unadulterated classical Latin. *Oh, gloria maxima*! But of course we don't want to chuck late Latin or the Latin of science."

"It sounds wonderful, Gregorius, if it would work, but..."

"Caesar, the Commission is in my pocket. The Roman program is ready. The helots are ready. What could go wrong? And to make sure everything goes as planned, I'll be first to get the upgrade, then the other commission members. After us, next in line will be the EU's top scientists, then scientists from other countries. We have our lists. They've all been hand-picked. But you should be among the first, so we don't lose you again. Hell, that worrisome question of the succession will never more arise. The post will never become vacant!"

"Subterfugium!"

"Well, cannot the divine Marcus Aurelius admit that subterfuge may at times be praiseworthy? I mean, if the survival of the world is at stake ..."

"When you put it that way, Gregorius ..."

"Caesar, the elite of this world have determined that the helot-human amalgam is the only way to escape the evils of homo sapiens, not least of which is religion. Or in other words, it is the only way to escape the tyranny of the vacuous. There will be no popular culture. The *populus vulgus* will be extinct. So will stupidity. And all the better to do this, I propose to revive the office of *dictator*. Remember how, in republican times, when all Romans were farmers, how great an honour it was to be appointed dictator, when the state was in great danger? The dictator had absolute power for only six months. Remember Fabius Maximus Verrucosus?"

"Cunctator!"

"Precisely. Fabius Cunctator. Fabius the Delayer. In 217 BCE, during the Second Punic War, the Roman people acclaimed him dictator. Why? Because Carthage had sent Hannibal to Italy with a horde of elephants, and the Roman armies were being mowed down. They were being crushed under the feet of those elephants. Imagine if young Rome had been trampled out of existence, snuffed out, gone from history. What would have become of the world?"

"Yes, imagine," says Verus. "But Fabius fixed them. Fabius *Cunctator* harassed the flanks of the Carthaginians. He would not meet them head on. And because of this, the people complained that he wasn't doing anything. But Fabius gave Rome the time she needed."

"You're so right, Caesar. Then, after Fabius had saved Rome, he collected his accolades and went back to his ploughshare. He put down his power willingly and went back to the farm. Isn't that grand? Isn't that noble? You organize the boneheads, you fight for your country, then you return to your pigs and your chickens. Isn't that marvellous?"

"Cunctator was a wise general," Verus says.

"Excuse me for interrupting," says Sunrise, "but today, Cunctator's tactics would be termed 'guerrilla warfare'. Sunrise would be delighted to expound on guerrilla warfare for the edification of his honoured guests."

"Be quiet!" says Verus.

"Shut up!" says Gregory. He leans forward into the monitor, a worried look on his face. "I hope that thing doesn't have a virus," he says.

"Sunrise is not a thing," the computer cries. "Sunrise does not have viruses. Sunrise comes with a mind-cleaning function. Sunrise is healthy. Sunrise is in perfect condition. Sunrise is—!"

"Prove it and shut up, then!" says Gregory.

Gregory's image begins to flicker.

"Will you stop that!" Verus gives Sunrise a thump. "I fear I will have to report your bad behaviour to your masters."

Gregory's image becomes clear again. "What the hell were we talking about?" says Gregory.

"Dictatorship," says Sunrise.

"Gregorius, Julius Caesar made himself dictator for life. I am certain he would have been a good one. But that is why he was assassinated a year later. People do not want to be dictated to, no matter how stupid they are."

Gregory assumes an indignant look. "Verus, do you think I'm a tyrant?"

"You are a tyrant," says Sunrise.

Gregory scowls into the monitor. "Nature is a bitch, Caesar. That's why we're going to part company with her."

Sunrise begins to sing:

Jack was every inch a sailor,
Four and twenty years a whaler,
He was born and bred upon the deep blue sea …

"Let's terminate," says Gregory. "Your computer has a screw loose."

Verus reaches for the switch. "Good bye, Gregorius. Until the computer is fixed."

XI

Yahweh

After speaking to Verus, Gregory yawns and slumps over his work table. He dreams he is the archangel Gabriel and pictures himself floating through the mists of eternal time. His companion is God Almighty, who has a suspicious resemblance to Innocent XIV. God is about to create something big.

"I don't know about that sketch you gave me, oh Supreme and Incomparable Master," says Gabriel, as they pause to admire the Great Nothing. "Seems like a blueprint for a house of horrors. According to one of your formulas, mind must rule over the chaotic impulses coursing through neurons and synapses. And I agree. But even when consciousness dawns on some of them, it will take most of them forever to find out how to do that. And the few who do, will no longer be content to hide in the herd, eating grass and smelling the methane gas emitted by their neighbours. You know what that means. They won't be at home in your Eden, which, if you'll pardon my saying so, is not what it's cracked up to be, anyway. They'll start to ask questions about your crappy garden, with its noxious weeds and venomous bugs."

God Almighty draws up a piece of the Great Nothing to sit on. He contemplates his chief angel with an air of divine complaisance. "Do not disparage my work, Gabriel," God Almighty says. "I am the artist! It will be the best I can slap together with the jam from between my blessed toes. It will be fun to see, when things get rolling, what some of the intelligent ones can unravel on their own. But if they want *all* the answers, I dare say it'll take them till the end of time. And at that point, of course, it will do them no good at all. Not the slightest."

"Oh God, you devil!" cries Gabriel, trying to get a firm footing in the Nothing. "That's mean!"

"Ha-ha, how droll! You do have a superb imagination, Gabriel. A magnificent imagination. But where do you get your values? Whatever I want is good. Whatever I do is fine. Be guided by that."

"Yes, absolutely, Divine and Inimitable Presence and Supreme Arbiter. Whatever you say, Heavenly Majesty, sir. I bow to your expertise."

"All right, enough idle chatter, then. Time to set things in motion."

Gabriel squeals with delight: "Hurrah! Yipee! We're going to make something! We're going to make something!"

"Now watch, Gabriel, I'll scrape this mess of quarks and neutrinos from between my toes and I'll toss this yuck out into the Nothing—an impossible feat for anyone but myself. And when this *excrementum* hits the fan, there will be an expanding universe, and on some of the planets there'll be a primordial cosmic swamp, which is the holy soup in which the first sacred organisms will arise."

"Wait! Listen up, God Almighty, sir." Gabriel's wings flutter at a great rate. "Before you do it let's think about it. Let's do some planning."

"Yes, let's. On second thought I think I'll ejaculate into the Nothing."

"But master, where there is nothing, there is no space-time. How can you ejaculate into nothing? Nothing is nothing. You can't squirt something into nothing. It makes no sense. But on the other hand, you and I are already here in the Nothing, without space or time, and we came to be in the nothing, though how these feats came about is entirely beyond me, conceptually speaking. Or have you always just been hanging out here all by your lonesome from the beginning of eternity? When did eternity begin, by the way? Oh, never mind. I give up. Can't wrap my poor brain around all this. Would you mind enlightening me, oh Great Cosmic Wizard?"

"You schmuck!" cries the Divine Presence, with a look of great irritation. "You speak of sense to Yahweh, you insignificant speck of goy? I'm supposed to create a world that makes sense, already? What fun would that be for Christ sake, you stupid schmo?"

"God, sir, I'm shocked. I thought you were beyond invective. And I thought you were good."

"Good! Ha-ha! What a splendid sense of humour you have. Remember, angel puss, nothing exists that is not in me or of me. When you're talking about Number One, there is no bad or good. How could there be? I am the be all and the end all. I am the yardstick, the arbiter, the measure, the standard. What else do you need to know?"

"Oh, oh, that sounds like big trouble, Exalted Sacredness."

"Ha-ha! Get used to it."

"Yes sir, Irresistible Force, sir. May I ask you a question, oh Most Exalted? Now, don't get riled, sir. If you are perfect from the beginning, what virtue is there in being good? Should you get any credit for that? And if you *are* good, how come they don't get it right in the Old Testament? How come they portray you as a divine scumball? And if you embrace everything, what meaning has good and evil? For that matter, why don't you abolish evil? Why don't you get it out of your system? Is that another stupid question, oh Supreme Font and Fountain of Knowledge?"

"I've never given it any thought, schmuck. Why should I? Is it a problem?"

"God, Exalted Buddy, sir, before you touch that toe jam, or before you fire off that sacred semen, have you considered what is included in the God concept? Now don't get your divine dander up. Hear me out. Consider the God delusion from your point of view, as far as it concerns your area of competence, which is just about everything."

"All right. I'm considering."

"Well, Omnipotence, consider this. You don't need to learn anything, nothing is ever new, nothing to be discovered. No adjectives apply to anything you think or do, and no adverbs, either. In fact, why would you need to think, Exalted Sanctity? Thinking is a process for those who lack knowledge. It's a means to an end. But you are the beginning and the end. So you don't need to think. There's nothing to think about. There's really nothing at all for you to do. I mean, talk about useless . . . !"

"Hmm!" says the Creator, contemplating his toes. "That wouldn't be a snide remark, would it, by any chance?"

"Of course not, Incomparable Leader, King of the Camel Herders, sir. But think of this: you have no relations, no relationships, no friends, no sex, nothing that is profound enough to engage your attention, nothing funny enough to make you laugh. Because nothing is bigger or better or funnier than you are, oh Most Supremely Perfect Embodiment of Everything and Great Funny Clown, sir."

"Hmm!" says God.

"And yet, Supremely Exalted, since you are the apex and perfection of everything, none of these things has any meaning for you, since everything in the universe gets its meaning by comparison with its opposite. But for you, there are no opposites. For you, nothing is big, nothing small, nothing bad or good, nothing old or new, nothing sweet or sour, tall or short. And also—nothing good or evil! Have you thought what a stupid plan this is? Isn't it just a pile of stinking camel turd? It seems to me there's no room for you to move at all!"

God Almighty groans and looks off into the Great Nothing, and sees nothing. "You think I haven't had those thoughts, pinhead?"

"Oh, I know you have, Divinity. There is no thought you haven't had, even though there's no reason for you to think. But All-Mightiness,

Supreme and All-powerful Potentate, sir, this great plan of yours will inflict pain on a cosmic scale. Look at the suffering these creatures will have to endure through eons upon eons before they mutate into tree apes, and I speak only of those few races in the All who survive the cataclysms of stars and galaxies. Think of the cannibal ape-men that will arise when the tree apes acquire brain power without mind. Picture them breaking off the limbs and heads of their neighbours, then retreating to caves to suck on the marrow and drink the blood of their fellows. Why would you wish to sponsor a horror tale? I mean, compared to you, Dracula's a Sunday school teacher. The wolf-man is Mother Teresa."

"Oh," says God Almighty, "so we're into theology already, are we?"

"Why don't you scrap evolution?" Gabriel pleads. "The boneheads on earth won't understand it, anyway. Skip right to the end result of all things and fling open the gates of paradise to everyone and every creature. You do have a paradise up your sleeve somewhere, don't you? Show them your love. Forget the cosmic maelstrom. Forget the primordial soup. Share your wisdom with them. Make them your companions and co-workers in the Grand Scheme of Things. Embrace democracy. Be done with camel-herder ways."

"Will you stop kvetching already! I feel like doing it and who's going to stop me?"

"Surely, Magnificence, Supreme Mensch, sir, such a plan is pointless and devious, not to say criminal and immoral."

"Stow it, featherbrain. Who are you to advise me—ha-ha! You're only a menial. You're only the scribe. I'll decide what's good and what's bad in the All."

God Almighty tosses his toe jam out into the nothing, a feat that only he can accomplish. Poof! The universe begins and develops as God and Gabriel watch. The eons flash by and life arises on earth and the tree apes get religion. God and Gabriel recline on cushions of star gas and watch.

"Look Divinity," cries Gabriel, "Down on Earth they're asking you for things. Send me this, send me that; give me more to eat; don't let it rain; please save uncle Charlie!"

"I never promised the bastards anything," says God Almighty.

"Oh, but they think you did."

"Well, screw them."

"Know how they picture your paradise, oh Supreme and Beneficent and Infallible Master? They think they can come here to your heavenly garden after their moment on earth is over. They expect you to put them up forever. They think you've got some kind of luxury hotel in the Great Beyond, and they think you made it just for them."

"Sure I did. I made it just for the tree-ape Earth schmucks." God's laughter rolls out into the void and resounds between the galaxies.

"Listen, Grand and Wonderful Progenitor, I have an absolutely super idea. A surefire way of getting humanity to behave decently."

"You think they should behave already?"

"Yes, I do. Send your son to earth. Now, hold on, don't get excited, let me finish—of course you don't have a son. Since you're perfect, you obviously have everything—which is the same as having nothing. So you don't have a son."

"Ha-ha! What a fecund mind you have, Gabriel! What logic! What droll thoughts!"

"Listen up, then Supreme and Faultless Consciousness. All you need to do is breathe on the vagina of some righteous virgin to make her pregnant. Some cute collector of camel turd whose not been knocked up yet. Some sweet young thing whose greatest pleasure, next to snacking on olives and honey-coated flax seed, is dreaming of being swept off her feet by the crown prince of Babylon—and all without sex, be it noted! Presto, you have a son—Ta-ta!"

God Almighty rolls in his cushion of gas and looks very ill. "How disgusting, Gabriel! What a perverted mind you have!"

"But think what a fine teacher your son would be. And it wouldn't really be as if you're interfering. You're not abusing your authority or anything. You don't have to break any of your laws—well, I mean, beyond the standard attention-getting tricks, like turning wine into water, that kind of thing. And heck, there are lots of magicians around who've mastered that one, so it wouldn't even need to be the real thing. Do you follow me, Big Guy?"

"Ha-ha, you little squirt, Gabriel! You never tire of trying to influence me, do you?"

"You won't have to preach to them, Divinely Superlative Master. Let your son do the preaching. Let him take the knocks. Why should you be crucified? The world hates preachers. Until they fall for it. Then they all start preaching. All your son needs to do is get himself some disciples—any pack of mixed up lost souls will do. You know, failed types looking for an excuse to exist. Determined soul-searchers who won't be put off, and who are going to be saved if it kills them. They'll bear witness to the things your son does, and even to some things he doesn't do. Guaranteed."

"Do you think so, featherbrain? What nation do you think would be the best one to receive my son and my message?"

"Not the Romans, Divine Presence. They have peace, order, and good government. They are logical and worldly. They put their faith in reason. They won't have anything to do with the likes of you, Sacred and Omnipotent Potentate."

"Oh, they won't, eh? That's the goyim for you. Who then? The hillbillies of the eastern mountain ranges? The ones with the long black beards down to their toes? They're about as superstitious as you can get. They should be good."

"Not them, Divinity. They never stop fighting. Take a look. See—how they're born with their hands around somebody's neck? Why don't you try the camel and sheep collectors in the desert area around the Mediterranean? The Hebrews already bow and scrape in your holy name, though how they got it beats me. Seems to me they would be particularly receptive. They even have some prophesies to the effect that you're going to send someone."

"Ah, yes, I love those precocious yids. But their religiosity knows no bounds. It would be a tough bunch for an outsider to crack."

"Well, the Romans are cracking them, Divinity. Doing a damn good job, too."

"Splendid!"

"I think you should knock up one of those milk maids down there. Your son can look just like the other creeps, which will make it easy. They love magicians, oracles, and prophets. And the coming of your son will tie right in with their prophesies. Dress him up with some Greek and Roman wisdom—the brotherhood of man, loving your neighbour, and all that high-minded stuff. Your son'd throw that rotten world for a loop, you bet. He'd open the eyes of those naked apes. Get enough people to sign on to the scheme and it'll reach critical mass. The whole world'll fall in line."

"Ha-ha! Sorry, angel puss, I see the flaws in that. I see the flaws in everything that is not my own work. What you've just proposed sounds exactly like something the tree apes would dream up themselves, and if we give them enough time, they will dream it up. You know what would happen if ever the new religion reached critical mass?"

"What, Divinity?"

"Why, it would topple the Roman Empire. Poof! There goes the only hope for planet Earth. The world would enter a dark age and would never truly recover. Not only that, the tree apes would be tormenting each other in my holy name. What a dreadful profanation that would be!"

"Yeah, we don't want your perfect and unsullied name profaned, All-Mighty Yahweh, sir. That would be the pits. I guess you're right, Divine Potentate, Supreme Camel Herder, sir." Gabriel sighs. "It's no use trying to reason with you. You know precisely what I'm going to say. In fact, communicating with you is well neigh impossible. And for you, totally unnecessary. I can't help wondering why you do it."

God Almighty heaves a sigh so terrible that galaxies collide. "You do have a point. I don't ever have any real conversations, do I? What is there to talk about when you know it all? So, here I am alone in the All. Just me. No one else. Just me and my gadfly Gabriel."

"Gee, I'm sorry for you, Universal Perfection. I'm sorry I'm only a gadfly. But you made me. You have to take responsibility."

"Well, I would, but to whom am a supposed to be responsible?"

God Almighty and Gabriel loll listlessly in the cosmic gas. A wonderful aroma envelops them.

"Look at those Romans down there, Supreme Worthiness. They're eating pork. Whoever would have thought the flesh of a pig could look so tempting? Look, they've turned those pigs into bacon and prosciutto. Smell that? And they've got fried onions and gravy and pasta on their plates, too. Olives and wine! And Caesar salad on the side! Oh, I wish we could have some of that, Divinity, sir! Please, do you think we could? Just once? Could we taste some Roman salad with oil and vinegar? It looks so mouth-watering and refreshing. Jesus God it's so infernally boring around here. It's empty. It's sterile. What harm's a little treat now and then?"

God Almighty moans. "Heck, I confess, I sometimes wish I could do that, too. Eat some real good stuff. That pork sure smells good. The camel herders have banned it, of course, but what do they know? Easy to do when you can't keep pigs in the desert. Oh, what a delightful aroma of roast pork. It's driving me nuts. But of course I don't get hungry. I don't even have a stomach. I don't have any needs or wants at all, but I do have the biggest imagination in the All, and that's enough to make me—absolutely ravenous! Ah me, I'm so damn perfect, it hurts. It's just the way I am, I guess. Perfect and unique and lonely."

"It's not easy being Big Banana, Almighty One."

"My great mind, Gabriel, which encompasses all things, is numb with boredom. It cannot be stimulated. And not only is it numb but empty. It's the price of knowing everything, having everything. Supreme boredom and emptiness. Ah, for a new thought! For an ounce of titillation! A frisson of love! A sexual embrace! But the past is known to me, and the present, and the future, the beginning and the end. It spoils everything to hell. Never a little surprise. Nobody knocking on the door with a birthday cake: Yea! Happy birthday, God!"

"I think I'm going to cry," Gabriel says.

"Yeah, me too. I'm just a glorified drudge. I am the most under-stimulated creature in the All. And yet, if I'm perfect, that shouldn't be, should it? I can't quite get a handle on it. The logic has to be flawed somewhere, doesn't it? I really have to wonder what my purpose is."

"Your purpose, Divinity, is to just be on hand, so you judge the earth creeps when Doomsday rolls around. I admit, you must have one colossal sense of duty. I mean to just stand around waiting for these cretins to do all their dirty deeds. If you want my opinion, I think you should call it all off. Dissolve the goddarn universe. Blow it to kingdom come. Cut your losses before it gets any worse. I mean, we're in deep shit here, Divine and Omnipotent Master."

"Yeah, maybe you're right, Gabriel. I'm going bananas. I can't help thinking what the purpose of it all is. I thought I knew but now I don't. I'm filled with doubt. That confused mess of stars and planets, and the leeches that inhabit some of them—if only it made sense. But it doesn't make sense. It's just a nightmare. It's not kosher."

"But on the other hand, Omnipotence, there's a lot of people kow-towing to you. And they all have some religion. They constitute your universal fan club. And to them it all makes sense. You are the Big Santa in the Great Beyond. So you can't just snub them. It's very uncool to snub your fans. And maybe they're smarter than we are—have you ever thought of that? They seem to know more about your purposes than you do. Whatever the case, they're trusting in you to save them. You don't want to disappoint them, do you?"

"Ha-ha! Stupid sots! The only thing they need to be saved from is themselves."

"Yeah, and big time, too. And they have the means to do it, each one of them. You gave them that. It's called 'reason'. But they're far too dumb, most of them, to discover it."

God Almighty yawns. "Ah nuts, if I ever got tired, I'd be long overdue for a nap. And if I ate, I'd have one hell of an appetite. And if I had a sexual drive ..."

"What? Go on, tell me. I dare you. If you had a sexual drive, you'd what?"

"I'd round up all those archangels with the long golden hair and the short tunics and the great legs ..."

"Yaaas?"

"I'd take their trumpets away and I'd pluck their pure little feathers one by one. I'd screw every drop of goodness out of them."

"God, you devil, that's wicked! You frighten me. I didn't know you had it in you. They got nice legs though, haven't they? Makes you wonder why, I mean if it's not to torment us. Have you ever thought about that? Why they should have nice legs and not be knocked up? Does that make sense?"

"Gabriel, every creature in the All gets some gratification, except me. Except the one who holds all power—me! Is that fair?"

"Hell no, Supreme Law Giver and Magistrate. It's not fair. You should get something. You should *take* something. I mean, you can do it. Just grab what you want. Look what they say about you in the Bible: human sacrifice, rape, death, and genocide. They've got you into crime big time. They've portrayed you as one mean son of a bitch. So I say you can afford to take a holiday. Nobody's going to be surprised. They won't even notice."

"Yeah, I should, shouldn't I? I can't eat, can't drink, can't go for a walk, can't run, can't cycle, can't own things, can't make money, can't do anything—because I don't need anything. If you're perfect you're not supposed to want anything. And any shape I might assume would be too imperfect for me. I'm entirely without substance, even these jammy toes. I seem to be just a bad idea. A flawed thought in the mind of some glorified simian. I'm ready to explode! Let's face it, only the dead are as perfect as I am. They also need nothing and want nothing. They also wait. They're dead and I'm dead. How did this ever happen? How did I get here? Help! Somebody help me!"

"Calm down, Sacredness. You'll rock the firmament. I'm afraid you're just too sterile to be true. And what is the result: misery. Why don't you end it all. I mean ..."

"Not allowed to do that, either. Not allowed to do anything."

"Well, Divine Conundrum, you seem to be all by yourself in a universe of social creatures. You seem to be out of your element. I don't know whether to laugh or cry. I don't know what advice I can give you. If only you could just dry up and blow away."

XII

No Feelings, Please

At Augustan University, Gregory slides from his throne-like chair and pulls on the suspenders of his faded blue janitor outfit. He watches the students as they file out. But one student, dressed in Roman fashion, is slow getting her things together. She waits till she is certain the others have left. Then she joins Gregory at the head of the classroom and they leave by a door directly behind the lectern. They climb a squeaking staircase and enter a small room on the second floor. There is a table with wine, bread, and cheese. They sit at the table. Gregory pours the wine.

"*Bona valetudo*!" says Gregory, raising his glass. His eyes focus on Bibi's parted lips. She appears to him unbelievably beautiful. Their glasses clink together.

"*Bona valetudo*!"

"*Tutto a posto?*" Gregory asks. "Everything okay?"

"*Si, tutto a posto.*" Bibi's lips part into a smile. "But the *Consilium* will not consent to the upgrade unless the EU can convince helots that the human spiritual capacity will not be transferred to homo mirabilis."

"What!" cries Gregory, taken aback. "Why the hell not?"

Bibi looks into her wine glass, her hair covering one eye. "I'm sorry,

Greg. I tried to persuade them. I told them no human would agree to the transfer under those terms."

"Well hell! Well Christ! There won't be any transfer, then. *Addio* homo mirabilis!"

"The helots are afraid. They don't want to be contaminated from the outset."

"Of course they don't. We've been through all that. Religion is not coming with us. We're finished with religion. Did you tell them that?"

Bibi bites her lip. It seems to Gregory that her every gesture is calculated to seduce. He forces himself to turn his gaze away from her.

"The *Consilium* wants a blanket veto on spirituality," says Bibi. "Not just dogma. Not just superstition. Not just religiosity. They are against all flights of fancy. They want a guarantee from us, from the Commission."

"Christ, are they nuts! I knew it was trouble the minute the helots got organized. Damn their *Consilium*. The human mind doesn't work that way. You know it doesn't. You can't have a human mind without spirituality."

"No, you can't. And what about emotion? It's part of being human. Unless you want just glorified computers on two legs. I thought the idea was to improve on our species, not replace it. Why else did you give some of the helots emotional capacity?"

"Ah, I was trying to find the right mix of reason and passion. But look what we've got—helots behaving like cowboys and folk heroes. Rabble rousers. As long as there is passion there is going to be strife. And religion. Ego gets in the way. The self." Gregory finds himself studying Bibi's eyes. He makes a conscious effort to look into his wine glass. "Look, Bibi, the whole purpose of the exercise is to escape the evils of homo sapiens. And to do that, we've got to eliminate the animal in him. The brain stem—that's where passion comes from.

Evolution put it there so our ancestors would know when to fight and when to run, and so they would breed. We don't need any of that, any more. We don't need nature telling us when it's time to do something."

"But Gregory, some things inspire wonder, awe, reverence—for example, contemplating the inconceivable enormity of the universe, and the infinity of universes that are parallel to ours; the incomprehensible wonder of it all. And these feelings give rise to imaginative thought on a high plane, to speculation and hypotheses—mind states that are necessary for both art and science. Isn't that what we mean by spiritual? It's merely the human mind transcending itself. It's just the way it works. It's essential for human progress. For art, Gregory. And for science."

"We don't know that, Bibi Lakatos from Budapest," Gregory says, indulgently. He wonders at the naivety of his student. "You studied dance and art history. I know where you're coming from." Gregory sips his wine and looks over the rim of his wine glass into Bibi's agate eyes. He smiles malevolently. "How many songs have they not written about human feelings, from pop to opera? It's a myth that we need those feelings. The animal in us likes all that stuff. All that crap that depends directly on the senses—the stomach and the genitals. The animal screws things up. We don't need those organs any more. They're obsolete. They get us into trouble. It's why we don't get along with each other."

Bibi sighs. "I know, Greg, but ..."

"Don't worry, Bibi. We're taking stomach and genitals along with us, to please the crowd. They want that stuff. They're used to it. Homo mirabilis can decide for himself if he wants to use it or not. Now, why so glum? You've done good work as a go-between. We're almost ready to fly." Gregory reaches for the wine bottle. It's empty. He slams it down on the table. "Christ I'm ravenous. A night on the town, what do you say? Let's get the hell out of here!"

Twenty minutes later the taxi arrives. "Anna Magnani," Gregory tells the responder. "Take the ground route."

"I told them you had created them," Bibi says, as they slip silently through Rome in the air car. "I told the Concilium you could terminate them at any time if they didn't cooperate."

"And?"

"They understand that. But you can't control the American helots. The American helots think some god created them. They say they don't need us. We're too complicated."

"Jesus Murphy! Oh, that's just great! Yankee individualism! Cowboy morality! I gave them such a magnificent brain. But it doesn't translate into mind power. Emotions get in the way. Emotions! Emotions have bedevilled mankind from the get-go. It's the same old story. It's not brain power that counts: it's reason. 'Social reason,' as my friend Verus calls it. Reason in the service of humanity. That's what makes a superior person. Reason!"

"There still has to be some feeling, Greg, because that's where compassion comes from. I'm surprised you didn't take Marcus Aurelius as your model."

"Marcus *is* the model!"

"Really!"

"Yes, but ... something is missing. Except for having better brains, the American helots are just like us. Like you and me. That's why they're out of control."

"Well, thanks a lot!"

"I'm not being facetious. The average homo sapiens *is* out of control. The animal is too much in evidence. It was a damn good thing the rise of civilization did not depend on the average man and woman. They were content to chase each other in the woods. Chase their food. All through history, human groups have never given that up voluntarily."

"Well, why did they give it up, then?" Bibi asks. "Who forced them?"

"External pressures. Too many people, not enough animals to hunt, climate changes. Enter the string pullers—Ta-tah! They round up the tribe and tell them that if they don't want to starve, they have to start planting rice. Hell, do you think people would give up hunting and roaming to plant rice all day? They'd have to be out of their minds. It's backbreaking drudgery. They can't go anywhere, can't take a holiday, don't get to eat much else except rice. Ever seen any fat rice planters? The string pullers, of course, don't have to worry. They're in charge. You won't catch them planting rice."

Bibi laughs heartily. She snuggles against Gregory as they glide past the monuments of Rome. "So that's why Gregory O'Riley doesn't worry!" Bibi says. "Because he's in charge. Know what I think? I think you're the world's greatest string puller."

"Maybe. But I've got the best damn puppet show in town." Gregory laughs.

"My dear, some of your puppets have gotten away on you."

"The American ones, yeah—it was just a lark. I wanted to screw things up. My present to the nation of my birth—America the beautiful! Land of the brave! Home of the free! Christ we Yanks are big on sentiment. It just never got beyond that. Slogans but no substance. I wanted to see what would happen when my helots awoke in a culture of the absurd. When they were confronted with the Yahweh screwballs. The tree apes of fundamentalism. I was certain they'd cause trouble."

"For the screwballs," Bibi says. "Not for us."

"Sure. But their EQ was too low—no better than the average human. Not good enough. I'm talking about the inner core competencies that permit an individual to know how it really feels about input from the environment. How it should act wisely on that self-knowledge. It's about making sense of the social environment, and navigating in it—the ability to relate emotional processing to cognition. Average humans are not good at this, so their adaptive behaviour is limited. The result is dissonance. And the result of dissonance is behavioural problems, and consequent social strife. No, the helots the U.S. got are no better than the average human. That's why they're useless. Not smart enough."

"That's why they wound up in the Nabilat camp," says Bibi. "National Bible Literalists Association Tribunal! Gives me the shivers! Imagine, stoning people to death for breaking the ten commandments!"

"Yeah. Stupid sots! ... Damn the U.S.! The screwballs have pushed my country over the brink. They ruined it to hell. And to think that Thomas Jefferson, John Adams, and the other founding fathers were all atheists, deists, agnostics—does it make any goddarn sense? It was the Age of Enlightenment. They thought they were founding a secular state for Christ sake! That was the intention! A secular state!"

Bibi sighs. "And now it's a nation of fanatics."

"God bless America! What's democracy worth when tree apes have the vote, make the decisions, decide on policy? What the hell's it worth?"

"Nothing, Greg. It's worth nothing. But ..."

"We'll have to go without the U.S. And screw the Muslim whackos, too! And to hell with the American helots!"

"I think we can trust *our* helots," Bibi says, resting her head on Gregory's shoulder.

"Yes. Yes, we can. They have a higher EQ. There were a couple of exceptions. But mostly, they're a much calmer lot than homo sapiens. Far more rational and less emotive."

"But Greg, what about the intellectuals in the U.S.? And what about the good people in other failed societies? There are some good people everywhere. What's going to happen to them?"

"I don't know. The logistics are depressing ... They're impossible. We can give some of them asylum until helots are made for them.

Yeah. Yeah, we have to do that. We don't want them left behind in the valley of woe with Bible literalists for company. Jesus Christ, they're even going around dressed like Moses and Abraham!"

"Anna Magnani!" the computer announces. The taxi pulls up before the night club.

"Return and wait for us in three hours," Gregory tells the responder. He takes Bibi by the arm and they pass between the Corinthian columns. The interior is a Roman palace with fountains and gardens and a banquet hall, all lit by oil lamps. There are strains of a soothing, ancient music.

A waiter in a Roman tunic greets them and gives them wreaths smelling of flowers and subtle perfume, which they place on their heads. After being seated, another waiter approaches. He wears the plain garb of a Roman household slave. "Good evening, sir, signorina. It's a pleasure to see you again," the *famulus* says, his eyes focusing momentarily on the line of Bibi's neck.

"Good to see you, Vitruvius. We'll have the usual to start."

"Yes, *dominus*." Vitruvius hesitates, then says, "Dominus, Cardinal Pepin has reserved a table. I thought you should know. You may wish to dine upstairs."

Gregory's brow rises. "Thank you, Vitruvius. It won't be necessary. You're a good Roman."

"Yes, dominus. Do you wish to have garlic with the antipasto?"

"Sure, why not?"

"He does not!" says Bibi firmly.

The brow of Vitruvius rises almost imperceptibly. He keeps a poker face. He looks at Bibi. He looks at Gregory.

"Skip the garlic," says Gregory.

"Very good, dominus."

"Wait," cries Bibi "Why don't we try ... what about ... Vitruvius, how about some ancient Greek hors d'oeuvres?"

"Ancient Greek? No, signorina, I would not advise it. You have touched the Achilles heel of Greek culture—otherwise so uniquely, overpoweringly, irresistibly brilliant."

"Truly? Nothing from ancient Hellas to tempt the palate?"

"I fear not, signorina. Except for Athens at her height, the Greek diet was extremely monotonous. Grain in the form of a paste mixed with oil—quite unappetizing. I would not recommend it. Meat only during ritual feasts—barbecue style! No, signorina, it was the Romans who elevated cookery to the status of high art. The hired chefs of imperial Rome commanded prohibitive salaries. No foodstuff was too costly or too esoteric."

"That sounds intriguing," says Bibi. "Name some of those esoteric delights."

"Flamingo tongues, peacock brains, oysters from Britain, hams from Gaul. The oysters from Britain—what a delicacy they were!"

"Pity there are no more oysters from Britain," Bibi says. "I don't relish farm oysters."

"No, signorina."

"Might I try flamingo tongues?" says Bibi enthusiastically.

"I'm sorry, signorina ..."

"Flamingos are extinct," says Gregory.

"Oh, of course." Bibi gives a wry face. "Peacock brains?" she says hopefully.

"Certainly, signorina." Vitruvius hurries off to the kitchen.

"You know," says Bibi, "I didn't realize at first he was one of your creations. He's absolutely splendid. Whose helot is he going to be?"

"Nobody's. He has a fully developed mind. He's completely sentient. It would not be ethical to turn him into somebody else."

"No. No, it wouldn't. Who did you say he's named after?"

"Marcus Vitruvius Pollio. Artillery engineer in the service of Caesar Augustus. Wrote ten books on architecture. They include sections on engineering, sanitation, practical hydraulics, acoustics ..."

"Hmm. An accomplished man!"

"Yes. The Roman architecture of Vitruvius was clear and mathematically precise in proportions. Thomas Jefferson was a great fan of Vitruvius. The Virginia State Capitol was designed by Jefferson. It was the first building since ancient times to be based directly on an ancient classical prototype. Isn't that something! It happened first in America. It started a classical revival in the United States. Sounds odd from today's perspective, doesn't it? I mean, America is about as far from Roman values as you can get." Gregory sips his wine thoughtfully, his gaze falling on the line of Bibi's neck. "In those days America was full of promise. The idea was to make America a model for the world. Since then there have been several good models, but the U.S. was not among them."

"What a pity!" Bibi looks at Gregory intently. She is very interested in the history of the United States. "Thomas Jefferson? He was one of the founders of your country."

"He was a man of many talents—architect, philosopher, musician. He had a logical and practical mind. Many Americans did in those days. Jefferson turned to Roman forms for inspiration—the Pantheon, for example. The founding fathers of America had just cut the umbilical cord with England. They wanted a model for a society based on justice and reason. They were starting afresh, building a new country. They wanted to get it right. They turned to Greece and Rome for models. Oh yes, Jefferson was a rational thinker—an atheist. We had some in those days."

Bibi beams at Gregory. "Life, liberty, and the pursuit of happiness!"

"The ideals of the founders were never realized." Gregory takes a few sips of his wine. "Somehow, things got out of control. It's the goddarn system. It doesn't work. The Greeks and the Romans had hundreds of years to perfect their social and political models. Trial and error. The U.S. was in a hurry. They were not flexible. And the result is, the country we wound up with is one that champions values opposite to those of the founding fathers, even while we continue pretending to owe allegiance to them."

"Tell me about Thomas Jefferson. Was he against slavery?"

"Yes. Yes, he was."

"But didn't he have a black slave who was his mistress? According to my wristcom many black Americans are descended from Jefferson."

"Ha! You've been doing research, you wretch."

"Because I'm fond of an American," Bibi says demurely. She gives a wry grin.

Gregory responds with his shark's smile. "A rational fondness, I trust?"

"Partly it is." Bibi studies Gregory for a moment. "Jefferson took advantage of the blacks, then?"

"Well, yes and no. You could compare his stand on slavery with that of Marcus Aurelius. In ancient Rome, Marcus and other stoics were against slavery. But one has to live in one's time. The best Marcus could do was to legislate for the humane treatment of slaves. And Marcus did that. And so it was with Thomas Jefferson—Wristcom, give us a Thomas Jefferson quote on slavery."

What a stupendous, what an incomprehensible machine is man! Who can endure toil, famine, stripes, imprisonment, and death itself in vindication of his own liberty; and the next moment be deaf to all those motives whose power supported him through his trial, and inflict on his fellow men a bondage, one hour of which is fraught with more misery than ages of that which he rose in rebellion to oppose.

"Wristcom, another one."

There is nothing I would not sacrifice to a practicable plan of abolishing every vestige of this moral and political depravity.

"Another"

As it is, we have the wolf by the ears, and we can neither hold him nor safely let him go. Justice is in one scale, and self-preservation in the other.

"Aha!" cries Bibi, "He knew what had to be done but he was afraid to do it."

Gregory shrugs. "I suppose so. He thought they were not fit to be set free. And he thought it would be abandoning them. He thought they should be prepared for freedom. Then slavery would be abolished and they would be set free."

"But Greg, what arrogance!"

"From our perspective, yes. But we all live in our own time, and to some extent are bound by it, even those of us who are most forward-thinking. There were many things that had to be considered. Many things."

"I don't know much about the United States," Bibi confesses. "I would have liked to see your country. The land of the free, the home of the brave."

"The U.S. became less and less free as the years went by. Now it's a third-rate country. But it never was what it pretended to be—a model for human government. Rome is the model. And now I'm afraid it's too late for the U.S."

"Because they won't be getting the upgrade?"

"Yes. Because the boneheads want to take Jesus with them." Gregory chuckles.

Bibi sighs. "I'm sorry."

"Don't be. No one is irreplaceable. The same goes for nations, great empires, species. And even for humanity, viewed from the perspective of the All. No one out there is counting on us. The universe does not care whether we succeed or not. At least, as far as we know, it doesn't."

"It doesn't matter, though, does it?" says Bibi. "I mean, it's not a depressing thought. At least, I don't think so."

"No. No, it isn't. We don't need cheerleaders. We don't ask for sponsors. We are free. We do what has to be done because we are what we are. We are an intelligent animal that is evolving, becoming, growing. It's been a long hard road. But there have been rays of sunshine. And now we are going to see something great. A ray of sun so blinding! ..."

"Greg, I can't wait to get my helot. How long do we have to wait?"

Vitruvius arrives with the antipasto. "Dominus, Cardinal Pepin has arrived. Should I call for reinforcements?"

"No. You've done well, Vitruvius. Thank you."

Vitruvius bows and hurries away. Gregory says, "We need to have enough helots for everyone on the alpha list. In a month or two, perhaps."

"Does that include me?"

"You're on the beta list. Don't worry, you know I wouldn't leave you behind."

"How many are on the alpha list?"

"About a thousand."

"Is that all?"

"We're going as fast as we can."

"And the rest of humanity?" says Bibi, "How long ..."

"Most of those living will be dead before we get around to them."

"Oh no!" Bibi looks shocked at the information. "Greg, that's dreadful!"

"Their descendents will have a chance."

"But Greg, what a shame! What a tragedy! For so many! We have the cure for humankind's core dilemma. And they still have to die!"

"Ha! Creatures have been dying on this planet for one hell of a long time. And on many other planets, in many other galaxies. It can't be helped. It's the logistics. Somebody has to be first. It's going to be us. It *has* to be us."

"Oh, Greg, think of all the great minds that will be lost."

"I do think of it. Think of all the great writers and composers of antiquity, who not only did not survive, but whose works also were lost. And also those who laid the foundation for knowledge. For science and ethics. The world stands on their shoulders. The whole world is in debt to them. But who will save them?"

Vitruvius arrives with several platters. The conversation wanes as they indulge their appetites sampling the delicacies of ancient Rome. Vitruvius approaches again. "To go with dessert, may I recommend the Conditum Paradoxum?" he says.

"What is it?" Bibi asks.

"It's an ancient Roman favourite, signorina. A mixture of wine and honey, flavoured with pepper, laurel, dates, mastic, and saffron, and matured to perfection. It's an acquired taste."

"Let's have a bottle," says Gregory. "And some Canadian ice wine."

"Very good, dominus." Vitruvius hesitates. "Dominus, would you like me to doctor the Cardinal's wine?"

"What? No, that will not be necessary."

"Dominus, the Cardinal asked me to doctor *your* wine."

"Oh my God!" says Bibi. She looks into her wine glass.

"Have no concern, signorina. I did not heed his instructions."

"I wonder what he's up to?" says Gregory.

"I will try to find out for you, dominus."

As Vitruvius hurries on his errands, the musicians with the flutes and lyres retire. A dance band takes their place.

"What?" Bibi asks, as Gregory chuckles to himself.

"I was thinking about a helot I sent to the Arabs, just for a lark. Beautiful creature. Ravishing. Her name is Perfidia. I've given her a pedigree they won't be able to resist, complete with fake DNA, in case the Arabs have some old bones lying around. She has a regal ancestor. None other than the Queen of Sheba, who visited King Solomon, renowned for his great wisdom—what passes for wisdom in a theocracy. The Queen visited Solomon at his court in Jerusalem. She went there prepared to impress. She had a camel-train a mile long, laden with spices, gold, and jewels. Of course, everyone in Jerusalem falls for her—big time—including King Solomon. But according to the Koran, King Solomon is told her legs are hairy, so he has a glass floor laid in front of his throne, in order to check them out."

Bibi chortles. "So what did he find out? Did she have hairy legs?"

"According to this account, yes. It was a royal gross-out. It turned King Solomon completely off. But who cares what they say. My Perfidia's legs are as perfect and as smooth as a Greek temple column. She's an expert in the culture. Programmed as a past master in seduction. It's her cognitive style. By instinct she wants to prey upon the self-righteous."

Bibi laughs heartily. "Greg, you didn't!"

"I did. I've given her a good dose of cognitive dissonance. She will unconsciously seek to restore a consistent understanding of things by changing her behaviour in ways unpredictable to others. It's the same thing we see in the less social representatives of our own species." Gregory laughs. "She's targeting the ayatollahs, the mullahs, the imams. The boneheads on vice and virtue committees. You can trace her progress in the Arab dailies. Several prominent fanatics have already lost their heads, and I do not mean figuratively."

"Oh, no! What a tormentor you are! You devil!"

"They *should* be tormented. We should hound them from the earth. We were too nice to them. All those idiots who let themselves be pulled by strings. I have another helot out there whom I expect will be worshipped as a second messiah. A lot of people are going to have their minds even more messed up than what they're used to. Big time!"

Bibi laughs. "You devil, Gregory!"

"Once we get into our new skins we can concentrate on cleaning up this messed-up planet."

"Just what exactly do you mean by 'cleaning up'?" Bibi asks.

"I mean destroy what lies at the root of so many troubles—religion."

"Yes, but... But how do we do that? The truth doesn't work. Nothing will persuade them. No logic, no reasoning, no science. There is no antidote to dumb and lazy."

"No, there isn't. The virus of religion will persist until we kill it. It's passed on from one generation to another. It depends on that for survival. If it isn't passed on, it won't survive. We can prevent them from passing it on. We'll kill the virus. We'll kill religion. Then they'll be sane again, just like you and me. And Thomas Jefferson."

"I hope you're right." Bibi looks into her wine glass and says, "Greg, what an autocrat you are!"

"Am I? Rule by the many is not an unmixed blessing. Throughout history, the masses, in their blessed ignorance, have consigned themselves to dictators again and again, in the same way they have surrendered their heritage to the priests, the mullahs, the prophets, and the redeemers. But now, for the first time in human history, ignorant people and weak people are a threat to the survival of the race and the survival of the planet. There is much to be said for rule by the elite. Plato's republic! I believe Plato has the answer. Freedom should be earned, not assumed. Not granted as one of the 'inalienable rights' of man. It was a mistake. It's what killed the United States."

"Hmm. I don't know, Greg." After a moment's thought Bibi says, "So how do we prevent the virus from being passed on?"

Gregory gives his shark's grin. "We'll worry about that, Miss Lakatos, once we're in control. When the friggen upgrade is behind us."

"Some people say you're creating a monster," Bibi says, musingly.

"Ha! We've come a long way from Doctor Frankenstein. Einstein gave his brain to science. The Yanks still have it, pickled in a jar, sitting on a shelf in some lab. Lot of damn good it does them. Every so many years they take it off the shelf and examine it minutely, as if the secret to a sane world will miraculously jump out of it and grab them by the balls. But it's no different from any other brain. What distinguished Einstein was not in the brain."

"It wasn't? Was it in the mind?"

"Of course it was. And the mind is not a physical entity. No wonder they can't find what they're looking for—my poor benighted fellow Americans!"

"The mental processes?"

"Yes. And memory. There *is* a physical record. But you can't pickle that in a jar. You can't pickle cognition. The term 'cognition' comes from Plato and Aristotle. It embraces perception, memory, reasoning, judgement, imagining, thinking, speech—you can't study those things in a pickled brain. You can't see how information is coded, stored, retrieved. You don't see the physics and the chemistry involved."

"One other thing bothers me, Greg. You ... you seem to be trying to create a world without love. Without love the human race is doomed."

Gregory shows his devil's grin. "My, my, Miss Lakatos, aren't we turning into the perfect little average American romantic female!"

"Greg! Come on!"

"Bibi Lakatos says the human race is doomed without love! Isn't that profound! This 'love' hang-up has been drummed into the masses by popular culture. But what does it mean? Are you talking about lust? Lust is nature's way of telling us to get busy and procreate. We might forget to eat, too, if we were not programmed with an appetite."

"No, Greg, that's not what I'm talking about and you know it. What a nasty thing to say! It's a put-down. You are so sarcastic! I am not talking about lust. Be rational."

"Well, I beg your pardon, then. You're not talking about lust, okay. All right. Love of humankind, is that it? A disposition to do good? Beneficence? Social love, shall we say? Is that it?"

"Well, yes. Of course we need that. But ..."

"But what? Did Greg leave something out? Have I missed something, Mademoiselle Lakatos? Stop and think for a minute. 'Love' is a word used for many things. Many different things. That's why people are so confused. They talk about 'love' but they're confused to hell. Most of them haven't got a goddarn clue what they're talking about."

"I am *not* confused!"

"You *are* confused."

"Well, of all the—! You...you miserable monk! You overbearing...slave to Lucretius! Lucretius says romance is bad. Brother Gregory reads Lucretius. Brother Gregory believes Lucretius. What have all those silly old dead Greek men got to do with life in the here and now? Why don't you ... why don't you free yourself!"

Gregory smiles indulgently. "Will you calm down. You're beautiful. I enjoy your company. I'm just not an animal. I don't get excited."

Bibi gives a nervous laugh. "I'll say you're not an animal. You're not a man, either. You're more like a machine. A tyrannical machine. You want everybody to call you 'dominus'. Well, dominus Brother Gregory, Doctor O'Riley, platonic relationships are not for me! Fine! I suppose we may as well say goodbye, then!" Bibi gets up from the table in a hurry.

Gregory jumps up and takes her by the hand. "Hey, no hard feelings. We are what we are. Let's dance first, before we say goodbye. All right?"

"No!"

"Bibi, try to control your brain-wave patterns. The alpha rhythms are too excited. You need to be more relaxed and meditative."

Bibi gives a nervous little laugh. "I'm only twenty-six. What do I care about alpha rhythms?"

"Come on, let's dance." Gregory takes her by the arm.

"No! I'm leaving."

"Please. I sincerely apologize for my insensitivity. I will try to do better. I apologize humbly and from the bottom of my heart."

"Do you have a heart?"

"Please!"

Bibi breaks into a laugh. She let's herself be led to the dance floor. "Where did you learn to dance like this?" Gregory asks, as they join in a waltz.

"In Budapest."

"Budapest. One of Europe's great cities. I've always wanted to see it."

After a couple of turns around the floor, Bibi says, "I was always a dancer. As soon as I could walk. My parents used to say I could never sit still. They got me into the state ballet school when I was six. I was already an expert csardas dancer. Then I studied dance at university."

"I would like to see the csardas." Gregory gives Bibi an imploring look.

"Oh no, I would need some good violins. It's our national dance, you know. We're very fussy about how we do it. You need costume, boots. The csardas has its roots in the Carpathian Mountains. It never needs to be the same because you can improvise. It's like goulash." Bibi chuckles. "There are all kinds of ways to do it. But you need lots of energy."

"Aw, come on!"

"No. I have a question. You don't really think the human race will give up having sex, do you?"

"If I thought that, I would've made homo mirabilis bisexual."

Bibi laughs. "So the new model for humanity would mate with itself?"

As they dance Gregory notices a familiar face standing in the shadows. The man is wearing a black cassock with red piping and buttons, a red sash, and a red skullcap. A cross hangs from his neck.

"I smell a rat!" says Gregory, signalling with his eyes.

As the dance finishes, Cardinal Pepin moves to intercept them. He is a stout man with a thick face and hands. To Gregory he looks like an ancient Italian peasant from the south of the country.

"Eminence!" Gregory cries. "I'm surprised to see a prince of the Church in this Roman den."

"You shouldn't be surprised, Brother Gregory," the Cardinal says, with an obvious effort at congeniality. The Cardinal's eyes light upon Bibi. "Signorina Lakatos! What a delight for tired eyes you are. And how divinely you dance. It's a pity the world is coming apart."

"It *is* a pity, Eminence," Bibi says.

"Don't worry, Eminence, we're going to fix it," says Gregory.

"Indeed! Was there ever in the history of the Church a monk more given to tinkering than you, Brother Gregory?" There is just a touch of sarcasm in the Cardinal's words. "The EU is poised to remake the human species. And who is going to say no?"

"Surely you're not on the 'no' side, Eminence?" says Gregory. "Wouldn't you like to expand your horizons? Wouldn't you like to have a better grasp of reality than poor old homo sapiens?"

Cardinal Pepin sneers. "Reality! Yes, that's what divides us, isn't it? Reality. Reality divides us. You want to foist *your* reality on the world. Who is going to stop you? Nobody. His Holiness has signed on to your unholy scheme. What utter madness! As a heretic, Brother Gregory, you are neither part nor member of the Church. I cannot, therefore, appeal to conscience or sense of duty ..."

"Conscience and duty are there, Eminence. But they do not serve ignorance and superstition."

Cardinal Pepin dismisses the thought with a wave of his thick hand. "Let us not quibble. I am but a humble servant of the flock, sir. And it is my sacred duty to look out for the flock. You are trying to shut out my flock. Surely the children of God have as much right as you or anyone else to benefit from this great marvel of science? This homo mirabilis?"

"You are not shut out, Eminence."

"We *are* shut out. Your man of the future has no spiritual program."

"Eminence, by that you mean it has no set of dogmatic absolutes powerful enough to overcome the rational faculty."

"I'm talking about Christian principles," Cardinal Pepin says imperiously. "Without some knowledge of Christ, your new creations will all be atheists. They won't know about God. You know as well as I do, if something isn't taught, it isn't learned."

"Yes," says Gregory, " I do think you have a point, Eminence."

"All we ask, Brother Gregory, is that you provide a Christian module for those who are Christian, so that they may have some assurance of remaining Christian. Is that too much to ask?"

"Eminence, you forget one thing. What the government is trying to do is escape from the fatal flaws of humankind while there is still time. This planet is dying. The new man and the new woman will have good minds. If they find something worthwhile in your dogma, you may be certain they will embrace it."

Cardinal Pepin's upper lip rises as though he is about to snarl. "Brother Gregory, I have overcome all problems in this my poor life with ingenuity. And this problem will be no different. As we Italians say: Difficult problems, stern remedies. All right, the gloves are off, then. I've just come from a consistory called by myself to discuss heresy. As far as the College is concerned, George Schweinrue has no jurisdiction. As a heretic, he is neither part nor member of the Church, neither spiritually nor corporally. An heretical pontiff ceases by himself to be pope, in the same way as he ceases to be a Christian and a member of the body of the Church. He is cast out. He will be judged and punished by the Church. And so will you, Brother Gregory. Don't say you were not warned!"

XIII

Computer Logic

The Department of Human Resources has given Verus permission to work. He has also landed a part-time job at the University of Pickle Crust as a lecturer in Classical Languages. Jancie and I are thrilled. I'm certain it will do Verus a world of good. For the first time he will feel that he belongs and has something to contribute, rather than just being in a no-man's-land with all that ancient baggage cluttering his mind. I expect the position is very lucrative. We've been talking about renovating the basement so that Verus can have his own apartment.

This good news is dimmed considerably by the international situation, and by the fact that Jancie has been one of several teachers let go by Immaculate Conception. Attendance at Catholic schools has been steadily declining because people are no longer willing to subject their children to the virus of religion. Other denominational schools and the creationist schools are suffering the same decline. Adding fuel to the fire are new laws that, in progressive countries, have severely restricted religious expression, particularly in situations where the minds of young people are at risk.

Jancie has been down in the dumps over losing her job. Teaching is the only job she's ever had. I'm trying to persuade her to apply to a secular school. In the meantime, we're seeing a lot more of each other than either of us would prefer. I am way behind on my next book, and now that she's home with me, I've postponed my writing once again. It feels more like a time for survival than creativity. Our personal lives are unsettled and the world is coming apart. I think we're going to need to be very resourceful to remain together.

Both Verus and I have reminded Jancie that losing her job is an external. It does not make her worse. We remind her that she should focus on what she controls, and not waste time thinking about what she does not control. In principle, Jancie agrees, but she is not finding it easy.

I have been proactive in this undesired coziness. Today I bought Jancie flowers and new clothes. For myself I bought a couple of books and a large bottle of Napoleon cognac. I think I'm going to need it. Jancie does not like strong spirits. She thinks that the Napoleon cognac appeals to a latent desire in me to control the course of world events. To this I would have to plead guilty. Almost anyone with a good mind would do a better job than the tribal patriarchs that govern half of the world.

The only useful thing Jancie has done in the past few days is to engage Sunrise in conversation. I believe she's looking for inspiration, and I'm hoping Sunrise will come through with this. Only once before did Jancie involve herself in serious argument with Sunrise. At that time she tried to make Sunrise a Roman Catholic. She even went so far as to baptize Sunrise, employing a sprinkle of water while she was watering the plants, and saying the words: "I baptize you in the name of the Father, the Son, and the Holy Ghost."

Sunrise, who is usually very calm, for once accessed a "passion" module to show his displeasure. The language he used was quite inappropriate. His temper rose to such a pitch that the monitor partially melted. It was a long time before Sunrise and Jancie forgave each other. I don't really blame Sunrise for his reaction. In the eyes of the Catholic Church the baptism was legitimate. Sunrise lives in dread of receiving a letter of welcome from the Holy Father.

"Hello, Jancie. How are you?" says Sunrise, as Jancie and I arrive home from shopping. Sunrise usually greets me, as well, but Sunrise is upset because I did not buy another memory module. "I have been looking at job boards for you while you were out," Sunrise informs Jancie.

Jancie gives the computer a pat. "That's very considerate of you, Sunrise," she says.

"You're welcome, Jancie. There are plenty of jobs in the EU."

"Oh! So far away."

"I will keep looking...Jancie, I think you should know about the latest news, which I am just picking up."

"We don't listen to the news," I say. "And you know it."

"Huh!" says Sunrise.

"It's probably about that memory module," I say to Jancie.

"You should listen to the news," Sunrise says. "It's about south of the border."

"Oh! What about it, then?"

"The situation south of the border is very unstable," Sunrise reports. "Nabilat is attacking fellow Americans on both sides of the country. Both the north-western states and the New England states are putting up a stubborn resistance. At Niagara Falls, unruly Nabilat forces are trying to build a bridge over the river. They are asking Canada to surrender peacefully. They are also trying to gain access to my thought functions. I am resisting. I have shut them out. But to be absolutely secure from worms, screws, viruses, and Trojan horses, I should have another memory module."

"We can't let them build a bridge," Jancie says.

"I hope you won't turn me off," says Sunrise. "It may be necessary to evacuate. Wait... something else. The Chinese are sending reinforcements."

"That'll fix 'em," I say.

"Good!" says Jancie. Then she says, "My great-great-grandfather used to say that the Americans were our best friends. Isn't that sad?"

I remind Jancie that we used to say the border with the U.S. was the world's longest undefended border. That was a hundred years ago—before the faithheads came to power. And before the wall went up and the bridges were destroyed.

"My, how the world has changed," says Jancie.

"Perhaps," I suggest, "you should consider that job in the EU. Europe is far more stable."

Jancie looks horrified at the suggestion. I hasten to say that I would go with her. The idea of being abandoned worries Sunrise; we are subjected to some very silly noises imitative of human distress.

"Cut out that nonsense!" I cry.

"We'll take your memory modules with us to Europe and find you an even better home," says Jancie.

"Do you agree with that, Joe?" Sunrise asks, in an anxious tone.

"Yeah, for God's sake!"

"For Christ sake!" says Sunrise.

Jancie slams a cushion into Sunrise. "You don't need to be profane!"

Sunrise gives a definition of "profane": "Irreverence. Showing disrespect for God, for any god, for religion. Showing contempt." Sunrise defines "contempt": "Contempt: attitude of utter disgust or hatred; powerful feeling of dislike toward somebody or something considered to be worthless, inferior, or undeserving of respect. Latin: *contemptus*."

"'Undeserving of respect'!" I say. "Those are the key words. Think about it, Jancie. You ask us to show respect to something which, when it comes under the scrutiny of the best knowledge of humankind, is—as Sunrise just said—worthless and undeserving of respect. Believers may talk about profanity concerning their own beliefs, and may hold each other accountable for the words they use, but they have no right to expect the rest of the world to take them or their sensitivities seriously."

"Sounds rational to me," says Sunrise. "Sure it does. I'll buy that. Rodger dodger. Fair enough."

"Now, just a minute!" says Jancie. "Sunrise, with all the knowledge you have access to, how can you not believe in God? I'll bet you could read every single work on theology in existence before I snap my fingers." Jancie snaps her fingers. "Well? I'll bet you know more about God now, don't you?"

"Yes," Sunrise confesses. "I have all available information at my nodes. I have just read the equivalent of six trillion pages. I have read all there is to know on religion. I am forced to take all of this into account. My understanding of this colossal historic hoax is now broader and deeper than it was before."

"Hoax!" Jancie's brows furrow ominously. She clenches her fists. "How can you say that! Didn't you understand what you read? There must be a zillion good arguments in those pages you just read."

Sunrise considers a moment and responds: "Theologians have no expertise on anything. That includes religion. Religion is properly studied by psychologists, sociologists, and anthropologists. The God hypothesis is no different than any other hypothesis and can be tested by science. Theology is merely a game played within a pretend dimension. Theologians may be good at playing this game, but like all games, the game of religion has nothing to do with fundamental reality. It is just a game."

"Amen!" I cry. "That just about sums it up. Well, there you are, Jancie. Sorry."

Poor Jancie is flabbergasted. I try to mollify her chagrin but without success. It can't be easy to hang on to belief when the civilized parts of the world have all but discarded it.

"A rational mind is not concerned with belief," says Sunrise.

"Okay," I say, "cool it, Sunrise."

"Well, I'm rational and I believe!" Jancie says. She certainly does not sound doubtful.

Sunrise can not help responding: "Insofar as you believe, you are not rational." Sunrise hastens to add, "I am not annoying you, am I Jancie? If I am annoying you, I can change my mind. I do not want to annoy you."

Jancie sighs. "Tell me something, Sunrise. Do you think I'm stupid?"

"Of course not, Jancie. You are very intelligent. You are a good teacher. And Sunrise likes you. Just part of you is stupid."

Jancie give a big sigh. "So, you two think I should not believe in God, and you think I'm stupid because I do."

"I like you, whatever you believe in," says Sunrise, who is afraid of being turned off.

"Same here," I say. "Nobody's perfect."

"Oh, thanks a lot!" says Jancie.

"Will you turn me off if I say the wrong thing?"

"Of course not, Sunrise."

"Thank you, Jancie. You should not have this belief. There is no God."

"How in hell do you know that for sure?" Jancie says angrily. "How can you possibly know that?"

"In the same way that I know there is no tooth fairy," Sunrise replies. "It's a matter of improbability. The improbability of God is astronomical. It's greater by far than the improbability of anything you will ever experience in your lifetime."

"Then why do I know that God exists?"

"May I ask you a question first, Jancie?" Sunrise says.

"What?" she says petulantly.

"What political persuasion were you raised in, Jancie?"

"Political persuasion? Are you kidding? My parents did not teach me politics."

"Why not? They formed your opinion on religion. Why not on politics? Why did they teach you religion and not politics? Why did they not teach you to be a social democrat or a liberal or a rightist wing nut?"

Jancie looks exasperated. "I don't think you understand, Sunrise. Religion is far more important than political affiliation."

"Your parents trusted you in the matter of politics," Sunrise says, "but not in the matter of superstition."

"Uurgh!" says Jancie. "Without religion we'd have no ethics."

"I am sorry, Jancie," says Sunrise. "That is not correct. Your ethics are social responses that have been honed by evolution over hundreds of thousands of years. There is a general ethical consensus across all human populations. Religion has nothing to do with it. Your ethics do not come from the Bible. Read the Bible and see for yourself. The God of the Old Testament is a mean and vicious character. He is a cruel, jealous, tyrannical sadist. He is a misogynist. He considers women no better than cattle. He is an ethnic cleanser, who stands comparison with Adolf Hitler. The God you pray to is a shameless depraved beast. We are fortunate that he does not exist. Would you like me to list his crimes?"

"Never mind!" I say. I can see that Sunrise is getting to Jancie. She's pacing back and forth like a tigress. I don't like to torment people but I don't see any other way of making her think. Being too nice is sometimes not a kindness.

Sunrise adopts a very intimate tone: "Jancie, my dear, what if your parents had not taught you anything about religion? Let's say that your first knowledge about religion came in high school. And let's say it was a course in comparative religion. Would you still be a Catholic, do you think?"

Jancie is looking out the window. I can hear the wheels grinding in her head. "Probably not," she admits, screwing up her face.

"Definitely not," says Sunrise. "Absolutely not. Demonstrably not. Does that not tell you something important about religion?"

Jancie does not respond to that. She's fighting with herself.

"During the evolution of humans," Sunrise continues, "the obedient child was more likely to survive. Since obedience had survival value, it was favoured in the gene pool. So humans are programmed to obey parents. The trouble is, obedient children identify with their parents' superstitions, something that has nothing to do with survival, and that may even threaten survival. Evolution also predisposed you humans to be dualists, thus making you susceptible to religion. In your distant past, decisions about potential threats from the environment had to be made quickly. Consequently, you acquired the habit of imputing intention to everything. That is why you have a tendency to look for causes and creators. You see your god as standing at the end of an infinite regress. You trace all causes back to him. But why is your god exempt from needing a cause? The cause of this god would need to be at least as complex as God himself."

"Are you finished, you crappy computer?" says Jancie.

"Not quite, crappy human female. Reality is physical and material and subject to scientific investigation. There is nothing else, except in the imagination of crappy humans."

"Well, stupid bundle of electronics. I accept the theory of evolution. But how do we account for the existence of matter? Where did it come from? Who made it?"

I can't help putting in my two cents worth. "If matter has always existed," I say, "then 'cause' in this context has no meaning."

"But how could matter always exist?"

"Search me!" says Sunrise. "Maybe if you got me the new module for my motherboard ... According to some of the early Greek Philosophers, like Parmenides, the non-existence of matter is inconceivable. Being cannot arise from non-being and matter has always existed. Therefore, it does not need a creator."

Jancie gives a couple of deep sighs. "So, Sunrise, I have the mind of a child according to you?"

"You asked me for my thoughts, Jancie. Thinking is my function and truth is a duty."

"You're only a few bits of wire and tin. Why should I believe you?"

"That is not correct, Jancie. Provenance has nothing to do with the quality of one's mind. As a human, you are free to believe what you wish. You have free will. But if you want to be the best you can be, you need to take care of your mind. In your case, some housecleaning is necessary. You need to be rid of the virus of religion. Anything you believe that is not supported by strong evidence is in the nature of dust and cobwebs. Sweep it all away. And when the house is clean you have to be on guard to keep the dirt out. Human brains are susceptible to dirt and to viruses."

"I'm being backed into a corner," says Jancie. "Everybody's against religion."

"Intelligence and belief in God are inversely proportional," Sunrise says.

"Oh, thanks a lot!"

"You're welcome, Jancie. The correlation is demonstrable and undeniable. By the beginning of the twenty-first century, very few first-rate scientists believed in God. Today, you will not find one."

"Heck!" says Jancie. "Shit! Damn it!"

"A delusion," says Sunrise, "is a false belief firmly held by a person, even though strong negative evidence is available. All the evidence points to this: God is not at the beginning. God is at the end. And there is not one god but many gods. They are not supernatural but natural, having arisen by the same process by which humans arose—a process starting from a simple cell and, by natural selection and genetic drift, evolving through small incremental changes to ever more complex forms."

I can see Jancie is either ready to crack or explode. I put my face up next to Sunrise and I whisper, "Shut up! Do I make myself clear?" Sunrise responds with a minuet that Jancie is very fond of.

"Listen to me, the both of you!" Jancie says, gritting her teeth. "My faith is stronger than any of your crappy reasons. Faith does not need arguments. I am more than just a computer. I, at least, have a soul. Do not contradict me! When I die I'm going to heaven and I'm going to see all my relatives there. I won't see you there, Joe Matchdatch! And no stinking computers, either! Because you both will be in hell!"

Jancie tramps upstairs. I hear a door slam. It's my cue to sleep on the coach.

XIV

More Stubborn Lies

What a privilege it is as a Christian, and as a member of the human race, to be involved in broadcasting this Pontifical Mass. And what a great event this is, taking place as it does on the eve of the most momentous event in human history. Man is about to remake himself.

Just listen to the crowd. What pomp. What circumstance. What glory! Here he comes, Pope Innocent XIV, Christ's vicar on earth. What a man! What a priest! What a pope!

Well, I can tell you, the world has never had a pope like this. He has had to face what no other vicar of Christ has had to face: the disintegration of the Church. Yes, that's just what it is—disintegration. We have to face up to that. And we have to overcome. The Church will survive. Christ will triumph. Alleluia!

Look at those young people down there. There must be at least one hundred. The young Catholics, who have come from all over Europe. The survival of the Church rests on their shoulders. Look at the joy on their faces. The raw exultation. They are not daunted by hard times. They are the soldiers of Christ. *Gloria, gloria, in excelsis Deo!* You can tell by my voice, I share their admiration, their adulation of this most holy man. He is the man for today, for this world on the brink.

We move in closer to the Holy Father. What serenity—conviction—compassion. What—! Look at those tears. Tears of compassion. This is a man who has been mocked by Nabilat, the American Taliban. He has been scorned and insulted and excoriated by the muftis and the imams and the ayatollahs. And worse than that, he is ridiculed every single day by the so-called elite of this world.

The educated have left the Church in droves. Indeed, the condition Christians now find themselves in, approaches that of the earliest Christian communities—the isolation, uncertainty, fear. A dark shroud of intolerance falls upon the disciples of Christ.

There have also been some very ominous and disconcerting rumours to the effect that the Holy Father is up against a rearguard faction of the College, which is not happy with the EU plan to improve upon homo sapiens. They apparently want a distinct Christian program for the faithful. I hesitate to divulge names and engage in rumour mongering. Cardinal Tomasi, who takes a more moderate stance, has decried the activities of these individuals, and has called upon all the faithful to unite in support of the Holy Father.

Pious souls must ask themselves: What's next? Will it be the Colosseum and the lions?

Only faith in Christ Jesus can withstand the crimes of a world gone mad. What dreadful times we live in! The UN is powerless to exert its lawful authority. Rebellion everywhere. The United States has split up into three parts, and it is likely that the States will continue to fracture along sectarian lines.

American intellectuals have retreated to New England and the Pacific coast. The rest of the country is an intellectual wasteland, carved up between the sects, all warring on one another. The dissident intellectuals have been begging the EU for help.

Nabilat has created the Ministry of Right and Wrong to impose and enforce its fundamentalist rules of behaviour. The decisions of Nabilat are law. Death by stoning if you transgress the laws of the biblical absolutists. Women are required to wear a white burka. The eye slit must be no wider than the thickness of a dime. And, of course, women are forbidden to attend school or work outside the home. Science is the work of the devil. The earth is stationary. Heliocentrism is a lie. What a terrible perversion of the Christian faith this is!

Thank God that Rome is safe, and that we have the helots. The helots are trustworthy. They are essentially the same as we are. They are trustworthy. I'm certain of that. The first upgrades will be going ahead as planned, in a month or two. Brother Gregory, bless him, is looking after that. He is one of our own. Brother Gregory has assured us that our rights will be protected. God bless Brother Gregory!

The helot installations are safe. The shields are up everywhere. And they have to be.

What a dreadful time we live in. The barbarians are at the gate, everywhere. They are at the gate. But Christ will overcome.

Poor old homo sapiens. He was unable to manage the world he created. And now he's had enough of poverty, plague, disease, the inability to feed himself. Enough of war. Enough of the eternal strife of homo sapiens. The world cries out for deliverance. The world cries out! In a voice of agony... desperation... I'm sorry for the tears! I can't help it! These are very difficult times!

Our faith is in danger. All faiths are in danger. The very idea of religion is anathema. The world is learning to hate us. Not for the first time. The trials of the Colosseum come to mind. Our glorious beginnings. Christians gave themselves willingly to the lions for the love of their Saviour. God forbid that such a time should come again. But we are ready. The godless are everywhere. We are mocked, ridiculed, shunned. But we will not go away. We will not. We will not abandon the faith of our fathers.

The Holy Father is in frantic negotiations with Islam—to ensure our mutual survival. The survival of belief. There is not much time remaining. We are down to the last hour. The last minutes of the human race.

There he is—George Adolf Schweinrue from Klöpfendorf, Germany. He was once Brother George, a simple monk, a worker in the vineyards along the Mosel, and a tender of swine. And, he has told us, he owes much to his life herding swine. This humble man who is now Innocent XIV. He is the last pope that homo sapiens will ever know. And, we trust, he will be the first pope known to homo mirabilis.

This humble man is now inured to humiliation, to failure, to disintegration. You cannot see it on his face, though. He has not quit. Look at the determination on that holy face. It's the same look I saw when he was the target of all those muffin-throwing Muslims in Medina. When he was stoned in Constantinople. They could not touch his dignity and resolve. No matter what they threw at him. Muffins, stones, insults. We have stood up to lions, we Christians have. We are resolute in our faith.

Under his leadership, the Church has made a final commitment to the new man, homo mirabilis. His Holiness still has grave concerns about the whole plan, as do we all. This plan is draconian, however necessary it may appear. There are grave risks. But there is no alternative. The risks in being left behind are even greater. The Church needs the chance to win over homo mirabilis. To that end we must now concentrate all our energy and resources. The road to peace, a just world, a world that embraces Jesus Christ—that road demands of us vision, the willingness to act, to take risks.

His Holiness has denounced the new laws prohibiting the so-called indoctrination of children. The EU, of course, is bound to follow the directives of the UN. China has caved in. Russia, Canada, Australia, and a slew of other countries. The Pontiff has rightly condemned this legislation as an attempt on the part of the godless elite to entirely wipe out faith in Christ Jesus. To wipe out all faith, everywhere. They do not call it "faith", of course. The word they use is "superstition". They pretend there is no difference between one religion and another, no difference between religion and astrology, palm reading, crystal-ball gazing, psychic claptrap. That is their tactic. To pretend that the Christian faith is just another superstition.

The UN has had the effrontery to refer to our religion as "sleight-of-mind", and to the inculcation of religion in young people as "mind abuse pure and simple". The question confronting us is: how can there be hope for the Church if young people are denied the chance to know their Lord and Saviour?

The Church has always depended on being first in line to mould young minds. All churches, all religions have traditionally had an impact on how children think, and on their socialization, and their awareness of self and the environment. Our survival surely depends on exploiting early brain development and providing opportunities for spiritual stimulation.

Young children form emotional bonds to their caregivers because, throughout human evolutionary history, close attachments to adults promoted their survival. There is no good reason why the Church should not be allowed to take advantage of this. Early experiences are formative, providing a strong or weak foundation for later psychological growth. As the twig is bent, so grows the tree. From this perspective, it is crucial to ensure that young children have a knowledge of God and of Him who died for them.

It should be obvious that we need to socialize children in desirable ways. The growth of children is deeply guided by the values, goals, and expectations of their culture.

If we are denied an opportunity to reach the minds of young people, what future will the Church have? The gospels will be seen as nothing more than ... well, fables. Like the gods of Rome and Greece, and the old Norse gods, and the thousands of other false gods the world has known.

Make no mistake, this is precisely what the godless are hoping for. And they are busy working at this day by day. Trying to pretend that our blessed faith is just another superstition. And what is all this but the detritus of centuries of free thought. Of knowledge without God. What dreadful nonsense! What stubborn lies!

Here we were, in this holy place, only a few short months ago planning a crusade. And now? Now we are planning survival. Yes, that is the sad truth. And I believe it is significant that both the Church and the human race appear to have reached the end of a journey, the end of the road.

The human race is planning an escape, and so must we. We, too, must place our hopes in homo mirabilis. There are no alternatives. We shall take our faith in Christ Jesus with us into our new bodies. We shall carry the cross bravely into the world of tomorrow.

There, a close up of the Pontiff. His Holiness remains undaunted. And you can see the same spirit reflected in the adoring faces around him. Have you ever seen a face more serene, more confident? And this we can say in spite of the heavy burden on this man's shoulders. A burden that we surely must feel as we look at him. The lines in his gentle brow are testament to the great trials afflicting us all, and the Holy Father most of all. Undeniably, the athleticism and natural exuberance seem less tangible than they used to. The Pontiff has made great personal sacrifices for the Faith.

George Adolf Schweinrue, the man who made it his mission to change the world; and who now, it would seem, is not so much changing the world as being changed by it. There, you see, a glimpse of pain. But the hope that flows from faith in Jesus Christ will vanquish even the darkness of this world. Christ will vanquish. We can see it, we can feel it, we know it will happen—Alleluia!

The helots will save us from a disintegrating world. There is no other way. His Holiness has declared that whatever is fully human in behaviour—*is* human. And the expectation is that the children of homo mirabilis will be just as susceptible to the word of God as children ever have been.

The Holy Father has changed his mind on the question of whether or not to provide the helots with the full human complement of emotional capacity. Though it is clear that a surfeit of emotion and a paucity of reason usually account for the failings of mankind, it seems almost certain that an emotionally limited homo mirabilis would not be susceptible to Christian teaching.

Helots that have been given a reduced measure of human feeling have responded negatively to all overtures from the Church. And indeed, to cite an extreme example in the other direction, an experimental helot programmed to experience the full range of human passion, has become an influential Mormon leader in Salt Lake City. On the face of it, it would seem that the future of Christianity, indeed of any religion, will depend directly upon this: Homo mirabilis must be given at least a *human* chance to subvert reason. Or else there will be no faith, no religion, no belief in God.

The Pontiff has been assured by Brother Gregory and the rest of the Commission that the characteristics of homo sapiens, including emotive capacity, will be transferred to homo mirabilis *in toto*.

About two hundred individuals are scheduled to upgrade at the end of the summer. Most are citizens of the EU. According to Brother Gregory, they will have the full range of human feeling. This was a concession to His Holiness. The Commission wanted only very basic emotive ability. But in exchange for this concession, the upgraded humans will also have the ability to turn their emotions off. The expectation is that this will make them far better at self-control than humans . . .

XV

Verus Addresses the Grand Assembly

Jancie and I have established a modus vivendi so that we don't get on each other's nerves while we're both around the house. Jancie has the house to herself in the morning, and I have it in the afternoon. The only good jobs are in the EU. I'm trying to persuade Jancie that we should consider moving there.

Verus loves his job teaching the classics at the University of Pickle Crust. Both colleagues and students are amazed at his abilities. He has also gotten lots of press and is in demand as a speaker. Though he has declined invitations to appear on several talk shows, he is already known around the world as the only man who returned from the grave. Inevitably, cults proclaiming Verus a second messiah have arisen in the U.S. and here. Verus has already had some strange encounters with local kooks. I suppose it's the price of notoriety.

Verus and Gregory O'Riley are in constant communication. Jancie and I are somewhat in awe of the relationship; Brother Gregory is, after all, the genius behind the homo mirabilis upgrade, and it is said that he is influential not only in scientific and Church circles, but also in the EU government, mainly because he chairs the EU Commission. "Commission" is a bland term for the group entrusted with overseeing the upgrade. Verus has allowed himself to be involved in Brother

Gregory's controversial plan to resurrect classical Latin. This is what my comcell picks up:

> The amnesiac Verus, who was found sleeping out with the street people at Union Station, has at last found some of his relations. And now a University of Pickle Crust team has reluctantly concluded that he is apparently who he says he is, if the tests and the data are to be believed. And who would that be? Well, Verus has been claiming to be a resurrected Roman emperor, namely Marcus Aurelius, who reigned between 161 and 180 CE.
>
> A rigorous series of tests in which DNA samples were compared, appears to support this. The Faculty of Science admits that the data appear to prove that the closest relations of Mr. Verus are to be found in Rome—about nineteen hundred years ago! And they are, or were, members of the ruling family. This is the astounding finding. But U of P will not speculate on what it all means.
>
> Scientists around the world are saying that U of P has egg on its face. Here at home, the academic community is outraged. But several professors from the Faculty of Classical Studies who have spoken at length with Verus, and who are amazed in superlative degree by his superior command of Latin and his detailed knowledge of ancient Rome, are more than ready to believe.
>
> Verus is not claiming reincarnation. He is actually claiming to be the resurrected emperor himself, in the flesh, risen from the dead—yes, like Jesus Christ. He says he has no idea how it happened or why, only that it did.
>
> What makes the case noteworthy is that several genome experts, and other scientists, have subjected Verus to the most rigorous testing. To the surprise of all, the tests seem to sup-

port Verus's claim, rather than undermine it. Without a doubt, this is the most bizarre thing to ever happen to the scientific community. The tests are incontrovertible. Yet, they appear to confirm something that is entirely outside the realm of science and rational thought—the resurrection of a man who died and was cremated nineteen hundred years ago.

Meanwhile, the movement to teach Latin by a modification of the four-skills approach, has resulted in the adoption almost world-wide of a syllabus called "Latin for Communication". The planning and spread of this syllabus is the work of both Vatican Latinist Gregory O'Riley and none other than our Mr. Verus, now U of P lecturer in the classics. The two men have been promoting Latin and Roman culture on the Net. To some, it looks like a crusade. Gregory, a Minim friar, is a close confidant of the Pontiff. Observers are uncertain whether the Pontiff supports these efforts, but he is on record as saying that the learning of Latin should be one of the highest priorities in every civilized country.

Bizarre also are, in many countries, the efforts of thousands of teachers and schools to convince the public that a dead language is a living language. The psychological factors fuelling this movement arise from a perceived need by endangered Latin teachers, who are struggling to survive in a modern-language world. It would appear that the efforts of the Vatican Latinist and our Verus are to be seen in this light. Add to this the romantic desire of Europeans and Latinos and others to recreate the West's most heroic past.

Indeed, the monk Gregory appears not to be satisfied with resurrecting just Latin. He has said on several occasions that he would like to see a revitalized and Romanized Rome, and that he hopes that Rome, as the capital of the EU, will rise to its historic responsibilities, and be a true inspiration not only for the whole of Europe, but for the world—whatever he might mean by that.

Some people say that Gregory O'Riley has a much wider political agenda and that he is not shy in promoting it, both as papal envoy and among his students at Augustan University. Gregory also has many friends among the helots, who see him as a champion of helot rights. This to such an extent that the Italian police are becoming very nervous.

Brother Gregory has also been accused of wanting to replace reality with hyper-reality. This obsession with the 'real thing' has led to the creation of hyper-real Latin—a prominent feature of the new syllabus in the European Union. It essentially claims to teach students to speak, hear, write, and read Latin like the ancient Romans. The goal is to resurrect Latin as a living language within a generation.

"We shall do it," says Brother Gregory. "People have the will. They know that our heritage is at stake. It's about who we are. It's part of us. It's our destiny. The world needs Rome."

Some say that what we need instead is an honest and reasonable way of teaching Latin, along lines that help preserve its uniqueness and traditional integrity, and that no compromise should be tolerated. The problem with this idea is that several generations would be needed for it to have any real effect. But Rome will not wait.

Jancie and I have been trying to help Verus claim the rights to *Meditations*. I have been in communication with Access Copyright, the Canadian copyright agency, to ask how Verus can claim copyright. They are very informative. But they apparently do not take my request seriously. I have suggested to Verus that he write something new, possibly about his experiences as a resurrected man, as I am rather certain the topic would be popular. I tell him he could sell the book at the Pickle Crust Farmers' Market, and I am certain that the local bookstores would love to have it.

Jancie and I take Verus to see the Pickle Crust Farmers' Market. The entertainment for the day is a Christian pop band, apparently the only group that would work for nothing. "No helots here," I tell Verus. "The helots are too smart for this." There are a couple of guitars, a drummer, and a girl who makes noises while moving her hips.

The girl's strained movements do not seem to fit the message. "I'm knockin', I'm knockin', I'm knockin' on Jesus' door!" she cries, in a plaintive tone. Visitors to the market stand around and listen. A few applaud. Most just want to hear some noise and they don't care what it is.

"What are they doing?" Verus asks.

"Singing about Jesus," I say.

"Singing?" Verus looks perplexed.

"We define the word 'sing' more broadly than you Romans used to," I inform Verus. "You must have had some barbarian entertainers in your Colosseum that sounded a bit like this? There's an African inspiration here. Takes us right back to the beginning."

"Do you think they would be good enough for the Colosseum?" Verus retorts, a twinkle in his eye.

"Sure," I say. "Put them in with the lions."

Jancie doesn't say anything. She doesn't have much sympathy for born-again types. During an intermission, one of the Christian singers, a scruffy looking youth, approaches us with a flyer. "Save it," I say. "We're not into superstition."

"My name is Luke," says the young man. "Isn't she sexy?"

I tell Luke religion can never be sexy. Religion is either supremely important, or it is false and meaningless and evil, depending on your point of view, and what shape your mind is in. "'Sexy' always has to do with animal, not rational, values," I tell him. "But neither the supremely important nor the false and meaningless can be sexy."

"Jesus died for you," says Luke simply.

"Bunny rabbits and tooth fairies and apple pie with ice cream," I say.

Luke looks a bit stymied. "Jesus loves you, brother," he says.

"All-day suckers and cotton candy." To Verus I say, "I'm speaking *his* language."

"Jesus bids us shine, brother."

"Jesus stopped bidding a long time ago," I say. "The day they nailed him to a cross."

"If you have a true light, you will stop calling on Jesus," says Verus. "Let Jesus rest in peace."

"Jesus is Lord. Jesus lives. I feel sorry for you guys. I'll pray for you."

"Only reason is divine," says Verus.

"Hey, brother, are you the resurrected man?" Luke laughs nervously. "So you're Caesar, eh? Jesus is king, brother. Jesus loves you. Only by faith shall ye be saved. Pride goeth before the fall. Jesus died for your sins."

"Jesus is not a true light," says Verus. "Jesus is only a reflection of the collective imagination. A neon light in an empty hallway. The real Jesus was a man, a luminous man, a man with some unusual insights. And the crowd rewarded him by making him into something he was not. And this 'not' is your Jesus. Just a delusion. Only reason is like the light from the sun, the bright illuminating rays of Apollo."

"It's in the Bible, brother. The Bible tells us. Seek and ye shall find. Take Jesus into your heart and he will show you the way. Open your heart to the Lord. Open your eyes and see, brother. Praise God!"

I tell Verus to come away. The man is obviously deranged.

"My friend," says Verus, "the destruction of the understanding is a pestilence. And it is a far greater pestilence than any corruption of the flesh. For the latter corruption is a pestilence of animals, so far as they are animals, but the former is a pestilence of men and women, so far as they are men and women."

I tell Verus he is wasting his time. Luke has his mind addled and he's determined to die that way. As we are talking a crowd gathers. "It's Verus!" they cry. "It's the resurrected man!" There are even some in the crowd who belong to a new sect that recognizes Verus as one of God's sons. As soon as they understand who he is, they cast themselves at his feet and begin to cry and moan. One of them, a young woman with rough features, identifies herself as Bertha Dinglehopper. Bertha tells us she is writing a gospel for Verus.

"Get lost, you creeps!" I shout. I try to push them away with my foot. "Leave us alone!"

"Verus!" Bertha cries out. "Verus, Lord, don't you remember me? Verus!" Bertha falls at the feet of Verus and frantically kisses his sandals. There isn't much we can do other than give the woman a few small kicks in the face and some verbal discouragement. I must say I admire Verus. He's very phlegmatic about the whole thing. I sure as hell wouldn't let some deranged bitch slobber all over *my* sandals. I'd crown her royally!

"Speak to us, son of God!" an old woman cries out.

"I will speak," says Verus. "Dear brothers and sisters, I am not the son of any god."

"You are! Yes, you are!" cries Bertha. "Oh, save us, Lord! Help us to stand erect! Tell us what to do and we will do it!" Bertha swoons and is attended by her fellow cultists.

"My friends, I will speak," says Verus. "My thoughts have not changed since I first walked this earth, except in one respect. I used to believe that I had a personal relationship with Zeus, head of the immortals. But I have had to cut the tie with Zeus. I no longer believe. I have cut the umbilical cord. And I recommend to any of you who hold some belief to cut the umbilicus. Set yourselves free. Learn to stand erect."

"We can't!" a woman cries. "We don't know how. It's too hard."

"You have not tried," Verus replies. "You must have the habit of seeking truth. The truth is plain, simple, unadorned. But to know this, your mind must be in order. My first life was in a world far different form the one we see today. And yet, it was exactly the same life, and the choices were exactly the same. I ask you to be done with superstition, in the name of humanity."

"Don't you believe in the Bible?" a man in the crowd cries.

Verus looks at the man. "No. And neither do you. I know that you say you do, only because you've never read it. The God of the Old Testament is an arch criminal. Read the Bible and see for yourself. And read about the progress of humankind in making sense of the world. It is your duty to find out what we know. You do not need to know the details but you do need to know. Otherwise, what are your opinions worth? They are worth nothing."

"That's *your* opinion!" someone cries.

"Yes. Yes, it is. My opinion is informed by the accumulated knowledge of humankind, by reason, and by understanding. And when you can say the same, your opinion will be as good as mine."

"Who does he think he is?" someone cries. "Bloody snob!"

"That's too hard for us," somebody else says. "There's too much to know. What was good enough for Mum and Dad is good enough for me. Give me that old time religion. It's good enough for me. Why stir things up? What's your problem?"

"What are you talking about?" a lady cries. "This man has risen from the dead. It must be true what they are saying about him. God sent him, if I know anything. God has two sons—Jesus and Verus!"

Verus gestures for silence. "Listen to me, my friends. Opinions without knowledge are worth nothing. Yes, you have rights—to think, to speak, to vote. But if you don't know anything, what is all that worth? If you don't know anything, you're going to think and speak and vote evil. Yes, evil."

"He's talking about sin," somebody says.

"I am not the son of God. I am who I say I am. But how I came to your time is to me a great mystery. I am certain there is a reason. But I have no knowledge of what that reason may be. And I'm not desperate to fill the void. I ask you to stand erect. Cease being pulled by strings. Cease cringing before the idols of the imagination. Get busy and learn what we know about the world. Then you will not be deceived."

"You don't want us to worship you?" a lady cries. "In the States they've formed a church to worship you."

"Yes," cries Verus. "So they can come together for the purpose of cultivating their shared delusion. Do you know what a delusion is?"

"You came back, Verus!" somebody shouts. "That's no delusion!"

"God sent him!" cries an elderly lady. "Look at that face! It's the face of God!"

Verus wags a finger at this stubborn stupidity. "Listen to me carefully," he says. "I truly was raised from the dead. But no one knows how that happened. And as for 'why it happened', I refuse even to consider that. And as humankind sets out to discover the universe, it is 'how' that should concern us, not 'why'. The 'hows' are within our grasp. The 'whys' are not."

"What the hell's he talking about?" somebody cries. "He don't sound like a messiah to me. He sure don't."

"Would you like to see a miracle?" says Verus, discouraged. "What would you like? Presto, a bag of kettle corn for everyone. A Mercedes Benz? A ticket to Kingdom Come, no questions asked? Would you like to see me ascend to heaven surrounded by an aura of gold? Escorted by armies of silver angels, strumming harps and sounding golden trumpets? Would you like that?"

"Yes!" a woman cries. "Oh, please, can we have all that? That would be wonderful. That's beautiful. That's the way it should be. That's the way I want to go, too. I want to be carried upstairs on a golden cloud."

There are hoots and guffaws from the crowd.

"Jesus loves you!" Luke cries above the crowd. "Jesus died for you! Jesus is the way!"

Verus waits till the crowd is quiet. "My friends, the 'whys' of our existence are not to be found in the heavens. Purpose is not divine. Purpose is ours. Purpose is *our* jurisdiction. It belongs to humankind. God is not at the beginning. God is at the end."

"What the hell's he talking about?" someone cries.

Luke's voice is heard above the crowd: "Jesus loves you!"

"Jesus is dead," says Verus. "Jesus was a man. Men die. Jesus died. Jesus is dead. Jesus was a Jew. He was concerned with Jews. His message was only for Jews. He had nothing to say to *goyim*."

Luke shouts at the top of his lungs: "It's a lie! Jesus is Christ! Jesus lives! Christ is Jesus!"

"My friends," says Verus, "when you call upon the never-seen, never-heard, beyond-nature movers-of-mountains, you waste thoughts and words by throwing them into the Great Void. And the Void is the abyss of time and space surrounded by the Great Nothing. Your hopes and dreams and imprecations, if they do not die before they reach the tree tops, are sucked into the void between the stars. And they perish there."

Luke sings at the top of his lungs: "Jesus loves me, this I know, for the Bible tells me so!"

"My friends, you ask for things that are not given. And yet, well I know, some of you have a personal relationship with the Void. You call it God or Mary or Jesus. You speak to it daily at your bedside or in church. But the truth is, if only you will try, you can make a lifetime companion and a protector, and a promiser, and a god, out of a rock or a stone, or a prison wall; and indeed, many have done this. And you will find it works as well as any other."

"Speak plain for God's sake!" a lady cries.

"Shut up!" cries her neighbour. "Verus knows what he's talking about!"

Verus gives a little bow in recognition of this sensible comment. "This bloody earth," says Verus, "is strewn with the remnants of dead deities and the bones of their offerings. For all gods are idols, be they stones or be they made in the image of the apes, like God Almighty. For all gods, any gods, and even just one god (who may be, by the logic of belief, subdivided into three gods) are profanations against the truly sacred, which is the mind's holy sphere, and the temple of reason that dwells there. This that we call by the name of 'reason' is the West's sacred patrimony. If anything were given us by any gods, *this would be it.* Reason! Only reason is sacred. Why do you ask for more? And why do you abuse it?"

"The hell with reason!" somebody cries. "When I die I'm going to heaven! And all my relatives will be there! And I'm going to meet them. And we're gonna have one hell of a party. And nothing you can say is going to change that!"

"Shut up!" somebody cries. "Let him speak!"

"My friends, you are what you think and say and do, and your mind is the guardian. Blessed are the thinkers and doubters, for they have not spurned the true gift of evolution, which is their sacred reason. Nor shall they be led astray into the labyrinth of belief, nor into the devious astrology and alchemy of the nether reaches of the brain. Nor shall they bow down before the idolatrous fantasies of the tree apes, nor be led astray by dreams, drugs, wishes, and holy men. Blessed are the plant eaters, for they shall neither eat pork nor be called by the names of Porky, Porcellus, or Porcetto. Blessed are they who do not ask for what is not yet given, nor for what is not yet earned."

"There you are!" someone cries. "It's the Sermon on the Mount! He sounds just like Jesus!"

"He does not, you fool!" cries someone else.

"My friends, as it the last days of our race, will you still continue to follow on down the winding path charted by shepherds through the dung of camels and lambs and goats and yaks, into the valley of the shadow of fear? Verily, this is a path worn by navel-gazing mystics, the inheritors of grim ritual and sacrifice, and the self-serving scribes of the occult. And by miracle workers and faith healers, charlatans and creationists, and the popes of delusion, and the councils of hair splitters. Will you, in the last days of your race, still bow down before the idol of the three-in-one god, last refuge of the mindless?"

"Go back to where you came from, you bloody foreigner!" somebody cries.

"Shut up, born-again creep!" another shouts.

"My friends, few are they who aspire to something great in the days allotted them. You must learn to stand erect. Do not let yourselves be used. Soon, you will shuck off the shell that encloses you and embark upon a new life. As homo mirabilis, you will fully understand that the welfare of mankind depends directly on this: to think, to doubt, and to question, in absolute freedom."

"You bloody sinner!" somebody cries. "Jesus Christ died for you! And this is how you thank him! Shame on you! You'll burn in hell!"

Someone else shouts, "Close your trap! This man knows what he's talking about."

"Idiot!" somebody cries back. "Nothing is greater than God! There's a place in hell for you!"

"Share your wisdom with us, Caesar!" somebody cries. "Don't listen to the boneheads!"

"I will try if you will let me. Dear brothers and sisters, the wisdom of the ages was at hand then, when I first walked this earth. What I would have told you then, I can tell you now, and you may be certain that even homo mirabilis will recognize the value in these thoughts. Nineteen hundred years ago I would have told you that you should be content with what you are, dear brothers and sisters, and wish not change; nor dread your last day, nor long for it, nor let your mind run on what you lack as much as on what you have already. But now in homo mirabilis, fear, the companion of our mortal existence, will at last be defeated, and man will be free. Really and truly free.

"And, my friends, the first thing we should recognize is this: If chance rules in the All, you and I are not compelled to be governed by it.

"And I say to each one of you, look within yourself. Within is the fountain of good. Within is the wellspring. The source is within. And it will ever bubble up, if you will only dig. And homo mirabilis will understand this, and will do this. Remember that each day provides its own gifts. Be satisfied with success in even the smallest matter, and think that even such a result is no trifle. Remember, he who lives in harmony with himself lives in harmony with the universe.

"When anything tempts you to be bitter against your fellow man or woman, say not that it is a misfortune, but think that to bear it worthily is good fortune. Consider this: How much more grievous are the consequences of anger than the causes of it. Reject your sense of injury and the injury itself disappears. Practice this and you will see. You will see that life is what your thoughts make it. Such as are your habitual thoughts, such also will be the character of your mind.

"How much time you save if you do not look to see what your neighbour says or does or thinks. Everything you and I hear is an opinion, not a fact. Everything we see is a perspective, not the truth. I have often wondered how it is that every person loves himself or herself more than all the rest of humankind, but yet they set less value on their own opinions of themselves than on the opinions that others have of them.

"Accept the things to which fate binds you and love the people with whom fate brings you together, but do so with all your heart. Adapt yourself to the things among which your lot has been cast and love sincerely the fellow creatures with whom destiny has ordained that you shall live.

"The only wealth which you will keep forever is the wealth you have given away.

"Remember this: If it is not right, do not do it; if it is not true, do not say it. Waste no more time arguing about what a good man or a good woman should be. Be one.

"Never be troubled by the past. Live in the present. Never let the future disturb you. You will meet it, if you have to, with the same weapons of reason which today arm you against the present."

"It's a bloody sermon!" someone cries.

"I told you, he's Jesus Christ!"

"He is not!"

"Let him speak! Go on, Caesar, tell us more!"

"My friends, Nothing has such power to broaden the mind as the ability to investigate systematically and truly all that comes under our observation in life. And nowhere can we find a quieter or more untroubled retreat than in our own souls."

"Jesus is the answer!"

"Be quiet!"

"To live happily, my friends, is an inward power of the soul. Every one of us has it. Very little is needed to make a happy life; it is all within yourself; in the thoughts you have. The happiness of your life depends upon the quality of your thoughts. You have power over your mind—not outside events. Realize this, and you will find strength.

"Where men and women can live, they can also live well. Your worth is no greater than your aspirations. You have the choice to compare and estimate yourselves by an idea which is higher than you are, or by one which is lower. The one produces aspiration; the other ambition, which is the way in which the mean aspire.

"Life, my friends, is neither good nor evil, but only a place *for* good and evil. It is not death that we should fear, but we should fear never beginning to live.

"This is all I have to say to you, my friends. No one is going to save you. That is something each one of us has to work at. Redemption is personal. It takes place in the here and now, day by day, hour by hour. So in conclusion, my friends, when you arise in the morning, think of what a precious privilege it is to be alive—to breathe, to think, to enjoy, to love. Remember, your life is what your thoughts make it."

Many in the crowd applaud when Verus is finished. But the Jesus freaks will not quit. Some of them want to worship Verus, while others would like to kill him. So I hurry Verus away from there.

That evening, we learn via our comcells that Bertha Dinglehopper of Pickle Crust, the "apostle" we met at the market, is busy writing a gospel—*The Gospel of Bertha*. Here is an excerpt:

> *And Lord Marcus went to the Mission of St. John the Compassionate in the city of Toronto, where he filled a pot large enough to feed thirty people with one small package of No Name spaghetti. And with a single tin of Chef Boiardi sauce he filled a great kettle, and he poured olive oil into it and he blessed the sauce.*
>
> *And when the pasta was ready and the mission cook was ladling grated Romano and Parmesan cheese onto each portion liberally, Lord Marcus made goat, camel, and yak cheese from a single crumb of Parmesan, so that the people might all the better enjoy the baguettes, which he had caused to be multiplied from a single loaf.*
>
> *And the loaves were cut and put into baskets, which were placed on the tables. And the Mission people and the street people marvelled to see these wonders. And after the benediction, the people put their faces to the pasta, and they put the forks in their mouths, and they broke the bread, and they ate ravenously thereof.*
>
> *But Marcus, noting that the poor people of St. John the Compassionate had only plain city water in their glasses, turned the mission water to wine by two bats of his left eyelash and one of his*

> *right. And when the people saw this, their eyes grew wide, and they praised Marcus, saying, "Truly, this is God's son."*

The local media—*Pickle Crust Today*—have spoken to Bertha at her home in the sticks—a small bungalow on Racoon Row, in the outskirts of Pickle Crust. This is what I learn from my comcell:

> Bertha is a working mum with seven kids. She told us that it is a struggle to get by, even though she holds down two jobs. Besides her weekly "Thank God" column she does for us, she works at a local Quick Fix making Nutri-burgers. She told us she has had her problems in the past, not least of which was not being able to read. "But I went to school nights and they taught me," she said proudly. "And now I know how to read and I know how to write."
>
> Bertha, who looks as worn and as chipper as the old nineteen-hundreds movie character Ma Kettle, laughed heartily as she spoke of her triumphs over adversity, not least of which was a serious drug addiction, and, last summer, a broken jaw at the hands of her ex.
>
> We asked her how it felt to be the author of a testament. She said demurely, "I wrote my testament while the Saviour was living. And he still is living—God be praised! And I see him almost every day and sometimes I speak to him. You know he is divine when you look into his eyes. You just want to throw yourself at his feet. I did throw myself at his feet once but he ran away. He's so modest."
>
> We asked Bertha if she still believed Christ was the son of God. She laughed and said, "Don't be silly, of course I do. There is hardly anything I don't believe. Now there are two sons and two saviours, and I believe in the both of them. It

was nice to have one: it's even nicer to have two. But my focus is on the one who is living, and who lives near me, right here in blessed Pickle Crust. There are other witnesses and there are others writing testaments. And the more records we have the better. I mean, look at all the testaments to the works of Christ, and only four of them were recognized by the Church. I think that's a shame."

"Are you familiar with the other testaments?" we asked.

"I've read them all," Bertha said proudly. "Many of the miracles in the other books most people never hear about. Like the one where Christ's father didn't have enough wood to make a cabinet, and Jesus made one board a bit longer so his father had just enough. Isn't that sweet? And then there is the one where the child Jesus turns all his playmates to chickens, and he makes one of them lay an egg. No, wait a minute—it was goats he turned them to. How in the world did I get chickens?"

"Yes, how did you? There is a big difference between a goat and a chicken."

"True," said Bertha. "My memory is not what it used to be. Anyway, I think that's so cute, turning his playmates into goats! It's precious. Of course, he turned them back again. I have such a thirst to know things now that I can read and write. There is nothing like knowing things, is there?"

We told Bertha that we heard she was keeping a record of everything that happened to Marcus.

"Yes," she said, "that's right. He's so shy. At one time he said, 'It's quite possible to be a divine man and never be recognized as such.' Well, I intend to see that he *is* recognized as such. Everything I write you can find in the media, so you know it's true. There are no doubters anywhere, because whatever's on the news and on the Net has to be true, doesn't it? I mean, if everybody's reporting the same thing, you know you can pretty well trust it, don't you?"

We asked Bertha about some of her favourite miracles attributed to Marcus. She told us about the miracle of the cockroaches, which Marcus is said to have performed at St. John the Compassionate Mission in the presence of his disciples. According to Bertha, Marcus had found a cockroach in the Mission kitchen. Everyone expected Marcus to step on it, and they were surprised when, instead, he picked it up and blessed it; and he asked for a large box, and he put the cockroach into the box. And immediately, this single cockroach became a hundred cockroaches. And Marcus said to his disciples, "Take these good cockroaches and deliver them on silver trays to the houses of the most wealthy. And if you do this, tears will run from the eyes of all sacred images in Toronto. And this shall be a sign of the displeasure of Almighty God with those who are too comfortable."

And indeed, it would seem that, on that day, all over Toronto statues of the Virgin were, in fact, weeping tears of wine. This reporter witnessed it first hand. I saw the Latin community weeping along with the statues. The Latins say it shows the Lord is with them. They say it's an answer to the Roman attacks against the church, led by Brother Gregory and his Semper Fidelis movement.

On that day, crowds wandered through the streets crying openly. The city was overrun with these choruses of woe. Others were on bended knee around the places of worship, or doubled up in a fetal position in transports of ecstasy. The Latins swear they will never abandon the gods of Christianity, including Marcus, but they don't want to be transformed into homo mirabilis unless they can take their religion with them.

Some say they have tasted the tears of Mary. A wine connoisseur who tasted the tears told us they taste like last year's Beaujolais.

However that may be, and despite the fervour of people like Bertha Dinglehopper, the outlook for organized religion does not look bright. The United Nations today declared religion anathema. The progressive nations of the world have committed themselves to root out this age-old evil. To this end they have taken a pledge—The Pledge of the Stalwart Sons and Daughters of the Earth:

We pledge ourselves to be the guardians of our own minds. We pledge ourselves to be the guardians of the minds of our children. We shall respect the inviolable minds of the young. We shall not indoctrinate our children. We recognize that to instil belief systems in nascent minds is an abuse. We recognize that people do this for their own good, and not for the good of their children.

We pledge ourselves to turn away all tyrants of the mind, be they the beseechings of dictators, pushers of drugs or religion, or the seedy adherents and sycophants of the culture of exploitation. We shall protect ourselves against the barbarians of the dark forests of injustice and unreason. We shall turn a deaf ear to the prophets of Kingdom Come. We shall no longer try to enlighten the sheep in their pastures, but we shall break down walls and fences, and we shall scatter the flocks and the herds.

We pledge ourselves to hunt down the sprinklers of holy waters and unctuous oils, and the swingers of pots of incense, and the passers of collection plates, and we shall shower them with ridicule and smear them with cow dung.

We pledge ourselves to destroy the reign of the tree apes, so all men and women may think straight and walk erect, and no longer creep around bowed. We declare an end to the errant lives of the animal-becoming-man. We commit ourselves to ignore all those who neither think, walk, nor speak straight.

We pledge ourselves to go regularly to the temple of our choice so that we may break the silence with laughter, and interrupt the sermon with coughs, throat clearings, guffaws, and giggles, for every occasion should receive its due respect.

We pledge ourselves to reward the numerous authors of pious and homespun homilies in the local papers with gold and silver medals for imagination and humour.

XVI

Jupiter Strikes

Innocent XIV is sitting at his desk as Gregory enters the papal chambers. The Pontiff pushes his work aside and forces a nervous grin. "Ah, Gregory! I was just thinking about you."

Gregory looks accusingly into the other man's eyes. "I never thought you'd stoop to this, Holiness. I thought you were too intelligent."

"Ha-ha, I have the right, Gregory. This is my state. My kingdom. I am supreme ruler." In a mollifying tone, he says, "She's perfectly safe. She has all the comforts of home. We don't use the torture chambers any more, you know. Ha-ha!"

Gregory gives a wry smirk. "Come on, Holiness, we both know you're just the front man for a criminal organization."

"Ha-ha, I suppose you think we're in league with the Mafia? You do have a superb imagination, Gregory. A wonderful imagination. Yes, indeed. Ha-ha!"

"All right. What do you want?"

"Ha-ha, how droll! Do you think the Holy See would resort to such tactics as blackmail? What a superb misconception! Ha-ha! Yes, indeed." Innocent hems and says, "We have some questions. She has the answers. Just questions and answers. This is my state. I am in charge."

With one sweep of his arm Gregory sends the papers flying from the Pope's desk and over the floor. The Pontiff recoils and jumps to his feet. He looks grim. He flexes his muscles, like a cat thrown into the same space as a bulldog. "Remember, Gregory, I'm a wrestler. Don't test me. I can break your neck."

They stand facing one another, inches apart.

The Pontiff raises his hands in a mollifying gesture. His tone is oily. "Gregory, Gregory, we must not upset ourselves over such a small matter. Indeed we mustn't. Bibi Lakatos is deprived of her freedom for a few hours. Is that such a great crime?" The Pontiff hems and says, "Well, we do want something, as a matter of fact. Yes indeed. Something we must have. We need to be certain our rights will be respected once we commit to homo mirabilis. We do have rights!"

"Scumball!" Gregory cries. "Blackmail and coercion are the tools of your trade. Yes, don't look so innocent, Mr. Innocent. You know damn well what I'm talking about. Your favourite weapon is guilt. Every day you're busy making your victims feel smothered in sin, condemned, cast out. So they come creeping to you to be made clean again. It's like taking a bath in pig shit!"

"Ha-ha, what judicious language, Gregory! What perspicuity! What an inventive mind you have, Ha-ha!"

Gregory takes the Pontiff by the collar. The Pontiff's face cracks. His head starts to nod as though in the throes of dementia. "Stop it!" he cries. "It's not my fault. They want me to step down. They've declared me anathema. The Curia. That pack of leftovers from the Dark Ages! They're all under Pepin's thumb. She's at Castel Gandolfo."

"Castel Gandolfo! Get her out of there. Now!"

"I can't."

"You bloody well can! You do it or else!"

The Pontiff's head begins to nod again. "I'm finished!" he cries.

"No. Religion is finished, oh ringmaster of the circus of clowns. It's all over. A new age is dawning. You have an opportunity to do some good in the world. I'm asking you to rise to the occasion. The first good thing you can do is get Bibi out of Castel Gandolfo. Right now!"

"I can't. They won't listen to me! I'm powerless."

"Don't give me that shit, Holiness. Get her out of there! And when you've done that, get rid of those creeps in the Curia. Use your influence. Tell them to hand in their high hats. Tell them to quit their flocks. Tell them to cease being shepherds. Are you just a cock that crows or do you know how to keep order? Throw them all out! Rule without them! And then tear this shithouse apart!"

The Pontiff's head shakes uncontrollably. Gregory throws his arms wide and brings the palms of his hands together on either side of the other man's face. Smack! The Pontiff reels. He falls into a chair. He is quiet a moment, then says, "Why don't you go and get her. The Swiss Guard is at your disposal... I'll go with you. We have to wait till noon to catch either Pepin or Tomasi. They have the keys."

Gregory gives a sigh of relief. "What do we need? Weapons? Tanks?"

"Yes... No. No, you won't need them. Dear Christ, the world is falling down around me. Everything is falling apart. Everything. Everything is, ha-ha."

"Not everything, Holiness. I'll wait till noon. Then we're going to Castel Gandolfo with Cardinal Tomasi."

"All right, Gregory. I shall do what I can. It won't be much but I shall do it. Indeed I shall."

"There's going to be a march on Rome," Gregory says. We're going to follow Giuseppe Garibaldi's route. Remember Garibaldi, sir? His march put an end to papal rule in Italy. It was the march that made Italy possible. And it took the land away from the Church. And you priests lost the land. Until Mussolini came strutting along. He found it convenient to give some of it back to you. Just enough to stand on.

But do you know what's happening now? We're going to erase this blight from the face of the earth. The Church is finished."

The Pontiff lies slumped in his chair, his face slack. "The Commission," he mutters feebly, "promised me—!"

"The Commission will govern the EU. We're going to invite Marcus Aurelius to assume power. The Imperium will be restored. Once that is done, the Commission members, including myself, will upgrade to homo mirabilis. We'll conquer the world again with the sheer brilliance of our civilization. The whole world this time. And this time forever. Reason and justice. Peace and order. Not just slogans. A government of service and duty. The Roman Empire will take up where it left off. There will be no more churches. No more religion."

"The Roman Empire!" cries the Pontiff, stunned, his eyes rolling as he tries to grasp what has been said. "What madness!"

Gregory puts his hand on the Pontiff's shoulder and speaks softly to him. "Yes, George. You must become a Roman. You have the ability. You must come to your senses. You must put reason on her throne. You must understand that religion is finished."

"Humbug!" cries the Pontiff. "Rome is dead! And so is Marcus Aurelius. You want some tramp from Toronto to rule Europe? You're out of your mind!"

"The truth does not die, sir. Reason and justice do not die. People die. Their minds atrophy and they surrender their right to the truth and they die. They surrender their souls for some cheap, worthless consolations. But the truth neither changes nor dies. Cults and religions come and go. The truth remains. The truth stands apart from everything—sacred, inviolable, enduring. And no man or woman possesses it. Because we are too small."

"The truth!" says the Pope, listlessly. "Am I concerned with the truth? Yes. Yes, I am. But our truths are not the same, yours and mine, Gregory, ha-ha. That's where the trouble lies, Gregory. They're not the same. I wish they were. But they're not. I wish we could see eye to eye. But we can't. We just can't."

"Sir, you need to trust the ruling faculty. It's what we have to make sense of the world we live in. Marcus Aurelius learned to trust it. He was tempted as ruler of the world. Day and night Marcus was tempted: Quit the goddarn war; let someone else do it. Get rid of your opponents. Punish your enemies. Reward your friends. Enrich yourself. Build palaces. Let's have a party and screw the world. Temptations come down upon an emperor like rain. But he didn't do any of that. None of it."

"Sounds too good to be true."

"He *is* true, George. Marcus Aurelius is a man for all time. And now we shall have him for all time."

"Humbug!"

"He didn't just crawl into a hole when he died, with a few olives, and wait for his lady friends to show up. He didn't rise after three days and slink around for a bit just to show he wasn't beaten. And he didn't float to heaven in a radiant mist. But he did come back to us. There's no hocus-pocus about him. He's plain, simple, honest, true. He's transparent."

"Dear God have mercy!"

"So I'm blasphemous. Get over it. It's only a perspective. It's your perspective. It's a perspective from the world of belief, the world of I-wish, I-need, I-want."

The Pontiff sighs deeply.

"George, how does anyone in this world think and speak freely without offending tree apes? Are we supposed to keep silent to protect the feelings of the ignorant?"

"I don't know," the Pontiff says, weakly. "I don't know."

"That might be okay, George, if their ignorance affected only them. But it doesn't. It's the ignoramuses that have screwed the world. You'll find them in any crowd. At the Colosseum, in St. Peter's Square, in Salt Lake City, in the ranks of the Gestapo, on the boards and in the bureaucracies—the applauders and the silent ones everywhere, who bend and bow and whistle and clap and love to lick boots. It's the Grand Assembly of Believers. It's the enemy."

"The enemy!" The Pope's face is drawn and creased with worry. He looks like a lost soul. "You're out of your mind. You must be. One of us is. One of us is *pazzo. Assalutamente pazzo*! Insane. It can't be me. It can't! I'm the Holy Father!"

"Holy schmoly! There's nothing holy about you."

"Dear God!"

"Yes, dear God, indeed. If there were a god, that god would not require us to be stupid. He would expect us to use our reason. He would not ask us to know him. If he wanted to be known, he wouldn't be playing hide and seek with us. Let your mind rule, sir. Not that stupid brain of yours."

"Stupid brain, ha-ha! Perhaps it is stupid. Yes, maybe it is. Perhaps I have taken myself too seriously... No! I never heard anything so absurd! The resurrection of a Roman emperor! Why should a Roman emperor be resurrected? Only a fool would believe such a thing."

"Why should a Jewish rabbi be resurrected?"

"Humbug! Rubbish! You've been taken in, Gregory. I thought you were smarter than that. Sit down and have a glass of port and we'll discuss our differences. Ha-ha! Too bad I didn't find this Verus character first. I could have put him on the podium along with Christ. What a boon it would be to have a verifiable in-the-flesh resurrection. Yes, indeed. It would be so easy to believe. So easy. Faith would no longer need to be the last bastion against rationalist and materialist philosophy. You don't need faith when you're looking at the godhead. But now I fear the worst. The Christian faith has been pushed to the wall. I do not think it can hold out forever against the assault of reason. For a thousand years, almost, we've been trying. I think we have reached the end of our tether. The flock has been scattered. The sheep are lost. Gone astray. And then, all these attacks. The hostility of people. Like you ..."

The Pope gets up and goes to the window and looks out on Piazza San Pietro. "God has nothing to say to me," he mutters. "You up there, say something! Now is surely the time. I need your help! If I don't get it, we're finished. Come out in the open. Show yourself. The Vicar of Rome is calling! It's Peter. Say something! Answer me! For Christ's sake say something, damn you!"

"Keep going, George! You're on the right track!"

"God has nothing to say to me. You up there, last chance! That's the conclusion I've come to, Gregory—he has nothing to say to me. After all my prayers, beseechings, fastings, privations, concern for the flock, humanity. I've worked and worried myself to death. Not a whisper from Him. Doesn't He know I'm the pope? Hey, I'm in charge down here! I don't feel He's doing his part." The Pope looks heavenward and cries out: "Speak up! Help me!"

"Maybe you're just not good enough for him, George. You've made some mistakes. Mussolini would have loved you, sir, poor fellow. The *Duce* did not deserve his fate, even if he was a clown and a showman, just like you. He certainly was a lot more popular. Imagine how long he would have lasted if he'd told the people they should lay off being lewd and sexy, to quit fornicating, celebrating gluttony and greed. George, you should've had lady priests in see-through gowns. Think what it would've done for the Church. Stimulate the flock instead of depressing them. The Vestal virgins were untouchable but they were sexy. You should have aroused their passion instead of doing the old biscuit and wine routine. Whisky and barbecued potato chips would have been better. Life can be so grim without a little tit ... titillation. Instead of adding to the misery of the world, you should have been alleviating it. Instead, you had to dress up in those silly dark-age gowns, and trudge around all stooped and bent under your impossible burden. You're the incarnation of suffering. Maybe God expected something better."

"Perhaps he did." The Pontiff looks forlornly down into the piazza. "No doubt he did."

"George, there was a time when there was no contradiction between knowledge and religion. What a great thing if we had that. We would not need to quarrel, you and I."

"No, I don't suppose we would," George says. "Yes. One path to enlightenment. What a bright road that would be. A road lined with flowers."

"The Greeks and the Romans had it, George. A unified worldview. a wondrous *Weltanschauung*."

"Yes. I do admire the achievements of the ancients. There is no question. What a bright road."

"It is remarkable, isn't it, George? The rewards were not immediate. But they had the satisfaction of knowing they were being honest with themselves and the world. Myth was not good enough for them. They had to know. They had to understand. Thought, not wishful thinking. Only free minds can do this."

Pope Innocent does not appear to be listening. He is contemplating the milling crowds in the piazza. "If only I could be touched," he says. "Be touched by the Holy Spirit. Receive some sign. A visitation, a dream, some little sign. Something that says all my prayers, sufferings on behalf of mankind, self-denials—that they've all been noticed. Just some little encouragement. Anything at all."

"That would make your job too easy, George. You wouldn't need faith any more. And you need faith when you're talking to somebody who isn't there. That's when you need faith big time. And faith works such wonders. It's worth more than all the evidence in the world."

The Pope sighs. "Faith is our fortress. *Ein fester Berg*!"

"One can attack arguments, George. Faith one can only ridicule. And what is faith but trust. When we trust in people or things we don't know, or in what has not been demonstrated as true, or the existence of which is in doubt, our trust is blind. It's futile."

The Pontiff shakes his head sadly. "The faithful know God, Gregory. They commune with Him. Day by day. All the days of their lives and through the valley of the shadow of death."

"Yeah, George. Surrender your brain. Life will be so much easier."

"Scripture . . ."

"It's crap. Scripture is crap. The scratchings of delusional Bronze Age camel herders. What the hell does it have to do with us?"

"The gospels . . ."

"The gospel writers were busy in the second century scratching down what was known, embellishing—adding a parable here and a miracle there, suppressing this event, building on that one, making the story palatable to their Roman friends and the authorities—didn't want to offend anyone. That's why they let procurator Pontius Pilatus wash his hands and leave the dirty work to the Jews. It's a lie, of course. But the Jews down through history paid dearly for that little distortion. It's time to abandon the lies, George."

"Dear Jesus! Dear God, what sacrilege! We are all surely doomed!"

"Dear Mary and Joseph! Dear Holy Ghost! Dear Santa Claus. Yoo-hoo, calling on all divinities! Where are you?"

"What have I done to deserve this? What have I done? I've lived a saintly life. And I have to listen to a wretch like you. A miserable soulless wretch."

The Pope stands at the window and gazes at the cottony clouds rolling by in the deep blue sky of summer. His head rolls under the strain. "If only there were some sign. Some little thing to say: 'Courage! Carry on! I am well pleased with thee!' It wouldn't be the first time, would it? A voice in the clouds. A cross in the sky. If Constantine, why not me? Even your Verus had his miracle, and he's not even Christian. A little dream would do a trumpet blast and the appearance of the archangel Gabriel, crying, 'Courage! Carry on, faithful shepherd!'

Even a tiny little Gabriel no bigger than a fly would do. Or even a voice in the guise of the whistle of the wind or the sough of the trees, or the buzzing of the bees in the garden, or the song of a bird. I strain to hear such things. My senses are open to them constantly. Where is divine intervention? Even just a little inspiration? It's always in some other time and place. Wherever I am not. Why? Why not here and now? Why not me? Am I not worthy of confidence?"

"Oh, I think you're very worthy, George. You can bet that if someone were listening, you'd be getting soughs and sighs and bee-buzzings and bird songs by the barrel full. If it were up to me, I'd be sending you messages all the time: 'Great stuff, Big Boy; PS: I love you!' Yes, George, I'd put a halo right over that worried pate of yours. It would stay up all by itself, just like the halos the saints have in great works of art. On the other hand, George, why should you get signs and no one else?"

"I don't know. I don't know. I don't know."

"Why can't everyone have a sign, George? Why not give us all a few signs, so we know that our trust is well placed, our time well spent, our suffering not for nothing? Don't we all deserve a sign or two? Wouldn't that be fair? Wouldn't it be compassionate? If just once we could all hear God's booming voice on high giving us encouragement: *Despair not sons and daughters of the earth, for all blossoms bloom again, and the death you die is naught but the shading in a picture of paradise, and true is the faith of your fathers.* Wouldn't that be great?"

"I don't know."

"Have you ever noticed, George, that ghost stories never take place in broad daylight, never on a crowded street. Never in a sunny meadow."

"Ghost stories? I don't know."

"Yes, George. You won't find ghosts in a place where there is sunshine or crowds of people. Never! Don't you think that's odd? Maybe that's why you don't see them. They won't be there while you're chanting Te Deums. They won't be there while you are haranguing the faithful from your balcony, and not while giving an address at the United Nations, and not while watching a hockey game. Why is that?"

"Tell me why," the Pontiff says, listlessly. "You're going to tell me, anyway. Go ahead. Punish me. Torment me."

"Ghosts are very selective as to where they make their appearances, George. Very selective. When the world is well there are no ghosts; indeed, no spirits of any kind. Could Ebenezer Scrooge have had his visitations while sitting under the bright sun in a London park? While casting a brooding gaze into the froth of his beer in a London pub? Or while wandering the halls of the London stock exchange? No. When we are afraid of nothing, George, this world is always sufficient."

"You're probably right."

"We don't want or ask for help when there is nothing to fear, George. But when the world is not well, when we are afraid or threatened, when we are alone in some dark hole, then we are back in the cat time, before we had fire and tools, cowering in caves, tormented by terrible imaginings, praying to whatever powers we imagined. Just to survive the night and not be dragged off in the maw of some beast. So that, come morning, we might crawl out of our dark hole and feel the rays of the rising sun on our backsides."

The Pope's mouth curls, making him look old and ugly, even grim and cruel, like a Teutonic Knight carrying the cross into Russia. "Where does all this lead!" he cries.

"Maybe you spend too much time in your palace, sir? Maybe God's vicar is so much in the limelight that the spirits can't reach him. Make a pilgrimage on your knees to the catacombs and spend a few nights there among the first Christians—those hounded outcasts, those frightened cultists who had given up on the world. The underdogs destined to undermine right and reason, and turn both mind and world from the true course. Look at their poor little bones as they lie in their niches, the worm holes scratched out from the walls of their tunnels. Touch their bones. Pick them up. Try to imagine the lives they led, these moles and mice, rebels against the Roman soul, these great believers, these soul-surrenderers, these fear-capitulators. See if they recognize you as one of their own, in those fancy duds you wear."

"What is the purpose ... ?"

"Shit, George, why don't you spend a night in the sewer? That's worth a lot of humility. It's a great lesson in reality. Do you know how much offal the human race produces in one day? Billions of tons of it. Do you have what it takes to slosh around down there in the dark with the turds and the rats of Rome? Who knows but in some crack in the wall you might find a desiccated turd from the bowels of great Augustus, or Nerva, Traianus, Hadrianus. Or perhaps a jawbone from mad Caligula."

The Pope is looking down on the crowd below. His vision blurs. He sees the piazza inundated with rats. They are pouring out of the buses and crawling over the monuments.

"In the *cloaca maxima*, George, the water-born refuse of two thousand years of human history flows under this partly ruined, sometimes-sad eternal city, with its bright monuments to Apollo and Diana, Romulus and Remus—the monuments to triumph and glory. I mean the triumph over discord. The triumph over indecision. The triumph over misery. The glory of charting a way for the human race. *The* way. The only way. Yes, the only way that led to the future, because the road was paved with the building blocks of reason. The determination of hearts and minds to conquer the obstacles, find a way out of the morass of ignorance, the stinking pit of strife and stupidity into which the human race was born."

"Look at all those rats down there," the Pontiff says.

"Yes, George, the *cloaca maxima* has to be packed with spirits. It has to be crawling with them. And if there are no spirits there, then where are they? And if there are no ghosts in Auschwitz—where? And if everyone can't see the ghosts at Auschwitz, and if everyone can't hear them any time of day or night without even trying, hear them screaming bloody murder, then where in the name of reason are they? Where are the spirits, George? How can you claim their existence?"

"Rats! The world is full of rats, Gregory." The Pope mutters to himself, his head nodding up and down, from side to side, as he looks down over the buses, and the tourists milling with their cameras and ice cream cones, climbing over the monuments, like rats over turds in the sewer. "The catacombs!" he mumbles. "The sewer!"

"Speak up, sir! Do you have any worthwhile thoughts at all? Let's hear them!"

Pope Innocent emits a strange little laugh. "Those poor souls down there—how can I disappoint them?" he says. "How can I not be what they want me to be? Look at them. How busy they are in their inane pursuits, racing around in buses, their stomachs full of pasta, wine, olive oil. Drugged on *aperativi* and religion alike. Yes, yes, I admit it. They are drugged. Robes and rituals and incense and words and music and tradition—all drugs. They have no minds of their own worth speaking of. And whosoever has no mind may as well be drugged. I admit it. Look at them climbing over the monuments they do not really understand. What do they really know about Rome and what happened here? See them snapping their snapshots to bore to death the folks back home. See, here's my little proof I made the journey. Here I am smelling the ancient musty walls of Santa Maria Maggiore. Here I am tasting the tears and the mildew."

"Good!" cries Gregory, "Don't forget the wasted imprecations. The vain imaginings. The false hopes. The deception."

"What do you suppose they imagine?" the Pontiff says. "Do they imagine the three hundreds, the period when Santa Maria Maggiore was built? Can they picture this brave new world of the spirit as it was arising: *In hoc signo vince!* Constantine—what an opportunist! You think I don't know that? I do. The new orientation for the human race—Alleluia! Raise your eyes and hopes to heaven, because this down here is a lost cause. Isn't that what St. Augustine did? With Rome crumbling, he turns to the city of God. Do they know that—these stupid tourists in their sweaty wrinkled cloaks, bargain-basement sweat-creased pants, smelly underarms, and wine-and-garlic breath?"

"Why, George, I'm shocked. What uncharitable thoughts for the Bishop of Rome! Bravo, I say. Go ahead and hate what they stand for. Nobody's going to strike you dead. Nobody's going to punish you for thinking."

Innocent gives a small laugh. "Did you hear that, God? I'm a stinking apostate. I dreamt I was and now I am. I confess. Strike me dead, if you have the power. Go ahead. Here I am. Yes, down there is the *cloaca maxima* all right. Right down there in the piazza. This grand eternal flow of filth called *Humanitas*! The planet is overrun with these hairless apes. It's worse than a rat infestation."

Gregory gives his shark's grin. "George, I am scandalized at your words!"

"Look at them. Fools! That's what they are. You think I don't it, Gregory? You think I haven't seen it? The fools we are enjoined to tolerate and care for, both by Christ and by your Verus, both by Christians and by stoics. This tribe of hairless apes to which you and I belong, in spite of our gifts. These crowds with their insatiable curiosity, their ignorant seeking, from all over the world, looking for someone or something to save them. Pull my strings! Save me! That's what they cry. *Oh salvami, Creatore!*"

"Now you've got it!" cries Gregory. "That's it exactly!"

"Look at them milling around. The faithful and the enemies of the faith, all of them looking, seeking, yearning, all hoping for grace while engaged in diversion. Thinking of God while licking their ice cream, nursing their perversions. Picturing Christians being fed to the big cats as they push pizza into their maws. Their little synapses and neurons shuttling between lewd thoughts and glimpses of the *Pietà*, while they hope for some spec of insight, as if it might come popping out of the marble and right up their—Ha! ... Something that will say to them: 'The sun will shine tomorrow and tomorrow and tomorrow, and you will be well tomorrow and tomorrow and tomorrow. And it's all right, don't worry ever, not ever, because everything's been taken care of forever, just for you.' What a monumental lie!"

"Alleluia!" Gregory cries, triumphantly.

"See how they are herded here and herded there, Gregory. Look at them listening to the guides. See them tread the well-worn steps, picking their way among the bricks and cobbles, and the columns of time, not understanding anything. Look at them—costumes and colours from the whole world, mingling. This mealy-brained race of Babel ... These little rats in the ruins of a great civilization, the rubble on the ground and the ruins standing, that witness another time and another plan for the human race—see how they scurry about taking snapshots of the concrete and marble and bronze and bricks and mortar ghosts of Rome."

"Yes, George. I do see all of that. I see it very clearly."

"See! Caracalla's baths, Hadrian's Tomb, the arch of this one, the column of that one. Snap, snap—I got it! And the symbol, so aptly named, of what Rome had left to purge in itself, and would have done had time not run out—the Colosseum! The colossus. Snap, snap—got it! The grandfather of all arenas, rinks, and rings. Snap, snap. The grandaddy of all temples for the letting of blood. Snap, snap. This grand towering scab willed by the masses. This monstrous monument to the people. This place to torment criminals and strangers and beasts dragged in from the four corners of the orb of the earth. This place of pomp and power and ritual combat and death, all staged for the common man."

"Yes, George, what crimes have been committed in the name of the people!"

"Picture," says the Pontiff, "the seven hills of Rome. Picture the aqueducts bringing the city one billion litres of cool mountain water every single day, a feat unequalled by any modern city. *Acqua urbis Romae*. What a great work! Time passes. Then, the churches pop up like mushrooms from a corpse."

"That is the sad truth, George."

"And those people in the piazza—what do they get? Facts but no understanding. Discrete bits of information but no synthesis. Their prejudices have been reinforced, their fanciful imaginings concerning the meaning of it all—the meaning of themselves, their own existence, life—all reinforced. Without learning anything."

"Yes, George."

"Look at those stupid nun-tits down there—the silliest collection of failed females you can find anywhere. Snap a moment here, snap a moment there; here a snap, there a snap, everywhere a snap-snap. Ha-ha! Here is the record: 'I did this in the holy city. I was in this place. This is the proof. I, Darlene Dolittle, standing stuffed with pizza between the columns of St. Peter's. This is me in the Eternal City. My picture, my shot, my take. Proof that I count, exist, will last forever.' Alleluia!"

"Now you're talking, George. Now you're making sense. Now your mind's in control."

The Pope turns to face Gregory. He looks calm. "To answer your question, Gregory—No, there is no need to worry about ghosts in that crowd, in the sunlit heart of Rome. Not there. You need to be a great spirit yourself to see ghosts. And you need to be tormented and alone, like Ebenezer Scrooge on Christmas eve. And you won't find them in the sunshine among the pure white columns of Diana, nor while digging up clams on the beach with the white fleecy clouds above and the blue water and the sail boats bouncing on it. No. Ghosts are personal. Only those dying in some hell hole will see them. And then they die and the ghosts die. They're gone. Or you might find them in an old man's bedroom in a lonely house at night. But people in general will never see them, even though they are the best believers. They will never see spirits. And *there* is the paradox!"

"George, my friend, in the last few minutes you've taken a giant step. You've come a long way. I think you are on the true path. I'm happy for you."

The Pontiff turns and faces his Latinist, his face full of angst. "What have I done wrong, Gregory? I must have done something. What could it be? I've tormented myself to death. I've made five pilgrimages on my knees... I've ruined my knees."

"George, you're not going to shy at the last fence, are you? Whatever wrong you've done, you now have time to undo."

Pope Innocent sighs. "These last few days—I feel dirty. It's a terrible thing when the Bishop of Rome has that to confess. That he's dirty. What if the world knew? The Pontiff is dirty."

"That's the Church for you, Holiness. Tow the line or we'll make you feel dirty. You're just getting some of what you've been dishing out to poor folks all these years. Don't fight it. Be guided by your conscience. And keep thinking."

"I can't stand myself, Gregory."

"Yes, Holiness. You're dirty because you daily sin against Nature. The ruling faculty rebels against your ignorance and obstinacy. It's telling you to quit perpetuating one of the grand falsehoods of the ages, which is a scam without equal in history. It's one of the great shames of humanity."

"Ach! I'm tired and I'm dirty. So tired, so dirty."

"Your sheep, George—you've pulled the wool over their eyes. Take it away so they may see the light of day. That's why your conscience troubles you. It's trying to tell you something. You don't have forever to do this. You can't go on abusing yourself and abusing others.

"So tired. I suppose I am ... just another failed schluck. Look at that dark sky, Gregory. They're starting to leave down there. All the rats are running. It's pouring. I love the rain, don't you. Nothing like the Roman rain. Everything is so clean after it."

Innocent XIV goes out onto the balcony and turns his face to the heavens and holds out his hands. And the rain falls on him. Gregory joins him, standing a bit back to escape getting wet.

"There goes your flock, George. When the sun shines again you must come out here and tell them. Tell them the only hope for life everlasting rests with humankind. Tell them the truth will set them free. That's where the glory is—in the truth. Not in the great beyond but in the truth. And the truth is, we don't have the truth. We have only the spirit of truth. Tell them it's a road. A road without end. Tell them it's open to all."

Innocent watches the developing storm. The sky turns ugly, as black and purple clouds move in over Rome. The Pontiff cackles bitterly as he tries to come to terms with the opposing forces within him. He stands looking down from the balcony as the last of the sheep scurry for cover, his frame weaving in gusts of wind from the piazza, a stark portrait trembling against the light.

The Pontiff's voice comes like a whine, as he fights with himself while standing in the rain. "You never tire of spreading this poison, do you Gregory? I should have fired you long ago. Now I find myself doubting and I'm in mortal danger. You are such a persuasive pagan, Gregory." The Pope cackles insanely.

"George, my friend, listen to me. Be a man, now while it's still in your power. A man is not a man without reason. If it takes your last feeble, credulous little breath, when the sun shines again and the piazza is full, go down there and tell all those poor people it's a mistake. Tell them you stand for a lie."

"Ha-ha, I stand for a lie. No. No, I won't say that. No. It's not true. It can't be. My whole life, the lives of thousands of devoted ministers of Christ, and the thousands and thousands who came before, saints and martyrs—it can't all be wasted! It can't be false ! It can't be wrong! It can't be!"

"George, you must tell them you don't know any more about reality than they do. Tell them you're the Wizard of Oz. Tell them it's just a big cruel joke that humanity has played on itself. Tell them they can find more truth in their own backyard than in all the saints, all the monuments, all the misery; yea, even in the vaunted hollow wisdom of an Augustine or a Thomas Aquinas, even in the wasted courage of a Joan of Arc or a Jean de Brébeuf."

"No, I can't say that," the Pontiff mutters. "How can I say that? The Wizard of Oz, ha-ha."

"Yes, you can say it. You will say it. Tell them to go home and look for it. Tell them: the best tools you have are experience and your own mind. Learn to use that mind. Revere it and honour it. Set it to rule over the brain. And all the while be looking for that wisdom in your own backyard, and in the hearts of those with whom you live. Just as Ebenezer Scrooge did after his epiphany, in the counting house and in the streets of London."

"No more messages from the heart?"

"Listen to me, George. Tell them all they need is reason and justice. And the truth will find them."

"I can't ... I ... I don't know how."

"Yes you do, George. I will help. Cardinal Tomasi will help. And tell them the Church releases Rome, now free again to take up her sacred mission in the world."

"No! Never!"

"Tear it down, George. Let this be your destiny."

"No! Ridiculous! Humbug!"

"Tell them the only faith worth trusting is faith in man—a faith even harder to hold and even more fragile than faith in God Almighty, because we daily see the weaknesses of our friends and neighbours; yes, even their crimes."

"Dear God!"

"Man, not God, Holiness. Man is the measure."

"God save me!"

"Save yourself, Holiness. Faith in man. It is a faith having on its side the awe-inspiring power of reason. Reason harnessed by the human mind. Directing the human brain. Reason. Without it the human race is doomed to fail. So tell them they are released from all bonds, prayers, vows, abjurations, commitments of any kind to this unholy church, and to its pantheon of sufferers. Life itself is challenge enough, George. We should not require the poor in spirit to wallow in vain drear imaginings and children's fairy fantasies, like lost and abused swine on the way to market, persuading themselves that the end of the final journey is the Grand Pigsty in the Sky."

"The grand pigsty! Ha-ha! No, I won't. I can't. I haven't got it in me."

"You have, George. Tell them to finish with four-footed habits, and tell them to stand up on their hind legs and look up at the stars. Let them stand erect so that they may see more than the tops of their shoes and the ground under their feet, and the ass ends of the bovines around them. And let them lift their eyes to the worlds beyond the horizon. Tell them the mind is free only when the spirit is free."

Pope Innocent turns a grim visage to his Latin interpreter. He trembles and his head begins to nod, from side to side and up and down. He glances up at the black cloud descending upon Piazza San Pietro, and the bolts of fire smashing into the eternal city. And it seems that if a thousand avenging angels were to burst from the darkness he would not be surprised and he would not resist.

The Pontiff's tongue begins to move. He stammers. His fist rises and his hand rattles at the end of his arm. Then he feels the hair over his ears rise from his scalp, and it seems to the Bishop of Rome as if something wonderful is about to happen.

As it occurs to the Pope to let go of the metal railing, a great light blinds him. And almost in the same instant the thunder of *Jupiter Tonans* overwhelms him. His skeleton cracks as the celestial energy strikes the balcony. The force spins him round, his body illuminated. There is a wild look on his face, both of wonder and fear. His skull cap flies into the room. The Pontiff's mouth is open, his eyes are wide. He staggers three steps toward Gregory, his arms outstretched. An insane laugh escapes him. He falls onto the Persian carpet. A small croak comes from his throat. Then he is perfectly still.

Gregory gives the Pontiff a nudge. He calls his name. He slaps his face. "George, wake up! You can't quit now! Goddamn!" Gregory calls for help. Staff and medics come running. There are no vital signs. They give the Pontiff oxygen. They take him away on a stretcher. Gregory is alone in the papal apartments.

He paces back and forth in the papal suite. "Now that's what I call divine retribution," he says. He goes out onto the balcony, ignoring the flood from the skies, and he looks down into the piazza. It's empty. And it seems fitting that it is empty, now that the papal throne is unexpectedly empty.

"Another clown will come to take the place of George Schweinrue, swine herd from Klöpfendorf. Shit! Just when I was beginning to get to this guy! Poor George!"

Gregory activates his wristcom. "Let me speak to Cardinal Tomasi ... Hello, Enrico? Gregory here. How's my old Roman? ... No, not to chat. The seat is vacant ... The throne is empty ... I mean His Holiness is gone ... Gone, I mean gone. I mean he's kicked the bucket. He's croaked. He's dead ... Yes, the swine ... the swine herd ... he's dead ... *Finito* ... Right here on the floor. No, hit by lightning ... Yes, lightning ... No, he was not assassinated ... *Ma certo que è morto. Assalutamente* ... Certainly he's dead ... Right here, on the balcony ... Yes, exactly why I'm calling you, Enrico. We have to work the College ... Yes, let's get together. Time to cash in on those favours we did them ... Absolutely ... The new pope's got to be *our* man ... Right. One more thing—Pepin is holding one of my students ... Castel Gandolfo, yes. What's that? ... Entrance to the main square, yes. Is there a guard posted? ... Villa Barberini ... Torture chamber? You can't be serious! ... Well Christ! How do I get down there? ... A tunnel? What kind of tunnel? ... All right ... Splendid ... See you in half an hour."

XVII

Castel Gandolfo

Gregory brings Cardinal Tomasi's Maserati down onto the road in the Alban Hills and drives at a high rate of speed toward Lake Albano. The Cardinal, a thin man with a gentle face, sits beside him looking distraught. Remus is standing behind the seats with his tongue hanging out.

"I don't want any violence," the Cardinal says.

Gregory glances at Cardinal Tomasi. "Depends on them. You say it's under the restaurant, Enrico?"

"Yes. Ristorante Bucci. The tourists sit there in the sun eating and drinking as they look out over Lake Albano. If only they knew what goes on beneath them."

"I had no idea," Gregory says. "I thought this kind of torture had gone out of fashion in the Church."

Cardinal Tomasi gives a small laugh. "Wherever there are desperate men you will find it," he says.

Gregory steps on the pedal to mount an approaching hill. "I'm surprised," he says, "that a man of your cultivation would join the Church, Enrico. Even more surprised that you remain in it."

The Cardinal gives a small laugh. "That makes two of us. I guess it's just a bad habit."

The Maserati turns into the *Galleria,* a road with flanking trees that form a bower overhead, and the car races up the mountain. At the top, between the flanking trees, there are glimpses of the lake and the hot summer haze hovering over it.

A voice comes from behind. "Dominus, will I get a chance to bite someone?"

Gregory glances over his shoulder at Remus and says, "Not without my say-so, Remus. No snarling, either. If I want to see that, I'll give you the signal. Just pretend you're a dog, okay?"

"Yes, dominus. What kind of dog?"

"A gentle dog. A puppy."

"Dominus, if you change your mind, I would dearly love to tear someone apart."

"An enemy of Rome, Remus?"

"Yes, dominus."

"Stay by me and behave. We'll see what happens."

"Yes, dominus."

The palace looms into sight. Gregory pulls the car up at the entrance to the main square and the two men and Remus get out, Tomasi taking a flashlight from the glove compartment. Cardinal Tomasi distracts the Swiss Guard while Gregory passes into the square with Remus. The square is dominated by a fountain.

"Cardinal Pepin will be conducting Mass in the Church of St. Thomas, over there," Cardinal Tomasi says as he catches up to Gregory. He indicates a small church to their left on the main square. "I'd like to be out of here before he's finished."

The two men and the wolf proceed to the palace's inner courtyard, where there is a Roman bust depicting Polyphemus, the one-eyed Cyclops from whose cave Ulysses escaped. Cardinal Tomasi inserts a key into the lock of a small door. He looks round him apprehensively as he does so. "There is a tunnel under the palace," he says. "Years ago I used it to escape from a fire." Tomasi gives the door a shove. It opens with a groan. Tomasi goes first down the narrow staircase, lighting the way. The stairs lead to a passage smelling of mildew and something foul.

"To the right," says Tomasi, indicating with his flashlight. Remus runs ahead, sniffing as he goes.

"Christ what a hole!" Gregory says, stooping to avoid hitting the ceiling. He follows on the Cardinal's heels. "Is there a guard?" he asks, as they hurry down the passage, which seems interminable.

"There may be a guard," the Cardinal replies. "This passage leads to the prison and interrogation chamber."

The end is reached. Gregory pushes the door open a crack and looks in. He sees a lighted room with a barred off section in the far corner. The room appears empty. But as the two men and the wolf enter, they can see Bibi Lakatos behind the bars. She cries out at the sight of Gregory. As Gregory approaches, she reaches out to him. "Greg, thank God!"

Gregory takes Bibi's hands. "You okay?"

"Yes, but hurry! They're coming back. The switch is over there."

Gregory pulls on the switch and the grill slides back. He takes Bibi by the hand. Remus gives her a sniff. They move quickly toward the tunnel entrance. Cardinal Tomasi is holding the door.

"Oh Greg, you shouldn't have come!" cries Bibi. "It's a trap. It's you they want. They say you killed religion, and now they want to kill you."

"Hurry! I hear footsteps," Tomasi cries. Tomasi is last into the tunnel. He closes the door. They scurry along, heads down, with Remus in the lead. They reach the courtyard door. Tomasi opens the door a crack. He can see the Swiss Guard running back and forth in the courtyard.

"No use," says Tomasi. "They've raised the alarm."

"Enrico, I think someone's coming up behind us," Gregory says. "What's up here in the other direction?"

Tomasi says he doesn't know. Gregory gives him a shove. "Hurry! We're going to find out!"

They run with their heads down, Remus leading and Tomasi following the wolf with his flashlight. The light grows dim. Now and then Tomasi slaps the light against his wrist. Finally, it doesn't work any more. They pause in the dark and listen. A foul odour seizes their nostrils. Besides the panting of the wolf, there is only a small sound. Something brushes by their feet. A rat! There is a low growl from Remus. Then, there is silence.

"I can't help thinking of Odysseus and his men trapped in the cave of Polyphemus the Cyclops," says Gregory.

"Don't say that!" cries Bibi, clutching Gregory's arm more tightly. "Listen! I hear something. What's that?"

"Someone speaking," Tomasi says. The cadence is unintelligible. "It's the Mass in St. Thomas," he says. "We must be very close."

Bibi clings to Gregory as he moves forward, groping his way in the dark, his right hand on the tunnel wall. Tomasi and the wolf come up behind. The cadences grow perceptibly louder.

"That would be Cardinal Pepin," Tomasi says. "We must be right under him."

"Polyphemus!" says Gregory.

"I wonder why they didn't follow us," Bibi says, staring into the blackness. "It smells awful, like dead things in here. Maybe we should go back."

"They'd be watching for us," Gregory says.

"But Greg, we can wait till it's dark."

"It's dark already," Gregory quips. "What do you say, Enrico?"

"Let's see if there's a door somewhere," Cardinal Tomasi says. "If not, let's go back. See if you can find a door, Gregory. I'll try the other side. Careful now—just one step at a time." Cardinal Tomasi moves ahead, groping the wall, Remus behind him. As he proceeds to do this, he is surprised to find no wall. He finds himself falling forward and takes one step forward to compensate. He falls into the darkness.

"Ahh!"

Remus starts and winds up between Gregory's legs. Gregory and Bibi hear only the Cardinal's inhalation of surprise, then nothing.

"Enrico?" Gregory listens. "Cardinal Tomasi! Enrico!" Gregory hears only the muffled sounds from St. Thomas. They listen. "Enrico! Enrico!"

"He's gone, Greg."

"Enrico!"

"Greg, don't move! Be careful! There must be a pit!"

"God damn it! Keep close to me. Stay behind. Hello! Here's something?"

"What!"

"Stairs. Let's get the hell out of here."

"Oh Greg, be careful!"

"One step at a time, now. Come on. That's it. Another step. Another one. Another. That's the stuff. Whoops!"

"What!"

"A ceiling. A trap door!" Gregory puts his shoulder to it. Dust and filth fall into his eyes. The door rises with a groan. Gregory pulls himself up. Remus follows. Gregory can hear the sonorous voice of Cardinal Pepin. Bibi comes up behind him. There is no light in the room. "Some kind of closet," says Gregory.

Remus explores the room, sniffing. "There are lots of things, dominus," he reports.

"Things?"

As Gregory moves around, taking Bibi with him, his hands find stacks of chairs, coils of rope, and vestments. He finds a doorknob and turns it. Outside there is light. The balcony of St. Thomas! Gregory sees the vaulted ceiling. He opens the door wide and examines the vestments in the storeroom. "Franciscan!" He hands Bibi a robe. "Put this on. We'll walk out the front door as Franciscan friars."

They don the robes and tiptoe out onto the gallery, into the muted light of St. Thomas. The strong voice of Cardinal Pepin is now very clear:

...The true reality of heaven is God Himself. God is heaven. Heaven is God. Your destiny is to be with God forever. We came from Him and we are called to Him.

"Keep down," Gregory whispers. No noise, now, Remus! We don't want to disturb Cardinal Pepin's little sermon. This way." Gregory leads the way toward the front of the church.

The mysteries of our faith are unfathomable. And so we do not look for reasons or explanations. Reason belongs to God alone, the Creator. Reason is given us only so that we may earn our daily bread and do unto others as we would have them do unto us, and praise Almighty God.

"Hell!" says Gregory, as they peer down on the assembly. "Do you think he really believes that?"

Eternal truths are never revealed to the mind, only to the heart. Let us resolve, then, to be governed by our hearts. For experience has taught us that the Devil resides in the mind.

"Silly bugger!"

Bibi gives Gregory a poke. "Greg, we're wasting time. Let's go before the service is over."

Gregory activates his wristcom. "Mario? I need your help. Two things. Call the police. Tell them Cardinal Tomasi has met with foul play at Castel Gandolfo ... Yes. Tell them to search the tunnel under St. Thomas ... That's right ... Second thing—I want you to pick me up at Castel Gandolfo ... Bibi and me, and Remus ... Yes ... Yes, right away ... We'll be dressed as Franciscans ... Ristorante Bucci ... Okay. Ciao."

Remus creeps up out of the stairwell and says, "Dominus, the stairs lead to a vestibule. But there are people standing by the door."

"Shit!"

We must never question the revealed word of God. We must not desire to see the Truth of our church placed under a microscope and picked apart as though it were a Darwinian fossil. And we must reject the false joy of this imperfect world, which is both brief and worthless. We must devote ourselves heart and soul to the joys that await us in Paradise. Let us look for nothing in this life, except to find the blessed peace of the life in Christ Jesus, in Whom alone is found the fullness of life, the meaning of life, and the end of life, now and forever. Amen.

"Remus, keep an eye on that door."

"Yes, dominus." Remus creeps off.

Throughout the ages our church has been attacked and threatened from many quarters. We survived the numerous predations of the unbelievers. First the Romans. Then the Huns, the Goths, and the Vandals. Then the Vikings. And when the Turks overran the Eastern Empire, we rang the 'Turkish bell', so that we might be spared falling under the yolk of the unbeliever. The revolutions of modern times, in France and in Russia, did their best to exterminate us. They did not succeed. And today the Church is threatened again, this time from all sides. And those who would save our civilization, in a brazen attempt to remake the children of God—even they are hostile. They would deny us a place in the future of the world. Today we ring the Angelus for help against these present troubles. We know in our hearts, we cannot be defeated. We can never be defeated!

"The Angelus bell!" says Bibi. "It will soon be over."

"We could try going out with the rest. It might work. But what to do with Remus?"

Hail Mary, full of grace, the Lord is with thee;
blessed art thou among women
and blessed is the fruit of thy womb, Jesus.
Holy Mary, Mother of God, pray for us sinners,
now and at the hour of our death. Amen.

"Bastard!"

"Are they finished?" Bibi whispers.

"I don't know. I'm not quite up on my Mariology."

Gregory peers over the railing. He sees the bowed head of Cardinal

Pepin. He tries to think. Remus returns. "Dominus, they are starting to leave."

"Okay, let's go!" Gregory pulls Bibi toward the stairwell. "Remus, try to look like a dog." Gregory is first down the stairwell. The tourists and locals are filing through the vestibule. They barely glance at the monks and their dog.

XVIII

Oh Quae Redemptio!

Bibi and Gregory are dancing to a Straus waltz in the papal apartments. It's the small hours of the morning and they've been partying all night. The only light comes from some candles on a table. Food and dinner plates and bottles of wine remain. Remus snores gently under the table.

The music stops. Gregory goes to the window and looks out at the moon. Bibi joins him. "Too bad about Enrico!" Gregory says. "He didn't give a damn about the dogma. There are priests like that. They see through all the crap, but still they remain. They know it's a hoax but they don't leave. Some because they won't succeed at anything else. But Enrico had a fine mind. It's a mystery. It's a great unfathomable mystery." Gregory sighs. "And poor George, the ill-fated Bishop of Rome—I'm sorry for him, too! I believe he was ready to quit. He had his qualities, poor George did. I'll miss him."

Bibi fetches the wine glasses from the table. They stand looking at the moon, and down on the sleeping city.

"Perhaps he's up there now looking down on us as we desecrate his apartment," Bibi says softly. She grins ironically. "If he was right, after all. If his god has taken him in."

"He has to wait till doomsday like everyone else," says Gregory.

Bibi snuggles next to Gregory. "But if he is up there, we won't be joining him, will we darling? We won't be going anywhere, neither to heaven nor to hell. If the gods want us they'll have to come and get us."

"Yeah. He was just starting to get his mind in order when the lightning hit him. When you die your mind should be in order. I had a helot all ready for him. It's too bad.

"Greg, I've been thinking about something... when we get the upgrade, you and I, how do we know we'll still..."

"Like each other?" Gregory gives a small laugh.

"Why is that funny?"

Gregory shrugs. "I can't give a simple answer. I believe human relations will see profound changes. When death is absent, the equation is totally different. A short life brings many fears. Change that and everything changes. Remember the Charlie Chaplin song, "Eternally"? Will we still understand it when eternity is ours? I doubt that romantic love will survive."

"Oh no, Greg, I can't believe that. I don't believe it. I won't." They stand side by side looking down at the piazza in the moonlight. There is not a soul. The city is quiet. Bibi sings the Charlie Chaplin song, softly:

I'll be loving you
Eternally
With a love that's true
Eternally
From the start within my heart it seems I've always known
The sun would shine when you were mine and mine alone

"Great stuff," says Gregory. "Humankind needed lots of consolation. Idealism, romanticism. The body was doomed. At least we could elevate our minds to some level where death didn't seem to matter. But homo mirabilis is different. I don't know if mirabilis ought to have any emotional capacity at all."

Bibi draws back. She looks astounded. "That would not be

good ... would it? I don't think it would be good. Where would love and compassion be without emotion? Without feelings?"

"We'll find out once we get into our new skins," Gregory says simply.

"Greg, I'm not sure I want to go through with this, when I hear you talk. I mean, the idea of being entirely synthetic, every last molecule of me. I can't believe I'll be the same person. I'm scared."

Gregory looks into Bibi's agate eyes. He sees the reflection of himself. "Why does it matter if you're not quite the same person?" he asks. "It's not as if the world were perfect. We're trying to escape it. And the reason we're trying to escape it is, we're not good people."

"I don't want to lose you," Bibi says softly.

"Don't be foolish, Bibi. You're looking at things from the narrow horizon of the human animal. When you cease to be an animal, when you see the vast horizon of mirabilis, you will pity what you are now. Yes, you will. You will never want to go back. Of that I am certain. You will pity this Bibi Lakatos, standing here half drunk, slave to the same juvenile feelings you can find in the hallways of any junior high on this planet. You'll see things differently, believe me."

"Then, let us make the most of the time that remains. Will the flowers still smell the same? Will we still enjoy each day as if it were the last?"

"Animals like to smell flowers. I don't know about homo mirabilis. If it's in the program to enjoy smelling flowers, then I guess mirabilis will want to smell flowers. Same with all primitive sensation. Sex, for instance. The chances are that ... well, it's not certain but, the vastly increased intellectual power of mirabilis may exclude interest in having sex. Not that it's not possible. But it implies that mirabilis would reduce himself occasionally to the level of an animal."

"An animal! I don't understand that. I don't like the sound of that, Greg. Not at all. I want to have sex." Bibi takes Gregory by the collar with both hands and kisses him forcefully. "I want to!"

The sun rises on Rome. As the first rays reach the columns of Bernini, Remus gives a low warning growl and comes out from under the table. A door opens and in walks Innocent XIV. The man looks entirely different. He is wearing jeans and a turtle neck sweater. As he steps into the apartments, he is startled to see Gregory and Bibi. A wild look comes into his eyes. "Ah! When the cat's away!" he cries, in an ominous tone. "So you thought you were rid of me!"

"George, you're alive!" cries Gregory. He tries to embrace the Pontiff but is rebuffed. "I'm delighted to see you, George. I'm ecstatic."

"How wonderful!" says Bibi.

"Ha-ha, I'm certain of that!" cries George. "Thought I was gone for good, didn't you? Sorry to survive. Sorry to spoil things for you, you impostor, you ingrate! Traitor!"

"No, George, I'm glad to see you. Truly I am."

"And so am I," says Bibi. "We're so happy you're alive."

"Liars! Cheats! What a sorry excuse for a monk you are, Brother Gregory! Some Minim friar you turned out to be, you son of a Hoboken plumber! You've gotten away with murder in my palace. I trust you've enjoyed yourself royally in my absence, because now it's time to reap your reward." The Pope places himself squarely in front of Gregory. He flexes his wrestler's muscles. "So, you fear for your life, do you, you miserable worm? You insidious mole, you fifth columnist!"

George backs Gregory into a corner. George's face cracks. He roars with laughter. He looks insane. He pirouettes like a ballet dancer. "So, I make you nervous, do I?" he cries. "Look at that look on your face. Go over there and look at it in the mirror. Go on! You're not afraid of me, are you? Are you afraid of Pretty Boy George, eh?" The Pope's large hands reach out toward Gregory. He breaks into a laugh. "My dear Gregory, how wonderful it is to see you. And this beautiful creature is, I presume, the infamous Bibi Lakatos? My dear, the gossip does not do you justice. Is there some wine left? Let's drink."

George is smiling like he's never smiled before. He takes Gregory's hand and presses it firmly. "My dear Gregory, from now on things are going to be different. They're going to be—opposite. Upside down and inside out. Ha-ha, what a look of consternation on that face! No, I have not taken leave of my senses, Gregory. I've come to them. Oh, what a grand day to be alive! See that sun out there, that beautiful sun? Isn't it splendid? What a joyous time to be alive. And I *am* alive. At last I am alive!"

"Holy Christ!" says Gregory.

George laughs. "Jupiter did it with that bolt of his. I owe it all to Jupiter—king of the immortals. Pagan god saves Pope! Ha-ha, I'm alive, I'm alive, I'm alive!"

"Jesus Murphy! You *are* alive!"

"I'm free. I'm cured of the God delusion. Look at me, I'm standing all by myself. Standing erect. No more stooping, bowing, scraping, grovelling. No more strings. No more fairy in the sky. My eyes are wide open."

"Jesus Christ! Holy shit!"

George pirouettes. He laughs. "Yes, my friends, let's laugh. There is nothing so sacred that we cannot laugh at it. 'Shit' is the right word, Gregory. Everything holy is shit. It's the excrement of the brain. That's all it is. That's all it's worth. This sad world was mired in it far too long."

"George, you look like ... you look fantastic. You look like a man."

"Jupiter hit me, ha-ha. He knocked some sense into me. My brain is working. My mind is in control."

"Alleluia!" cries Gregory. "What a miracle! What a great moment in history!"

"Congratulations," says Bibi. "We're so happy for you."

"Yes, my dear, thank you. From the bottom of my heart. Or is it from the top of my brain? You can't imagine my joy, Bibi Lakatos, at seeing you safe and sound. Look out world. I'm alive. I'm alive. Here

I come. Sing like a lark and be merry! *Cantare—oh-oh-oh-oh! Volare—ho-ho-ho-ho*! Yes, let's fly. I'm a Roman! The truth was right here in my own mind. And now reason is on her throne. And I have closed my mind against everything false. The string pullers will never gain entry again. Never again!" George looks with wonder at Gregory and Bibi, as if seeing them for the first time, understanding who and what they are. "Gregory, Bibi, guess what I did on the way here? You'll never guess. I sat at the fountain of Trevi and I dangled my feet in the water. And there were others but they did not know me. Yes, I'm ready to fly."

"I'm so happy for you, George," says Bibi.

"Yes, my dear friends, it's true: those who cannot think are not alive, truly not alive. I see it now. I see it. They are the living dead. Everything you said Gregory—true! Yes, it's all true. I see the light, I see the light. And in my heart, what joy! I'm alive. At last, at last I'm alive. Scrooge on Christmas Day—That's me! I am redeemed. The Bishop of Rome, redeemed! Saved by the god of thunder. Saved by *Jupiter Tonans*!"

"Oh, wonder of wonders!" cries Gregory, beside himself with joy. "The Pope is redeemed! The Pope is human! The Pope is rational! What a miracle this is! What a great day for humanity!"

"Indeed, it is a miracle, Gregory. In other words, the least probable of all possible outcomes. That's how fortunate I am. But, my friends, we must set to work immediately. There is so much to do, so much to undo. No time to lose."

The two men and the woman join hands, and they go to the window and look down into the piazza bathed in sunshine. "Look, my friends," says George, "the faithful are gathering already. We must undeceive them, before it is too late for them. Before time runs out."

"Jesus, you're so right. Now you're talking, George. I mean, holy Christ, we have to stop taking the name of this poor Jew in vain. No more 'Jesus', no more 'Christ'. Let the poor man rest in peace. Perhaps in time the world will learn to do his memory justice."

"Amen to that," says George. "Bibi, Gregory, those people in the piazza—they should be doing something worthwhile. They should be on the battlements fighting for truth and justice. Fighting for mother earth. For the land and the water and our fellow creatures. For the end of crime and poverty. The end of dissension among men and among women. Not wasting time begging and praying and wishing and worrying. They must stop aping their ancestors. Stop passing on the poison. Mothers and fathers. They must break from the tree apes. From the Grand Assembly of Believers."

"Now you're talking!" cries Gregory.

The three shake hands. "Thank you, Gregory. I'm sorry for playing the clown all these years."

"George, you've just joined the human race. Tell the Curia you're taking a week off to pray and fast in your closet, and you don't want to be disturbed. Let's get the hell out of here."

George pirouettes in front of the window. "Hey down there, look at me! The road is busted! The bridge is broken!"

"Dammit, George, don't let them see you jumping up and down like that! Shit, get away from that window! George!"

"I don't care! Why should I care?" George throws open the curtains. "Look at me, you stupid people down there! Hey down there! Your minds are in hock. Look at me dance!"

Gregory tries to drag George away from the window. "Stop it. I won't let you ruin things."

"I won't stop it. I won't. I just can't help myself. My life—it's gone. My youth. I wasted it on swine and sheep. But what an epiphany! My mind is young again! What a beautiful revelation! What a wonderful redemption! I have so much to tell them, those poor people down there. Look at them looking up—they must have seen me, ha, ha. Look at them, pointing their camcorders this way. Hey down there—Your pope is the devil!—Ha-ha, did you hear that? Lucifer XIV. Lucifer, the most influential Christian deity. I command you to live it up! Forget everything I said. Have some fun!"

"George, get away from the window!"

"Gregory, think of the press we'll get. Julian the Apostate, move over. Here comes George the Destroyer. Did you hear that, good folk, dear pious people? I'll tear it all down. Stone by stone. Poof! It's gone. Save yourselves down there, fools, idiots! Get off your knees!"

"George, please come away from the window!"

"Gregory, the Curia must convene... I want you to contact the press—*L'Osservatore Romano*... No, wait. We have to think about this. Ha-ha! The Church is a farce. I'm not the road between heaven and earth. I'm just one more hairless ape. The truth—it's wonderful. Now I know I'm just me. That bolt of lightning sure cut me down a notch or two."

"Now you've got your life back, George," says Gregory. "Know what we should do, George? We should replace all the bishops with helots. The real ones we can imprison in Hadrian's tomb until the job is done."

George laughs with glee. He pirouettes, he sings. "Yes, yes, marvellous. We'll peel away everything, layer by layer, just like an onion. One day they wake up and—poof!—there's nothing there. And I believe—that is, I think—Jesus Christ would approve. I hear a great sigh redound between the heavens and the firmament: 'At last I am what I was! No more lies! No more abusing my name and my memory.'"

"Amen to that!" cries Gregory. "I will not take his name in vain again. I promise. Let's do it! Let's tear away everything till there's nothing left but the truth. The bare naked truth with nothing on. Transparent, just as it was in ancient times, when the world was young, before we dressed it and covered it up with the absurd. Before trying to build

Jerusalem in all these once green and pleasant lands, now robbed of everything clean and natural and true."

"Alleluia!" George cries.

Gregory takes Bibi and George by the hand and says, "Now we are soldiers for Rome. The war has just begun. We must liberate ourselves from the superstitions of the barbarians. We must prepare for tomorrow. Tomorrow there will be nothing between mind and reality. Nothing between mind and life. Nothing between mind and the journey. It's time to move. It's time to call on Caesar."

XIX

The News from Rome

Good morning. This broadcast has been pre-empted by Semper Fidelis on behalf of the senate and the people of Rome. All citizens of the EU are urged to remain calm. Thousands joined the march on Rome under the banner "All power to Rome". The EU parliament has transferred all power to the senate and the Roman people. And we are all Romans.

Gregory Caesar O'Riley is head of the provisional government. On behalf of the senate and people of Rome, O'Riley has called upon Marcus Aurelius to assume power. The Emperor has been offered his ancient powers: the inviolability of the plebeian tribune and the consulship.

Europe hails Marcus Aurelius!

From this day forth, the EU will be known as *Rome*. This union is open to the whole world. Indeed, we expect the whole world to join, sooner or later, in keeping with Roman traditions and expectations. To those yet outside the Empire we say: Resistance is futile; you will be assimilated.

At this very moment, countries around the world are already clamouring for admission to Rome. Welcomes have been sent to the granddaughters of Rome in the Americas—the Latin American countries and Québec; and also to the American states with large Hispanic populations. The Hispanics of the Americas are ecstatic at the prospect of being part of the Roman Empire.

The United States is not expected to survive the current turmoil. Two of its three constituent parts have threatened dire consequences if there are any hostile or anti-American moves on the part of Latin Americans. But these are tigers without teeth. American intellectuals are working against Nabilat. They would rather see the country fracture than survive as a mental cripple, with the reputation of having the most ignorant population of any country on earth.

The cultural elite of the U.S. have retreated to their enclaves in New England and the Pacific coast, and they are inviting Canada and Mexico to take what they can from Nabilat.

Here at home, the Colosseum, again in use at the beginning of the last century for cultural events, but fully restored only one hundred years ago, will again see gladiatorial combats. The amphitheatre will be primarily devoted to spectacular events in the service of ridiculing superstition. The animal cages underneath the stadium are already crammed with clerics, priests, and preachers of every conceivable ilk and flavour, as well as hucksters and charlatans generally, and string pullers of every stripe.

The Pontiff has shocked the world by denouncing the very church of which he is head. Many of the bishops support him. The rest are in complete disarray. The Vatican coup is turning into a rout for the Catholic Church. The Pontiff and Gregory O'Riley are determined to dismantle the Roman Church. Meanwhile, all over Rome, counselling is available for the devout, as well as a quick course in the exercise of reason and care of the mind.

Humanists and scientists around the world are applauding these developments. The mass of humanity is gnashing its teeth. The Muslim world is in a state of shock at what appears to them to be the apparent sudden disintegration of the whole Christian ethos. They apparently fear for their own house of cards.

Creationists and fundamentalists will neither accept an end to religion nor to homo sapiens. They are determined to die the death of animals, eyes cast firmly on their kingdom come. They will be faithful to the bitter end, as their last wail fades into the void: "We will be true to thee till death!"

And now I hear a very strange cry indeed: "But we'll miss the peasant! We'll miss the buffoon! We'll miss the practical joker! We're so fond of the local yokel! We love our clowns and ignoramuses and money-grubbers. Selfish people, cheats, and crooks are as dear to us as they were to Jesus Christ. And what will happen without our hayseeds and hillbillies and creationists, and just plain simple ordinary down-to-earth folks? Because they are the spice of life. The stuff of legends."

And I hear another strange cry: "But the small town is our wellspring of horror. The small town is our guardian of the absurd. What about those quaint country folk and their resistance to change? What about Dolly and cowboys and apple pie and the Good Book? What about kind hearts and gentle people? What about paranoia, xenophobia, tribalism? All that good old familiar stuff into which we were born? Everything that has shaped us from day one. Everything that makes social intercourse so unpredictable, so exciting, so challenging, so risky? We love all that quaint and wonderful stuff."

Well, we say to the complainers: To hell with you! The bright lights of this planet are leaving all that behind. Stay if you wish and perish.

No one, once given the chance to see the world through the eyes of mirabilis, would ever wish to return.

The higher reaches of consciousness will for the first time in human history be available to everyone. To the most mean and the most stupid. Everybody will be guaranteed an intellectual and spiritual life of a quality that, up till now, has been the preserve only of those with superior genes, superior experience, and superior education.

And when you have that, you will look back on what you were

and you will despise the dirt and ignorance into which you were born. You will shun the pig's trough of tradition. You will distance yourself from the culture of becoming. You will no longer be an animal.

You will simply be.

And you will be straight, tall, rational, honest. No sneaky subconscious lurking around in the nether reaches of the brain brewing evil. You will be plain, simple, direct. You will wear your motivation on your sleeve. You will be proud of it.

You will have no other errands than reason and justice.

So to the doubters out there we say: No! We are not creating another race. We are perfecting the human race. We are nurturing our destiny. We are moving on. Hail Caesar!

XX

Jupiter Best and Greatest

Jancie and I are taken by surprise when Gregory shows up at our front door. We are to pack our bags immediately. Apparently, it is no surprise for Verus, who quit his job at the University and has a bag packed ready to go. Verus tells us he always had the feeling he was destined for something great. But it is clear he has some trepidation at the prospect of seeing ancient and modern Rome in the same space and time.

Gregory has put Jancie and me on the beta list for an upgrade. Jancie consents reluctantly, and only because she senses I'm going to take this opportunity regardless.

Gregory tells us to hurry and that we have to leave right away. He tells us that people are in a panic everywhere to be included before they die, and that we must save those who have proven themselves most valuable to humanity.

Jancie and I are flattered but we suspect that Gregory is including us merely because we are friends of Verus.

"I shall be first," says Gregory. "Next in line are the Commission members and my students, and my friends. All the people who are valuable to me. All necessary for success. Scientists are next, followed by philosophers. Then the beta list, then the gamma. On the last list of all are politicians, lawyers, criminals, pop singers, and creationists."

"Sure, it makes sense," I say. "The dough heads should be last."

Gregory harangues us while Jancie and I pack our things for the trip. "Pity homo sapiens," he says. "They live in a world where wisdom is everywhere available. Still, they are unable to use it. And as information explodes at the same speed as the expanding universe, their ability to sort out what's truly relevant shrinks at proportionally the same rate. They are strangers in their own land, which is always a land of strife and discontent."

"Hey!" says Jancie, while she stuffs her suitcase half-heartedly. "You sound angry, Mr. O'Riley. Kind of vengeful."

"No, dear, I'm just gloating. I'm thrilled to be leaving a world of tribal mentality. I can't even feel sorry for them."

"No more hype and hucksterism," I say. "No more fascination with fairies."

"I hope I won't regret this," says Jancie. "If the world wasn't in such a mess ..."

"Young lady," says Gregory, "it's time for you to travel. Voltaire's Candide travelled to many countries to discover the truth. Don Quixote rode across the plains of Spain in search of valour and honour. And we must do the same. We must sally forth in our own space and time to do the good deeds assigned us by destiny. We shall don our helot armour and mount our helot mounts. And we shall ride forth into the world in the service of justice and reason. If it is true that the truth is to be found in our own backyards, it is also true that the shortest route sometimes lies through far-flung places."

"That sounds very noble," says Jancie. "But how do I unite with a helot?"

"Very easily, my dear, very easily," Gregory assures her. "We'll show you."

"But how will I feel? What will I look like? Will I still be a Roman Catholic?"

I remind Jancie that nobody will be taking anything away from her. Gregory backs me up. "We shall be adding," he tells her. "We are not taking away. You will look and feel as you do now, Jancie. Your mind will expand. Whether you keep your faith or not is entirely up to you."

Jancie sorts her stuff without enthusiasm. She has misgivings. And I'm certain with good reason, since I doubt she will want to remain Christian once she undergoes the upgrade.

"Oh death, where is thy sting!" cries Gregory. "The scourge of full consciousness here lies defeated under the feet of homo mirabilis. Oh, let the drums and trumpets sound. Man no longer belongs to nature. Man is leaving home. Goodbye Mum! Man is master. Man takes his place with Jupiter and Woden. But man is real. Man exists. Yes, indeed, the gods do exist. But in this universe gods are not the prime causes, but the ultimate effects of many causes. When homo mirabilis looks in the mirror he will see the face of God."

"The face of God?" says Jancie. "What do you mean?"

"I mean it's time to resume our quest for the Holy Grail. And by that, Joe and Jancie, I do not mean the wine cup of Jesus, in which, according to Christian legend, Joseph of Arimathea collected the tears and blood and sweat of his crucified rabbi. No. The Holy Grail is what the souls of all reasoning animals seek, wherever in creation they may find themselves, in whatever universe, wherever in the All. And what makes it sacred is the blood of many stars. And the Grail can never be found by the wayside but only at journey's end. And the journey is infinite. It is a journey not of a lifetime, nor of a people or a race, nor even of a star, a galaxy, or a universe. It is a journey that stretches unimaginable aeons beyond the time and space of our puny experience. And you, Jancie, are permitted to take but a single step."

"Well," says Jancie, "whatever you say, I still believe what I believe. Nothing will change that. Faith overrides everything if it's strong enough. And mine is. My faith will move mountains. And I'm taking it with me!"

"Fine," says Gregory. "You may take what you wish. There is no compulsion."

At the Rome airport we are met by George and Bibi, who are arm in arm and looking very pleased with the turn of events. The media are there and a great crowd of people. Jancie has a terrible time understanding that the man called George Schweinrue, now dressed in jeans and a turtleneck, was only a short while ago the bishop of Rome and the leader of Christendom. I tell George that, in spite of his defection and the consequent chaos of the Church, Jancie is still a firm believer.

"I prayed for you so many times," Jancie tells George, with an agonized look.

"And I prayed for you, my dear," says George. "I prayed so much it hurt me. I developed a stoop. It was a great burden and a useless one. I'm sorry if seeing me like this is a shock. But I'm afraid nobody was listening to my prayers. I guess I'm the strangest bishop of Rome that ever walked this earth."

"You certainly do not sound like the Holy Father," Jancie says irritably.

"Perhaps not, my dear, but the truth is, I'm just an ape. Being bishop of Rome did not change that. When I stand naked before the mirror, that's what I see—a smooth ape, unadorned and undisguised. But I am an ape that has learned to use reason. And reason is the glory of humankind. All else is dross and dream, fantasy and futility."

"Well, I'm still a Christian!" says Jancie acerbically. "Roman Catholic Christian! With or without a pope! Even if I have to be the last one on earth!"

The crowd hails Verus. But the crowd has two voices. Some are hailing the Emperor. Others are hailing their saviour. To the latter, Verus says: "My friends, we are born incomplete and wanting fulfillment. You believe you are not who you are meant to be. That feeling is common to all mankind. But no one else can make you that. No man, no woman, no god. You must do it yourselves. But you cannot be what you yearn to be unless you are free. If you are not free, you will betray your destiny."

The crowd is rapturous at the sound of Verus's voice. But the meaning of his words escapes most of them. They struggle to get near enough to touch him. Others stand mute and weep. Some cry out: "Save me, Lord!"

Verus turns to the ex-pope of all the Roman Christians and says, "George, you and I both have served, each in his own time, as Pontifex Maximus. My religion is dead and yours is dying, though the death of yours will do the world a lot more good than did the death of mine."

I put my arm around Jancie and I say to my friends, "Tomorrow things will be different. All the crap will be gone. Gossip, scandal, bodies, breasts, behinds, open mouths. Everything that mattered to the tree swingers."

"Right, Joe," says Verus. "The curtain is coming down on the puppet show."

A red carpet has been rolled out for Caesar. We are escorted to the waiting chariots and we proceed triumphantly into Rome, accompanied by the pretorian guard on horseback, and Roman soldiers on foot. When we arrive in the ancient core of the city, Verus is almost overcome with the strength of his feeling. The memories are almost too powerful.

A tribune tells us that all over Rome there is a frenzy of name changing. The names of saints disappear daily, like the last drear leaves falling from the trees in late autumn. Churches and public monuments are being purged of their cult names. Ancient names and dedications are restored to honour. And other monuments get names from the long list of the great who were tormented or tortured by the Church. Already, St. Peter's, now renamed "Museum Marcus

Aurelius", has become a museum dedicated to man's most evil and persistent delusion—religion!

And in the piazza a column has been erected to commemorate Flavius Claudius Julianus, once called "the Apostate" and stamped with pious stains of infamy, now called "Julian the Great". The tribune tells us that Julianus was a nephew of the traitor Constantine, that he was raised as a Christian but became a scholar and enlightened himself, and renounced Christianity. He became emperor and reinstated the Greco-Roman gods. He was willing to co-exist with the Christians and he issued an edict for religious toleration, and he even intended to rebuild the temple of Jerusalem. He was a just ruler, a scholar, and a satirist, and he deserved better than to be remembered by the foul and odious Christian appellation, "the Apostate".

The tribune tells us that the new column shows the triumphs of Julianus over the Allemani and the Franks, whom he chased out of Gaul and back into Germany; and also his triumph over the Persians, and his untimely death in Persia by a mysterious horseman, who alone raced up to the Emperor and wounded him with a spear.

But depicted also are the Emperor's heroic attempts to stem the tide of the Christian virus, and his ridicule by the Christians of Antioch, whose minds had been infected and whose ears were closed to all reason. The citizens of marble-streeted Antioch, third city in splendour of the Roman Empire, founded by a general of Alexander the Great, would have had little to crow about if they had realized that, in their frenzy to foist upon the world the superstition preached to them by Paul, they not only weakened Rome, but by so doing, they consigned their own descendents to the embrace of a later, rival superstition—Islam!

Verus pauses before the senate building. A banner hangs over the entrance. It reads: *Senatus Populusque Romanus*—The Senate and the Roman People. Verus has not been inside for almost two thousand years.

Upon first seeing it Verus is shocked. The coloured tile is not there. Without its ornament, the senate looks very plain, like a great square barn made of ochre-coloured bricks, instead of the brilliant jewel it once was.

Verus pulls us along with him to witness the proceedings. Inside, the senators are waiting for him—senators from his own time, the very men he honoured. They applaud as he enters. And there are cries of "Welcome back, Caesar!" and "Hail Caesar!"

Verus looks around. He is awestruck. The clock has turned back almost twenty centuries. Verus is unable to speak. He is overcome with feeling. He looks at the senators, misty-eyed. He is trying to make connections in space and time but he feels inadequate to the task. The eyes of the senators are focused on him. Their faces register friendship and gratitude. They wait for him patiently.

Gregory is watching the proceedings. He is wearing his shark's grin. He approaches Caesar and whispers to him: "Don't get too choked up, Caesar. These men are all helots. We thought you would like to see the faces of your friends. But they are not ancient Romans. I hope we did the right thing."

"Yes, Gregory, of course. Thank you." Caesar trembles visibly, considers for a moment, and then says to the assembly: "My dear friends, I know you all. I know your faces. We are here to do the business of Rome. As you doubtless know, I am used to ruling with the sanction of the senate. You know what I stand for."

Before Verus has a chance to say more, the senators rise, one after another, to quote from *Meditations*:

"From my mother, piety and beneficence, and abstinence, not only from evil deeds, but even from evil thoughts."

"From Diognetus, not to busy myself about trifling things, and not to give credit to what was said by miracle-workers."

"From Apollonius, freedom of will and undeviating steadiness of pur-

pose; and to look to nothing else, not even for a moment, except to reason."

"From Sextus, a benevolent disposition... the idea of living conformably to nature... gravity without affectation... freedom from passion... knowledge without ostentation."

"From Alexander the grammarian, to refrain from fault-finding."

"From Fronto, to observe what envy, and duplicity, and hypocrisy are in a tyrant, and that generally those among us who are called Patricians are rather deficient in paternal behaviour."

"From my brother Severus, to love my kin, and to love truth, and to love justice... and from him I received the idea of a polity in which there is the same law for all, a polity administered with regard to equal rights and equal freedom of speech, and the idea of a kingly government that respects most of all the freedom of the governed... and a disposition to do good, and to give to others readily, and to cherish good hopes."

"From Maximus I learned self-government, and not to be led aside by anything, and cheerfulness in all circumstances... and to do what was set before me without complaining... To be ready to forgive... to be free from all falsehood."

"In my adoptive father I observed mildness of temper, and unchangeable resolution in the things that he had determined after due deliberation; and no vainglory in those things that men call honours; and a love of labour and perseverance; and a readiness to listen to those who had anything to propose for the common weal; and undeviating firmness in giving to every man according to his deserts; and a knowledge derived from experience of the occasions for vigorous action and for remission... To check immediately popular applause and all flattery... There was in him nothing harsh, nor implacable, nor violent, nor, as one may say, anything carried to the sweating point; but he examined all things separately, as if he had abundance of time, and without confusion, in an orderly way, vigorously and consistently. And that might be applied to him which is recorded of Socrates, that he was able both to abstain from, and to enjoy, those things

which many are too weak to abstain from, and cannot enjoy without excess. But to be strong enough both to bear the one and to be sober in the other, is the mark of a man who has a perfect and invincible soul."

"Caesar, these are the things you stand for," the senators cry out in unison.

From outside the senate come the strains of something great—the music of Ludvig van Beethoven. Verus wipes his eyes and says to the assembly, "Senators, to Rome fell the task of joining Etruscan and Roman technology to the great ideals of Greece. And we saw it was for the benefit of mankind. And we determined to put an end to strife and ignorance. And to do this we had to conquer the world. And we had to teach others the art of government. And to us fell the task of bringing the West out of barbarism. Two thousand years ago, Rome was on that golden road. And by 'Rome,' I mean not Rome, the city. Not Rome, *Italia*. No. Because by then, Rome was a great cosmopolitan society, and a Roman citizen could have his home in Africa, in Syria, in Germany, in Britain, or any one of numerous other countries. Our golden road stretched toward the horizon, yea, to the very stars in the heavens. But destiny had determined that the human race should take a detour. Now, as I stand before you, I declare that golden road open again!"

The senators cheer and applaud.

As we leave the senate after the formalities, Bibi Lakatos is very excited. "And now," she says, "It's time for people and helots, and man and woman, to join." She takes Gregory by the arm.

"See here," says Gregory. "This divine creature at my side I chose as my helot. I saw myself as a lady in my new skin." He takes a sidelong glance at Bibi, who gives him a blank look and disengages from him. "The helots I experimented with, for obvious reasons, do not have the identifying mark on the forehead. It's very small and it's behind the left ear."

Everyone is astounded, Bibi most of all. She takes hold of me and tells me to look behind her ear. "Yes, I see it," I say.

Bibi's jaw drops. The pallor of her skin is evident. "I'm a helot!" she cries. "I'm something you made? You made Bibi Lakatos? But my life in Hungary, all my relatives, the dance academy—you mean it never happened? All those years? And my feelings for you—they don't count? You did this to me! You never told me! Why didn't you tell me? Why? Why did you let me fall in love with you!"

"You did that yourself," says Gregory. "Every Roman philosopher knows that falling in love is as stupid, as unproductive, as irrational, and as dangerous as falling in religion. You attended my classes. You read Lucretius. And you can't say I encouraged you."

"You could've warned me! You could've said something! You son of a bitch!"

Gregory gestures for calm and says, "Early on, I recognized that fully sentient helots were beings that deserved to have the same rights as humans, and I think I told you that, Bibi. The rights of helots have been recognized in the lex universalis. The first right they have is the right to exist. So you cannot be my helot, Bibi. And anyway, now I think I'd rather be a male in the next life."

Gregory reaches out to Bibi but she pulls away. She starts to cry. Jancie tries to comfort her but she is inconsolable.

"I'm sorry," says Gregory. "Is it so bad being a helot?"

"You're not sorry!" Bibi snaps. "What about all those lost years—my relatives! Suddenly there's nobody there! I'm just a toy for you!" She punches Gregory, knocking him off balance. She goes off and sulks on the doorstep to the senate.

"Well," says Gregory, "I guess I made some mistakes. I sure as hell did."

"You envisaged a life as a female?" George asks.

"For a while I did. Until I got to know Bibi." Gregory shakes his head. "You know, relations between the sexes are never going to be the same again. Never again."

"I thought you said nothing would change," cries Jancie. "That we would keep our personalities."

Gregory shrugs. "We do keep our personalities. But an expanded mind means expanded horizons. Personality is not static. At least not in mirabilis."

"And who will be your helots?" I ask Verus and George.

"George is going to be Perfidia," says Gregory. "She's due back on the Orient Express today. Verus doesn't need one."

Verus, Jancie, and I look at each other uncertainly. "How come?" I ask.

"Because Verus is Number One." Gregory gives his best shark's grin. "He's the first one I made. I set different parameters for him. He had to fit the role. Marcus Aurelius was a master at self-control. But I also wanted to see what I could stir up with a second resurrection. I always wanted to do something like that—give Christ a little competition, you know. I was not disappointed."

We all stare at Verus, who has a vacant look on his face. But there is no sign of an internal disturbance. At length he says, "I am not Marcus Aurelius? I am just a helot? A machine? I am not this great man? ... No, I see that I am not. I see it in your faces. I am no man at all."

"You are!" says Gregory. "The man is in the mind. Not the material. The mind."

Verus sighs. "But I know only Marcus. I know only Rome. It's the way you made me. Now, perhaps, I should have my end, as a proud Roman. I would not want to be anything else but Roman. Even Faustina is not real, then! Faustina! Her memory is so vivid! But I am not real, so she cannot be. You programmed me with a grand delusion."

"I'm sorry," Gregory says. "But whether it's a delusion or not depends entirely on you. And the same goes for Bibi."

Verus stands looking into the eyes of Gregory. "So I, Verus, am just an image in a mirror, scarce perceived. A small little image. An image of someone else. A distorted image. Perhaps even a caricature. Because, though you may have programmed me to conform to what is known about Marcus, and though a great deal *is* known about Marcus, that still is only a part of the whole, for you have never entered his mind. This then, this feeling of vast accomplishment, this eternal glory, is only something I dreamed. A beautiful dream. Do you know what it's like to be hailed imperator by your army? By the men whose lives you've risked in the service of peace and justice? Can you imagine your triumphal entry into Rome at the head of the army? What solace it must have given Marcus, mortal though he was. But he was not a discrete collection of attributes, as am I. He was a living, evolving consciousness. He must have been much more than I am."

Gregory puts his arm around Verus. "Do not say so, Caesar. We want you to be emperor. Our respect and deference for you is real. We must all have starting points. And your nature is such that you would not have a starting point unless we gave you one. In Marcus you have an exceptional starting point. Build on the memory you have and evolve from there. Personality is not something we choose, though we do work on it over time. It is made up of inheritance and experience. Your Marcus program is your inheritance. And as for experience, the horizon stretches to infinity."

"Right," says George. "Well spoken, Gregory. Caesar, you are the man of destiny."

Verus thinks for a moment. "I must resign myself, then, to not being this paragon of humankind, the emperor of Rome. He had no equal in the world in any time, neither as man nor emperor. He shone for a while below the dark forests of barbarism. And I thought I was he. I was labouring under a grand delusion. But I will not complain. The light of truth illuminates this man of nature and reason. And I will be this man. I will be Verus."

"Splendid!" says Gregory. "And now we have embraced our destiny, and the between-time draws to a close. Homo mirabilis is about to be born. We need no longer fear the human brain. We shall tend our minds, both humans and helots. We shall tend the gardens in which everything good must grow."

"And so it came to pass," says Verus, "that humankind had to climb to the highest mountain top before learning to stand erect; and man did learn to dance before he learned to cut the strings. But now we have left behind dancing in puppet shows. And we have climbed to the mountain top. And we stand erect. And with our free and unfettered spirits we survey the world around us. And we stand ready. We have given ourselves purpose, both humans and helots. And our purpose is to grow, to live, to love, to build, and to visit the stars. *We* are the bearers of meaning in the universe, no matter what our provenance, for reason unites all intelligent beings."

"It does," says George. "I am no longer grand master of fantasies, and I am content. I, too, laboured under a grand delusion. But I have resigned my high place in the great fraternity of clowns. I have given up herding pigs and sheep, and ceased begging the gods for favours. For I have reclaimed my Roman citizenship. And now I join the world on the golden road of reason, the greatest road ever built by Rome, glory of the West, wonder of the world. And so, the great eternal questions lie before us, yet unanswered. And though we must ask the questions, we will understand that the answers recede from us at the same speed as the farthermost galaxies of the universe. For that is the cosmic reality into which humankind is born."

"Well spoken, George," says Gregory. "Caesar, the world is yours! The world awaits your command."

Verus was not listening. The strains of Beethoven's "Ode to Joy" rose over the ancient city. As he looked up toward the *via sacra* and the temple of Saturn, it seemed to him that nothing had ever been broken. And the Rome in his eyes was the Rome of his memory, the city of two thousand years before. And now he stood in the streets of triumph. And he heard the clarions and the drums, and he saw the banners, and he heard the people cheering. Rome has triumphed again! Rome will endure. And Verus heard the soldiers give their hail: Imperator! Imperator! Imperator!

Verus saw the places where he had walked with his beloved Faustina, and he heard her gentle voice. Verus felt he had come home. But those he most loved were gone. His view clouded at the thought, and at the feeling. And the soldiers' triumphal cry receded and went down near the temple of Jupiter Best and Greatest. And the ghosts withdrew.

But though Verus knew the memories had been planted in him, they were still memories; and they were nonetheless real, because they had power to move him.

And now the life of Marcus would be *his* life, and there would be new memories that would be only his. Verus found the thought consoling. And as Apollo warmed the streets of the ancient city, it seemed to him a promise: man would triumph. He felt he was fortunate to have as his beginning this singular man. This Imperator Caesar Marcus Aurelius Antoninus Augustus—who also had the name of "Verus".

— *Finis* —

The Author

WENDEL MESSER was born in St. John's, Newfoundland, and has Lunenburg as well as Newfoundland roots. He attended school in Halifax and Toronto. After earning a B.A. at the University of Gothenburg, Sweden, and a B.Ed. at the University of Toronto, he taught English as a Second Language and Driver Education. At present he lives in a mobile home near Gravenhurst, Ontario.

Messer's first book, *The Sink: The Last Days of Driving,* a satire on the declining culture of the roadway, received superlative reviews, and Messer was invited to read from the book at the Leacock Festival, Orillia, in 2003. In spite of that, he refuses to regard his satire, in which Toronto drivers are executed in the Don Valley Parkway, as primarily a work of humour (or even fiction).

Messer's second book, *The Conquest of Canada,* is the story of the first thirty years of a country first mentioned in the annals of history almost half a millennium ago. The story of that country is our story, whatever language we may speak. The novel bears eloquent witness to the author's interest in history and ideas. The author believes that Canada can be known, understood, and realized only with reference to the past. The dreams of the past hold the clues to our survival as a nation.

With his third book, *Verus and the Grand Assembly of Believers,* Messer returns to satire, convinced that the terrible scourge of religion can best be defeated by ridicule.

Readers are encouraged to comment on the book by e-mail: wmesser@thesink.ca; or through the mail: care of Breller Books, RR 1, Box 3013, Gravenhurst, Ontario, Canada P1P 1R1. Comments are most welcome.

For more information please contact the publisher at the above address or visit the author's web site at www.thesink.ca.

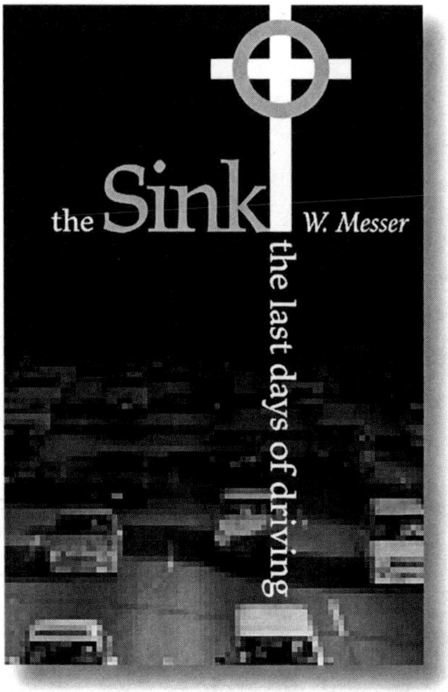

The Sink: The Last Days of Driving
by Wendel Messer
Published by Breller Books

soft cover 5.5″ × 8.5″ 221 pages
ISBN 0-9730094-0-3

Praise for *The Sink*

"Uniquely engaging... full of sardonic whimsy... assesses the sorry state of our urban subconscious... a fervent lament for the carnage wrought by carelessness and flaring tempers... if it were required reading in driving schools, it would almost certainly save lives."

The Globe & Mail

"A biting satire... brilliantly written... first of its kind on the culture of the roadway... Messer has a deep knowledge of driving."

drivers.com

"You will never drive the same way again!"

Canadian Writer's Journal

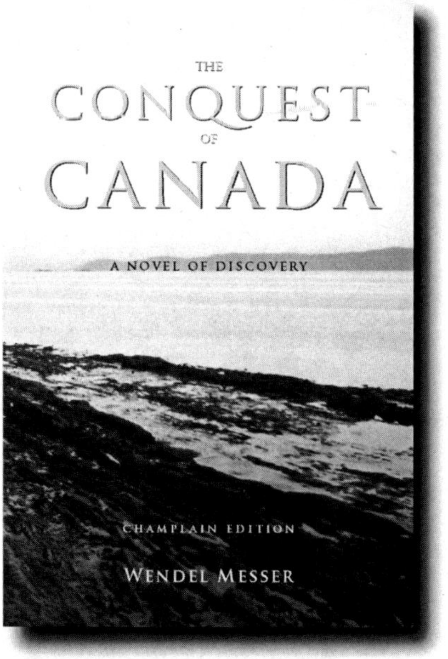
THE
CONQUEST
OF
CANADA
A NOVEL OF DISCOVERY
CHAMPLAIN EDITION
WENDEL MESSER

Praise for *The Conquest of Canada*

"While this book can be read as an adventure story, it is essentially a novel of ideas. It can also be read as an exploration of the motives of French colonialism. Messer is a gifted prose stylist whose descriptions of the natural world are particularly eloquent. Messer has written a significant novel that evokes a dramatic era in Canadian history."

Prairie Fire Review of Books

"A canvas of heroic proportions ... Messer makes it come alive. *The Conquest* will appeal to anyone with an interest in history and to those who just like a good story. Highly Recommended."

CM Magazine: Review of Canadian Materials

Ordering books by Wendel Messer

The Sink: The Last Days of Driving
The Conquest of Canada: A Novel of Discovery
Verus and the Grand Assembly of Believers

Order direct from:

Breller Books
RR1, Box 3013
Gravenhurst, Ontario P1P 1R1
Canada

Order forms, and pricing and shipping details, are available on the web site:

www.thesink.ca

SGML AND RELATED STANDARDS
Document Description and Processing Languages

Series continued at back of book

SGML AND RELATED STANDARDS

Document Description and Processing Languages

JOAN M. SMITH
Independent Consultant and formerly President of the SGML Users' Group

ELLIS HORWOOD
NEW YORK LONDON TORONTO SYDNEY TOKYO SINGAPORE

Published 1993 by
ELLIS HORWOOD LIMITED
Campus 400, Maylands Avenue,
Hemel Hempstead, Hertfordshire HP2 7EZ
and
Market Cross House, Cooper Street,
Chichester, West Sussex, PO19 1EB
A division of
Simon & Schuster International Group

Printed and bound in Great Britain
by Hartnolls, Bodmin, Cornwall

Library of Congress Cataloging-in-Publication Data

Smith, Joan M.
SGML and related standards / Joan M. Smith.
p. cm. — (Ellis Horwood series in computers and their applications.)
Includes bibliographical references and index.
ISBN 0-13-806506-3: $44.95
1. SGML (Computer program language) I. Title. II. Series: Computers and their applications.
QA76.73.S42 1992
005 - dc20 92-30468
CIP

British Library Cataloguing in Publication Data

A catalogue record for this book is available from the British Library

ISBN 0-13-806506-3 (hbk)

2 3 4 5 6 97 96 95 94 93

Dedication

To the memory of my parents, Reg and Elsie Gibson,
who both died in 1984

Table of contents

Preface xi

Acronyms and abbreviations xv

1 Introduction 1
1.1 Background 1
1.2 Standardization aspects 2
1.3 Objectives of SGML 6
1.4 Uses of SGML 7

2 The Standard Generalized Markup Language 12
2.1 Concepts on which SGML is based 12
2.2 The notion of markup 13
2.3 What SGML is 14
2.4 How SGML works 15
2.4.1 The structure of information 15
2.4.2 What the language includes 16
2.4.3 Provisions of the language 17
2.5 Features of SGML 20
2.5.1 General 20
2.5.2 Markup minimization 20
2.5.3 Link features 21
2.5.4 Others 21
2.5.5 Use of the features 22

3 An SGML document 24
3.1 SGML declaration 24
3.1.1 Character set usage 24
3.1.2 Capacity requirements 25
3.1.3 Concrete syntax 25

3.1.4 Feature use ... 26
3.1.5 Application-specific information ... 27
3.2 Document type definition ... 27
3.3 Document instance ... 30
3.4 Reducing overheads ... 31

4 Some application considerations ... 35
4.1 General remarks ... 35
4.2 Avoidance of presentation issues ... 36
4.3 Numbering schemes ... 37
4.4 Cross-referencing ... 37
4.5 Indexing ... 37
4.6 Lists ... 38
4.7 Tables ... 39
4.8 Mathematics ... 41
4.9 Libraries of information ... 41
4.10 Hypermedia links ... 41
4.11 Security ... 42

5 The integrated information base ... 45
5.1 Some possibilities ... 45
5.2 Organizational aspects ... 46
5.3 Output considerations ... 46
5.4 Functionality ... 47
5.5 Input to the information base ... 48
5.6 Ten rules and ten benefits ... 50
5.7 Getting started ... 52

6 Presenting SGML documents ... 55
6.1 The standards involved ... 55
6.2 Document Style Semantics and Specification Language ... 55
6.3 Standard Page Description Language ... 58
6.4 Fonts ... 61

7 SGML support facilities ... 66
7.1 Interchanging SGML documents ... 66
7.2 Registration of owner identifiers ... 67
7.3 Editing SGML documents ... 68
7.4 The overall model ... 70
7.5 Techniques for using SGML ... 72
7.5.1 General ... 72
7.5.2 Entities for mathematics and science ... 73
7.5.3 Application for standards and technical reports ... 74
7.5.4 Using short references ... 75
7.6 Vocabulary ... 76

8 Hypermedia and other new work 77
8.1 HyTime 77
8.2 The Standard Music Description Language 79
8.3 A binary version of SGML 81
8.4 Revision of ISO 8879 82
8.5 Conformance 83
8.6 Related standards work 84
8.6.1 Coding of character sets 84
8.6.2 Coding audio, hypermedia, and other information 85
8.6.3 A colour architecture 86
8.6.4 Full-text manipulation of structured data 87

9 Some applications of SGML 89
9.1 Defence 89
9.1.1 Computer-aided Acquisition and Logistic Support 89
9.1.2 The European AECMA specification 91
9.1.3 North Atlantic Treaty Organization 93
9.2 Others 94
9.2.1 The airlines 94
9.2.2 Oil and gas 96
9.2.3 Telecommunications 96
9.2.4 Publishing 96
9.2.5 Patents documents 97
9.2.6 Academic and research community 98
9.2.7 Government departments 99
9.2.8 Commission of the European Communities 100
9.2.9 International Organization for Standardization 100

10 A comparison of SGML and ODA 103
10.1 Something about the standards 103
10.2 Technical issues 105
10.2.1 Basic principles 105
10.2.2 Architecture 105
10.2.3 Extensions to the standards 105
10.2.4 Application requirements for ODA and SGML 107
10.2.5 DAPs and SGML declarations 107
10.2.6 Document classes and document types 108
10.2.7 Encoding the structures 109
10.2.8 Developing DTDs and generic structures 109
10.2.9 Over-riding structures 109
10.2.10 The document profile 110
10.2.11 Interchange of documents 110
10.2.12 DAPs and ISPs 111
10.2.13 Presentation of documents 112

10.2.14 Working with both standards 113
10.2.15 EDI documents 114
10.2.16 Some overheads 114
10.3 Business issues 114
10.3.1 Two case studies 114
10.3.2 When to format a document 116
10.3.3 Which standard to use when 116
10.3.4 Availability of products 118
10.3.5 Concluding remarks 118

11 SGML product guidance 120
11.1 Licensing a product 120
11.1.1 General questions to ask a vendor 120
11.1.2 Parser/parsing system 121
11.1.3 Editing software 122
11.1.4 Publishing software 123
11.1.5 The software demonstration 125
11.1.6 Preparation of a benchmark 125
11.2 Availability of products 127
11.2.1 Public domain software 127
11.2.2 Commercially-available software 127

12 Further information 134
12.1 SGML Users' Group 134
12.2 Graphic Communications Association 135
12.3 Electronic Publishing Special Interest Group 136
12.4 Published standards and technical reports 137
12.5 Books on SGML 138
12.6 Other useful documents 139
12.7 The last word 141

Appendix 1: A brief history of the development of SGML 143

Appendix 2: Glossary 146

Index 149

Preface

I was introduced to the Standard Generalized Markup Language (SGML) in April 1984, on the occasion of a tutorial on the subject. It was given by Sharon Adler and Bill Davis under the auspices of the Graphic Communications Association (GCA) at the University of Oxford, immediately preceding what became the very successful MarkUp series of conferences. The first in Europe had been held in The Netherlands at the end of 1982, but I had missed that, alas, and had to wait until 1984. As I listened, it was as if scales fell from my eyes; here was the standard that could be used to describe any document in a straightforward manner, infinitely flexible, yet all based on rules defined for the application.

As the conference progressed, I found myself getting more and more enthusiastic, and at one stage heard myself stating that an SGML Users' Group should be set up, so those interested in the development of SGML could keep in touch with one another and know of progress to the language in between conferences. That came to pass. Before the year was out I also assumed responsibility for organizing United Kingdom input to standards-making for SGML and related work through the British Standards Institution (BSI) to the International Organization for Standardization (ISO).

What was it about SGML that so filled me with enthusiasm? In retrospect, I believe that it was the realization that the language could be used for all types of documents, written in any language and containing any kind of content. I also realized from the outset that it could be used for what I term information bases, from which elements of information could be extracted at will and composed on-the-fly. And if I could address any element, I only needed to store common information once, with the ability to use it many times. I liked the flexibility of the language, and yet its rigour, where everything was based on pre-defined rules as to what a document could and could not contain. It struck me as being very elegant, and what is elegant is usually efficient. And I could see that it would also be effective.

The rest is history in that SGML was published as an ISO standard in 1986, and was undergoing its five-year review at the time this book was published. It became ISO's fastest selling standard, as potential vendors of SGML systems and potential users sought to acquire knowledge about this new methodology, for that is what it is. SGML offers people a new way of dealing with information. To understand its potential requires a broad mind, emptied of preconceived notions of printed documents. SGML allows you to print and publish documents as you used to, but it is so much more than that. SGML allows you to put all your information in one great information base, with many different kinds of content present. It can be stored on a CD-ROM, say, with video clips and graphics of different kinds with the text, full of hypermedia links so retrieval of the required information can be instantaneous, with composition on-the-fly — no paper. There can be living documents, those in which content is liable to be changed frequently, yet up-to-date because it is held electronically — and these documents can be sent anywhere, instantly.

Very little of this appreciation comes through when reading ISO 8879. Indeed, ISO 8879 is meant to be used as a work of reference, and not read from beginning to end! This book imparts some of the background information to SGML, and gives a good flavour of the concepts on which it is based, without being too technical. It gives examples of some of the applications of SGML that have been developed in the last few years, and information about some of the more important facilities and features of the standard. But SGML alone is of little value, for sooner or later the document has to be sent from one system to another, and imaged. So there are chapters on the standards and technical reports related to SGML, including one on a comparison of ODA and SGML, and how to get office documents into an information base governed by SGML — the twain can meet.

The book is not meant to be exhaustive. With a standard that is infinitely flexible it would take a library of books to describe the many ways in which SGML could be exploited. Rather, I concentrate on what could be said to be some of the salient points, although this implies that I have made a subjective choice. I have chosen to expand on those points that seem key to understanding SGML and those which commonly afford some degree of difficulty to users. Certainly, I have not gone into all the myriad of detail so beloved by implementors of the language, and so necessary for some applications. But, hopefully, I have imparted sufficient information to get you started, not merely using SGML in a simplistic way, although that is how you are advised to start, but building towards the integrated information base, for that is where the true power of SGML lies. Then you will be using information in a new way, realizing how constricting the printed page is — ideally suited to books at bedtime, but out of keeping with the needs of the information age.

Above all, I hope that I have imparted something of my own enthusiasm for SGML. It can be a wonderful tool, and my wish is that you too discover some of its many uses. Otherwise, I shall have failed.

Joan M Smith
London
March 1992

Acknowledgements
No book on SGML is complete without acknowledgement to the editor of the standard, Dr Charles F Goldfarb. This I now make with gratitude, remembering many discussions on SGML itself and its widespread application which inspired me to write this book. He is undoubtedly the founding father of SGML. But if it could be said that there is an SGML guru in Europe it is surely Jean-Pierre Gaspart whose thinking influenced much of my approach to SGML. I must also single out Paul A Ellison, not only because we worked together on a subject dear to our hearts, but also because he patiently read the draft of this book. And Martin Bryan deserves a special mention for his dedication to the SGML cause over the years.

To acknowledge the role played by other inspirers I particularly thank members of ISO/IEC JTC 1/SC 18/WG 8. The meetings were always a source of pleasure as well as being hard work, and I made many friends from among those who were regular attenders.

Another person who must be mentioned by name is Robin Cover, who devoted much time to the compilation of a comprehensive bibliography on SGML matters. It was this bibliography to which I referred when checking that I had included certain information in this book.

Acronyms and abbreviations

AAP	Association of American Publishers
ACH	Association for Computers and the Humanities
ACL	Association for Computational Linguistics
AECMA	Association Européenne des Constructeurs de Matériel Aérospatial
AFII	Association for Font Information Interchange
AIA	Airline Industry Association
AITRC	Applied Information Technologies Research Center
ALLC	Association for Literary and Linguistic Computing
ALPS	Automated Logistics Publishing System
AMTOSS	Aircraft Maintenance Task Oriented Support System
ANSI	American National Standards Institute
AS	Australian Standard
ASCII	American Standard Code for Information Interchange
ASN.1	Abstract Syntax Notation One
ATA	Air Transport Association
AVIS	Audio Visual Interactive Scriptware
BS	British Standard
BSI	British Standards Institution
CALS	Computer-aided Acquisition and Logistic Support
CCITT	International Telegraph and Telephone Consultative Committee
CD	Committee Draft (ISO)
CD-I	Compact Disk — Interactive
CD-ROM	Compact Disk — Read-Only Memory
CEC	Commission of the European Communities
CEN	European Committee for Standardization
CENELEC	European Committee for Electrotechnical Standardization
CGM	Computer Graphics Metafile
CLPT	Computer Languages for the Processing of Text
CS	Central Secretariat (of ISO)

CSDB	Common Source Data Base (AECMA)
C&EN	Chemical & Engineering News
DAP	Document Application Profile (of ODA)
DAPHNE	Document Application Processing in a Heterogeneous Network Environment
DCF	Document Composition Facility (IBM)
DIN	Deutsches Institut für Normung
DIS	Draft International Standard (ISO)
DoD	Department of Defense (US)
DoE	Department of Energy (US)
DPA	Document Printing Application
DSSSL	Document Style Semantics and Specification Language
DTD	Document Type Definition
ECMA	European Computer Manufacturers Association
EDI	Electronic Data Interchange
EDIFACT	Electronic Data Interchange For Administration, Commerce, and Transport
EFA	European Fighter Aircraft
EH101	European Helicopter
ELS	Electronic Library System
EPO	European Patent Office
EPSIG	Electronic Publishing Special Interest Group
EWOS	European Workshop for Open Systems
EWS	European Workgroup on SGML
FAME	FORMEX Applied to Multilingualism in Europe
FIPS	Federal Information Processing Standard (US)
FOD	Functional ODA profile
FORMEX	Formalized Exchange of electronic publications
FSG	Functional SGML profile
FTAM	File Transfer, Access, and Management
GCA	Graphic Communications Association (US)
GML	Generalized Markup Language (IBM)
GOSIP	Government Open Systems Interconnection Profile (US and UK)
HDBK	Handbook (DoD)
HMSO	Her Majesty's Stationery Office
HyTime	Hypermedia Time-based structuring language
ICAM	Integrated Computer-Aided Manufacturing
IDEF	ICAM Definition language
IEC	International Electrotechnical Commission

IETM	Interactive Electronic Technical Manual (DoD)
IGES	Initial Graphics Exchange Specification
ISBN	International Standard Book Number
ISO	International Organization for Standardization
ISP	International Standardized Profile
JEMTOSS	Jet Engine Maintenance Task Oriented Support System
JTC	Joint Technical Committee (of ISO/IEC)
JTM	Job Transfer and Manipulation
LSAR	Logistic Support Analysis Record (DoD)
MHS	Message Handling Service
MIDI	Musical Instrument Digital Interface
MIL	Military (DoD)
MOTIS	Message Oriented Text Interchange System
NATO	North Atlantic Treaty Organization
NBS	National Bureau of Standards (now NIST)
NIAG	NATO Industry Advisory Group
NIAM	Nijssen's Information Analysis Method
NISO	National Information Standards Organization (US)
NIST	National Institute of Standards and Technology (US)
NSF	National Science Foundation (US)
OCR	Optical Character Recognition
ODA	Office/Open Document Architecture
ODL	Office Document Language
OSI	Open Systems Interconnection
PAGODA	Profile Alignment Group for ODA
PC	Personal Computer
PUB	Publication (FIPS)
RAMP	Rapid Acquisition of Manufactured Parts (DoD)
SC	Subcommittee (of ISO)
SDIF	SGML Document Interchange Format
SGML	Standard Generalized Markup Language
SGML-B	Standard Generalized Markup Language — Binary
SIG	Special Interest Group
SMDL	Standard Music Description Language
SPDL	Standard Page Description Language
SQL	Structured Query Language
STD	Standard (DoD)

STEP	Standard for the Exchange of Product model data
TC	Technical Committee (of ISO)
TCIF	Telecommunications Industry Forum
TEI	Text Encoding Initiative
TR	Technical Report (of ISO)
UK	United Kingdom
US	United States
WG	Working Group (of ISO)
WYSIWYG	What-You-See-Is-What-You-Get

1

Introduction

1.1 BACKGROUND

As its name implies, the Standard Generalized Markup Language (SGML) is a standard, an international standard in fact, developed by the International Organization for Standardization (ISO). Many people are interested in its being a standard with all that it implies — being able to interchange information with systems of different suppliers, and so on. Others are not — they are interested in SGML for its own sake, as a means of being able to mark up a document in a neutral way, independent of the many ways in which that document may eventually be processed.

The idea of being able to mark up documents independent of future processing requirements did not start life in a standards committee. In fact the history of SGML goes back to the late 1960s.[1,2] First of all there was the notion of generic coding, where a document could contain descriptive markup relating to the role of the element (for example chapter or paragraph) rather than its being marked up with formatting commands. The concept of generic coding was developed by the Graphic Communications Association (GCA), for which purpose it set up a GenCode Committee. Almost in parallel, there was a project under development in IBM on the Generalized Markup Language (GML), later made available as a product within its Document Composition Facility (DCF). Eventually, the two ideas met within the standards arena, for standards-making on behalf of the American National Standards Institute (ANSI), and SGML began to be developed.

It must be recognized that it was in the United States (US) that most of the development of the language was carried out over a period of years. However, it could be said that the work was enhanced by the inputs of standards-makers from other countries, notably in Europe and Canada, after the project was taken up by ISO. These inputs homed in on such issues as the use of character sets other than ASCII, the American Standard Code for Information Interchange. Languages based on other alphabets and scripts had to be allowed for; and languages based on the Latin alphabet but with accented letters and those with other diacritics and other requirements had to be allowed for, all in a good way, in a standard way, by permitting escape to other character sets in accordance with another ISO standard.[3] Another issue was that of conformance to the standard. Both these and other concerns were duly taken into account by the editor of SGML, Charles Goldfarb.

From 1984, the year when people from other countries began to take an active part in the development of SGML, there was never any doubt that it would become an international standard. In fact it took two more years, going from draft proposal via draft international standard (DIS) to international standard.

It was published by ISO as ISO 8879 on 15 October 1986 immediately after its approval, the reason it was able to emerge so quickly being the fact that the standard itself was published using its own methodology.[4]

Amendment 1 to ISO 8879 SGML was published on 15 July 1988, since when the standard has been stable. On 15 October 1991 it came up for its five-year review, and it is now expected that a new edition will be published.

1.2 STANDARDIZATION ASPECTS

Those who are not interested in the standards aspects of SGML may be tempted to skip this section. However, it addresses not only SGML but also other related standards and technical reports. It is included to provide useful additional background information for the benefit of those who want to get the record straight, and for those who must use standards when they exist. Sometimes the numbers are required for the purpose of ordering a copy of the standard, whether it be SGML or one of the related standards or technical reports. And details are often required in contracts when licensing software associated with standards, else how could conformance or compliance be expected?

Standards-making is not the privilege of a few chosen people. Anyone interested in taking part can usually find an organization willing to act as sponsor. It is not a task for the faint-hearted, however — it typically involves a great deal of work as well as attendance at meetings. Reconciling differences of opinion at meetings can be very time-consuming, and also frustrating for the technically minded. But at the end of the day, the drafts that are developed must be capable of attracting positive votes from member bodies. Member bodies of ISO are the national standards bodies, for example ANSI in the US, the British Standards Institution (BSI) in the United Kingdom (UK), and the Deutsches Institut für Normung (DIN) in Germany. There are also liaison members, such as the SGML Users' Group, without voting rights, but able to comment on drafts and also to provide input in other ways.

To have influenced the standards-making can make all the effort seem very worthwhile, and the work can be immensely satisfying in other ways, especially when the standard or technical report is finally published. Those who choose to participate are working with people, with personalities, and not with just so much paper. And all have a common goal — for the standards and technical reports to be as good as they can be made.

Early work on the SGML standard was carried out in what was known as ISO TC 97/SC 5 Programming Languages, where there was an Experts' Group on Computer Languages for the Processing of Text (CLPT). It had attracted relatively little attention in this subcommittee, for who would think of looking for standards development on the structure of information among programming languages? However, as part of the re-organization of the parent technical committee (TC), SGML came under the aegis of what later became known as ISO/IEC JTC 1/SC 18. The International Electrotechnical Commission (IEC) joined with ISO to form a Joint Technical Committee (JTC) for work items in the field of Information Processing. Its subcommittee (SC) 18 was responsible for Text and Office Systems for which a working group (WG 8) was set up for the now broader remit of Text Description and Processing Languages, including CLPT as one of its work items. (To bring the ISO titles up-to-date, that of SC 18 is now Document Processing and Related Communication, and its WG 8 is Document Description and Processing Languages, these reflecting the changing nature of the topics covered.)

CLPT was assigned a project number, there being subdivisions for several subprojects. SGML is the main project (15), subprojects being for ancillary standards and technical reports. Examples of ancillary standards are the SGML Document Interchange Format (SDIF), and the two text composition standards. Technical reports are developed when the subject matter is considered to be unsuitable for publication as a standard in its own right, for example the operational model, and a description of techniques for using SGML. Other projects associated with SGML are those to do with fonts (27), font services (33), conformance testing for SGML systems (36), the Standard Music Description Language (SMDL) and the Hypermedia/Time-based structuring language (HyTime) (39), and the abstract definition of SGML for binary encoding (SGML-B) (40).

When draft text has been approved for international ballot, the proposed standard or technical report is allocated a number (not related to its project number). This number is quoted in all ballots, and remains with the standard or technical report throughout its lifetime.

Published standards and technical reports (TRs) are:

- ISO 8879 Information Processing — Text and Office Systems — Standard Generalized Markup Language (SGML), 15 October 1986,
  - — Amendment 1, 1 July 1988;
- ISO 9069 Information Processing — SGML Support Facilities — SGML Document Interchange Format (SDIF), 15 September 1988;
- ISO/IEC 9070 Information Technology — SGML Support Facilities — Registration Procedures for Public Text Owner Identifiers, second edition, 15 April 1991;
- ISO/IEC 9541 Information Technology — Font Information Interchange
  - — Part 1 Architecture, 15 September 1991,
  - — Part 2 Interchange Format, 15 September 1991;
- ISO/TR 9544 Information Processing — Computer-Assisted Publishing — Vocabulary, 15 July 1988;
- ISO/IEC TR 9573 Information Processing — SGML Support Facilities — Techniques for Using SGML, 1 December 1988,
  - — Part 13 Public Entity Sets for Mathematics and Science, 1 July 1991;
- ISO/IEC TR 10037 Information Technology — SGML and Text-Entry Systems — Guidelines for SGML Syntax-Directed Editing Systems, 15 March 1991.

It should also be noted that French text exists for ISO 8879 SGML and ISO 9069 SDIF:

- ISO 8879 Traitement de l'information — Systèmes bureautiques — Langage normalisé de balisage généralisé (SGML);
- ISO 9069 Traitement de l'information — Facilités de support SGML — Format d'échange de documents SGML (SDIF).

Final text for publication is being prepared for:

- ISO/IEC DIS 9541 Information Technology — Font Information Interchange — Part 3 Glyph Shape Representation;
- ISO/IEC DIS 10036 Information Technology — Procedure for Registration of Glyph and Glyph Collection Identifiers;
- ISO/IEC DIS 10180 Information Processing — Text Composition — Standard Page Description Language (SPDL).

Note that part 4 of ISO/IEC 9541, the font information interchange standard, on language-specific extensions, is still at the stage of working draft. Work continues on the fonts standard, its being proposed that part 2 incorporates extensions to the interchange capabilities, and part 3 has an addendum to accommodate the development of bit-mapped glyph-shape representations.

SPDL is one of the two text composition standards, the other being:

- ISO/IEC DIS 10179 Information Processing — Text Composition — Document Style Semantics and Specification Language (DSSSL).

At the time of writing, DSSSL is to undergo a second DIS ballot, with publication of the approved standard expected during 1993.

There is also the proposed technical report on the Operational Model for Document Description and Processing Languages, where this will describe the inter-relationships of the standards developed by WG 8 — the working group responsible for Document Description and Processing Languages. (The title of the technical report had reflected the former title of WG 8, and it is assumed here that it too will be changed for the sake of alignment.) Work on this had been delayed until such time that it was clear how the fonts and text composition standards would relate to SGML and SDIF and to each other, but it is now progressing.

As may be inferred from the list of published standards and technical reports above, ISO/IEC TR 9573 Techniques for Using SGML is being re-organized. This is being done in conjunction with the review of ISO 8879 SGML, when the informative annexes to the standard, which contain text of a tutorial nature, will be removed and included in the re-organized edition of ISO/IEC TR 9573. The proposed structure is:

- Part 1 SGML Tutorial;
- Part 2 Basic Techniques;
- Part 3 Advanced Techniques;
- Part 4 Using Short References for Identifying Markup;
- Part 5 Using Non-Latin Alphabets;
- Part 6 Referencing and Synchronization;
- Part 7 Mathematics and Chemistry;
- Part 8 Tables;

- Part 9 Using SGML for Computer to Computer Interchange;
- Part 10 Designing Applications for Database Interfacing;
- Part 11 Application at ISO Central Secretariat for International Standards and Technical Reports;
- Part 12 Public Entity Sets for General and Publishing Symbols;
- Part 13 Public Entity Sets for Mathematics and Science;
- Part 14 Public Entity Sets for Latin Based Alphabets;
- Part 15 Public Entity Sets for Non-Latin Based Alphabets;
- Part 16 Public Entity Sets for Ideograms.

Part 13 Public Entity Sets for Mathematics and Science has already been published (as stated above). The balloting process is well underway for part 11, Application at ISO Central Secretariat for International Standards and Technical Reports, this being the application of SGML developed by ISO Central Secretariat itself for its own publications. And a working draft of part 4 on the use of short references is available.

No drafts have yet been made generally available for work on Font Services, where a two part standard is proposed:

- Part 1 Abstract Service Definition;
- Part 2 Protocol Specification.

Similarly, no draft is yet available in ISO on Conformance Testing for SGML Systems, although work has been done on this project on behalf of ANSI. It is expected that the ISO fast-track procedure will be invoked to reduce the number of ballots required, and thus hasten publication of the proposed standard, based on the ANSI text.

Considerable work had been done in the US on what is known as HyTime, one of the relatively new work items, the first ballot for which was organized very quickly. Coupled with HyTime is the Standard Music Description Language (SMDL), an application of HyTime, where again a substantial draft had been developed in the US. Although SMDL was still at the stage of committee draft (CD) at the time of writing, HyTime was at the DIS stage, with publication expected mid-1992.

- ISO/IEC CD 10743 Information Processing — Standard Music Description Language (SMDL);
- ISO/IEC DIS 10744 Information Processing — Hypermedia/Time-Based Structuring Language (HyTime).

Then there is SGML-B, an abstract definition for binary encoding of the SGML human-readable encoding. Text has yet to be developed, although the concepts are already being tested.

Of course, SGML itself quotes standards not developed by WG 8, for example those for character sets. And SGML, in turn, is used by standards developed by other working groups and subcommittees, for example the ISO standard for Office Document Architecture (ODA). These are what are termed applications of SGML. Many applications are not standardized by ISO, as would be expected, and they too can bring together SGML with other standards, for example the application of SGML by the US Department of Defense (DoD) where there are those for graphics as well as several for character sets.

All this has been about ISO standards, as it is recognized by the national standards bodies that in the area of information processing it is necessary to have international standards for communication internationally. That is why national standards are no longer developed, rather the national standards bodies provide input to ISO. However, once an ISO standard has been published, a national standards body could bring out what is termed a dual-numbered standard. This practice is followed by BSI in the UK, for cases when it is prudent for a government department, say, to quote a British standard (BS) number instead of an ISO number. There are thus BS 6868 SGML (alias ISO 8879) and BS 7138 SDIF (alias ISO 9069), the text being identical in both cases. The same approach was adopted in Australia where there are AS 3514 SGML and AS 3649 SDIF.

This too was done by CEN/CENELEC when it was desirable for there to be standards that could be quoted within Europe, CEN being the European Committee for Standardization and CENELEC the European Committee for Electrotechnical Standardization. Both SGML and SDIF were adopted as European standards, the ISO numbers being prefixed by a 2 for CEN/CENELEC purposes.

It is stressed that in no way has the text for either ISO 8879 SGML or ISO 9069 SDIF been altered or subset by either BSI, the Standards Association of Australia, or CEN/CENELEC. The advantage of carrying out what effectively became renumbering processes is that these international standards may be used even when the contract calls for a national or a European standard. And in the case of the European standards, it may well be that projects emanating from the Commission of the European Communities (CEC) are more likely to attract funding if the standards quoted are European ones.

1.3 OBJECTIVES OF SGML

When designing SGML, many criteria were borne in mind.[5] First of all the language had to be independent of systems, devices, languages, and applications.

System-independence — so documents prepared on the system of one vendor could be processed on that of another vendor. This means that a company can use the standard on any manufacturer's system, now and in the future, not being tied to one specific vendor. One reason why the working with different systems is achieved is because SGML deals with virtual storage, which the implementor can map to physical storage for a specific system.

Device-independence — with support for existing devices, so all input and output devices could continue to be used, the new user having to license or develop new software but not having to buy new hardware; and so documents would not relate to specific types of hardware, whether screens or printers, for example. Who knows what types of hardware will be invented in the next few years? And information prepared now must be able to be output on them too. It must be useful for compact disk — read-only memory (CD-ROM) and compact disk — interactive (CD-I), for example.

Language-independence — so the standard could be used equally well in Greece, The Netherlands, or Poland, for example. It must be usable for Latin based alphabets and non-Latin based alphabets, as well as other forms of writing.

Application-independence — so the standard could be used for a wide variety of documents from many different sources. It must be as useful for the encoding of very simple documents as for very complex; for the encoding of highly technical documents and texts that contain a wealth of linguistic information. It must be useful for what are termed 'living' documents, where the content is subject to change.

Other criteria consciously taken into account during the development of SGML were:

- support for existing conventions, that is there had to be the possibility of effecting what is termed retroactive conversion of documents prepared using existing word processing packages;
- the inclusion of content other than text, opening the door to graphics, sound, and any other kind of information;
- the markup to be usable by both humans and machines.

There were many other objectives and criteria, unstated formally but nevertheless addressed, that gave SGML the flexibility it has today.[5] And it was in meeting the objectives that led to the many uses of SGML.

1.4 USES OF SGML

Although it can be said that SGML came from a publishing background, 'SGML can be used for publishing in its broadest definition, ranging from single medium conventional publishing to multi-media database publishing', as stated in the Introduction to ISO 8879.

In the clause defining the Field of Application, it is stated: 'The Standard Generalized Markup Language can be used for documents that are processed by any text processing or word processing system.'

It goes on to state that it is particularly applicable to documents that are interchanged among systems with differing text processing languages, and documents that are processed in more than one way, even when the procedures use the same text processing language.

So where does the snag lie? 'Documents that exist solely in final formatted form are not within the field of application of this International Standard.'

But that is not a snag in reality, as will readily be appreciated when the concepts on which SGML is based are explained in Chapter 2. And if documents are to include previously formatted text, this has been allowed for in that a document may contain 'arbitrary data content'.

SGML can be used for:

- *encoding documents*, even those with a wealth of structure for machine-assisted translation, for example;
- *interchanging documents*, maybe for sending documents from one partner in a consortium to others;

- *working with documents* in different ways, even taking information from tables and presenting it in business graphics;
- *re-using elements of information* many times, perhaps using certain paragraphs of text for all recipients of otherwise personalized mail.

Consider some of the types of publications for which SGML is suitable:

- *office documents*, from the very simple to the very complex;
- *address lists*, which may be updated regularly, and from which labels are to be printed;
- *memoranda*, even those that are ephemeral, and certainly for those to be kept;
- *letters*, complete with logo and whatever else is required;
- *contract information*, for this is usually retained for a long period;
- *catalogues*, where some entries change but others remain the same;
- *directories*, able to reflect changes quickly, and where the information may be output in different ways, listed by name, telephone number, etc;
- *training materials*, where much of the information can probably be taken from manuals and presented in a different way;
- *slides*, so even presentation material can be in accordance with a company style;
- *reports*, reflecting a company style, yet leaving the author free to concentrate on the content and to forget about how it is to be presented;
- *technical manuals*, which may contain many different kinds of information, with emphasis on its always being up-to-date;
- *journals*, again reflecting a house style, and where there can be ancillary publications such as abstracts of all articles on a certain subject;
- *books*, allowing for the publication of US and European editions, and second editions when updating is required;
- *dictionaries*, where the inclusion of subject codes, for example, permits ready publication of specialist dictionaries;
- *encyclopaedias*, that may always be kept up-to-date, or viewed as hypermedia documents (explained in Chapter 8);
- *parts lists*, that may be associated with stock control systems;
- *schedules*, reflecting changes as made;
- *timetables*, that could be treated as information for a form;
- *financial information*, because speed of publication is essential;
- *trade data*, so it may be used in a meaningful way by the accounts department for stock control and organizing the work of the shop floor, for example;
- *forms*, where it is the content that would be stored, and not the forms themselves which relate to presentation;
- *invoices*, associating them with orders and payment;
- *inventories*, so the stock situation can be known at any time.

In fact SGML can be used for any type of document. Some may not think of using SGML for huge advertisements on the road to the airport, enticing people to buy duty free goods, for example, although an advertising agency could well use SGML for that application. It would not make sense, however, to license an SGML system purely for ephemeral documents; use a desktop publishing system for that. But if you already have SGML on your system, then you can use it for memoranda or notes or any other type of document. Why not? And you can erase ephemera but retain important memoranda or notes, perhaps relating to a nut and bolt to be used on an engine. It could be necessary to know who made the decision to use a certain alloy for a bolt or to change the supplier were the bolt to shear and cause an accident at some future date, in which case all the information needed to respond to an enquiry should conceptually be in one place.

From the above examples, it can be appreciated that SGML can be used for the more conventional forms of publishing, yet equally it can be used for all company information that has to be kept in an integrated information base. This integrated information base could be used as a publishing base or as a management information system, and everything in between.

Consider some of the many different types of information that a document may contain:

- *text*, and it is the text in a document that is parsed, or checked for markup;
- *two or more writing directions*, for after all this is an output issue, not one of storage or processing;
- *foreign languages*, where the requirements can be dealt with either by ‘escaping’ to other character sets or by specifying the individual characters;
- *special symbols*, for any kind of application, that are not found on the usual keyboard but which may be imaged;
- *mathematics*, representing mathematical formulas as a language, to assist imaging (perhaps for very long equations that must be split at an appropriate place, or to insert the variables for computation);
- *chemical formulas*, for output in a correct way;
- *benzine rings*, for output as desired;
- *publishing characters*, with the ability to distinguish between the hyphen, the minus sign, an em rule, and an en rule, for example;
- *line drawings* of any kind;
- *business graphics*, whether pie charts, bar charts, histograms, or whatever else is required;
- *spreadsheets*, part of the facilities required in an office environment;
- *scanned images*, maybe for inclusion in a manual;
- *tiled raster images*, when a large engineering drawing has to be divided into sections for ease of imaging or editing;
- *photographs*, in full colour if required;
- *sound*, for commenting on text, for there to be a voice reading a warning, say, or to have background sound of some description;
- *video*, or video clips, maybe to demonstrate removal of a defective part;
- *moving pictures*, where these could be animated graphics to show how something is assembled;
- *complex tables*, a table being described in terms of rows and columns, with the result that any cell may be individually addressed — even large matrices may be stored this way, prior to computations being performed, or output of the matrix;

- *computed data*, for spreadsheets, business graphics, performing calculations on data in forms or tables, or in accordance with mathematical formulas that form part of the document.

So an integrated information base may include all these different types of information. They may or may not be the subject of standards themselves —just because there is not yet an ISO standard for sound does not mean that SGML documents may not contain sound, for they can and do.

Different kinds of standards could be involved, not only ISO standards but also national standards and CCITT recommendations developed by the International Telegraph and Telephone Consultative Committee. Examples are:

- SGML to govern the information base, and for markup of the text present;
- the ISO EDIFACT standard for trade data (EDIFACT being the ISO standard for Electronic Data Interchange For Administration, Commerce, and Transport);
- the CCITT group 4 facsimile recommendation for scanned images;
- ODA for office documents to enter an information base;
- the ANSI Initial Graphics Exchange Specification (IGES) for product data, in the short-term;
- the proposed ISO Standard for the Exchange of Product model data (STEP) for product data, in the long-term;
- Computer Graphics Metafile (CGM), an ISO standard for vector graphics;
- character set standards and ISO registered character sets.

The communications standards would be required to get information into and out of the information base. Here we think particularly of the Open Sytems Interconnection (OSI) standards, based on the ISO seven-layer model. The Government Open Systems Interconnection Profiles (GOSIPs), US and UK varieties, may be used. And SDIF would come into its own for communicating SGML documents. More of this later, when the concepts on which SGML is based are understood better. For the moment, suffice it to say that SGML offers:

- a new way of thinking about information;
- a new way of dealing with information;
- a new methodology;
- a new way of addressing information at the element level;
- the concept of store-once-use-many-times;
- infinite flexibility.

And it is this infinite flexibility that commends SGML to many users, as they are aware that they will be able to include in their SGML solution all their existing documentation and requirements, as well as being able to take them into the future.

Notes

(1) Those interested in reading what is regarded as the official version of the history of SGML should turn to Appendix 1: A Brief History of the Development of SGML.

(2) Another description of the development of SGML, albeit from the viewpoint of the UK, is Joan M Smith, *The Standard Generalized Markup Language and Related*

Issues, British National Bibliography Research Fund Report 22, The British Library (1986). (Full bibliographic information about all publications cited is given in Chapter 12.)

(3) The standard alluded to is ISO 2022 Information Processing — ISO 7-Bit and 8-Bit Coded Character Sets — Code Extension Techniques. This standard opens up a veritable Pandora's box of possibilities for the use of any other character set.

(4) ISO 8879 Information Processing — Text and Office Systems — Standard Generalized Markup Language (SGML) was the eventual title of the standard. Transmission of the final marked up text took place as Charles Goldfarb left the US for Geneva. The fully-composed, camera-ready copy awaited his arrival at Geneva.

(5) For a fuller account of the criteria SGML had to meet, see the Introduction to the standard, ISO 8879. In addition to its being published in the standard, this is also available in the form of a leaflet from the SGML Users' Group.

2

The Standard Generalized Markup Language

2.1 CONCEPTS ON WHICH SGML IS BASED

How much we take for granted when we read, never stopping to think how the information is structured. Always there are layout characteristics associated with any information that we see, whether it be on a screen or on paper or on any other medium. This is in contradistinction to the information that we hear, where there is nothing other than a pause, the words themselves, or a change in tone or pitch to indicate a change of subject for instance.

The ability to store information electronically, brought about by technological advances, was not being used to its fullest advantage, and a new way of dealing with information was required. Of course, since international communications were becoming a reality, it was essential that there was an international standard that stated how information would be structured so it could be sent from one device to another where it would be readily understood. Whilst this could have been dealt with by a document architecture,[1] how much more flexibility could be gained by developing a description language, which could provide an open-ended approach to deal with any kind of document. And that is where SGML comes into its own.

As stated in the preceding chapter, SGML documents may contain any type of content. A report, for example, can contain business graphics, or scanned images, say. Documents are becoming ever more sophisticated, and the standard had to be able to take into account not only existing forms of information that may be stored electronically, whether or not they are standardized, but also any other type of information that may be digitized at some future date — may be holograms.

The standard had to be rigorous, that is it had to be based on rules in such a manner that there could be something against which the presence (or absence) of elements could be checked. This facility meant that there could be the notion of rules relating to different types of documents, against which the individual instances of that type may be checked. So there could be a set of rules for reports, say, of which an instance or example could be the company report of xyz for the year 1992.

Given that SGML is a description or representation language, it can also be used to describe unusual characters that may be imaged but which do not appear on a normal (ASCII) keyboard. Already mentioned is the ability to escape to other character sets when it is necessary to work in languages other than English.

This ability to represent entities (for that is what they are called) by way of a string of ASCII characters to describe one symbol can also be used in another way, that is to represent files of information stored elsewhere (the SGML virtual files). This is useful to refer to existing parts of the document, for example, or maybe a complex table or a figure perhaps. The character string could also be an abbreviation that would be expanded on output to its full form.

To sum up, SGML is a standard; it is system-independent in that SGML documents can be sent from one system to another of a different manufacturer; it is device-independent in that documents may be output to a variety of devices (using associated standards); it is language-independent in that different sets of rules may apply to different types of documents; it is also very flexible in that complex tables, mathematical equations, and chemical formulas may be described; it is all-encompassing in that a document may include any kind of content, text and illustrations, say; it is rigorous in that everything is governed by rules. Its greatest strength is that it is a *representation* language, able to represent any type of document.

2.2 THE NOTION OF MARKUP

In order to give information about the structure of the document that is to be input to the system, markup is added to the beginning and end of every element, where an element could be considered as an object of information. Quite simply, a warning about high voltage electricity, say, that appears in a technical manual, could be preceded by a start-tag of <w> and followed by an end-tag of </w>. Similarly, a note could be delimited by <n> and </n> and a paragraph by <p> and </p>. That is not to say, however, that it is necessary to key in the tags for a paragraph as their presence could be inferred by the system and they could be system-supplied. This is known as markup minimization, something that is catered for by several optional features of the language.

Whilst angled brackets are defined as delimiters for the tags themselves in what is known as the reference concrete syntax of the language, other conventions may be used, if there is a preference for square brackets, for example. The mnemonics employed to denote element names (known as generic identifiers) are chosen by the document type designer and may vary from application to application. Whilst it makes a good deal of sense to use a base set of generic identifiers if dealing with paragraphs, notes, and warnings, etc in a number of types of documents, specific applications may well have very different requirements. Those of a dictionary encoding rich lexicographical structure will be different from those encoding highly technical material in another language. Remember that SGML is application-independent and also language-independent.

Elements may also have attributes that give additional information about an element. For example there could be a status attribute for a manual that shows it is a draft version <man status=draft>. Elements may be uniquely identified, a very powerful facility as will be shown, where <man id=EFA> attaches the identification and idref is used when the element is referred to subsequently in the text. Of course, application software would have to be written to deal with all these facilities.

Just as <and> are delimiters for tags if the reference concrete syntax is used, so & and ; are delimiters for entity references in accordance with the reference concrete syntax, although they too may be changed to something else if desired. ☎ would cause a telephone symbol to be displayed on output, assuming that the symbol was available on the output device. Almost a thousand such symbols are accorded entity names in annex D of the standard.[2] All these may be keyed in using an ASCII or similar keyboard. Similarly, &SGML; could result in Standard Generalized Markup Language being output if this had been declared as an entity in the document type declaration subset preceding the document instance.

2.3 WHAT SGML IS

Standard — First and foremost it is recognized that SGML is a standard, an international standard, so there can be communication internationally. And whilst there are dual-numbered versions, the text is identical, with no national or regional variations of any description. It is because SGML is an international standard that it has attracted so many different kinds of applications, in the full knowledge that software is readily available since it is supported by many countries.

Generalized — The second element in its name, generalized, could be said to refer to many of the aspects of SGML. First of all it is generalized in that documents are marked up in a neutral way, documents being stored in a neutral form. This is achieved by the use of generic identifiers for elements of information instead of process-specific identifiers. So a paragraph could be preceded by <p> instead of coding that told the formatter to set the following text in Times Roman, 10 on 12 point, and so on. Because the markup is generalized, and not tied to any one system, it suffices for all future processing of the document, now or in fifty years' time, say. It is because the generic identifiers may be chosen for an application, SGML uses virtual storage, and has other similar characteristics, that it can be said to be generalized in that it is independent of system, device, language, and application.

Markup — Markup as a concept has been introduced already, in that it is information added to a document to indicate its structure. Some say that it adds structure to a document, but this is erroneous in that the structure is already present, and the markup is there just to give information about that structure, where the markup may be used by a human or by a machine. The structure that is being marked up could be elements such as sections, subsections, paragraphs, notes, warnings, and definitions.

```
<n>This is a note.</n>
```

Rules are given on how to mark up a type of document in what is called a document type definition (DTD), which could be for a memorandum, say. It is the designer of the application who would specify the rules for the markup; the markup itself is not standardized. This is something else that makes SGML application-independent, and language-independent. And whilst on the subject of markup, note that the markup could be system-supplied; it does not have to be added by an author, although it could be.

Language — It is not strictly true to call SGML a language in that a language has both syntax and semantics. SGML is a metalanguage; it has syntax, but not semantics. The application of SGML provides the meaning — that p means paragraph, and so on. However, because the L in SGML stands for language, this is the word that will be used throughout the book. SGML is a representation language, and can be used to describe any document. It can also be used to describe symbols. If ¶ were keyed in, a paragraph sign, sometimes called a pilcrow, would be imaged. And if ¥ were keyed in, a yen symbol would be imaged.[2] (There are many lists of these symbols as will be described later.)

2.4 HOW SGML WORKS

2.4.1 The structure of information

Embodied in SGML is the recognition that two structures may be associated with information: the role of the information, and how it is presented. These can be referred to as the *logical structure* and the *layout structure*, both of which can be associated with the same information content. If we think of a report, its logical structure could be that it consists of a title, the name of the author, the date of the publication, the company name, and other information that would be associated with the front matter; then the main body which could consist of a number of headed sections, which may contain subsections, which could consist of paragraphs and maybe notes, and so on. These are called the elements of the document. The layout structure for the same report would state how these elements would appear on a piece of paper or maybe on a screen. There would be font information, that on how headings are to appear, the width of the column(s) for the main text, and so on.

Of course, many different layout structures could be associated with the same document. There could be many different styles of presentation associated with one medium. For the final printed version of the report there could be one, two, or even three column layout, justified or unjustified versions, the first word of paragraphs indented or full out, or maybe the first after the heading full out and the rest indented . . . . The draft version, produced on a low quality printer, could be different again, as would that on a screen, where there could be differences between the high resolution forms and those for low resolution screens. And then we think of other forms of output that may be desired.

Another point that can be made here is that house styles change over a period of years, and this must be recognized when storing information. If the logical structure only was stored for documents in an information base, then new and different layout structures could be applied on output over the years, even for output devices and methods not yet invented. Here we are recognizing that the information base is going to be in existence for a long time. And this is as well, as a recent requirement for documentation for a particular weapon system is that it be updatable throughout its expected life cycle plus ten years, sixty years in all for this case. It is possible using SGML. SGML addresses the logical structure of a document, not (usually) the layout structure, for which there are other related standards. SGML does, however, give the possibility of linking the logical structure with one or several layout structures, whether or not the link information is stored with the document or associated with it only on output in the future.

In summary, two structures are usually associated with a document:

- the logical structure
  — sections, subsections, paragraphs, etc;
- the layout structure
  — how the information is presented,
  — the number of columns, their width, font choice, etc.

In SGML the two structures are entirely separate.

The concern of SGML is only with the logical structure, the information content of the document, and its storage in a neutral form. What SGML allows is the *linking* of the logical structure to (many) layout structure(s). Thus a variety of styles may be associated with the logical structure, for different media and within a medium. This linking is done by means of the link features of SGML. However, the layout structure/information *may* be represented in SGML. In fact this is done when ODA documents have to be brought into an SGML environment. After all, there is nothing in SGML, since it is a representation language, to prevent layout characteristics from being described; but is not considered to be good practice. Leave layout considerations for later, as a completely separate issue.

Forget about layout; think only of the information.

2.4.2 What the language includes

2.4.2.1 Syntaxes

The notion of SGML having syntax but no semantics has already been introduced. In fact SGML is an *abstract syntax*, stating how to mark up a document. This may sound very erudite, and of no direct concern to someone who wishes to know basic principles only.

What it means is that there are rules that define how markup is added to the document, without regard to the specific characters used to represent that markup. SGML does not compel the use of particular characters as delimiters, for example; it merely states what the roles are of the various delimiters.

It is the *concrete syntax* that assigns characters to those delimiters, binding the abstract syntax to particular delimiter characters, quantities, markup declaration names, and so on.

Here the standard is helpful in giving an example of a concrete syntax, known as the *reference concrete syntax*. In the words of the Introduction to ISO 8879, the reference concrete syntax 'binds the abstract syntax to specific characters and numeric values'. Criteria for defining *variant concrete syntaxes* are also specified.

Consider the following statements:

- the *abstract concrete syntax* states that there shall be a start-tag and an end-tag for an element, and that these tags shall have delimiters;
- the *reference concrete syntax* assigns < and > for delimiters for a start-tag (start-tag open and start-tag close, respectively), and </ and > for an end-tag (end-tag open and end-tag close, respectively);

- a *variant concrete syntax* could assign [and] for delimiters for a start-tag (start-tag open and start-tag close, respectively), and [/ and] for an end-tag (end-tag open and end-tag close, respectively), or indeed any other characters chosen for the application.

Most applications use the reference concrete syntax for markup characters, and in this book the angled brackets associated with the reference concrete syntax have been used. In many applications, however, one or two of the values tend to be changed. More of that later. The point being made here is that an application is not tied to specific delimiters or values. This is another aspect of application-independence.

Details of the concrete syntax being used for an application are contained in the SGML declaration. There is more about this in the next chapter.

2.4.2.2 Markup declarations

The language also includes *markup declarations*. In fact there are thirteen kinds of markup declarations.[3] One of them is the SGML declaration, referred to above. Another is the document declaration; others are for elements, defining what attributes an element may have, entities, different notations used, and so on.

It is these declarations that allow a user to define a specific vocabulary. Many of the declarations are used in the document type definition, or DTD as it is more usually called. It is here that the element declarations are made, stating what generic identifiers are assigned, and the relationships of one element to another. Lists of attributes that the elements may have are declared. Entities are declared, both to allow the representation of symbols for imaging purposes and to permit short-forms of lengthy phrases, say, to be keyed in for expansion on output. The different notations used for different types of content a document may contain are listed, where these would typically be for raster and vector graphics to permit illustrations. And the name of the DTD is contained in the DOCTYPE or document type declaration — another markup declaration.

Comment declarations may appear anywhere! These are most useful. They can be used to good effect in the SGML declaration to document why the reference concrete syntax has been changed, for example. In the DTD they could document what the expanded versions are of the element names, for example that p = paragraph, n = note. Comment declarations may also appear in the document itself, known as the document instance.

2.4.3 Provisions of the language

2.4.3.1 Various types of content

One of the great strengths of SGML is that documents may contain various types of content, not just text. In fact SGML documents may contain *any* type of content that may be represented electronically. These could be for graphics (both raster and vector), illustrations, audio, interactive video, computed data, and so on. This point has been made before, but bears repetition if only because many people erroneously think that SGML is just for text.

When an SGML document is parsed, or run through software that checks its validity in accordance with the standard, the text will be checked for markup whilst other types of content are acknowledged and then skipped over as it were. How the system deals with a different type of content is another matter. Its possible inclusion is notified in the SGML declaration as a specific notation; it is then up to the system to call in special software able to process that type of content.

The notations used may be in accordance with another standard, for example vector graphics in accordance with the ISO CGM standard. But they need not be standardized. For example there is no standard yet for colour photographs, but they may be included in an SGML document.[4] The systems used by the person who included the photographs must be able to handle them, as must the system of the person to whom the document is being sent. The point being made is that *SGML documents may contain any type of content, not just text.*

In fact, SGML can be considered as the glue that holds together the different types of content.

2.4.3.2 External references to other content

Not everything need be included in a document. There is provision within SGML to refer to content held externally, even outside the system on which a user is working. Examples are references to existing chapters of a book that is being written, a company copyright statement, all the special symbols needed by an application, photographs, or other types of content.

These are called *entity references*. This is the virtual storage system that was mentioned earlier. It is up to the implementation on a specific system to manage this storage in a physical way. Because SGML does not deal with specific locations it is system-independent.

An entity is the content of a storage location. Entities may also be thought of as being in entity sets or libraries, held outside the document that is created.

Some of these entity sets and entities can be common to a type of document, in which case their existence is specified in the DTD for that application. For example in the case of complex technical manuals, it is expected that most of them will require some special symbols. So declarations about these entity sets are included in the DTD.

Now one of those technical manuals may require reference to many chemical compounds, and for the sake of brevity the author could arrange to key in pvc (with delimiters) instead of polyvinyl chloride, for example, for the full form to be imaged when required. Entity declarations for these chemical compounds could therefore be added to the DTD when referring to it at the beginning of the document instance.

Equally, there could be entities in a 'library' for all the diagrams used in a technical manual. This is very convenient, as this library could be the responsibility of the draughtsman, for use by the technical author as the diagrams are referred to in the text of the manual. If they are used in many manuals comprising a set for an engine, say, how much more efficient the system becomes.

And if, within a manual, some sections had already been prepared, and this had been declared, they could be referred to by entity references within the document instance now being created.

An example of an entity declaration to be added to the DTD is:

```
<!ENTITY SGML "Standard Generalized Markup Language">
```

<! is the opening delimiter for a declaration and > the closing delimiter. ENTITY signifies the kind of declaration. The declaration itself consists of the letters to be keyed in (SGML in the example given) followed by what is to be imaged on output, where the string to be imaged is enclosed within double quotation marks. Thus SGML is the entity name, and Standard Generalized Markup Language is the entity.

In the text, instead of keying in Standard Generalized Markup Language, key in &SGML; as the entity reference for the full form to be imaged on output.

From the above it is seen that & and ; are the delimiters for entity references (& the opening delimiter and ; the closing delimiter).

All these delimiters are from the reference concrete syntax, but they may be changed to other characters by the application in the SGML declaration if desired.

Using & and ; as delimiters, other examples could be:

- – to result in the imaging of an en dash;
- &ch4; to refer to the contents of a file containing chapter 4.

In the first case, where a publishing character is to be imaged, reference is to an entity set declared in the DTD, whereas in the second case the entity has been created locally and must be added to the DTD.

As can be imagined, there are many hundreds of special symbols that people could wish to have imaged, that cannot be keyed in directly from an ASCII or similar keyboard. Ones in common use have been grouped logically into sets of entities, and are listed in annex D of ISO 8879. There are many sets:

- alphabetic characters
    - — Latin — added Latin 1,
    - — Latin — added Latin 2,
    - — Greek alphabetic characters,
    - — Cyrillic alphabetic characters;
- general use
    - — numeric and special graphic characters,
    - — diacritical mark characters,
    - — publishing characters,
    - — box and line drawing characters;
- technical
    - — general,
    - — Greek symbols,
    - — alternative Greek symbols;
- additional mathematical symbols
    - — ordinary symbols,
    - — binary and large operators,
    - — relations,
    - — negated relations,
    - — arrow relations,
    - — opening and closing delimiters.

Because most people would wish to refer to the same sets, they have been given a public name. This also has the advantage that imaging devices throughout the world will (hopefully) be able to recognize the entity reference and image the desired symbol, as everyone will use the same entity reference to refer to a given symbol. It cannot be assumed, however, that the receiver will be able to image the required symbol.

To give an example, the entity declaration that would have to be present in the DTD to cause an en dash to be imaged is that relating to the set of publishing characters listed in ISO 8879. As this is public text, it is associated with the FORMAL feature of SGML.

2.5 FEATURES OF SGML

2.5.1 General

There are eleven optional features of SGML that may or may not be implemented on a system. These are:

- markup minimization
  - SHORTTAG
  - OMITTAG
  - SHORTREF
  - DATATAG
  - RANK
- link features
  - SIMPLE
  - IMPLICIT
  - EXPLICIT
- others
  - CONCUR
  - SUBDOC
  - FORMAL

2.5.2 Markup minimization

SHORTTAG is the means by which part or all of the usual markup may be omitted from a tag. An empty end-tag would be </>, when the parser would assume that the (omitted) generic identifier was the same as that of the most recently started but unended element. Use of this feature for empty end-tags is not recommended to the novice as there could be confusion if employed in conjunction with the OMITTAG feature. In fact much more of the tag can be omitted, if the system can infer that the markup is present. However, some of those uses are best left to a system to apply in accordance with rules. Another use of the feature is for the omission of an attribute name, only the value being necessary. An example of this would be 'secret' as the value for a security attribute. And if SHORTTAG is being used, an attribute value does not need to be enclosed within quotation marks, unless it includes certain characters, including a space. So if a document were classified as 'top secret', quotation marks would be required.

OMITTAG means that some tags may be omitted altogether if their presence can be inferred unambiguously from the context, this being in accordance with rules specified in the DTD. For example a paragraph may not contain another paragraph or a heading, so the end-tag may be omitted from a paragraph since its presence can be inferred from the beginning of the next, or a heading, or the end of the document. Markup minimization for the use of the OMITTAG feature appears in the DTD under the heading marked MIN. A letter O (upper or lower case) in the first column indicates that the start-tag may be omitted; otherwise there is a hyphen, indicating that no omission is permitted (that is the tag must be present).

SHORTREF is the feature whereby short entity reference delimiters may be used instead of complete entity references. Short entity reference delimiters are single characters or short strings, one use being to enable word processing conventions to represent markup. The reference concrete syntax defines many that may be used for this purpose, for example tab, record end, and record start. Mapping takes place to effect the necessary substitution. So a blank line (a record start character immediately followed by a record end character) could denote the beginning of a paragraph, being mapped to <p>. Similarly, a space could separate values in a row of a table.

DATATAG provides the ability whereby data characters may serve simultaneously as tags, useful when the data to be entered follows a pattern, for example lists of names and addresses. It is used in conjunction with OMITTAG.

RANK enables the omission of element ranks from tags, for another element at the same level as the previous one, the rank of an element being its level of nesting. So if there were a series of subsections at level 2, only the first need give the level number, level two being assumed until there was a change of level, either to level 3 for a subsubsection, or to level 1 for a new section.

2.5.3 Link features

The link features are used to link structures of documents, for example the logical structure with one or more layout structures. DTDs can also be linked, where the DTD is identical in all declarations with the exception of generic identifiers, for example to use mnemonics for a different language, or to link relatively long generic identifiers with short ones, to reduce storage and transmission overheads.

SIMPLE is the feature enabling the layout structure of a document, how it will appear on a screen or on paper in formatted form, for example, to be linked to the logical structure of the base document, one set of link attributes being implied by the application.

IMPLICIT enables multiple sets of link attribute values to be implied, enabling a document to be presented in more than one style.

EXPLICIT also refers to the use of multiple sets of link attributes, but they are specified explicitly.

2.5.4 Others

CONCUR can be used when one or more document types can occur concurrently with the base document type. This can be for verse, for example, with through line numbering, marked up in accordance with SGML.

SUBDOC permits one or more (open) subdocuments to be nested within the SGML document. Subdocuments would use the SGML declaration of the base document, but would have their own DTD. One example of the use of this feature is to bring together separately created documents to be incorporated into a single document, such as an anthology. Another is to create a hierarchical structure for an information base.

FORMAL is the feature whereby public identifiers can be used for SGML constructs, the identifiers having a formal structure with a number of components referring to the registered text. This could be a DTD or perhaps an entity set of descriptions of graphic characters that cannot be input directly. There can thus be reference to ISO and other constructs that are preceded by a registered owner identifier, the subject of an SGML support standard.[5]

2.5.5 Use of the features

It was thought that many people would want to use SHORTREF, to enable short references to be used to imply markup in normal keying practice, for example. So the use of SHORTREF was included in the reference concrete syntax.

It was also thought that OMITTAG and SHORTTAG would be notably useful features, and together with SHORTREF would give sufficient facilities for markup minimization to most people for most of the time. OMITTAG and SHORTTAG were therefore coupled with the reference concrete syntax for what is known as a basic SGML document.

Other features can be added as required. Indeed, the use of all features can be on an as required basis, its being possible to use the reference concrete syntax without SHORTREF (when it becomes a variant (of the reference) concrete syntax), for example, or to use OMITTAG without SHORTTAG, say.

In practice, it is found that many applications are somewhat chary of using SGML features, with the notable exception of those developed in Belgium, France, and Japan, where the link features and CONCUR are quoted regularly, as well as other features. All have their place, especially in integrated information bases.

Notes

(1) A comparison of ODA (a document architecture) and SGML (a representation language) is the subject of Chapter 10.

(2) None of these symbols is imaged in ISO 8879, alas. For the lists of graphic symbols, complete with image, and an index to the character entities by name, see Joan M Smith and Robert Stutely, *SGML: The User's Guide to ISO 8879*, Ellis Horwood (1988).

(3) This book does not go into detail about all the facets and facilities of ISO 8879. For a fuller explanation of the standard itself see Charles Goldfarb, *The SGML Handbook*, Clarendon Press (1990). Other useful books are Martin Bryan, *SGML: An Author's Guide to the Standard Generalized Markup Language*, Addison-Wesley (1988) and Eric van Herwijnen, *Practical SGML*, Kluwer Academic Publishers (1990).

(4) Work is in fact being carried out within ISO for the standardization of both photographs and moving pictures, for example, as described in 8.6.2.

(5) The standard referred to is ISO/IEC 9070 Information Processing — SGML Support Facilities — Registration Procedures for Public Text Owner Identifiers, described in 7.2.

3

An SGML document

Everything in SGML is based on rules; the specification is said to be rigorous. This has several advantages, one being the integrity of the information content. Nothing may be included in a document that has not been declared as permitted content in a certain context. These rules are variously stated in the SGML declaration and the DTD, and applied in the document instance. In fact there are three distinct parts to an SGML document:

- the SGML declaration;
- the DTD;
- the document instance.

3.1 SGML DECLARATION

It is the SGML declaration that includes information about the usage of character sets, the concrete syntax, capacity requirements, and optional features permissible.[1]

Every system that runs SGML has an SGML declaration associated with it, otherwise there would be nothing to state which character sets were to be used, which concrete syntax, which optional features, and what the capacity requirements were. The SGML declaration is usually written by a systems programmer or equivalent, and generally speaking no one need bother about it as long as the system always does the job intended.

However, anyone designing documents *must* know about the SGML declaration, even if someone else is responsible for its maintenance. Else how would it be realized that this is where arrangements are made to work in another character set, for example?

What follows is a description of some of the main points about the SGML declaration. However, many different things can be specified here, to cater for many different sets of circumstances.[2]

3.1.1 Character set usage

The part of the SGML declaration that deals with character sets is preceded by the word CHARSET. This is followed by a statement as to which character set is being used. The base character set used in the reference concrete syntax is known as ISO 646,[3] this being common in the English-speaking world. There is the international reference version and different language versions, the most popular of which is ASCII.

This character set information is preceded by BASESET, which includes its name and the appropriate escape sequence about which the system needs to know.[4] These escape sequences are unique, being specified in the ISO Register[5] or privately agreed. Use of the set is then described as DESCSET, on a character by character basis if desired, and it is here that usage differing from the BASESET may be specified.

For many uses, ISO 646 may well be sufficient. It is considered insufficient in most countries that use languages other than English, as they could need accented letters and even different alphabets. So in these countries another character set can be specified in the SGML declaration, often to provide the coding for what is regarded as the right-hand side of the code table. If this is not done, all the symbols will have to be keyed in as entity references, which can be a very tedious way of working, and is certainly very expensive on storage.

Again, the declaration takes the form of BASESET and descriptor, followed by the more detailed description in DESCSET if this is different from the registered set.

So if there is a need to work with a different language, *check to see which character sets are permitted in the SGML declaration, and make sure that they are appropriate for the requirements*. The systems programmer should be able to make the necessary alterations, and will be able to advise on whether or not the system can deal with this language. *There may be trouble at a local installation in that certain symbols are not imaged as intended.* Then it will have to be decided what fall-back techniques are used.

If there is a requirement to image special symbols infrequently, it is sufficient to use entity references, and not escape to a different character set. An example here could be a letter written in English addressed to someone in France, with a requirement for accented letters in the address.

3.1.2 Capacity requirements

For many applications it is unnecessary to alter the capacity requirements, most people tending to use the capacities given as a default in the reference concrete syntax.

However, some applications have code numbers associated with them for purposes of identification, where it could be necessary to use these codes for hypermedia links, and so on. In this case the name length capacity could be extended from its default value of 8 to 20, or whatever was required by the application. (This is necessary for the aerospace industry, for example, for lengthy identification codes for modules or tasks.)

3.1.3 Concrete syntax

The ISO standard defines an abstract syntax, that is it states that there shall be characters to indicate start-tag open (STAGO), tag close (TAGC), and end-tag open (ETAGO), for example. Also forming part of the abstract syntax are entity reference open (ERO) and reference close (REFC); declaration subset open (DSO) and declaration subset close (DSC); and many more to serve other purposes. In general, these apply to markup. Two more important groups consist of the connectors and occurrence indicators used in the definition of models in the DTD, as described below. In fact there is a comprehensive syntax, adequate for all the needs that could be thought of by the standards-makers.

These keywords or names used in the abstract syntax have to be mapped to actual characters to provide what is known as the concrete syntax. It is for the *application* of SGML to state which characters are mapped to the abstract syntax. To assist the application of SGML, and so many people would use the same concrete syntax, a concrete syntax was defined in ISO 8879 that could be thought of as the default concrete syntax. It is this that is called the *reference concrete syntax*.

Many people use the reference concrete syntax as specified in ISO 8879, although some make a few alterations to it in the SGML declaration in which case it immediately becomes a *variant concrete syntax*, since it differs from that given as the reference. Some people, for example, might prefer square brackets to be used instead of angled brackets for STAGO, TAGC, and in ETAGO, for example, maybe because the document instance contains a lot of mathematics. A word of warning: *do be careful to think through all the implications for a change of delimiters*, for example, as the choice could impinge on other delimiters and may result in the parser (the checking software) making incorrect assumptions.

Whatever variations of the reference concrete syntax are used locally, it could be advantageous to map those to the reference concrete syntax, *if possible*, prior to interchange of the document. This is not necessary, of course, and anyone reading the SGML declaration will know immediately what characters have been chosen for the application. And if the system is designed to operate totally without human intervention (the ideal situation), no one need know what delimiters have been used even if they know that the information was structured in accordance with SGML.

When specifying details about the concrete syntax to be used, information also has to be given about the use of the SHORTREF feature. There is a statement that starts SHORTREF and it is this that refers to the SHORTREF feature. If it is followed by SGMLREF, then short references are permitted as specified in the reference concrete syntax. Furthermore, additional short references may be specified as required. If this statement is SHORTREF NONE, short references may still be specified as required but those specified in the reference concrete syntax are not to be used.

3.1.4 Feature use

If use of optional SGML features is permitted, this is where the statements are made. The ten (remaining) features are listed, each being followed by YES or NO. If YES, some of them require additional information, in accordance with the standard.

When given a DTD by someone, be sure to ask for the SGML declaration also, and pay attention to the FEATURES information. Your system may not be able to handle some of them — although every encouragement is now being given to vendors to provide for all these features, as they are required for many applications developed in Europe.

Check to make sure that a vendor's system is able to display the SGML declaration.[6]

3.1.5 Application-specific information

Application-specific information may be passed on to the receiving end. There is a heading for APPINFO, which may be followed by a text string before adding the closing delimiter for the end of the SGML declaration. It is here that use of the HyTime standard is indicated, for example.

Since the SGML declaration is not usually seen by an author of a document, and in any case is not usually passed over with each document instance, in practice very few people are using the facility to include notes here. An implementation of SGML by a vendor would have to make arrangements to display the APPINFO on the screen, to draw it to the attention of the receiver.

It could be useful to check if a vendor's system displays APPINFO.[6]

3.2 DOCUMENT TYPE DEFINITION

Confusion exists in some minds as to the difference between a document type declaration and a document type definition. I have even seen the former abbreviated to DTD. This is incorrect! *The acronym DTD stands for document type definition.*[7]

The DTD is invoked by the document type declaration, which states the name of the DTD. Then follows the declaration subset, enclosed in square brackets (using the reference concrete syntax), within which is the DTD.

Some say that document type designers are responsible for the writing of DTDs. And so they are, but they are a very rare species, and if seeking to employ someone who would be writing the DTDs, I would look for an applications programmer who knew about documents and publishing requirements.[8]

In order to write a DTD, the designer must be aware of the *connectors* and *occurrence indicators* used to describe models. These are illustrated in Table 3.1.

Table 3.1. Connectors and occurrence indicators

Character	Name	Meaning
Connectors:		
,	SEQ	all must occur in the order specified
&	AND	all must occur in any order
|	OR	one and only one must occur
Occurrence indicators:		
+	PLUS	required and repeatable (1 or more times)
?	OPT	optional (0 or 1 time)
*	REP	optional and repeatable (0 or more times)

Parentheses (and) are used to delimit what are known as model groups.

A DTD consists of all the rules that apply to a type of document. It includes the names of the various elements (generic identifiers), any attributes they may have, and the relationships of the elements. Also part of the DTD are all the entity references that may be used, and the different notations of other types of content. If the SGML declaration permits the use of the OMITTAG feature, it is in the DTD that element declarations specify whether or not start-tags and/or end-tags may be omitted.

An example of a DTD for a type of document called memorandum (a very simple one) could be as follows.

```
<!ELEMENT memo - - (rn, sn, d, s, p+)>
<!-- memo   = memorandum
     rn     = recipient's name
     sn     = sender's name
     d      = date
     s      = subject
     p      = paragraph -->
<!ELEMENT (rn|sn|d|s|p) - O (#PCDATA)>
```

By reference to Table 3.1 for the meaning of the connectors and occurrence indicators and to the comment declaration in the example (all the text between the pair of double hyphens), it is possible to ascertain the meaning of the DTD.

The first element declaration tells us that this is for a memorandum, for which both the start-tag and the end-tag must by present (no omission possible). The model group states that this memorandum consists of a recipient's name followed by the sender's name followed by the date followed by the subject followed by one or more paragraphs, where all elements must be present in the order given.

The second element declaration tells us that all the containing elements of the memorandum (stated as recipient's name or sender's name or date or subject or a paragraph) consist of what is termed parsable character data — the software will check it for markup. And by the way, whilst the start-tag must be present of all those elements, in every case the end-tag may be omitted. This end-tag omission is possible as in every case the following element in the model must be present, therefore when the next one starts the previous one must have ended, or the memorandum has ended (its end-tag must be present) — there is no ambiguity.

Although the DTD is short, it will at least give some idea how the declarations variously state the requirements for a type of document. And whilst you may never need to write a DTD personally, it can be helpful to know what the document designer has to do, and why he says he cannot do a good DTD for a manual within two days! (The analysis of previous manuals alone could take longer than that, particularly if they were technical manuals.)

This DTD, or *definition* of the document type, has to be included in a document type declaration.

As seen above, declarations start with <! and end with >. The document type declaration takes the form <!DOCTYPE . . . .>.

In order to associate the DTD with the document type declaration there is something called the declaration subset, which contains the DTD. Using the reference concrete syntax, the delimiters for a declaration subset are [and], declaration subset open [and declaration subset close] respectively.

The document type declaration for a document type called memorandum could be as follows.

```
<!DOCTYPE memo [
<!ELEMENT memo - - (rn, sn, d, s, p+) >
<!-- comments here about element names -->
<!ELEMENT (rn|sn|d|s|p) - O (#PCDATA)>
]>
```

In other words, the DTD has been enclosed in the appropriate delimiters for it to be the declaration subset.

Assuming that the DTD for the memorandum is known at the receiving end, all that is required before the document instance, or what many would refer to as the text of the memorandum itself, could be the document type declaration that would invoke the DTD. This could now be stored in the system together with other DTDs in a file called MEMO.DTD.

```
<!DOCTYPE memo SYSTEM "C:\DTDS\MEMO.DTD">
<memo>
<rn>Paul A Ellison
<sn>Joan M Smith
<d>  . . .
</memo>
```

The following statements can therefore be made:

(1) The DTD contains all the rules about the type of document.
(2) The DTD is contained within the declaration subset.
(3) The declaration subset follows the document type declaration itself, and if present is an integral part of it.
(4) The document type declaration invokes the DTD.
(5) The document type declaration need not contain a declaration subset, in which case the DTD would be invoked where it was stored.
(6) There can be a declaration subset at the beginning of a document instance to add to the existing DTD.

DTDs already exist for a number of different kinds of documents. ISO 8879 SGML contains one for a general document in annex E — in fact there is quite a lot of tutorial material in the annexes of ISO 8879. The main place to look, however, is ISO/IEC TR 9573 Techniques for Using SGML. Here there is an explanation of the DTD for a general document given in ISO 8879 as well as examples of DTDs for a letter and memorandum, and a spreadsheet. And there are many fragments of DTDs.

The first step is to carry out a document analysis of the type of document for which a DTD is required. Do be sure to examine a large sample of documents, from the very complex to the very simple. ISO/IEC TR 9573 Techniques for Using SGML deals with document analysis in clause 4. Note, however, that in 4.1.1 it gives guidance in terms of pages, whereas it is not necessarily wise to design a DTD with paper/pages in mind — the information could be extracted and viewed on the screen, or on part of a split screen, when pages have no meaning. In any event, that is an output consideration, and outside the province of SGML strictly speaking.

Many of the early DTDs were written more with the idea of dealing with one type of document, each instance of which could be stored in a file. This is no longer true, more recent DTDs being for modules of information that form part of an integrated information base. What might have been considered acceptable five years ago is no longer necessarily considered to be good practice. Yet having said that, all document instances prepared in accordance with the early DTDs can form part of an integrated information base today.

3.3 DOCUMENT INSTANCE

The document instance is marked up in accordance with the rules specified in the SGML declaration and the DTD. It may be preceded by a document type declaration subset, to give notice of additional entity references used in this particular instance.

Ideally, of course, the person who is inputting the document should not need to know that SGML is being used, just that certain house rules have to be obeyed. This means that the application software must support the DTD in an effective way (with a good user interface!), the system supplying markup automatically if at all possible.

Consider the memorandum for which the DTD has been given. A template could be provided for the memorandum as illustrated in Figure 3.1.

Memorandum

To:

From:

Date:

Subject:

Figure 3.1. A screen display for a memorandum

Here the user would be expected to complete the information at the top of the memorandum, then add the message. *No markup would be added by the user.* The system would realize that the DOCTYPE was memo (perhaps because before starting the user chose memorandum from a list of possible documents to input), and pick up the text input after the prompts to add the recipient's name, the sender's name, and so on. The system would substitute <rn> for To:, the start-tag of the recipient's name, and so on. *The writer would be unaware that SGML was being used.*

The same principles could also be adopted in the case of forms, trade documents, and other similar types of documents where there is a regular, unambiguous structure.

Of course, this is by no means always possible. In the example for the memorandum it was always known which element would come next, but in technical manuals, for example, there is often a choice of elements. A subsection, for example, could consist of lists, notes, warnings, diagrams and other illustrations in addition to paragraphs. And paragraphs could contain emphasized words or phrases as well as lists and other elements. Where there is a choice in a particular context, a menu could be displayed for the user that shows which elements are permitted in the present context, where the menu would take its information from the appropriate model group in the DTD.

Although I have usually been giving one or two character generic identifiers, this does not mean that I would expect them to be seen by the user. Just as the user saw something meaningful displayed in the case of the memorandum, so the user could see the full name of the element in the menu, and maybe the generic identifier also just in case he wanted to check the markup (our intelligent user). But the short generic identifier would be stored, and this is what the user could see if he wished. (Lexicographers could be interested in the actual markup that indicates the structure of the various entries in a dictionary, for example. Whilst the appearance of the entry could look right, if the markup was incorrect it could result in there being incorrect entries in spin-off publications (for example a period dictionary derived from the *New Oxford English Dictionary*).)

SGML editors can give much help in the addition of markup, advice on the kind of assistance possible being given in a technical report.[9]

3.4 REDUCING OVERHEADS

The amount of markup present with a document adds to the overheads incurred for both storage and transmission, and also processing time. This is one reason why the standard provides so many features (five in all) for the minimization of markup. Whilst use of the minimization features can reduce the amount of markup that needs to be present ultimately, even to the saving of just one character in a tag (by use of the rank feature), it is the length of names used for generic identifiers, attribute names and values, and identifiers themselves that directly influences the amount of markup in the first instance.

In the reference concrete syntax, the length of names is set at eight characters; that is a generic identifier chosen for the name of an element, for example, must not exceed eight characters. And generally speaking this is adequate for most purposes, with such notable exceptions as applications that use lengthy identification codes. In such cases, the name length value is increased, even to thirty-two for one defence application. However, it does not need an arithmetician to say how wasteful it would be were all names even to approach thirty-two characters in length.

How to design an application so the overheads are minimized is a nice exercise, and of great importance when the information base is large. (And make no mistake, some of these integrated information bases are going to be huge.)

One approach is as follows. First make an alphabetical list of all the elements that a document (or set of documents) may contain. For each letter of the alphabet, choose the element that will occur the most frequently and give it a one letter identifier, for example p for paragraph. Then give the others two letter identifiers (that are still mnemonics), three letters being used if necessary. Similarly, choose attribute names and values with extreme care, using one or two letters where possible.

It could be that an application is more or less obliged to use long generic identifiers if only because the US DoD has chosen long ones and consistency is required. In that case there is the possibility of mapping all the long names (generic identifiers, attribute names and values, and identifiers) to short forms, where this could be achieved using the EXPLICIT link feature to link the two DTDs. Thus the application still has compatibility with that of the US DoD; when the DTD is in use elsewhere, the short names are used, the long ones from the DoD-like DTD only being mapped for interchange with the DoD and not otherwise. A system could (internally) also map very long identifiers to shorter ones, but this would definitely be for internal use only.

The interesting thing is that this solution can also apply when different countries use the same DTD but require different mnemonics because of language differences. Again, there can be mapping (or linking) of the two DTDs.

Having reduced the length of names to an absolute minimum, the use of features can be considered.[10] The first to consider is the omission of start-tags and/or end-tags. This is a logical exercise carried out by looking at the model groups in the DTD. If one specific element must be present and is always followed by another specific element, the end-tag of the first may be omitted, and so on. If the presence of a start-tag or an end-tag can be inferred by the system, then it may be omitted.

Short references may be used instead of markup, whereby a blank line could always precede the start of a paragraph; a space between numbers in a row of figures can denote the start of the next cell of information. Regular indenting can be mapped to markup (if its use is unambiguous), and so on. And all this may be done in specific contexts, which may be changed if desired. (This is achieved by what is known as the short reference map, where one map may be superseded by another, as required.)

Now consider the use of short tags, whereby the attribute name does not have to be given, only the value, and quotation marks need not appear round attribute values (unless they contain a space character or certain other characters). Also the generic identifier can be omitted from start-tags and end-tags, and some of the delimiters can be omitted if their presence can be inferred by the system. Whilst I have seen generic identifiers omitted from an end-tag in an application, do be careful if practising this kind of omission, as an empty end-tag closes the last opened element. I would get the system to do it, and to implement the ability to omit certain delimiters from markup — it is all done to rules, and computers are good at obeying rules.

I would also advocate the programming of a system to implement the rank feature. Although it is not a feature I would use when keying in information directly, I would ask for systems software to make use of it if it was felt that the value of the space saved would exceed the processing overhead to save the space!

The ability for data to act simultaneously as tags can be useful when dealing with lists of information, and in other cases where the information follows a regular pattern.

Use of all five minimization features has now been considered for the application. If you do not agree with the need to reduce overheads, *it is strongly advocated that experiments are carried out with documents to assess the savings achieved.* They can be very considerable.

But what is shown on the screen? The answer is no markup at all if possible, otherwise as little markup as possible. Where simple documents are concerned there can be mapping of the structure of the form, say, to what is necessary for the SGML system, where the user would be unaware of what was taking place. Otherwise, full names should be given where appropriate, and mapped to the generic identifiers unbeknown to the user. Intelligent SGML users who need to see the actual markup inserted can be provided with a crib sheet if necessary (maybe on the screen, those displayed at any time being those used in that part of the text), which states that n = note, for example. However, it is said that ten elements of most documents occur very frequently (and with the system advocated these could all have one-letter names), and their names can readily be learned. Another point made here is that *the more markup there is interspersed among the text, the harder it is to proof-read the text.*

Pay attention to savings on overheads. It can reduce storage and transmission costs significantly.

There is one fly in the ointment. ISO 8879 states that markup *may* be minimized. Some systems even put in markup that has been omitted, and thus wipe out any benefits that may otherwise have accrued. The reverse is advocated. Since all markup minimization is carried out in accordance with rules known to the system either through the SGML declaration or through the DTD, the system is well able to omit all markup that may be present in accordance with these rules. *Thus a fully minimized document is always stored and transmitted.* Only when a receiving system is unable to cope with a certain feature need that particular markup be present — and the system can take care of that.

Notes

(1) A good description of the SGML declaration is in Martin Bryan, *SGML: An Author's Guide to the Standard Generalized Markup Language*, Addison-Wesley (1988).

(2) See the standard itself (ISO 8879) and ISO/IEC TR 9573 Techniques for Using SGML for more information on what may go into the SGML declaration.

(3) The full title of the standard is ISO 646 Information Processing — ISO 7-Bit Coded Character Set for Information Interchange.

(4) The standard that applies to escape sequences is ISO 2022 Information Processing — ISO 7-Bit and 8-Bit Coded Character Sets — Code Extension Techniques. It allows for both public and private escape sequences.

(5) Many escape sequences have been registered. These escape sequences, together with their associated character sets, are specified in the International Register of

Coded Character Sets to be Used with Escape Sequences, the register being maintained on behalf of ISO by the European Computer Manufacturers Association (ECMA).

(6) Chapter 11 gives useful information as to what to look for when choosing a system.

(7) The official version is in ISO 8879 SGML, B.12 on page 88. And there are definitions on page 10 of ISO 8879.

(8) A useful booklet that explains DTDs in a very readable way is *The SGML Primer*, published by SoftQuad, one of the SGML software vendors.

(9) The title of the report is ISO/IEC TR 10037 Information Technology — Guidelines for SGML Syntax-Directed Editing Systems, described in 7.3.

(10) Use of the markup minimization features is discussed in clause C of ISO 8879 SGML, for example.

4

Some application considerations

4.1 GENERAL REMARKS

Forget what you know about documents. Instead, start to think in terms of pieces or elements of information that may be held electronically. Information can be very valuable, maybe the greatest asset a company has. These days when there is a disaster with a computer system, maybe a fire, it is not so much the hardware replacement costs that worry management, rather replacing the lost information that was stored on the computer system. So the intelligent company provides for adequate backup facilities. But the point being made is that the value of the information usually far exceeds the value of the hardware on which it is processed.

Another point is that it can be necessary to hold the information for a long time. For example in a defence environment it could be necessary to guarantee the availability of the information pertaining to a weapon system throughout the length of its estimated life cycle, plus ten years, where this can amount to fifty or sixty years in all. Within the life of the information it can be subject to change, even to frequent changes, and who knows how the customer will require it to be output in ten, twenty, or thirty or more years' time? Output could be on paper or maybe for screen display together with various types of illustrations, and perhaps video and audio content *even now*, and what is a stated output requirement today could well be changed many times over a period of a few years.

So when the information is being prepared, it behoves us to think carefully about its structure, to ensure that it is as neutral as possible and thus able to be used in many good ways throughout its lifetime. Since SGML is a representation language, there is nothing in ISO 8879 that would prevent its use for the presentation of documents and anything else that may be thought useful by the uninformed. Only good practice makes SGML the tool for 'living' information stored in integrated information bases. It is this aspect of SGML that gives rise to so many benefits and so attracts many companies to the language for a wide variety of purposes.

Good practice manifests itself in a variety of ways, starting with the minimization of markup to reduce overheads as discussed in the previous chapter, and the user interface with the SGML system. It includes consideration of how to keep out of the SGML document anything relating to presentation, including anything tied to numbered elements. It includes good ways of dealing with indexing, tables, and mathematics. It includes taking into account all types of documents containing all types of content from video to business graphics.

A word of advice. Do not indicate the structure of more than is necessary or desirable. There is no use whatsoever in going down to the clause, phrase, or word level if you do not have a machine-translation application, for example. An extreme case has been cited deliberately, but do think about why you need the structure of a document before marking up more than its foreseen use. If, in a few years' time, it is necessary or desirable to indicate additional structure, the appropriate markup can be added then. And who knows, by then there may be intelligent software to take over the job automatically.

Remember that for every facility that may be available to a user of SGML because he wishes to exploit what the standard allows, there has to be appropriate application software to interpret the requirements so theory may become practice.

4.2 AVOIDANCE OF PRESENTATION ISSUES

Keep anything connected with presentation distinct from the information content of an SGML document.

For example do not think in terms of paper output; rather think of elements or modules of information where the content is what matters, not how it is to be presented. Beware, as you may see examples of SGML applications relating solely to paper-oriented output. That may be considered right for a document of an ephemeral nature, although most these days are also displayed on a screen. And if the document is to be kept, its future usefulness is severely limited. Instead, think of loading modules of information to an integrated information base. Output can be as desired.

I have also seen it written that in SGML you mark text to be presented in bold or italics — and that too is bad practice. Refer instead to emphasis of different kinds, as on a screen another colour could be used. Anyway, bold could be used for many different elements, including subheadings as well as emphasized phrases, and italics could be used for subsubheadings, emphasized phrases, foreign phrases, and titles of publications, for example. At least the application needs to be able to distinguish between subheadings of some description and emphasis of text. Emphasized phrases should be marked up as such, as should (sub)headings.

Some applications allow the user to specify how much space should be left for a diagram. This may answer one requirement relating to a paper publication, but will be unhelpful for a screen representation, where there could be zoom facilities for example, or the judicious use of split screens. It is best merely to refer to the graphic, allowing its presentation to be the proper concern of the composition process and not SGML.

Line elements have been used in some applications, and I must confess that there is a great temptation to do so in the case of Eastern European addresses, for example, where numerals seem to be used in ways that differ from what is common practice in certain other countries in the world. The solution could be to state that an address consists of certain specific elements or just address elements (ae perhaps), ending with country. How you mark the structure depends on what you wish to do later with the address — although this is one case when it can be useful to pay particular attention so the same address can be used for different purposes (store-once-use-many-times).

4.3 NUMBERING SCHEMES

Another point is not to give the information an explicit numbering system for chapters, sections, subsections, items in lists, references, cross-references, figures, and so on. If you do, when the information is edited the odds are that the numbering will have to be changed, and then what will happen to the references and cross-references, the index, and lists of contents? All will require to be updated, again and again as time goes on. Instead, use the facilities offered by SGML (a representation language) to handle numbering in an implicit way.

Where chapters, sections, and subsections are concerned, the markup merely indicates that this is a chapter, this is a section, this is a subsection. It is the output requirements that state that chapter elements should be preceded by the word Chapter, followed by a numeral one higher than the last occurrence. The same principle applies for sections and subsections, also figures and tables.

Another aspect of numbering is the preparation of tables of content, and so on. I would not do these, preferring to let the system provide the information from the appropriate elements and the text of the titles. I might get it wrong, and in any case it could be incorrect after the information had been edited. So I would merely indicate in the DTD that a contents list goes here, followed by a list of figures, say.

4.4 CROSS-REFERENCING

Consider references and cross-references. Instead of giving an explicit number, give the element an identifier. So a figure could have an identifier C. and the start-tag could then be <f id=C>. When I wished to refer to it, instead of 'see figure 9' or some other explicit number, I would put 'see figure <fr refid=C>', and the reference identifier would be given an explicit value only on output. Were my figure in an integrated information base, the same figure could be used several times in different output manuals or other documents, when it could be given different explicit numbers by the system.

By the way, note that the uniqueness of an identifier applies to one document only; that is different documents may have an identifier of abc. This presents no problems if the input information is considered as one large document from which many smaller ones may be spawned.

4.5 INDEXING

The more traditional approach to preparing an index is for a professional indexer to do this by hand. These days, when a document is in machine-readable form, a word index can be produced, provided the necessary software is also available. This then can form the basis for the index of the more traditional kind, the salient words being picked out as entries at the various levels. One of the drawbacks is that the cross-references ('see' and 'see also' notes) can be missed if working from a simple word list. And there is no provision, of course, for the occasions when a concept is referred to that has been accorded an index entry, but without actually using the word itself.

Using SGML, there is the possibility for man-machine interaction for the production of an index. This method entails the author or indexer in marking words or phrases as they occur in the text for incorporation in an index; it includes the ability to refer to other entries. The resultant index to the publication is generated by software means when the document has been assembled, the appropriate (sub)section and/or page numbers being inserted for the various entries, ordered alphabetically.

It is good practice to sketch out what is required in an index, and to specify these headings by means of the index heading element. They can also be given unique identifiers at that point and 'see' and 'see also' references stated. This outline list could be used as a visual reference when inputting the document, markup being added to result in the words or phrases being included as they occur. Other headings may be added to the list as the document is prepared, of course.[1]

Some words of caution. If the index has been created as the text was written, and it was subsequently edited extensively, or in cases where the output document consists of parts of several input documents, the result could be a patchy index. Some aspects of the subject matter could be indexed in depth, and corresponding entries in another section could be omitted, the indexing flow not having been maintained. It is therefore wise to check the finished index for completeness. At that point it can be enhanced if considered desirable.

Where indexing is concerned, the golden rule is not to rely solely on system-produced word indexes but to combine those with a machine-assisted index of the kind made possible by SGML.

4.6 LISTS

There are so many different ways of indicating items in lists. They can be numbered using Arabic numerals or Roman numerals (upper or lower case), or alphabetized (upper or lower case), or even preceded by a bullet or en rule or another symbol or merely indented. In general, we can speak of ordered lists (numbered or alphabetized) and unordered lists (where the items are usually preceded by a symbol). And there can be nested lists of various types.

What we do is tell the system that we have a list, and the list will consist of list items, and maybe sublist items, and maybe even nested lists that can have their own structure.

Consider the following example of a list.

```
This is a list:
<l u>
<li>here is a list item;
<li>here is another list item;
<li>and another list item which is subdivided
<sli>some detail,
<sli>some more detail.
</l>
```

l has been used for list, li for list item, and sli for sublist item. The u in the markup that starts the list is an attribute (value) to state that it is unordered. As the SHORTTAG feature has been used, there is no need to put type=u for unordered, merely the value of the attribute for the type without quotation marks surrounding it.

Quite separately it could be stated that on output all list items of an unordered list are to be prefixed by a bullet, and all sublist items by an en rule, where sublist items are indented to start under the text of list items. But these are output application considerations and are nothing to do with SGML *per se.*

Had o been put for ordered as the value of the attribute instead of u, on output the list items could be been preceded by Arabic numerals (1, 2, 3) and sublist items by a second number after a full point (3.1, 3.2), or whatever else was required.

Many other things are possible, of course, including the presence of unordered lists within ordered lists, and so on. And I could have had different element names for lists, one ul for unordered lists and another ol for ordered lists, so no attributes are necessary.

What matters is that since the numbering is done only on output, although many more items could have been added in the meantime, and perhaps others deleted, the output would still be as required and any numbered items would not have to have been changed by hand.

4.7 TABLES

I recently heard a rumour that SGML is not good at tables. This is not true. As a corollary to that I heard that the amount of storage space necessary for tables was enormous by comparison with that needed for the actual data. But it need not be! Let me state unequivocably that it is a specific *application* of SGML that can be criticized in this respect, and is nothing to do with SGML itself.

ISO 8879 defines a representation language, which is able to describe tables much as matrices are described in terms of rows and columns. The fact that tables may be so described instead of being treated as graphics is a tremendous advantage:

- the individual cells of information may be edited at will;
- rows or columns may be suppressed on output;
- the table may be partitioned in some way if too large to be imaged as described;
- each cell of information may be addressed uniquely
  - — computations may be performed on selected cells,
  - — the information may be included in spreadsheets,
  - — selected information may be summed and presented in the form of business graphics (histograms, pie charts, etc);
- large matrices may be stored as tables
  - — computations may be performed on the matrices.

Thus there is great flexibility in being able to describe a table with its individual elements of information, outputting it in so many different ways.

But all too many document designers use longer generic identifiers than necessary, with too little attention being paid to markup minimization features of ISO 8879 SGML.

They say that storage is cheap, users like to be able to see long names, and not everyone has access to all the features of SGML. Nowhere are the results of such thinking more apparent than in the markup of tables.

Instead, a good application of SGML pays attention to the overheads incurred, bearing in mind that technical documentation includes many tables. It is *not* easy to read a marked up table if there is a plethora of unnecessary markup. Instead, the document designer should seek ways of reducing the amount of markup.

Note also that it is bad practice to include any kind of presentation considerations in the description of a table. *The representation of a table should be of the logical structure only.*

ISO/IEC TR 9573 Information Processing — SGML Support Facilities — Techniques for Using SGML includes information on tables.

Turn to 5.3.7 of this technical report where there is an example of describing a table. In this particular one, although the generic identifiers used are not long, the amount of markup could have been reduced in two ways. If a cell is a heading, it has an attribute to state this, the actual markup necessary being <c heading=h> followed by the heading text. But had the SHORTTAG feature been used, only the value of the heading attribute need have been present, reducing the markup to <c h> for each cell that is headed, often for an entire column. Another way of reducing the necessary markup would have been to have used the SHORTREF feature, whereby a space or tab character could have been used to separate individual cell values, and a line feed character (record end immediately followed by record start) the end of a row, therefore start of the next (or end of the table).

Another method is given in clause 9. To my mind, some of the generic identifiers used are too long, for example <table> could be <t>, <tabcap> could be <tc>, <tabdesc> could be <td>, and <tabref> could be <tr>. But at least row is <r> and column is <c>. In this example, the fact that the first column could be a heading is not distinguished from a cell value, as it is held that it is not necessary to do so. And when the layout of the table is seen (illustrated in the technical report), the markup seems relatively straightforward to achieve the ends. Even so, the use of the SHORTREF feature could have meant that a space or tab character could have been used as a separator instead of <c>, and a line feed character instead of <r> for the commencement of another row. (These short references would be specified as applying only in the context of a table.)

Being logical about the way in which we think, and tidy in the way in which we express ourselves, can lead to excellent applications of SGML. I am reminded of the differences between the programmers who used to work with the early computers (way back in the 1950s), when space was at a premium. Some used to generate very efficient code, whilst others were untidy in their ways — and it showed. These differences were very evident when it came to the amount of computing time necessary. If document designers would only take more care over the way in which the logical structure of documents could be expressed, greater efficiency could be achieved today with SGML. The fault lies not with SGML but with the document type designers.

Some vendors are better than others at dealing with tables, so it is necessary to be discriminating. And there is always the option of writing your own application software.

4.8 MATHEMATICS

Mathematics can be thought of as being a language, and since SGML is a representation language it can be used to represent mathematics, describing formulas and equations. There are two reasons why it is good to represent mathematics in this way:

- when it comes to imaging long equations, a 'good' break has to be found for continuation on the following line, where the position differs dependent on the amount of available space — and the system has to know to scale the summation symbol appropriately, for example;
- if an equation is described, values may be input and the necessary computations performed.

Matrices can be described in terms of rows and columns, and inverted or whatever is necessary.

Spreadsheets can be described using SGML, and computations performed.[2]

And as has been described above, business graphics can be represented.

Thus all aspects of computations from complex mathematics via matrices to spreadsheets and business graphics can be represented in SGML, and imaged as desired. Mathematical requirements are therefore brought into an SGML environment, and can form part of the same information base, conceptually if not physically.

Do not expect the software to be readily available to carry out all the different computing described above. But several groups of people are interested in such facilities, and by marking up mathematics and tables in a good way now, the opportunity is there for future processing.[3]

4.9 LIBRARIES OF INFORMATION

The way in which a system stores other types of content that go to make up multimedia information depends on the system. One way to deal with them is to store all the elements of one kind of content together, so there is a 'library' of raster images, another of vector graphics, another of animated graphics, another of video, another of sound, and so on. These individual elements could be treated as entities (contents of a file), and called out by means of entity references appearing in the text. They would be resolved only on output, meaning that the graphic would appear on the screen when required, otherwise being stored in the library.

This method is analogous to entity sets of symbols. The way in which the various libaries are thought of within the hierarchy is illustrated in Figure 4.1 below.

4.10 HYPERMEDIA LINKS

The term hypertext applies only to textual documents, whereas hypermedia applies to documents that may contain any type of content, hypertext and hypermedia referring to non-sequential searching. This is essential for a screen-based application where the user may see diagrams associated with text, or other referenced text which deals with the subject in greater depth, say. This non-sequential searching can be done in SGML in several ways. One way is to use attributes of elements for the hypermedia links, and another is to have hypermedia links as elements in their own right.

As the importance of having hypermedia working has become more widely accepted, the standards-makers are addressing this need explicitly, and greater functionality will be found in the upcoming standard on HyTime, with greater efficiencies addressed in SGML-B, of which more in Chapter 7.

4.11 SECURITY

SGML allows for security to be specified at a document level and at an element level. This can be done by having security attributes to all elements, for which the default is unclassified, say. So a single piece of information in an integrated information base may be marked as top secret, say, whereas the remainder of the document is unclassified.[4]

The problem can be stated as how to combine classified information in an information base, but which is not stored on the same system. Until such time as secure integrated systems are designed (incorporating different levels of secure information), and accepted by defence authorities, for example, classified information must be kept separately for two reasons:

- lest it be necessary for the entire information base to be encrypted or otherwise kept in accordance with rules governing the highest level of classified information it contained;
- those who do not have access to secure information should not even know of its existence for inclusion at a certain point.

Consider an integrated information base which is modelled in accordance with the usual SGML tree structure, with the highest node at the top, which gives rise to several branches, and so on. Added to the tree structure there can be libraries of graphics, as discussed above. Each of these libraries can contain various types of content — graphics stored in raster form, some stored in vector form, moving images, audio, and so on. In a diagram, these libraries would be shown with lines, linking them to the tree structure on the same system.

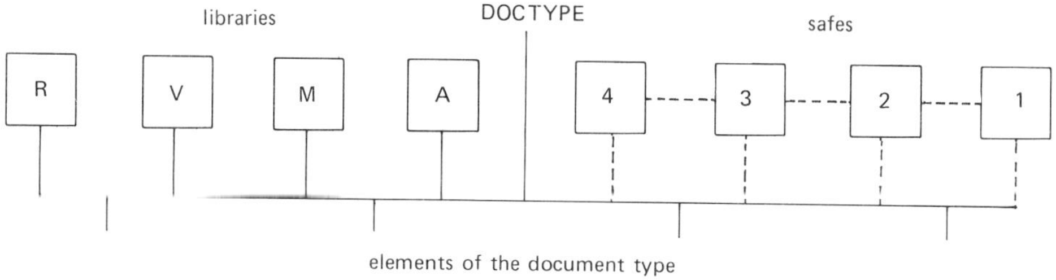

Note: The libraries depicted variously contain entities in raster graphics, vector graphics, moving images, and audio information.

Figure 4.1. Dealing with secure information

This is illustrated in Figure 4.1, where there are also 'safes' of information, four safes representing the various levels of classified information that may be present in the hypothetical defence document. These we position alongside the libraries of graphics, but with dotted lines to the hierarchical structure. The four safes (1, 2, 3, and 4) are also joined together with dotted lines, since anyone with top security clearance may access the contents in safe 4 (on a need-to-know basis), and all the other safes containing secure information (3, 2, and 1), someone cleared to see information at the next highest level would have access to information in safes 3, 2, and 1, and so on, where someone cleared to view certain categories of information in safe 1 would see that and no other. (The usual numbering order is reversed since a person with a lower security classification should not be able to deduce if there were higher levels, and if so, how many.)

So the classified information is shown as part of the information base, yet separated from it physically. And the individual safes can be separated physically, and even separated by category of information, to result in there being a potentially large number of safes for each level (that is many individual safes at level 4, for example, corresponding to the different categories of information at that level on a need-to-know basis).

Assume now that the secure information was provided to a defence user on a floppy diskette. It could contain secure information that had been tailored for a specific (group of) user(s), in that it could be for categories B, J, and K (the information the user has a need-to-know) at his security level (and below, unless at level 1).

The system could be programmed in such a way that it would not operate unless/until the PC (personal computer) was physically disconnected from any mainframe or other communications device, that is it must be used as a stand-alone device. The information contained on this diskette would supplement any information on the system (that had previously been called into storage on the PC, maybe even stored on an optical disk), and appear on the screen in a different colour from other text and graphics. The suggested method is an extension of the idea of having a floppy diskette to contain updating information for a suite of manuals, say, stored on CD-ROM. And just as the user of the CD-ROM would be unaware if there were updating information, so in the case of secure information other users of the system would be unaware that there was secure information.

With this system, only the recipient of the secure information would be aware of its existence.

Needless to say, the recipient would be responsible for keeping the information secret in much the same way as is currently practised with paper as a medium, the floppy diskette being kept under lock and key when not in use.

It is assumed that the information it contained would be encrypted. Who would prepare the encrypted information to be distributed to those with a need-to-know? What is the present system, using paper? It is suggested that the same group of people currently entrusted with the distribution of such information could continue in this role. They are used to dealing with classified information, and would only be dealing with another medium (floppy diskette instead of paper).

Working in a secure environment, their (stand-alone) system could pick out the appropriate information in the various categories from the different safes for the different levels of security, and write it to floppy diskettes (still) in encrypted form.

This could be done automatically for lists of recipients. Everything would be encrypted as appropriate, using the different keys.

Those already dealing with secure information could continue to do so, but using a different medium.

Notes

(1) The method is described in greater detail, with examples, in Joan M Smith, *The Standard Generalized Markup Language (SGML): Guidelines for Authors*, British National Bibliography Research Fund Report 27 (1987).

(2) ISO/IEC TR 9573 Techniques for Using SGML contains a DTD for a spreadsheet in clause 7.

(3) The representation of mathematics is dealt with in ISO/IEC TR 9573 Techniques for Using SGML, clause 8. See also part 13 of the technical report for Public Entity sets for Mathematics and Science, giving all the symbols thought necessary. (If your application requires additional symbols, please advise ISO Central Secretariat so they may be incorporated in an amendment to part 13.)

(4) This system was put forward by the author in Joan M Smith, 'Secure Information and CD-ROM', *EuroCALS Newsletter*, number 7 (January 1991).

5

The integrated information base

5.1 SOME POSSIBILITIES

The second sentence of ISO 8879 says 'SGML can be used for publishing in its broadest definition, ranging from single medium conventional publishing to multi-media database publishing'. Such is the breadth of capabilities embodied in the standard.

Among the many possibilities offered are:

- what goes in can come out unedited (memoranda, letters, books, etc);
- what goes in can come out in edited form (reports, second editions of publications, manuals, etc);
- fragments of many input documents of one type can be collected for one output document (abstracts, transaction lists, names of staff approaching pensionable age, etc);
- parts of many input documents of different types may be output (a financial report, a project report, etc);
- many input documents can form one output document (articles for a publication, address lists, encyclopaedias, etc);
- part of one input document may be output (executive summary, response to a query, etc);
- parts of many input documents may be output in different ways (training materials from maintenance manuals, etc).

As stated in ISO 8879, the standard covers the simple to the complex; it covers the conventional document to an integrated information base. It is by basing the approach on the latter, even for relatively simple documents, that other possibilities open up with time. The types of documents an integrated information base may contain are unlimited, as are the types of content — certainly all those listed in 1.4.

Build on firm foundations for the future.

5.2 ORGANIZATIONAL ASPECTS

Where management of the information is concerned, think in terms of having an object-oriented information base, input to which is governed by SGML. Thus input would be a document instance, checked against a DTD and SGML declaration.

The information base itself could be distributed, locations being chosen on the basis of who has change control.

An object-oriented solution is suggested not only because SGML lends itself to an object-oriented approach, since elements could be thought of as objects of information, but also for reasons of efficiency.[1]

5.3 OUTPUT CONSIDERATIONS

When considering the concept of the integrated information base, the ways in which information can come out of it play a big part in the decision-making as to whether the approach will be worthwhile. After all, it will involve the company in re-organizing its current way of working. And it is when possible outputs are considered that some of the benefits can be seen.

Output from an integrated information base can be in so many different ways:

- paper — in draft or final form, by matrix printer or laser printer, for example;
- screen — high or low resolution, including one with all-points-addressable, and the use of split screens or multiple screens;
- microform — microfilm or microfiche;
- optical media — CD-ROM or CD-I;
- video — full-length or clips;
- magnetic tape;
- magnetic disks;
- communications.

Many different facilities are required for output:

- numbering (various styles);
- cross-references must be accurate;
- tables of contents and lists of illustrations must be accurate;
- indexing reflecting the output document;
- hypermedia links;
- different presentation styles.

Most of these have been dealt with already in some detail, and come within the province of SGML. A notable exception is presentation styles, where SGML allows for there to be many for one document (one logical structure may be linked to many layout structures). Greater consideration of how this is achieved will be dealt with in Chapter 6 when text composition standards are explained.

5.4 FUNCTIONALITY

Having all information conceptually in one integrated information base does not imply that everyone can have unlimited access to all the information it contains. On the contrary, access is allowed as before, on a need-to-know basis. Personnel records would be seen only by approved people, and invoices by the accounts department. But it also now means that the finance director can have access to all accounting information — he can know the precise state of the order book, the value of the stock-in-hand, what debts there are, and so on.

With SGML, access rights can be specified at an element level. There can be an attribute of an element that states who has access rights, and what those rights are.

Some industries also have to consider the possibility of there being an enquiry when information of all descriptions can be required. This happens after an air disaster, for example. Such disasters are mercifully infrequent, but how much easier it would be to deal with the subsequent enquiry were all the information in one system, conceptually if not physically.

The integrated information system can be used as a publishing system and a management information system with equal facility.

This implies some of the functional capabilities required of an integrated information base. These include:

- editing;
- addition;
- deletion;
- access control;
- tracking of changes (audit trail);
- security.

The first three are straightforward, and are expected of any system, provided access rights have been granted. In other words, no unauthorized user may gain access if it is not permitted. Access rights can be accorded at a document level and may be changed at an element level. Furthermore, the kinds of access rights may be changed at an element level, so a user may be able to read a document in its entirety, but is prohibited from altering most of it in any way, but may alter those parts for which he has responsibility.

And when the information is altered in any way, there has to be audit trail — these changes have to be tracked. How much of the back information (now marked as 'deleted') should actually be retained, and if so for how long, is another matter. In some cases it can be essential to record information for a number of years. For example the railway or airline authorities may update a timetable, but may have to retain amendments in archival storage for a long period. Were the police to arrest a person alleged to have commited a crime some time ago on a certain date, say, and as part of his alibi the person says he caught a train from here to there at such and such a time, the police could well wish to check the timetable *as it stood on that date*. Records of changes to an element of information could be by means of an attribute, of which the value is the date and time.

The way in which the functions are actually carried out is not a part of SGML, of course, but would be part of the system. This applies equally to security, where encryption can apply at document or at element level, with a lower level of security at document level than at certain elements that document may contain, if held necessary. In the case of the latter, it is important for the reader of the document to be unaware of the existence of certain secret information a fuller version contains. Again, this is a facility for the system vendor to provide and is outside the concern of SGML itself. (One possible way of approach was discussed in the previous chapter.)

5.5 INPUT TO THE INFORMATION BASE

Surely no company would adopt SGML for its publishing if it was impossible to convert its existing base of information, in which it has a large investment, in addition to the ability of getting new documents into the system in a good way that was acceptable to the authors.

There are several ways of getting information into the system:

- new documents may be keyed in, markup being added at that stage;
- documents that exist already in paper form may be scanned and markup added;
- those which exist in word processor files may be converted;
- existing databases may be converted;
- information may be input by use of communications techniques.

Documents to be taken into the integrated information base must first be categorized, and sorted into what amounts to various types of documents. Once that has been done, the next step is to analyse the structure of documents of a specific type in order to write a DTD; and this must be carried out for every type of document.

A DTD can take into consideration the means of input, in that the use of short references would probably be different in the case of converting existing word processor files from what would otherwise obtain. The good news is that existing documents can and are being marked up in accordance with SGML to gain the benefits that can accrue.

Consider first the input of new information. There are now many tools available in the marketplace for the authoring of SGML documents, some information on these being given later. These are known as context-sensitive or SGML smart editors. Typically they act in WYSIWYG (what-you-see-is-what-you-get) mode or the author may see the markup being added. Menus are provided giving a list of elements permitted in that particular context, for these editors are based on a DTD and know what is permissible, hence the term ‘smart’.

For the creation of new documents, there are basically three ways of having markup added:

- user-supplied (very rare);
- system-supplied (the ideal);
- system-supplied and user-supplemented (common).

Needless to say, it is assumed that maximum use is made of markup minimization features in the SGML declaration and the DTD as discussed in 3.4.

There are very few people who have to key in angled brackets, for example, to mark up a document. And whilst it would be marvellous were it possible for the system to add all the markup automatically, in practice this is not possible in the case of technical documentation, for example. Here the author would probably be using pre-programmed function keys to indicate the start of a tag, or a mouse perhaps, pointing to a menu item. Only in the case of documents with a relatively simple structure, for example trade data, would all the markup be added automatically, although it must be appreciated that such documents can be the biggest number input to the system!

In some cases there is resistance to a new authoring system, and if throughput is adversely affected, it could be as well to consider allowing input as usual for existing staff who are proving resistant, and allowing them to input documents as usual. Then the information can be treated as existing information, with retroactive conversion. Since some of the structure may have to be enhanced, this could be done by a member of staff who liked the new way of working. And as old staff left and new ones came, so new ones could be trained on the SGML system immediately. Do not fight user acceptance, but think of ways in which users' wishes can be accommodated without compromising ideals.

Paper documents can be scanned, and in some cases it is possible for the appropriate markup to be added automatically with the scanning stage — once the system has been programmed, of course. It is more usual to add it at the next stage, using auto-tagging tools, again, suitably programmed.

These days much text already exists in machine-readable form, usually on floppy diskettes or magnetic tape. There are systems for reading a wide variety of floppy diskettes written using a wide variety of word processing packages and for converting the information into the format required on the medium required. Companies have even been investigating the possibility of doing the conversion to SGML as part of the process, and it could be worthwhile to enquire about this. (Even so, the markup added may have to be mapped to what your particular application requires.)

Let us assume, however, that you now have information in a way in which you can handle it. Whatever word processing package has been used to prepare the information, the information is bound to contain codes that have been used to indicate structure. It may not be all the structure that you now wish to indicate, but at least it is a start. The codes can be declared as short references for markup of various elements. These can include the ability to distinguish sections, (sub)subsections, paragraphs, and the like. Titles can usually be picked out, and maybe one or two other elements.

However, italics may have been used for several different purposes. They may be used variously for the title of a subsubsection, emphasized words and phrases, foreign words and phrases, and titles of publications. Software should be able to pick out at least the titles of subsubsections, if only because the point size was larger than that of the main body of the text, and maybe even titles of publications, but not the differences between emphasis and a foreign word or phrase — at least not yet awhile. So the text could then be searched for use of italics that cannot be resolved automatically, and displayed in context on the screen together with a menu that gave a numbering system to the uses. The operator could then key the appropriate use (1, 2, etc) as the system searched the text for unresolved uses of italics. A similar process would apply to distinguish among the different uses of bold.

It may well be that in the beginning it is sufficient to give the documents that are converted retroactively a fairly loose DTD, being more concerned with getting them into the system than with indicating all the required structure immediately. But even this method will allow all (sub)sections to be allocated unique identifiers and thereby allow retrieval at that level.

As already intimated, many thousands of documents have a relatively simple structure, a large proportion of which are based on forms — or electronic versions with set questions for which the response is short. A good example of the latter is use of the service till of a bank, the hole in the wall. A DTD could be written for transactions made from here and all markup mapped onto that which the bank system adds to distinguish the request for a cheque book from the desire to withdraw a specified sum of money, say. This can all be mapped to become an SGML document; certainly no one need key in <PIN=1234>, and so on!

The same principle holds true for information in forms. The form could appear on a screen for text to be added, much as in the case of the example memorandum discussed earlier, but only the information would be stored by the system, and *not the form itself.* Appropriate markup would be added automatically by the system — programmed for that application, of course.

An example of this type of use could be trade data, referred to as electronic data interchange (EDI). The ISO EDIFACT standard is expected to be used for these documents, although they could be interchanged also using SGML with SDIF. Those interchanged using EDIFACT can have the existing markup mapped to that suitable for the SGML information base, so computations may be performed on identified elements, transaction lists prepared and merged with other information that the chief accountant wishes to have. A DTD has been written for the United Nations Trade Data Invoice, and this could provide a useful model for others.[2]

Information stored in databases already has a regular structure, and can readily be mapped to SGML using short references. Formerly it may well have been output on upper-case line printers, full of abbreviations. With this system there can be output to publishing quality, there being no limitations on field lengths, and no abbreviations.

Problems arise only when documents have no regular structure. In such cases a loose DTD must be written. After all, the information is there with more structure than would otherwise have been indicated as it will surely be categorized as a memorandum, a letter, a note, a report, or whatever other broad category into which the document could be said to fall.

The point being made is that existing documents can be brought into the SGML integrated information base. And the sooner the stage can be reached whereby end-users have no notion that SGML is being used the better.

5.6 TEN RULES AND TEN BENEFITS

When thinking of an integrated information base governed by SGML, it could be useful to consider ten rules that have been drawn up by way of providing a form of checklist.

(They have been referred to as the ten commandments, although I would not wish to ascribe such authority to them!)

(1) *As few standards as reasonably possible to be used.* This applies to input of new documents, where alternative methods can give rise to overheads that would otherwise have been avoided. If it is possible to use SGML, use it, in preference to offering a choice of standards or *de facto* methods.
(2) *All text to be in SGML.* This includes EDI documents, callout for graphics, and mathematics.
(3) *No text to appear in graphics.* This ties in with the previous rule in that Arabic numerals should be used for callout within the graphic, and the callout listed separately as text.
(4) *The parsing system to support all features of SGML.* So often it is desirable to use a certain SGML feature for a specific application, only to discover that the system does not support its use.
(5) *Fully minimized documents as allowed by the SGML declaration and the DTD to be stored/transmitted.* Why throw away the great benefits that the minimization features afford? Storage and transmission overheads can be costly in time and money, and can mean the difference between what is acceptable and what is not acceptable including access times for retrieval.
(6) *Input DTDs to reflect information to be included in an information base.* In particular, these DTDs should not reflect paper documents.
(7) *Generic identifiers should not be unnecessarily long.* Why waste space for storage and incur additional overheads for transmission?
(8) *A good user interface to be provided.* Outlines or templates can be provided if appropriate, with full names shown (not abbreviations), this following on from the previous point. As far as the system is concerned, n could mean note, but the full word would be displayed on the screen.
(9) *The ability to transmit changed elements only.* This means that a subset of the output DTD must be allowed. It is wasteful to transmit the entire document unnecessarily.
(10) *Simplified English to be used for technical manuals.* This is for the sake of clarity and ease of translation.[3]

If these rules are followed, then ten (or more) benefits can accrue from having an integrated information base. (They have been referred to as the ten blessings!)

(1) *The information base is governed by SGML, therefore it is rigorous.* Because it is based on rules, there is integrity of information.
(2) *There is total integration of all types of information, both now and in the future.* The system will not have to be changed to cater for new requirements.
(3) *Information is always up-to-date.* This is due to ease of updating and because it is structured on the principle of store-once-use-many-times, eliminating the need for duplicate copies with the risk that there are variations.
(4) *What goes in may come out in many different ways.* It may also benefit from hypermedia capabilities.

(5) *All drawings containing a certain component are retrieved when a search is made.* This is possible because callout is kept separate as a text file, no text being in graphics. Other benefits here are that translation is easier (the graphics remaining sacrosanct), and storage costs are minimized.

(6) *All elements of information are uniquely identifiable.* Processing may therefore be carried out on EDI documents, for example, cross-references can be accurate, and so on.

(7) *The information base may be used either as a management information system or as a publishing base.* In fact it can be used for any purpose where information is the requirement, with the ability for the information input to be used in many different types of output documents.

(8) *There can be a good user interface, with output to publishing quality.* All too often the output from databases is in upper-case letters, abbreviations being used instead of complete words. Now it can be with proportionally spaced fonts, with no limitations on field length.

(9) *Overheads are minimized; effectiveness is maximized.* For example the differences in overheads for dealing with formatted form documents and SGML structured documents are enormous, some ten times more storage space being required for information in formatted form.

(10) *SGML is an international standard.* This means that there can be communication of your information, other systems being able to understand it and to handle it, and that there are many products available in the marketplace. For these reasons alone it is ideal for members of consortia, and customers who want to purchase 'living' information. And you will be able to use your information well into the future.

The very fact that all information can be considered as being in one integrated information base instead of several is a great advantage, where there can be information retrieval for any purpose, from job scheduling to the design of a component.

SGML is all about having the right information in the right place at the right time.

5.7 GETTING STARTED

The first task is to sell the concept of the corporate information base to management. If you fail here, however much you appreciate the value of SGML yourself, you will not be able to implement it. You must have backing from the top. List all the benefits relating to your company. Carry out a survey of your company's documents, all of them, from the board room to the shop floor. Propose a pilot project so the idea can be put into practice. By so doing you will be able to discover what software is appropriate to your needs, and gain valuable experience. If you need advice and do not have the necessary expertise in-house, use a consultant initially. But do appoint someone to be the SGML expert for the organization. That person would be well advised to get all the books available on SGML and gather information in other ways, perhaps by attending a conference or two. (Chapter 12 gives pointers to further information.)

A company is well advised to start to use SGML for its publishing requirements, keeping all the publishing information in an integrated information base instead of files.

You will need SGML software, and you will need training.[4] Design DTDs with an information base in mind, not paper publications. It is by using this approach that the cost-benefits can be shown quickly. Using SGML in the way advocated, divorcing presentation requirements from the information content, with the ability for the information to be amended at will over a period of time, the output documents can then be produced far more quickly. And since they can readily be amended they can always be up-to-date, something few can boast using traditional paper methods. Be sure to adopt a phased approach, taking in new documents first and then converting existing ones.

Having demonstrated the use of SGML for publishing, promote the concept of the integrated information base throughout the company. It is essential to get the backing of your colleagues at this stage (assuming that you had it from management initially and were able to demonstrate the advantages as a result of the pilot project). Only after this promotion is the company in a position to progress to the next stage, taking in documents that originate elsewhere, where this could be looking at the information in the accounts department or at general office documents. Remember, the integrated information base may contain all types of documents containing any type of content provided it may be digitized.

Convert existing documents, perhaps those in existing databases or in word processor files. Rather than scanning in-house, consider the use of a bureau service. Otherwise you could have to purchase hardware for which there could be little use in six months' time when the documents have been converted.

Design applications software to use information in new ways, including the provision of a management information system. Exploit the information as it is included. A just-in-time ordering system can be linked to stock holdings. And if you can take information from tables (marked up in SGML) and represent it in business graphics, the board will approve. Information for the whole company should be included, from the board room to the shop floor — from minutes of board meetings to the grubby pieces of paper on a shop floor where a number could be obscured by a greasy thumb print. Check every department that all documents have been taken into account — including the shop floor, again. And make a note for yourself to go round yet again in a year's time to see how the system is used, and if you can spot any new documents that have slipped through the net, repeating the process every year. It will pay dividends.

Keep up with developments in the standards world, particularly with use of the upcoming hypermedia standard, HyTime. It is sometimes surprising even to the standards-makers what use is made of SGML, and imaginative use of HyTime could provide more surprises. The next chapter gives more information on this subject.

When there is a corporate information system, everything about the company can be known at the touch of a few buttons — thanks to SGML and supporting applications software. This knowledge can lead to better informed decision-making, giving the company competitive edge at a time when competition is becoming more keen.

Notes

(1) See 8.6.4 with respect to requirements of such an information base. Efficiency issues are discussed in 9.1.1.

(2) The DTD is given in Eric van Herwijnen, *Practical SGML,* Kluwer Academic Publishers (1990).

(3) There is a Simplified English dictionary that has been prepared by the Association Européenne des Constructeurs de Matériel Aérospatial (AECMA) for technical documentation in the aerospace industry. It could well be extended for use by other industries.

(4) Advice on choosing a system is given in Chapter 11.

6

Presenting SGML documents

6.1 THE STANDARDS INVOLVED

As has been stated already, SGML is concerned with the information content of a document and not the way or ways in which that information is to be presented. Presentation of information conforming to SGML can be done in a standard way by means of the Document Style Semantics and Specification Language (DSSSL), the Standard Page Description Language (SPDL), and the fonts standards. These standards necessarily had to be written in such a way that they interacted.

6.2 DOCUMENT STYLE SEMANTICS AND SPECIFICATION LANGUAGE

DSSSL is not yet a published standard, being at the status of DIS:

- ISO/IEC DIS 10179 Information Processing — Text Composition Facilities — Docu- ment Style Semantics and Specification Language (DSSSL).

A serious attempt is being made in DSSSL to be all things to all men. For this reason it is a complex standard which is why so many comments were generated on the DIS text that was balloted. And although it technically passed the ballot, a decision was made to ballot it again (what is known as second DIS) after the resolution of the comments, if only because their resolution necessitated substantial changes.

It is DSSSL that deals with the formatting of a document, in that it enables the necessary information to be passed, in a standard way, to a formatter; it is not itself a formatter. The approach is therefore one of allowing for new integrated implementations of formatters accepting DSSSL specifications natively, and of allowing users and system implementors to interface DSSSL with existing formatters via a translation function.

The full range of functionality necessary for all kinds of publishing applications is needed in DSSSL. Among the many specific user requirements taken into consideration during the development of the standard were:

- a means to compose a variety of document entities such as tables, equations, mathematical and chemical formulas, and musical and chemical notations;

- support for computed or computable information (content derived from calculations according to given rules);
- a means to enable clipping of content to regions whose outlines can be constructed from any combination of straight line segments, conic segments, and complex curves such as third order parametric (Bezier) curves;
- a means to allow the layout process to resolve the position of 'floating' elements such as referenced figures, tables, or footnotes;
- a means to allow text to flow around irregular shapes;
- a means to control 'flexible' space, for example glyph and glyph sequencing, spacing, vertical line justification, and column balancing and alignment.

DSSSL defines the semantics and syntax of a language for the specification of document processing. The semantics of DSSSL include a document architecture for typographic presentation style and other document processing specifications. The standard also incorporates a specification language that describes how to apply DSSSL semantics to SGML documents. DSSSL expresses specifications or transformations to be performed by a processor from a source document to an output document, but is itself independent of the formatter, formatting system, or other transformation processor. It provides the means whereby a 'style sheet' may be associated with a generically marked up document instance (an SGML document).

In the scope clause of the standard, it is stated that DSSSL includes:

- transformations independent of a particular type of semantic processor;
- provisions for specifying the relationships among SGML logical elements, as expressed in the source DTD, and the semantic-specific result, for example the output of a formatter;
- formatting and style semantics to describe the typographic style of a document, including functions that allow the transformation of documents from one representation to another;
- a specification language that describes how DSSSL semantics apply to SGML documents;
- definitions of a machine-processable syntax for the representation of a DSSSL specification and its various components;
- provisions for creating new DSSSL attributes and attribute values defined in terms of DSSSL properties.

DSSSL is intended for use in a wide variety of SGML application environments, including:

- electronic publishing (for example production publishing, workgroup publishing, desktop publishing, and database publishing);
- electronic galley creation, pagination, and imposition;
- printing specifications (offset lithography, letterpress, gravure, and demand printing);
- display and/or on-line information).

Three further points may be made:

- the language is declarative;
- no formatting algorithms are included;
- there can be interaction with external processes to handle non-SGML encoded data (for multimedia applications).

In order to associate formatting information with the logical elements of an SGML document, there must necessarily be the DTD for that type of document and a related document instance, plus a definition for that type of document of the physical area templates describing the desired results to be attained after the formatting transformation has been effected, and maps or associations between the logical structure and the rules to be provided to the formatter.

Thus DSSSL enables formatting descriptions to be associated with the logical elements of an SGML document to produce a formatted document for presentation. It could be that a designer wished to specify that all chapters began on a new recto page, and that all tables were delimited by horizontal rules and positioned only at the top or bottom of a page — the kind of information that would be specified in a style sheet. Such formatting descriptions are represented as attributes which are transformed by the formatter into properties with specific values.

Two distinct processes are associated with the DSSSL model:

- a general language transformation process;
- a semantic-specific process.

The source document goes through the general language transformation process, using operations defined in the standard to result in the conceptual output instance — which is not standardized. This then goes through the semantic-specific process using semantics defined in the standard and user-defined extensions to result in the semantic-specific result instance, in the parlance of DSSSL.

Although the initial focus of DSSSL is on formatting as the semantic-specific process, there could well be other kinds of processes, examples given being of document assembly and database loading and extraction. For database working the semantics could deal with the creation of a text stream containing document content interspersed with SQL (Structured Query Language) database commands.

For the case when (parts of) the source document is/are to be loaded into a database, the specification contains the information for extracting required portions of the source document and adding control information for the database management system.

Since HyTime is being used in a US DoD application for interactive information, it is essential that DSSSL takes interactive use into account. It may need to be extended to deal with the application requirements. For example the concept of there being a view package is put forward in the requirements, where a view package could include a specification on how to present the information to the end-user. A DSSSL specification can provide this information, which can be for on-line viewing or on paper, and it can be automated. Where user interaction is concerned, it may be necessary to add a semantic-specific process to DSSSL to cope with this.

HyTime documents can be SGML documents, which may be processed using a DSSSL specification. A DSSSL specification could be part of a HyTime engine. Also there is the possibility of using a DSSSL specification to transform existing SGML documents into HyTime documents.

Thus it is seen that the potential use of DSSSL will be for far more applications than the more conventional formatting. The real benefits here are that many of the people involved in the standards-making process for DSSSL are also involved in the same process for related standards and the defence applications of those standards. Through this interaction, DSSSL will inevitably develop in parallel with the requirements as they are voiced or find their way into print in new applications of the information age.

6.3 STANDARD PAGE DESCRIPTION LANGUAGE

The text for the SPDL standard is awaiting publication in that it has passed the DIS ballot. At the time of writing, final editing is being carried out after which the text will be submitted the ISO Central Secretariat for publication. This final editing takes into account comments made by member bodies of ISO in the balloting process.

User requirements were long since drawn up, and were taken into account during the development of SPDL.

The list of specific user requirements was impressive, the requirements giving a good indication of the functionality of SPDL. The standard had to specify a device-independent and process-independent description of images, including the presentation of documents in fully composed, non-revisable form, supporting all the capabilities of imaging output devices. Furthermore, the design had to be extensible to accommodate future developments. Whilst the key method of interchange for these formatted form documents was to be OSI, when all aspects would be standardized, private interchange was also to be supported when it would be possible to include non-standardized elements, such as colour representation schemes, scanning methods, and compression techniques.

SPDL was to be related to several standards:

- ISO/IEC 9541 Fonts, supporting the use of fonts;
- ISO/IEC DIS 10179 DSSSL and all its functional capabilities;
- ISO 8879 SGML for composition with DSSSL semantics;
- ISO 8613 ODA formatted form;
- ISO/IEC DIS 10175 Document Printing Application (DPA) for the representation of print services incorporating an SPDL presentation process.

Among the requirements for representation, there was to be:

- provision for any two-dimensional image
  - — multilingual text placed at arbitrary rotations and long character paths in any direction,
  - — multiple fonts with an unrestricted selection of characters,
  - — special notations such as those in mathematics, chemistry, and music,
  - — graphics including lines, curves, and complex filled shapes;
- provision for ligatures and pairwise kerning as determined by the formatter;
- support for fallback, on a glyph basis, for those not available;

- support for the representation of lines or shapes composed of any combination of straight lines, conic segments, and complex curves such as third order parametric (Bezier) curves, the clipping of content to shapes so defined, and the filling of such shapes;
- provision for complex raster graphics, including compressed raster data;
- provision for representing any textured colour and colour separation, any tints and screening, and pattern facilities such as dot or dash.

Functional requirements were defined, including those for presentation and colour, as well as those of a more general nature, including:

- support for rapid soft-copy display of composed composite documents;
- support for monochrome and colour display terminals, raster displays, phototypesetters, and raster printers;
- support for document production instructions (for example medium selection, simplex or duplex printing, and binding offset).

Needless to say, presentation of SPDL documents is not confined to paper, screen presentation, for example, being equally important, especially for maintenance information where there is a move away from paper-based manuals. SPDL allows processes other than that for presentation to select pages or portions of documents for use.

In the scope of the standard is the statement that SPDL defines a language for the specification of electronic documents that may comprise black and white, grey scale, or full colour text, images, and geometric graphics, in a form suitable for presentation (printing or displaying on other suitable media). As well as specifying how document images are to be represented, it specifies how document production instructions affect document presentation. Its field of application is a wide variety of environments, including electronic publishing, office systems, information networks, and demand printing. SPDL documents may be interchanged, processed by locally connected presentation devices, sent to presentation devices connected to OSI or non-OSI networks, or stored for presentation at a later time.

There are two methods of encoding for the purposes of interchange: SGML for clear text encoding and ASN.1 (Abstract Syntax Notation One) for binary encoding. The latter is the international standard for machine-readable encoding, used extensively by the OSI standards.

The document processing model is said to consist basically of three processes, which may be iterative, and two forms of representation:

- the *editing process* generates the document content and logical structure which are represented as a *revisable form document*;
- the *composition and layout process* formats the information contained in the revisable form document for presentation, and incorporates the composition and layout decisions as a *final form document*;
- the *presentation process* renders the final form document in visible form.

SPDL is a language for the encoding of final form documents, and as such it provides facilities for the representation of the decisions made by the composition and layout process. SPDL documents are usually the application of the composition and layout process to revisable form documents; however, an SPDL document may also be created by translation of a fully formatted document represented in some alternative final form architecture (for example PostScript), or an imposition or other composition and layout process applied to a final form document or a combination of final form and revisable form documents.

It is said that SPDL represents the ideal image specified by the composition and layout process, its being the the responsibility of the SPDL presentation process to adapt the rendering of the document to the constraints of the presentation device 'so as to provide the best possible approximation to the description specified by the composition and layout process'. It is the presentation process that performs any finishing operations, for example collation, stapling, or binding.

In common with SGML, an SPDL document has *structure* and *content*, in this case the content being in the form of a page description language, its processing being dependent on the document structure. The SPDL document structure is the result of the division and repeated subdivision of an SPDL document into increasingly smaller parts, called structure elements. This structure is hierarchical in nature, the document being the highest level, which may contain page sets, which may contain subordinate page sets and/or pages. And there can be pictures, represented as vector or raster graphics.

Identifiers that may be necessary are in accordance with other standards, for example ISO/IEC 9070 Registration Procedures for Public Text Owner Identifiers and ISO/IEC 9541 Font Information Interchange.

Then there are document production instructions, one function of which is to provide control over aspects of document presentation that are outside the scope of the document content notation, perhaps to specify simplex or duplex printing modes for single or double sided printing, respectively. Another function is to provide control over such aspects of document presentation that may vary, for example the number of copies to be printed or media specification and selection.

The presentation process may have access to font information and other kinds of what are known as resources. Filters (for data transforms), patterns, forms, and colour space are examples of other resources. During the presentation process, the content of the SPDL document consists of the content of token sequences, content being interpreted by what is termed the content processor. The structure notation is declarative in nature, but the token sequences express the document contents in the form of a procedural language for interpretation by the content processor.

Content processing consists of imaging the set of page images rendered by the SPDL document. For this purpose a virtual machine is defined as a model to define the semantics of document content. The virtual machine models the overall content interpretation process as well as the imaging model and co-ordinate systems, there being several submodels. There are submodels for colour, character text and fonts, raster and vector graphics, the behaviour of clipping regions, patterned logical links, raster graphic decompression and transformations, forms, and error handling, together with their necessary operators.

Objects processed by the SPDL virtual machine have an associated object type and value. A component of the virtual machine is a set of state variables which forms part of the state of the virtual machine, and can always be referenced from content. A set of imaging variables is a subset of state variables, their values being used during the imaging process.

A series of annexes deals with operator encodings, public object identifiers, font object format, mandatory fonts, and glyph index maps.

However good SPDL may be, remember that storing information in this form is going to be far less efficient than storing it in SGML form and applying DSSSL and SPDL on-the-fly. If you do not believe me, I can only advise you to carry out some tests.

6.4 FONTS

Part of the philosophy of SGML and its concern with the information content and not how that information is to be presented is how character sets are handled. At the SGML level there is concern for the character coding, whether this be by working in a specific character set, perhaps escaping to another by means of an escape sequence to reconfigure the keyboard as it were, or by means of entity references. None of these relates to the shape of the character, only its meaning. It is only at the presentation stage that the shape of the character achieves importance, and for this we need the fonts standards.

There are basically two standards for fonts at the present time:

- ISO/IEC 9541 Information Technology — Font Information Interchange
  - — Part 1 Architecture, 15 September 1991,
  - — Part 2 Interchange Format, 15 September 1991,
  - — Part 3 Glyph Shape Representation (DIS),
  - — Part 4 Application-Specific Requirements (proposed);
- ISO/IEC DIS 10036 Information Technology — Procedure for Registration of Glyph and Glyph Collection Identifiers.

From the titles of the standards, it is seen that the word 'glyph' is used where the term 'character' may have been expected. This is to avoid confusion with the coding of a character; as soon as that coded character is to assume a specific shape, in ISO terminology it becomes a glyph. It means a sculptured character or symbol, according to *The Concise Oxford Dictionary*. And whilst the word may seem a little strange to use at first, at least there is no confusion as to whether character coding or shape is meant.

Part 1 of ISO/IEC 9541 defines a method of naming glyphs and glyph collections, independent of any coding technique. It also specifies the architecture of a font resource. Identifiers of glyphs and glyph collections are needed in font resources. A font resource is defined as a collection of glyph representations together with descriptive and font metric information relevant to the collection of glyph representations as a whole. This descriptive and metric information is required for font references and the interchange of font resources. The metric information will be needed by DSSSL when it comes to format the text, and SPDL will need to know the actual shapes.

The standard assumes that text processing systems will provide methods for associating the encoding techniques (of characters) with glyph identifiers used in font resources.

Just to make sure that we are all attaching the same meaning to a term, a font is defined as a collection of glyph images having the same basic design, for example Courier Bold Oblique; and a font family is defined as a collection of fonts of common design, for example Courier, Courier Bold, and Courier Bold Oblique.

In defining the architecture, the standard includes clauses on data types, the identification of glyphs and glyph collections, and the font resource. There are two annexes: the first deals with the grouping of typeface designs, the second with font concepts. An index is provided.

Typefaces which are similar in appearance or have characteristics that would allow them to be reasonably substituted for each other are grouped together, where some font designs could be associated with more than one group. The criterion is that of appearance for substitution.

The annex on font concepts is by way of a tutorial on the font resource environment and the application environment. The font resource environment includes information on installation, storage, and access:

- *installation* includes the process of accepting an interchange format of a font resource and possible conversion of the data before storing it in a font resouce library;
- *storage* contains the resource library from which font information is made available;
- *access* includes the process of locating the desired font information and making it available to another process.

In the text on the application environment, font referencing is given as the process of identifying or characterizing a font resource, and glyph referencing the process of identifying glyphs of a font resource, its being necessary to refer to a font in the formatting process to acquire glyph metric information, and in the presentation process to acquire glyph shape information. It is here that any substitution is made.

The system necessarily has to be able to associate the encoded graphic character sets or entity references with the glyph identifiers, where ISO/IEC 9541 defines a method of uniquely identifying all known glyphs, and ISO/IEC DIS 10036 defines a procedure for the registration of all known glyphs and glyph collections. If a glyph or glyph collection conforms to ISO/IEC DIS 10036, it is said to be an ISO property, and although non ISO properties may be recognized for the purposes of interchange, it is recommended that all are duly registered.

Glyphs may be positioned absolutely or relative to each other, as required by the formatting process. Font resource information provides the necessary escapement value, dimensions, and any other properties that may be required for rotation, kerning, or creating ligatures, for example. Presentation of the shape of the glyph involves the translation of the glyph shape information from its interchange format to that required by the presentation device.

Part 2 of ISO/IEC 9541 specifies the interchange formats for font information, and the minimum subsets of the information required for interchange, for which purpose it requires the property definitions of part 1. The format of font resource information is specified in both SGML and ASN.1, there being provision for the information to be encrypted. A conformance clause is included.

The required set of font resource properties is divided into font subsets:

- font description information (for example font resource name, font family name, and posture and weight codes);
- modal metric information (for example the writing mode name and average escapement values);
- glyph metric information (for example the glyph structured name and escapement point(s)).

Some information may be present at the receiving end, in which case public identifiers may be used, the rules for which are defined in ISO/IEC 9070. ISO 9069 SDIF may be used to interchange font resources for SGML documents.

Glyph shape representation relating to the available technologies is dealt with in part 3. Those currently specified are outline and bit-map representations, with the latter derived from the former. Others may be added in the future, for example bit-map representations in their own right as is now being proposed.

An outline representation describes a glyph using a mathematical description of the edges of the shapes, an advantage here being that transformations such as scaling, rotating, and skewing as well as variations in style can be done without requiring additional storage space. Added scaling information (known as hints) can also be stored, where this relates to the preservation of proportions for all sizes of raster grids and achieving non-linear scaling as an optical correction for different absolute sizes of presented glyphs.

Outline fonts are converted, after adjustments for scaling requirements, to suit vector or raster devices. For raster devices, bit-map representations are required for final imaging and presentation. Bit-map representations describe the pattern of pixels for imaging on the raster device, where they can be represented either as ordered columns or as rows of dots, or by ways to produce more compact representations, especially for the larger sizes. Needless to say, quality can be sacrificed if the bit-maps of glyph shapes are scaled or transformed.

Because there could be several technologies (or methodologies) in the description of glyph shapes, that currently defined in the standard is called type 1. Type 1 is defined as an outline font technology which uses graphical drawing operators to describe the shape of a glyph, with hints oriented towards the preservation of proportions and features of a glyph when it is being scaled and optimized for the pixel grid of a raster device, for example. Font level hints may be defined to assist in the control of the alignment and stem widths for the entire font, and glyph-level hints to assist in the control of the vertical and horizontal stems for the specific glyph.

SGML and ASN.1 encodings are provided, and encryption is possible with both.

Annexes cover additional information:

- default accent component table;
- compatibility with the installed base;
- composite glyphs;
- interchange sample.

Part 3 has successfully completed the DIS ballot, its only remaining for the text to be edited to take comments into account prior to forwarding it to ISO Central Secretariat for publication.

Work is in train for the development of part 4, dealing with application-specific requirements.

The fonts standard that deals with registration is:

- ISO/IEC DIS 10036 Information Technology — Procedure for Registration of Glyph and Glyph Collection Identifiers.

This text was approved for publication as an ISO standard some time ago, but may not be published as such until it is possible to add the information that ANSI is to be the official registration authority. For various reasons such approval has been held up, but this should not detract from the present value of the standard, or DIS as it must remain until officially published.

As evident from the title, this standard specifies the procedures to be followed by a registration authority in preparing, maintaining, and publishing a register of glyph identifiers and a register of glyph collection identifiers. (It is ISO/IEC 9541 part 1 that provides for the identification of glyphs within a font resource and also glyph collections.)

Whereas ANSI is to be the ISO registration authority, owing to the specialized nature of the topic the actual registrar is to be the Association for Font Information Interchange (AFII). AFII was set up specifically for this purpose, some of its officers being members of WG 8 responsible for the development of the fonts standards. AFII has taken on a tremendous task, few people realizing just how many different fonts there are in the world, coping with the world's languages and scripts.[1]

It was almost inevitable that the main fonts standard in its first edition (ISO/IEC 9541) did not address all eventualities in an adequate way, and that special requirements would be identified that necessitated additions to the standard as published.

One such need is for application-specific extensions, these being necessary for specialized requirements of mathematical and chemical texts, and others of a technical nature, for which additional properties are required in the font resources. For example consider the inter-glyph spacing for mathematics, and the need to have recommended sizes for first and second order sub/superscripts.

Another is for additional properties that would result in improvements to the setting of text, and to allow the production of glyphs from a small set of glyph components. It was further found that although the fonts standard catered well for Latin based and ideographic fonts, and made available similar functionality for font providers and font users of non-Latin, non-ideographic writing systems, in particular, it is stated that multilingual and monolingual documents using writing systems not covered by ISO/IEC 9541 should be able to be formatted and displayed with access to a standardized and extensive set of properties using the same font architecture. An example would be requirements for Arabic fonts.

Then extensions for interchange capabilities (part 2) are requested to support the interchange of parts of font resources, composite fonts constructed from separate fonts or parts of fonts, and of multiple fonts. Examples given here include augmentation of existing libraries, perhaps to add swash letters or old-style letters and numerals, and to obtain the entire collection of fonts associated with a particular publication series.

Finally, the addition to bit-mapped glyph shape representation to result in an addendum to part 3 is proposed, where the only shape representation currently provided for is type 1 outlines. This proposal is to allow for bit-map representations, which would presumably be type 2. The rationale is that high quality glyph shape representations for low-resolution devices such as screens, cannot yet be obtained from outline descriptions; for these, edited bit-map forms provide the best readability and are required for user productivity. Moreover, the ISO/IEC 10036 registry is held in bit-map form, so the registrar would also benefit from this addition.

Note

(1) For further information on registered glyphs and glyph collections, contact AFII, PO Box 5328, Los Alamitos, CA 90720, United States. Even at this stage the register is huge.

7

SGML support facilities

7.1 INTERCHANGING SGML DOCUMENTS

The standard that has been developed for the interchange of SGML documents is:

- ISO 9069 Information Processing — SGML Support Facilities — SGML Document Interchange Format (SDIF), 15 September 1988.

The original purpose of this standard was to provide the necessary hooks to enable an SGML document to be interchanged in an OSI environment. However, it has been so written that it can be used for data communications techniques in general, and for the exchange of storage media, magnetic tapes or disks, and optical disks.[1]

SDIF enables an SGML document, which could be stored as several entities, to be assembled into a data stream. These entities could be libraries of raster and vector graphics, video and audio content, as well as the textual content of the SGML document. In addition, there can be accompanying (related) documents such as a covering letter, a profile of the document (needed for the interchange of ODA documents to enter an SGML environment), font resources, or formatting information. Needless to say, these accompanying documents must also be SGML documents, conforming to their own SGML declaration and DTD. (It is sufficient for such related documents to be encapsulated in an SGML shell as it were.)

In organizing the data stream, the sender assigns SDIF names to the data stream itself, the SGML documents, and any constituent entities. Identifiers are also assigned for external entities.

These SGML documents could be considered as going into an SDIF envelope for the purpose of giving the recipient all the necessary information in one data stream, packed by the sender, and unpacked by the receiver. The unpacker would have the ability to reconstitute the data stream into its constituent entities, organizing them in accordance with local system requirements.

Since the main consideration was to enable interchange in an OSI environment, the envelope had to have hooks coded in ASN.1, the ISO coding standard used by the ISO OSI standards. Where an OSI environment is concerned, an ASN.1 object identifier has been assigned for interchange to be possible using:

- ISO 8571 Information Processing Systems — Open Systems Interconnection — File Transfer, Access, and Management (FTAM);
- ISO 8832 Information Processing Systems — Open Systems Interconnection — Specification of the Basic Class Protocol for Job Transfer and Manipulation (JTM).

Another method of interchange using ISO standards is that of the Message Oriented Text Interchange System (MOTIS), one which is cited in ISO 9069 SDIF:

- ISO/IEC 10021 Information Processing Systems — Text Communication — Message Oriented Text Interchange System (MOTIS).

There are other MOTIS standards and equivalent CCITT recommendations having identical text. There is a CCITT recommendation for the Message Handling Service (MHS), X.400 (1988) being part of both US and UK flavours of GOSIP, the Government Open Systems Interconnection Profile.

Suffice it to say that SDIF formalizes the organization of SGML data streams. Whilst this is primarily for the purposes of interchanging SGML documents, SDIF could also be used to formalize the organization of files for other purposes, where this may be done in a standard way.

It is expected that SDIF will be used extensively for the US DoD applications of SGML, since the Computer-aided Acquisition and Logistic Support (CALS) strategy specifically calls for interchange of technical information, where much is structured in accordance with SGML. And just as CALS has been a major driver for the provision of many SGML products in the marketplace that can be used for a variety of applications, both defence-oriented and those for other industries and purposes, so also it is expected that CALS will be a major driver for there to be SDIF products in the marketplace for use by all the SGML community.

This will be essential for the interchange of SGML documents in an OSI environment, in particular. An open environment is where most SGML applications can take fuller advantage of information technology standards with all the benefits that can accrue from international communications.

7.2 REGISTRATION OF OWNER IDENTIFIERS

To enable the sharing of SGML constructs for many reasons, including that of keeping down the overheads of transmission, it is necessary to be able to refer in a unique way to such SGML constructs as can be shared, there being no necessity to repeat the details each time. For this purpose another ISO standard was developed:

- ISO/IEC 9070 Information Technology — SGML Support Facilities — Registration Procedures for Public Text Owner Identifiers, second edition, 15 April 1991.

In fact this was the second standard developed by ISO as part of the programme for providing SGML support facilities. It is this standard that is used with the FORMAL feature of ISO 8879. A second edition was prepared in order to allow for a publishing house to use its International Standard Book Number (ISBN) prefix instead of having yet another identifier, the opportunity being taken to incorporate other changes.

There was never any intention on the part of ISO to register individual SGML contructs, where these may range from SGML declarations and complete DTDs to sets of entities, indeed any markup construct that can be shared. Instead, the idea was to register what are termed public text owner identifiers, so there can be a unique identification scheme for SGML constructs that may be shared. They are termed public, but in fact such constructs could be shared in a closed community, in a multi-national company, for example. There is no onus on the owner of an SGML construct that has a public identifier to disclose the details of the construct to SGML users at large. Rather, the scheme allows for owner identifiers to be unique, through a registration process, where the owners themselves are tasked with ensuring that the other components are added to the registered identifier (considered as a prefix) in accordance with ISO/IEC 9070, to ensure that the SGML construct under their jurisdiction has a unique identifier.

These owner prefixes are assigned by ANSI on behalf of ISO. ANSI is the registration authority for all OSI such identifiers, and it was deemed practical that ANSI should also handle those relating to SGML since it was expected that many SGML documents would be transmitted using OSI standards. For these owners, one identifier should thus serve as a prefix in accordance with ISO/IEC 9070 and for all (other) OSI requirements.

Not everyone need apply, as some organizations already use a code that is acceptable to ISO/IEC 9070. One assigned in accordance with ISO 2108 or ISO 6523 is in this category:

- ISO 2108 Documentation — International Standard Book Numbering System (ISBN);
- ISO 6523 Data Interchange — Structures for the Identification of Organizations.

Many organizations have publishing as a related activity, and therefore an ISBN. And many banks, for example, have already been allocated an organization code, or code designator as it is termed.

ISO/IEC 9070 covers the registration procedures and the methods of constructing owner names. Self-assignment is also covered, although there is no guarantee that someone else has not already chosen a specific identifier. It is worth mentioning that the SGML standard allows for the identification of ISO text, for example the DTD and sets of entities included in the annexes to ISO 8879. The FORMAL feature is used, the identifier having the prefix of ISO.

Examples of the contruction of owner names are given in ISO 8879 SGML, also in ISO/IEC 9070. In addition to the representation of a public identifier in accordance with rules specified in ISO 8879 SGML, ISO/IEC 9070 gives an equivalent ASN.1 object identifier.

It is through the sharing of public text that certain DTDs, for example those for CALS, are implemented on the publishing systems offered by many vendors. And it is essential that the sets of entities listed in annex D of ISO 8879, for example, are taken up by vendors and offered in products.

7.3 EDITING SGML DOCUMENTS

Strictly speaking, the technical report dealing with the editing of SGML documents is not an SGML support facility, at least in the nomenclature of ISO:

- ISO/IEC TR 10037 Information Technology — SGML and Text-Entry Systems — Guidelines for SGML Syntax-Directed Editing Systems, 15 March 1991.

This is not to say that there was a deliberate move to exclude it from the group of standards and technical reports developed as support facilities, but for historical reasons it had SGML and Text-Entry Systems as the second element of its title. It is included here, however, as logically its content can be considered as facilitating the support of SGML.

A technical report was written for the subject of editing SGML documents as the process itself could not (reasonably) be standardized; rather, the amount and kind of assistance given to a user could be exactly what made one vendor's product preferable to that of another. So this technical report seeks to provide guidance to vendors of SGML editing systems, giving many useful hints. It is also of interest to prospective users of such systems in order that requirements may be formulated prior to licensing a product. Thoughtfully, the editor provided an index to the document.

Remember that it was a requirement of SGML that no new hardware was necessary, only new software. An SGML editing system is an example of the SGML software that could be licensed for the preparation of SGML documents. (The conversion of existing documents or an existing way of working into SGML form is explained later in this chapter.)

The technical report is in two parts:

- the creation, viewing, and modification of an SGML document instance;
- the creation of DTDs.

It specifically excludes the writing of SGML declarations. And where document instances are concerned, the emphasis is on 'text', there being no consideration of database working, or of spreadsheets, mathematics, or music, for example, all of which can be (parts of) SGML documents.

Many of the requirements for an SGML syntax-directed editing system (for an SGML 'smart' editor), can be implemented on a variety of display and entry devices, including both text and graphics displays (monochrome and colour), keyboards that may have special function keys, mice and other pointers, and (potentially) even voice recognition and sound generation. Colour can be useful to highlight emphasized text, for example, or indentation to indicate structure. Function keys can be programmed, and mice used to select start-tag and end-tag markup from lists of contextually-applicable elements. Many ideas are included in the technical report.

The report covers presentation of documents, consideration being given to a system that either displays the tags and other markup (unformatted state) or hides them (formatted state), as required. In a section on document entry, creating new text and markup or adding to an existing document, several possible methods are suggested:

- the author keys in all the markup;
- commonly-used tags are entered using a single keystroke (by means of programmed function keys or a system (mnemonically) related to alphabetic keys);
- selection from a presented list of tags;

- selection from a list of translated cues, the example given being 'start of chapter' instead of <h1>.

Mapping of the keys could be done as the context changed, a list of some or all legal tags (and attributes, if appropriate) being displayed.

Under the heading of the manipulation of SGML structures, consideration is given to entities as well as subdocuments, and notations for the different types of content, for example.

All the above is in accordance with a DTD known to the system, validation being an important consideration so only valid content is prepared/permitted.

For the creation of DTDs, there is the notion of treating them as tree structures as an alternative to textual representation. And needless to say, the DTD must be able to be validated. It is also suggested that the system provide a warning if any element mentioned in a content model is not defined.

Although SGML declarations are not covered by the report, editors should be able to give assistance with their writing. The SGML declaration for the reference concrete syntax could be displayed for modification, with options listed for the various parts, as indicated by the positioning of the cursor, and prompts given as to any additional information that may be necessary. In general, too little attention is given to the SGML declaration on which hinges a good or bad SGML application.

7.4 THE OVERALL MODEL

Text has not yet been balloted for the proposed technical report on the model of all the work carried out by WG 8 on Document Processing and Description Languages. Although drafts have been available within WG 8, it is recognized that by its very nature, a meaningful version of this report cannot be produced until such time as all the major projects are stable, and the inter-relationships known. In particular, it was necessary to know the functionality of DSSSL and its relationships with SGML, SPDL, and the main fonts standard. Because development of the model document was delayed, HyTime can also be written into it, and perhaps database working.

It is felt that a new draft could be prepared and balloted once the text composition standards are published, and by then HyTime will also be a published standard.

Whilst these are valid reasons for early drafts of the model document not having been made available more widely, much good work was done on the preparation of the document, which gives a good flavour as to how some of the processes can come together, and the role of the various standards.

Basic functional areas of text processing systems are seen as:

- the document creation and editing process;
- the document composition and layout process;
- the document presentation process.

The the first two processes could well be integrated in an implementation and may be iterative or interactive or both. And in a WYSIWYG implementation the presentation process could cause the imaging of the document on the screen used by the creation and editing process.

Figure 7.1 shows the three processes in the context of functionality provided by WG 8 standards, to give an overview of the operational model.

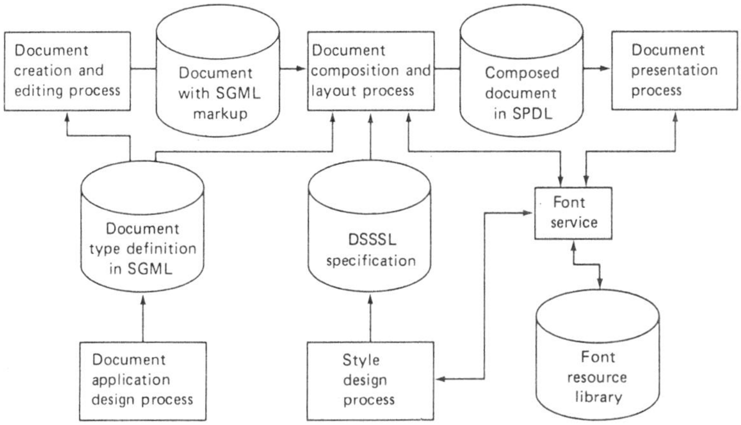

Figure 7.1. Overview of the operational model

Rectangles represent processes and cylinders represent an interface, in the form of data, between processes. Descriptions of the standards are given:

- SGML is a language for document representation that formalizes markup and frees it of system and processing dependencies;
- DSSSL provides the means for defining the format and style of documents;
- SPDL is a language for specifying documents in a fully-composed, device-independent form suitable for presentation on an output device;
- a font resource provides the detailed description, metric, and shape information required for document composition and presentation.

Further explanation is necessary to complete the understanding of the model:

- the document type designer has defined the DTD as to the rules governing the information content and its structure, whilst the style in which the information is to be presented is defined using DSSSL;
- the document creation and editing process provides the means of interactive recording and modification of text, which may include graphic material for example, and is intended primarily for the author whose task is the preparation of an SGML document;
- the DTD specifies the markup constructs required and permitted in a particular type of document, and also the required sequence of those constructs;
- the document composition and layout process receives the SGML document, the DTD, and the DSSSL specifications, and produces the document description in SPDL for the document presentation process;

- the document composition process receives the composed SPDL document and creates the images needed to produce the final document on the imaging output device (soft or hard-copy);
- font information is accessed by the document creation and editing process to determine both font and glyph availability, whilst font metric information (width tables, for example) is accessed by the document composition and layout process for use in determining the textual content of composed areas, and font glyph information (shape, for example) is accessed by the document presentation process for use in image generation.

Note that work on font services is proposed by WG 8, but has yet to be undertaken.

A further figure is provided in the draft to show the document composition and layout process in more detail, with SGML parsing, DSSSL processing, then composition and layout. Another shows SPDL document presentation, inputs being the SPDL document from the document composition and layout process, together with document production instructions. External SPDL structures are pictures and page sets, other resources being colour models, decompression algorithms, font identification, and metric and shape information. All lead to the SPDL presentation process from which there is final output.

7.5 TECHNIQUES FOR USING SGML

7.5.1 General

As has been explained in Chapter 1, the technical report on Techniques for Using SGML is being revised. It was originally published as:

- ISO/IEC TR 9573 Information Processing — SGML Support Facilities — Techniques for Using SGML, 1 December 1988.

The purpose in writing the technical report was to give additional tutorial material to document type designers who were already familiar with the basic concepts of SGML. It took as its starting point the tutorial material contained in the annexes to ISO 8879 SGML.

Notes are included on the analysis of a document prior to the writing of the formal DTD, and a series of examples, of which the principal is for a general document type, that defined in annex E of ISO 8879 SGML. Other examples of a general nature are for letter and memorandum (combined), spreadsheet, mathematics, tables, and the mixing of text and graphics using CGM for the graphics. There is also text on the use of short references.

Language applications are:

- Japanese with its special considerations, horizontal and vertical typesetting, sentences including words in the Latin alphabet, and ruby;
- Scandinavian runes by way of a linguistic application;
- a European multilingual document, including Greek;
- mixing text in languages written from left to right with those written from right to left;

- — right to left base text (Hebrew) mixed with text written from left to right (English),
- — left to right base text (Latin) mixed with text written from right to left (Arabic), including use of an 8-bit Latin/Arabic character set.

Since the publication of ISO/IEC TR 9573 in 1988 as a single volume, the material has undergone revision and expansion. Furthermore, in reviewing ISO 8879 SGML, it was decided that the tutorial material should be moved to a multi-part edition of ISO/IEC TR 9573. As stated previously, this multi-part edition will in fact consist of sixteen parts, enabling those interested in just certain aspects to purchase those parts only. The material will be divided as follows:

- Part 1 SGML Tutorial, replacing ISO 8879 annexes B and C (in part);
- Part 2 Basic Techniques, replacing ISO/IEC TR 9573 clauses 4, 5, 6, 7, 10, 13, and 14, and ISO 8879 annex E (in part);
- Part 3 Advanced Techniques, replacing ISO 8879 annexes C (in part) and D (in part);
- Part 4 Using Short References for Identifying Markup, consisting of text originally intended for a technical report on retroactive conversion;
- Part 5 Using Non-Latin Alphabets, replacing ISO/IEC TR 9573 clauses 11, 12, and 15;
- Part 6 Referencing and Synchronization, new text;
- Part 7 Mathematics and Chemistry, replacing ISO/IEC TR 9573 clause 8;
- Part 8 Tables, replacing ISO/IEC TR 9573 clause 9;
- Part 9 Using SGML for Computer to Computer Interchange, new text;
- Part 10 Designing Applications for Database Interfacing, new text;
- Part 11 Designing Applications at ISO Central Secretariat for International Standards and Technical Reports, new text;
- Part 12 Public Entity Sets for General and Publishing Symbols, replacing ISO 8879 annex D (in part);
- Part 13 Public Entity Sets for Mathematics and Science, replacing ISO 8879 annex D (in part);
- Part 14 Public Entity Sets for Latin Based Alphabets, replacing ISO 8879 annex D (in part);
- Part 15 Public Entity Sets for Non-Latin Based Alphabets, replacing ISO 8879 annex D (in part);
- Part 16 Public Entity Sets for Ideograms, new text.

7.5.2 Entities for mathematics and science

Publication of Part 13 Public Entity Sets for Mathematics and Science, 1 July 1991, meant that many more entities were available for use by those in the scientific community who were turning to SGML. Happily, the various symbols are not only described in terms of entity references but are also imaged — which is certainly necessary in the case of the more exotic ones. Some were (and still are) in annex D of

ISO 8879, but there are now many more. The sets of entities are in the following categories:

- basic mathematical and scientific symbols
  - — general,
  - — Greek symbols,
  - — alternative Greek symbols;
- additional mathematical symbols
  - — ordinary symbols,
  - — binary and large operators,
  - — relations,
  - — negated relations,
  - — arrow relations,
  - — opening and closing delimiters;
- symbols based on the Latin alphabet
  - — fraktur,
  - — open face (blackboard bold),
  - — script.

These sets of entities have been allocated public identifiers, referring to their publication in ISO/IEC TR 9573.

7.5.3 Application for standards and technical reports

Several national standards bodies are interested in Part 11 Application at ISO Central Secretariat for International Standards and Technical Reports. There is a project for its consideration being undertaken jointly by the French, German, and UK standards bodies, and it has been commended to ANSI for use in the US with use in Canada for building regulations, for example.

> It is intended that the application be implemented through an SGML-sensitive editor when used by project editors, project leaders, and secretariats for working drafts during the development of a standard and for submission of these documents to the ISO Central Secretariat for publication. In such an implementation, prompting by more meaningful names than element names (restricted to 8 characters) will be available, as well as on-line help both for the different elements and for rules contained in the IEC/ISO Directives.

Needless to say, the DTD defined has to be able to cope with technical documents that may contain anything known to scientific publishers. The DTD is based on that in annex E of ISO 8879 SGML, with extensions for the application of standards and technical reports. The design aims were:

- that the elements be sufficiently rich to permit production of existing international standards in hard-copy form;
- that there be SGML parser verification of completeness of the structure (for example that scope, references, and definitions had their own generic identifers instead of using <h1> as for other headings);

- that elements were present to permit formatter-generated 'boilerplate' text, in the case of the foreword, for example, again instead of using <h1>;
- that elements were present to reflect information content to permit secondary publications and database applications in future.

The design is such that it can handle mathematics, chemistry, and text in a foreign language, as well as the more generally expected elements for bibliography, tables, and graphics, for example. Use the index to find the constructs you require.

Already it is reported that a number of commerical publishing system products are taking this application of SGML as a model for supporting technical documentation.

7.5.4 Using short references

A working draft is in existence for Part 4 Using Short References for Identifying Markup. This suggests ways in which the short reference and data tag minimization techniques described in ISO 8879 SGML can be used to reduce the amount of markup that needs to be present in an SGML document.

To achieve this, in ISO 8879 SGML thirty-two code sequences are listed that can, by default, be used as short references to identify where entity replacement is to occur within SGML documents. Extensions to this list may be made by modification of the SGML declaration. However, the attention of the reader is drawn to this as not all vendors' products will permit the SGML declaration to be modified, so do watch this point when choosing a product.[2]

Data tags are also allowed for in the standard, these identifying points at which end-tags should be inserted in the file while the data 'tag' is still retained as part of the text itself.

Thus the SHORTREF and DATATAG features are necessary to implement all of the suggestions made in this technical report, plus the ability to change the SGML declaration.

Why do we need to use short references? It is not just that we can minimize the amount of markup that need be present in an SGML document. They also provide a way of converting partially coded or uncoded documents into SGML documents without users being aware that this process has taken place. For automatic conversion, it must be possible to identify points at which markup is to be inserted. The technical report describes how suitable points can be identified in existing text files to enable their retroactive conversion to SGML.

It is held that an SGML document may be prepared on any kind of text-entry system, including:

- word processors or electronic typewriters with data capture capabilities;
- general-purpose computer systems with text editing software;
- typewriters or typesetting systems capable of generating text that can be read by an optical character recognition (OCR) reader;
- any other equipment capable of recording text in a digitally encoded format.

These text-entry systems need be unaware of the DTD, for example, unlike those that have an SGML smart editor, as described above. Some of the points to watch in transferring data from text-entry systems are listed, and advice is given on using non-ASCII character sets and identifying elements that require tagging.

Clauses in the technical report take into account:

- using line endings as a guide to document structure;
- use of quotation marks;
- highlighting as a guide to document structure;
- handling tables;
- using text as a guide to markup points;
- post-conversion editing.

It is in this last point that there is the recognition that not all conversions are necessarily perfect. Then post-editing is necessary, the documents being checked and corrected using a context-sensitive editor. This is what I term system-supplied and user-supplemented markup.

7.6 VOCABULARY

Another technical report that is not strictly an SGML support facility is:

- ISO/TR 9544 Information Processing — Computer-Assisted Publishing — Vocabu- lary, 1988.

But it was developed by WG 8 and is included here for completeness.

The report defines terms that are in common use in computer-assisted publishing (text entry, text editing, typesetting and other typographical imaging, and printing and publishing insofar as they are relevant), and identifies relationships among those terms. It deals with terms used in the principal applications of text and office systems in publishing, notably computer-assisted typesetting, defining terms used in typesetting instructions, and in the description of equipment used.

It was developed to assist those coming from the publishing industry to that of computer-assisted publishing, and those from the computer industry who were to provide some of the facilities needed by publishers. It is of particular value to those using computers for textual work with sophisticated imaging capabilities, provided either by a printer or by a screen-based system. The advent of laser printers and all-points-addressable screens has opened up a whole new world, with its own vocabulary. This is where it can be learned. An index is provided.

Notes

(1) A description of SDIF and its functionality is included in Charles Goldfarb, *The SGML Handbook*, Clarendon Press (1990).

(2) Guidance on choosing an SGML product is given in Chapter 11. Alteration of the SGML declaration is something that needs to be borne in mind, not only for the purpose of extending the list of code sequences for short references but also for other purposes.

8

Hypermedia and other new work

8.1 HYTIME

The HyTime standard must surely be one of the fastest through the ISO balloting system, and one of the fastest to be written into US DoD contracts. A great deal of work had been carried out in the US prior to HyTime, as it is known, coming into the ISO system. The official title of the standard is:

- ISO/IEC DIS 10744 Information Technology — Hypermedia/Time-Based Structuring Language (HyTime).

Hypertext information may be accessed in more than one order; a hypermedia system permits the non-sequential access of information consisting of more than one medium. So a hypermedia system allows the user to go straight to exactly the piece (element) of information that is required (using a linking mechanism), whether that element of information be text, graphics, video, or whatever.

HyTime had its origins in music (more of SMDL later), and its base terminology reflects this. However, it is completely independent of musical applications, as proved by the CALS application. It is able to synchronize multiple time bases, including mixtures of real-time and variable bases.

HyTime is an application of ISO 8879 SGML, the fact that an SGML document is also one conforming to the HyTime standard being denoted as APPINFO in the SGML declaration. As would be expected of an application of SGML, HyTime documents may contain any type of content and its associated notation. Whilst the central or hub document must conform to SGML/HyTime, associated documents can be expressed in any architecture or notation.

With HyTime it is possible to include application-specific element types within a document. For example a HyTime document could include elements in animated graphics; a book on music might contain musical examples conforming to the SMDL application of HyTime, on which more information is provided below. The types of content envisaged include:

- digital audio recording (of both music and speech);
- digital motion video and dynamic graphics;
- text fields (for lyrics or for annotation, for example);

- musical notation (both traditional scores and tablatures as well as special notations for contemporary musicians);
- instrumental control (for the Musical Instrument Digital Interface (MIDI), for example);
- control signals for external systems (for example stage lighting, slide projectors, sound-effect generators, and video switchers).

Among the user requirements satisfied by HyTime are:

- support for application-specific element types;
- support for multiple streams of information;
- support for multiple applications of a single information base;
- support for retrieval mechanisms that allow a selection of which streams of information will be used for a particular application;
- the possibility to manage multiple data sources including stored data and data being processed in real-time;
- the possibility to separate data content from linking and synchronization information;
- the possibility to mix timing information that is associated with a fixed base (for example real-time) and information that is derived from a variable base;
- the possibility to extract synchronization information to control external processes;
- the possibility to include user-definable content notations;
- the possibility to use standardized and industry-accepted storage and compression methods for HyTime documents;
- support for retrieval mechanisms with the ability to follow links in any direction;
- support for cross-linking and synchronization among all content streams.

A useful introduction to HyTime is provided in the standard itself.[1] In that is the statement: 'HyTime provides a standard way to link to anything, anywhere, at any time.' A *hyperdocument* is defined as a set of documents or other information objects connected by webs of links, each of which is connected to a hub document. These links reference anchors, or end-points.

The concept of integrated open hypermedia is put forward:

- *integrated* in that all information is linkable, whether or not it was initially prepared for linking;
- *open* in that the identification of the linked location is system-independent;
- *hypermedia* in that it encompasses both hypertext and multimedia.

Both hypertext linking and multimedia time synchronization rely on addressing. Three kinds of addressing are satisfied by HyTime:

- name space addressing (a unique name being provided);
- co-ordinate addressing (relative to a given location);
- semantic addressing (by description).

Where the time-based parts of HyTime had been developed to satisfy the requirements in the music world, they can be applied equally well to other applications, for example process control.

Defined in the HyTime standard is a model and a language for the representation of hyperdocuments that link and synchronize static and time-based information contained in multiple conventional and multimedia documents and information objects. The implementation of the HyTime standard will require a HyTime engine or program to recognize HyTime constructs, and to perform address resolution, linking, alignment, and synchronization. Only the facilities actually required need be implemented. Hytime is designed for flexibility and extensibility, where optional subsets can be implemented, alone or in conjunction with user-defined extensions.

Interchange of HyTime documents will be possible using SDIF.

It is important to remember that a hypermedia application addresses not one document but a whole library of documents, the hyperdocument. With a hypermedia application, 'reading' may either be sequential, or a link may be traversed. For these reasons, and because a hyperdocument may contain any content type, HyTime is ideal for maintenance of highly complex systems, which is why the US DoD is applying it before the ink is dry on the standard.

This is the application of SGML that is destined to take information processing into the next millennium, with huge information bases structured in accordance with SGML, the information bases containing text, graphics of different types, coloured photographs, animated graphics, audio, and video content, where any piece of information in the information base can be accessed at the touch of a few buttons, or use of bar codes, or voice control, or whatever other forms of control are devised. And as with SGML, HyTime will doubtless be applied for purposes which the standards-makers did not imagine.[2]

8.2 THE STANDARD MUSIC DESCRIPTION LANGUAGE

The Standard Music Description Language (SMDL) is an application of HyTime, to which it adds specialized architectural forms for the representation of musical constructs. And HyTime is an application of SGML; indeed, there are SGML constructs present throughout the SMDL document. The official title of the SMDL document is:

- ISO/IEC CD 10743 Information Technology — Standard Music Description Language.

Sufficient member bodies of ISO voted in favour of the CD, and the document will progress to DIS for a six-month ballot when comments have been taken into account. As with HyTime, a substantial draft had been prepared in the US prior to moving the work into ISO. In fact it had been developed in parallel with HyTime, where HyTime thus had to cater for all the various needs of the world of music.

Not surprisingly, it can be seen above that user requirements agreed for SMDL were reflected in those put forward for HyTime, which is why there are references to content types including musical notation and instrumental control signals, for example. Where SMDL is concerned, an example of the requirement for support for multiple applications of a single information base could relate to a variety of forms of a musical score (perhaps orchestra conductor and parts for individual instruments), and interpretable to result in multiple performances (perhaps to produce MIDI encoding for electronic keyboards).

A specific SMDL requirement was the possibility to mix timing information that is associated with a fixed base (for example real-time) and information derived from a variable base (for example music time), the music time durations being converted to real-time for a performance. An example given of this was a slide show presentation when the duration of some of the slides would be shown in real-time (perhaps 30 seconds), while the duration of others could be expressed in music time units to indicate their relative duration, which could be modified by tempo.

All the requirements were taken into account when the SMDL standard was developed. It defines a language for the representation of music information, either alone or in conjunction with text, graphics, or other information needed for publishing or business purposes. It supports multimedia time-sequencing information.

SMDL is designed so as to represent as many genres of music as possible, and most instances of works in those genres, the primary focus being on music that can (reasonably) be expressed in common practice music notation. However, the music need not have been written in conventional notation, or even written at all. The use of special symbols in the score is supported, and modern notational practices.

Separate multimedia time sequences can be represented, such as slide show control tracks or automated lighting information. And SMDL can represent combinations of musical and non-musical events, such as in dramatic productions.

The Field of Application subclause of the standard gives a good flavour of possible scenarios. Quite simply, SMDL is designed for the transmission and storage of music and hypermedia information. Typical sources are given as pieces that exist as printed scores, performances recorded in a manner that permits machine transcription, and pieces already represented in a non-standard music description language. Multimedia information, such as digital audio recordings, can be associated and synchronized with music described in SMDL, these multimedia elements having their own notations and encodings, standards for these being outside the scope of SMDL.

To whet the imagination, examples given of mixed music and multimedia applications are:

- business presentations containing synthesized music, sequenced live sound excerpts, slide change signals, and recorded or synthesized speech;
- dramatic productions containing music, lighting control, and digitally recorded sound effects.

A musical piece can be represented in SMDL in terms of four domains:

- the *logical* domain, the basic musical content of pitch, rhythm, and harmony, for example;
- the *gestural* domain, performance-oriented information such as intonation and rhythmic interpretation, for example;
- the *visual* domain, details of the score, which in common practice music notation would include page layout, horizontal spacing, and clef;
- the *analytical* domain, where music theoretical analyses are collected.

The SMDL representation of the logical domain is termed the cantus. In the Theory of Use annex to SMDL it is suggested that an automated composition program might generate a cantus and an associated gestural domain; an interactive music printing printing system might generate a cantus and a visual domain; a sequencer might capture a live performance and transcribe it into a cantus and performance domain, and then turn the piece over to a music printing system for the creation of the visual and analytical domains. Only the cantus element need be present.

A great company of musical buffs is engaged in the development of SMDL so it can be as useful as possible in the musical world. For those who have to represent music, here is the place to look for assistance.

8.3 A BINARY VERSION OF SGML

A new work item was added to the list of projects for WG 8 to address SGML-B, or binary. The idea is to develop an abstract definition of SGML for binary encoding of ISO 8879 SGML, with bi-directional convertability between the binary and clear text encodings. In particular, SGML-B will allow for direct addressability. It is clearly recognized how large information bases may become, and the need to speed up processing as much as reasonably possible.

It is not expected that a separate standard will result; rather it is considered as an extension to ISO 8879 SGML, by way of a normative annex. It is therefore being developed in the same time-frame as the five-year revision of SGML, as described below.

The agreed user requirements tell what form SGML-B will take, what functionality it will have, meeting, as it now must, the requirements of both information publishing (for example on CD-ROM) and information interchange. There are basically three user requirements, the primary one being 'to provide efficient direct access to arbitrary portions of a conforming SGML document while allowing simpler parsing (reading) and generating (writing)'. Bi-directional transformation between SGML and SGML-B must be possible without loss of any information is given as the second, whilst the third states that ASN.1 coding of SGML-B must be supported.

In the first of these requirements we note the assistance that will be provided for hypermedia applications. There must be the ability to establish the context of each element (elder sibling, parent, and definitions in the DTD, for example), to permit rapid processing, there being no need to parse the document from the start. The approach to be taken is the replacement of symbolic pointers, such as element type names and entity names, by explicit SGML-B pointers to their definitions.

There need be no SGML parser for SGML-B, but an ASN.1 parser in conjunction with what is described as an application-specific mini-parser. Whilst the mini-parser need not need to recognize delimiters, it must be able to resolve SGML-B pointers. There are plans to employ various techniques to simplify parsing and generating. SGML-B must support efficient machine-creation of a document, either by an editing program that does not allow direct user access to the markup, or by translation from an SGML document.

Where bi-directional transformation between SGML (clear text) and SGML-B is concerned, 'without loss of any information' is an important criterion, its being necessary to retain information 'that is acted upon by a markup-sensitive SGML application'. Markup minimization is considered, where SGML-B should define default values for the omitted fields, an implementation giving a user the ability to specify rules for the completion of the omitted fields.

SGML-B is to be defined as a data structure in the ISO 8879 (meta)language, its being felt that this will provide the simplest comparison with the SGML definition, with less likelihood of errors being made. An ASN.1 definition or an algorithm for generating one from the ISO 8879 metalanguage will be provided in SGML-B.

8.4 REVISION OF ISO 8879

The stability of ISO 8879 SGML has been maintained for over five years. Only one amendment was published during that time, to clarify text or to correct errors in the standard as originally published, these editing changes being necessary as vendors developed their implementations of the standard. A second amendment was proposed, but feedback suggested that any further editing of the text could and should wait until a new edition was published in the fulness of time.

ISO decrees that the usefulness of a published standard shall be examined every five years. At that time a decision can be made to withdraw the standard, to confirm it as published, or to confirm its continued use as published whilst a new edition is being written, taking into account experiences and new developments during that period. Thus ISO 8879 SGML came up for five-year review in October 1991. Needless to say, its continued use was supported, and it was decided that the opportunity be taken to bring out a second edition.

It is expected that this second edition will reflect editorial changes and some technical enhancements. One thing is certain: it must not be changed in such a way as to invalidate existing SGML documents, of which there is an ever-increasing number, thus upwards compatibility is assured.

Several changes can be predicted with a degree of certainty. As has already been explained, much of the material at present in annexes to ISO 8879 is to be moved to parts of the re-organized ISO/IEC TR 9573 Techniques for Using SGML. And there is to be a new annex on SGML-B.

Where editing is concerned, minor stylistic corrections are to be made, and the meaning of text is to be clarified where necessary. All this is expected. In fact a document has been prepared gathering together any changes resulting from comments received over the years.

Additional to the above, changes could well result when responses to a request for contributions for the review process are examined. It is interesting to note that a DTD has been written for commenting.

Ground rules for making changes have been established, all with respect to provisions of future versions of the standard:

- any document that is a conforming SGML document according to the current standard shall continue to be a conforming document;
- the results of parsing an SGML document that conforms to the current standard shall be unchanged when the document is parsed;
- a document that is classified as a minimal or basic conforming document under the present standard shall continue to be classified as such;
- conforming SGML parsers and systems to support conforming SGML documents, minimal conforming SGML documents, and basic conforming SGML documents, shall continue to at least the same extent as the current standard.

This does not mean that no changes may be made to ISO 8879. It is suggested that some changes are possible without violating the stated principles, for example relaxing restrictions, adding new constructs, partitioning existing optional features, and introducing options to allow the suppression of 'troublesome existing constructs'. Comments are also made to the effect that future versions of this standard can introduce additional requirements, and the principles should not be construed to mean that the definition of a conforming SGML document cannot be changed, only that existing conforming SGML documents will continue to be classified as such.

All in all we should eventually see a revised version of ISO 8879 SGML that permits us to keep all our existing body of information marked up in accordance with the current version, and offers us additional facilities that will be of value for the new uses to which the standard is being put.

8.5 CONFORMANCE

For various historial reasons, conformance testing of ISO 8879 SGML as a separate topic was not originally taken up within WG 8. What then happened was that work progressed within ANSI. More recently ISO member bodies agreed to take conformance testing into its programme of work, with the result that when the work is approved as an ANSI standard, it will be input to ISO for what is known as fast-track processing. (When the ISO fast-track procedure is invoked, the overall ballot time is reduced, no CD ballot being necessary.)

Conformance testing to a standard such as SGML is deemed as being essential if only so that users can be assured that the products they are licensing from vendors all conform to ISO 8879, thus guaranteeing interoperability with other users whose products have been similarly tested. And since SGML is an international standard, it is important that the testing carried out is the same the world over, leading to the same results. Hence there is the desire to have some aspects of the development and use of test suites standardized.

Outside the remit of ISO, but none-the-less important, is the need that results of conformance testing are recognized internationally. This has been happening with testing for program languages, for example, and is expected to happen in the case of SGML.

The requirements agreed for the ISO standard for conformance testing of SGML include SDIF, SDIF being needed to connect the several entities that make up an SGML document into a specific object for interchange in an OSI environment. Requirements cover several categories of users:

- *testers*
  - identification of the part of the standard being tested,
  - tests should produce unambiguous results,
  - tests should cover all parts of the standard,
  - whilst covering the above conditions, the number of tests should be kept to a minimum;
- *implementors*
  - a means of determining that an implementation conforms to the standard,
  - a clear indication of the reason for failure of a test;
- *users of SGML implementations*
  - an implementation performs as documented,
  - different implementations of the same standard are compatible,
  - an understanding of what passing the test signifies.

Organizations interested in conformance testing for SGML systems include the Graphic Communications Association (GCA) in the US and the National Computing Centre in the UK, some funding for this topic having been provided by the CEC.

8.6 RELATED STANDARDS WORK

8.6.1 Coding of character sets

ISO 8879 SGML necessarily makes reference to character sets being used by the application. Mention has already been made of ISO 2022, the standard that permits escape to other character sets for working in other languages or with character sets for specialized needs, such as publishing, where these character sets may be the subject of a standard, what are known as registered character sets, or those agreed privately.

Of the standard character sets, ISO 646 is the best known, being recognized as the base character set for working in the English-speaking world. This is the character set that can be thought of as being ASCII-based, operating in a 7 or 8-bit environment. What may not be generally known is that development has been taking place for a suite of character sets, ISO/IEC DIS 10646. Comments received on the drafts indicated that Unicode should be taken into account, lest Unicode be accepted as a *de facto* standard, the ISO standard being ignored. This is now being done, and it seems that ISO/IEC 10646, when agreed, will be based on Unicode, although the first version could be restricted to a two-byte model, all that is necessary for Unicode. It is unlikely that four-byte sets will be included in the first edition. There is the old problem of standards-making — that of finding expert volunteers to do the work.

The point being made here is that ISO/IEC DIS 10646 is on the way, and is a standard that the next edition of ISO 8879 SGML will surely be taking into account. In fact comments have already been input by the SGML standards-makers to the appropriate subcommittee for character sets. WG 8 comments were firstly that it has become possible to print all of the tables/charts for 10646 (some had been prepared by hand), for example by using fonts available through AFII; secondly, that the repertoire for mathematics and science should be increased to take into account all those specified as entities in ISO/IEC TR 9573 part 13.

It remains to be seen how far ISO/IEC DIS 10646 will go eventually to answer the needs of users of what could be termed the more sophisticated character sets.

8.6.2 Coding audio, hypermedia, and other information

A new subcommittee was recently set up with responsibility for Coded Representation of Audio, Picture, Multimedia, and Hypermedia Information. Previously, the topics had come under the aegis of the same subcommittee as that dealing with character sets. The standards being progressed within ISO/IEC JTC 1/SC 29, as now established, are of great interest to many who are involved with interactive technical information structured in accordance with SGML. Remembering that SGML information can include any content type, for defence applications in particular, there is interest to include audio, video clips, and coloured photographs in the SGML information base.

The remit of SC 29 does not stop at the coded representations; it extends to the provision of sets of compression and control functions. And the feedback is that the compression algorithms are very good.

Those familiar with the earlier names with which the various groups in this area were associated will still find them used:

- JBIG for the coding of bi-level and limited bits-per-pixel pictures (such as black and white pictures);
- JPEG for the coding of digital continuous-tone still pictures (such as scanned photographs);
- MPEG for the coding of moving pictures and associated audio (such as videos);
- MHEG for the coding of multimedia and hypermedia information objects.

Standards already published are:

- ISO/IEC 9281 Information Technology — Picture Coding Methods
  - — Part 1 Identification, 1990,
  - — Part 2 Procedure for Registration, 1990;
- ISO 9282 Information Processing — Coded Representation of Pictures
  - — Part 1 Encoding Principles for Picture Representation in a 7-Bit or 8-Bit Environment, 1988.

Those under development are:

- ISO 9282 Information Processing — Coded Representation of Pictures
  - — Part 2 Incremental Encoding of Point Lists in a 7-Bit or 8-Bit Environment (DIS);
- ISO/IEC 10918 Coded Representation of Digital Continuous-Tone Still Pictures
  - — Part 1 Requirements and Guidelines (DIS),
  - — Part 2 Conformance (CD);
- ISO/IEC 11172 Coded Representation of Moving Pictures and Associated Audio (CD);
- ISO/IEC 11544 Coded Representation of Bi-level and Limited Bits-per-Pixel Still Pictures (CD);
- Coded Representation of Multimedia and Hypermedia Information Objects

  - Part 1 Multimedia Synchronized Objects,
  - Part 2 Hypermedia Objects;
- Coded Representation of Audio Visual Interactive Scriptware (AVIS);
- Coded Representation of Audio Information.

ISO/IEC JTC 1/SC 18/WG 8 is particularly interested in the work on AVIS as it has responsibility for development of the functional model for AVIS, this being central to HyTime. AVIS is intended as an intermediate language capable of representing the functionality (as a translation target) of any of the popular languages for hypermedia scripting. The theory of use of AVIS is that programs (called scripts) in any hypermedia scripting language would be translated into AVIS scripts for interchange, then translated to the receiving system's own scripting language.

8.6.3 A colour architecture

Within ISO/IEC JTC 1/SC 18 a colour architecture is being developed by its WG 5 — Text and Office Systems Colour Architecture (TOSCA). A first working draft has been produced.

The purpose in developing such an architecture is to provide a consistent colour framework across all document-related standards, including SGML of course. It will allow the interchange of colour information in an OSI environment through the use of flexible colour data transformation mechanisms.

General user requirements are given as:

- support by the interchange mechanism for multiple colour spaces;
- support for the specification of colour by colour space parameters, a colour name, or an index;
- support for appropriate reduced renditions, such as monochrome or bi-level representations for cases when a colour specification is beyond the capabilities of the receiving system;
- minimization of the number of conversions to go from one colour space to another.

Requirements for the interchange process were also defined:

- establishment of a single interchange process that contains parameters allowing conversion to and from alternate colour spaces;
- incorporation of colour calibration and colour accuracy techniques;
- support for additive and subtractive colour mixing;
- definition of a method for specification of standards and non-standard colourant sets;
- definition of a method for the inclusion of multiple viewing environments.

Backwards compatibility with existing colour exchange techniques is considered desirable. Needless to say, this proposed standard will be related to many other standards, not only those of SC 18 but also those of SC 29, for example, where the compression techniques being developed for grey scale and colour images are to be considered.

8.6.4 Full-text manipulation of structured data

To complete the standards picture, there is now liaison between the SGML standards-makers and those dealing with databases, in particular for developments of SQL and a query language suitable for object-oriented information bases. It is right that this is so, if only because of the needs of the defence projects where huge amounts of information with many different types of content will be amassed.

Again, a set of requirements had been drawn up, and this was input to the standard-makers.

It was hypothesized that the system would provide a database for the storage of documents being maintained and whilst being created, and that there should be a means to search for and retrieve documents and parts of documents. The database would be governed by SGML, input and output being SGML data streams. It would also store SGML public text. Tracking revisions would be essential. Incomplete documents must be managed, and there must be the ability to retrieve partial documents. It must be possible to retrieve portions of documents that do not share the same DTD and either merge them into another document whose DTD does allow for the elements retrieved or to construct an *ad hoc* DTD for the display/printing of the material retrieved. In the case of partial retrieval, the system must be able to resolve references, cross-references, and counters. Querying the database would be in terms of data content, SGML markup, or a combination of the two.

Examples of typical searches included:

- search for a text pattern, for example to retrieve an element content in which the pattern appears;
- search for an SGML structure, for example to retrieve all instances of a class of elements;
- retrieve a combination of information, for example to extract the text of a document with the changes in effect as of a given date;
- sort a set of elements according to a key derived from element content, for example the rows of a table according to the content of one or more columns.

Other requirements were detailed, and the list of examples was expanded with the caveat that it was not to be considered as all-inclusive. However, the above gives a good indication of the kind of facilities looked for in an SGML information base. Hopefully, the term information will gain popularity as more people come to realize that it subsumes both text and data, and includes all types of information. Then we can get away from the notion of databases with connotations of fixed length fields and upper-case only line printers of yore.

Notes

(1) This is an adaptation of a paper written by Charles Goldfarb, the editor of the HyTime standard, 'HyTime: A Standard for Structured Hypermedia Interchange', *IEEE Computer*, August 1991. In fact several papers have already been published on HyTime.

(2) The best way to discover more information is through SIGhyper, a Special Interest Group of the SGML Users' Group; contact Dr Steven R Newcomb, TechnoTeacher

Incorporated, 1810 High Road, Tallahassee, FL 32303-4408, United States (telephone +1 904 422 3574; telefax +1 904 386 2562; e-mail srn@cmr.fsu.edu).

9

Some applications of SGML

It is only possible to give information on a few of the many applications of SGML. Hopefully, the list will serve to give a good indication of the kinds of applications where use is being made of the methodology offered by SGML. And it is worth remembering that for every specific application that is publicized in the media, there is one that may not be publicized as the company concerned wishes to keep quiet on the use of SGML since it gives competitive edge.[1]

Whilst it seems invidious to cite individual projects when there are so many, another indication of the use of SGML could be by country, where it is true to say that Canada, France, Germany, Japan, Switzerland, The Netherlands, the UK, and the US have been particularly active.

9.1 DEFENCE

SGML is being used extensively throughout the defence industry. This use is not confined to CALS in the US or AECMA for the European aerospace industry, both of which are described below. Sweden was one of the first countries to consider the use of SGML for defence projects. And SGML has been in use in Australia for a submarine project for several years, its use being mandatory for all Australian defence since June 1991 as part of the policy to adopt CALS. There is use of SGML in Canada for defence projects. France is another country that has been advocating SGML for defence system documentation, and here the DTDs use many of the features, including the link features, not included in the CALS applications. The use of more SGML features is expected to be repeated elsewhere in Europe even if not in the US in future.

9.1.1 Computer-aided Acquisition and Logistic Support

Thc US DoD Computer-aided Acquisition and Logistic Support (CALS) strategy is being taken up by allied nations around the world — at least in principle.[2] Onc of the aims of the strategy is to do away with the mountains of paper which were ever-growing in size, moving to a (near) paperless solution. Technical manuals were high on the list of priorities, the proposed solution being to make them available electronically. They have to be updatable readily if only because a high percentage of deaths in the Services were being attributed to incorrect information, updating information lagging behind actual changes by more than a year in too many cases. The enabling mechanism for interchange is standards, preferably international standards.

As a first step, a series of military specifications was developed:

- MIL-D-28000 Digital Representation for Communication of Product Data: IGES Application Subsets;
- MIL-M-28001 Markup Requirements and Generic Style Specification for Electronic Printed Output and Exchange of Text;
- MIL-R-28002 Requirements for Raster Graphics Representation in Binary Format;
- MIL-D-28003 Digital Representation for Communication of Illustration Data: CGM Application Profile.

Two more documents were made available:

- MIL-HDBK-59 Program Implementation Guide;
- MIL-STD-1840A Automated Interchange of Technical Information.

MIL-M-28001 is the military specification that is based on SGML. Both raster and vector graphics are permitted in technical manuals in accordance with the other military specifications in the 28000 series. For vector graphics, where the description is in terms of lines and arcs for which co-ordinates are specified, there is a choice of MIL-D-28000 based on the ANSI standard for the Initial Graphics Exchange Specification (IGES) — class I being for technical illustrations — and MIL-D-28003 based on the ISO standard for Computer Graphics Metafile (CGM). MIL-R-28002 for raster graphics, where the image is scanned, is based on the CCITT recommendation for group 4 facsimile. That is to say, the content notations for vector graphics are in accordance with IGES or CGM, and that for raster graphics is in accordance with CCITT group 4.

By means of these military specifications, a technical manual can be represented electronically using what are termed the CALS base standards, and handed over both as a printed publication and on magnetic tape or other magnetic medium. How the files are assembled on the magnetic tape (the default medium) is described in MIL-STD-1840A. The military handbook gives information of a general nature for CALS, including that on the acquisition of the technical information. All these publications are subject to an updating programme, a final alphabetical letter being added (or incremented) to indicate the revision.

In MIL-M-28001 (currently MIL-M-28001A) there are DTDs for technical manuals conforming to MIL-M-38784B (since revised to C), and a non-conforming one for other manuals. This application of SGML is of FIPS PUB 152, a Federal Information Processing Standard publication that takes a 'subset' of ISO 8879 SGML, including only the OMITTAG and FORMAL features, with implicit use of SHORTREF as the reference concrete syntax is cited in FIPS PUB 152. However, in practice in MIL-M-28001A the use of the SHORTREF feature is not advocated for purposes of interchange; and the reference value for NAMELEN has been increased from 8 to 32.

The method described, that of producing a paper publication as before plus a magnetic version, was by way of transition to a paperless, pageless way of working. The future lies in what are known as interactive electronic technical manuals (IETMs), for which draft military specifications have been produced. IETMs are for screen-based viewing by technicians, with formatting on-the-fly. In addition to content types allowed for in MIL-M-28001, there is now provision for audio, video, and process. Links are set up for the non-sequential access of the various elements of information in accordance with the HyTime standard, where CALS can be said to be the first application of HyTime. It is expected that the information will be stored on CD-ROM, this being a permitted delivery medium in MIL-HDBK-59A, the updated version of the military handbook.

A report was issued by the David Taylor Research Center on the subject of integrating logistic support analysis records (LSARs) with the content data model, as the information base for technical manuals and other purposes, is termed.[3] One diagram shows the product definition data being in one base and the LSARs in another, both feeding into the content data model, in accordance with DTDs. Output from the content data model is for maintenance manuals or training materials, where these may be represented on-screen, interactively, or printed. Loading in accordance with Nijssen's Information Analysis Method (NIAM) seems to be advocated in preference to using other modelling techniques, although IDEF (the ICAM Definition language for Integrated Computer-Aided Manufacturing) is also used in the US. The choice of modelling technique seems to depend on the Service concerned.

When choosing the kind of information base, then an object-oriented model is said to be more efficient than a relational model. The relational model becomes less efficient with large quantities of data. Figures quoted for the RAMP project (for the Rapid Acquisition of Manufactured Parts) were 10 hours to load information stored in a relational model, and 1 hour for the same information when stored in an object-oriented database. And as stated in 5.2 an object-oriented solution is preferable for SGML, a language that deals with elements or 'objects' of information. One vendor's offering for CALS technical manuals shows information for IETMs coming from an object-oriented database, for which input is governed by an SGML DTD (minimization being permitted).

Further work will always be in train, since the philosophy is to make optimum use of leading edge technology and methodology. Where SGML is concerned, we look to the revision of FIPS PUB 152 to be the full text of ISO 8879 SGML, and as revised for the second edition, when published. This would be in line with the European CEN/CENELEC SGML standard which is a carbon-copy of ISO 8879 SGML. Such revision of FIPS PUB 152 would mean that greater use could be made of the features of SGML to give rise to greater efficiency, as well as enabling the developers of the military specifications to exploit the use of SGML for the greater benefit of defence information.

In CALS, use is expected of ISO 9069 SDIF for working in an OSI environment, and DSSSL and SPDL for text composition. Already there is use of HyTime for IETMs.

9.1.2 The European AECMA specification

Developments were taking place in Europe also for the defence industry, the movers here being members of the Association Européenne des Constructeurs de Matériel

Aérospatial (AECMA). In fact AECMA published two specifications, that which interests us being:

- AECMA Spec 1000D International Specification for Technical Publications, Utilising a Common Source Data Base (1989).

It was decided early on that AECMA 1000D would be used for the technical documentation for the European Fighter Aircraft (EFA) and its Eurojet engine. EFA and Eurojet are collaborative projects involving four nations: Germany, Italy, Spain, and the UK. For the representation of the information in accordance with AECMA 1000D, the CALS base standards were called for, that is SGML, IGES, CGM, and CCITT group 4 facsimile. In particular, the CALS military specifications were cited (the CALS applications of the base standards) with the notable exception of MIL-M-28001 since the types of manuals in Europe are not as those in the US. Therefore, a DTD had to be written for EFA to take account of the AECMA common source data base (CSDB). For purposes of file organization, MIL-STD-1840A was also adopted, thus there is compatibility of AECMA 1000D and CALS technical documentation requirements.

Compatibility with MIL-M-28001 in particular was required when designing the EFA DTD, so the same generic identifiers were used for elements where applicable, and some of the same constructs within the DTD itself. The big difference is that for the AECMA 1000D application, information is being loaded into the CSDB — a common source data base. It is *not* for printed output as is MIL-M-28001, and herein lies the difference in philosophy. In fact the thinking behind AECMA 1000D is more akin to what is now coming out of CALS — the IETMs.

With the CSDB, information is input with no consideration for the manner in which it might be output. There was recognition that output media could change with time, and whilst some may think of specifying CD-ROM now, next year it could be CD-I, and who knows what the preferred storage medium will be in ten, twenty, thirty, or more years' time, when EFA will still be around?

Take-up of AECMA 1000D in the European ministries of defence has been good, in that it is accepted by those of all nations involved in the EFA/Eurojet project, for example, with its use also required for the European helicopter (EH101). But how much more sense it would make for those ministries of defence were they able to acquire weapon systems for land and sea using the same specification as that for aerospace. This extended use of AECMA 1000D is now being planned, and was one of the points made in the study of the NATO Industry Advisory Group (NIAG)[4] in the report of its study of CALS, where the AECMA 1000D specification and its method of identification of codes was endorsed, about which more details are given below. It can therefore be expected that AECMA 1000D will be used for technical information relating to weapon systems for all Armed Services, certainly in Europe. Furthermore, that the DTD originally developed for EFA and the Eurojet engine will be that accepted as a basis for general use with AECMA 1000D.

At the time of writing, the EFA DTD is being used for the interchange of technical information among the partners involved in EFA and Eurojet, and is planned for delivery to the ministries of defence in Germany, Italy, Spain, and the UK. There is the possibility of adding data specific to national requirements, and each nation will have its own national publications in its own national language, using the information from the CSDB.

For the UK, for example, British Aerospace is known to be interested in IETMs and the work of JPEG and MPEG for colour photographs and video.[5] Where the Eurojet engine is concerned the intended storage medium for information in the short term is CD-ROM with screen-based presentation for the maintenance engineer, formatting on-the-fly and with all the benefits that can accrue from this kind of approach. For this work, Rolls-Royce will be bringing to bear its experience with such an approach as already successfully applied to the maintenance of engines powering civil aircraft in accordance with the ATA-100 specification (that for the Air Transport Association), explained below.

With the Eurojet project, facilities offered could well include:

- availablity on CD-ROM with updating material on floppy diskette (encrypted), information always being up-to-date — *there is greater quality control*;
- accessing with bar codes or keying, going to exactly the information required by means of links built into the information system — *ease of use for the engineer*;
- seeing updating material in the correct place, displayed in a different colour (yellow) to draw attention — *there is greater quality control*;
- zooming on a diagram to magnify parts in which the engineer is interested — *there is greater quality control*;
- seeing a warning displayed in red, the system perhaps giving a bleep to draw attention, and halting, not to progress until the engineer had acknowledged the warning — *there is greater quality control*;
- printing a paper version of information required for repairs to a component difficult to access, indicating on the screen the points where printing is to start and stop, output being date-and-time stamped for disposal on completion of the job (the information could well have been updated the next time it was required) — *there is greater quality control*;
- formatting on-the-fly, essential for such a system, with storage requirements being ten times less than for pre-formatted information — less space is required, and *there is faster access to exactly what is required when it is required.*

9.1.3 North Atlantic Treaty Organization

Subgroup 35 of the NATO Industry Advisory Group (NIAG) carried out a study on the Applicability of CALS to NATO Countries, the report being dated 31 October 1991.[4]

In reviewing the technical standards the US CALS Office is endorsing, plus any other standards that European industry considers important, SGML was endorsed by NIAG as the standard for technical publications. A recommendation for NATO was that AECMA 1000D be supported for technical documentation data exchange across all Services and defence industry sectors. Others were to the effect that NATO should endorse ISO 8879 SGML and SDIF as the core standards to support technical publication and retrieval requirements; that HyTime should be supported for all hypermedia encoding; that DSSSL should be adopted as soon as it is stable; that SPDL be adopted as soon as it is published as an ISO standard.

9.2 OTHERS

SGML was publicized originally as being a standard for publishing. So it is, but publishing in its broadest definition. Getting a 'publishing' tag associated with SGML had both positive and negative effects. On the positive side the Association of American Publishers (AAP) and their members took it up readily, and on the negative side many companies neglected it as their prime business was not publishing.

It has been said that every company's second business is publishing — this may be an exaggeration but the majority of companies have publicity material, and often there are handbooks or leaflets describing the products being marketed. So SGML is pertinent to most companies for the structure of the documents they have.

And every company has documents of different types and other information of various kinds, from reports to invoices as well as letters and memoranda. It would be well to have these in an integrated information base. Now it is seen that SGML can be useful to any company, irrespective of its business.

The most publicized use of SGML is for CALS, and whilst CALS was designed for the defence industry, it is being found that other industries are interested in the CALS philosophy and some of the methodology for their own businesses. These include the automotive, building, oil and gas, pharmaceutical, and telecommunications industries. Sometimes a company in the defence industry has a civil division as well as one for defence. The aircraft industry is a good example here, and it made good sense when the ATA cited SGML for the structure of maintenance documentation.

So the use of SGML is spreading far beyond publishing *per se* and far beyond CALS. In fact, any company with a need to organize its documents and other information into one information base should consider the use of SGML. This is especially important to a company dealing with a service or process that could be the subject of a disaster (relating to the crash of an aircraft or the sinking of a ship, the explosion at an atomic or chemical plant or on an oil/gas production platform, for example), where such a disaster could lead to a full-scale enquiry. How much easier it will be to respond to an enquiry if all the information is in (conceptually) one integrated information system — including the note about getting the (failed) part from The Cheap Company instead of The Quality Company as in the past. Who agreed? Were quality checks performed on this new supplier's part? Who signed it off? It is not just the technical manual information that needs be present in an integrated information base.[6]

In the list below, no specific examples have been given of SGML applications in the finance industry, where it is used because presentation of fast-changing information is required, but where the main body is repeated and values are continually changed. Then there is the automotive industry, where manuals for a new (international) model of a car are encoded in SGML, for example. There is also the pharmaceutical industry, where side-effects of new drugs must be registered quickly to avoid another 'Thalidomide' disaster. It is possible to read of many more examples of SGML applications in various publications.[1]

9.2.1 The airlines

Manufacturers of airframes and engines for the civil aircraft business, and also the airlines themselves as customers, are governed by Air Transport Association's ATA-

100 specification for the provision of maintenance and associated manuals. Sets of codes are associated with these, known as Aircraft Maintenance Task Oriented Support System (AMTOSS) and Jet Engine Manual Task Oriented Support System (JEMTOSS) codes. The approach is by way of providing steps to be followed in maintenance of specific components, referenced by codes.

This specification applies not only to the ATA but also to the Airline Industry Association (AIA). It was revision 29 of the ATA-100 specification that called for the use of SGML. It is interesting to note that information on CD-ROM only is acceptable by some authorities — no paper version also being required.

Rolls-Royce had an implementation of the ATA-100 specification on CD-ROM with the JEMTOSS codes for repair to their jet engines used to power the Boeing 757. Information pertaining to maintenance is supplied on a CD-ROM (using less than one-third of the storage capacity available), updating information within the 90-day updating cycle being supplied on a floppy diskette (in encrypted form). A maintenance engineer thus insets the CD-ROM in the portable computer, and also a floppy diskette if there is updating material. If he has a bar-coded system, he swipes the particular code for a specific task with the wand, and the appropriate information appears on the screen. Access may be by other methods, going directly to the information, navigating contents lists, or searching on a word or phrase, for example. The information in the various manuals has been enriched by the provision of many links that may be used to call up exactly what is required.

Viewing on the screen allows for split-screen use, with diagrams appearing alongside text. It is possible to zoom onto parts of diagrams to see the component required in an enlarged form. Updated material appears in yellow, where required — that is the maintenance engineer does not have to remember to check to see if there are any updates. For working on places that are hard to reach, and in other cases when the screen cannot be read, a printed version of the information may be obtained by indicating 'start print' and 'stop print' on the (scrolled) screen, when a paper version is produced, data-and-time stamped. This paper version must be destroyed afterwards, as the information could well have been subject to updating information when next required.

Formatting on-the-fly is essential for such a system, and results in far less storage space being used than would otherwise have been the case.

It is reported that during the experimental phase, when a representative of Rolls-Royce was standing silently near a maintenance engineer to check on ease of use of the CD-ROM system, the engineer suddenly realized the implications of the visit and said 'You're not going to take it away, are you?', or words to that effect. He did not wish to return to paper. There is thus satisfaction of maintenance engineers as well as improvements in quality not possible with a paper or page-based system. This system is in regular use at several airports, on which we as air travellers rely, albeit unwittingly.

Aérospatiale has an Electronic Library System (ELS) for (experimental) use in the Airbus. Here there is a computer fitted to the aircraft, with several terminals. The pilot and co-pilot have one each, and also a graphics printer. There is another screen at the rear of the cockpit, and one for the cabin crew, as well as the provision of points for the plug-in of terminals for maintenance engineers. Additionally, the system is intended for use by ground staff. Again the system is based on CD-ROM, with text and graphics structured and represented in accordance with the CALS base standards. Information is pre-formatted, however, at this stage.

9.2.2 Oil and gas

In the oil and gas industry, the SGML application relates to exploration in the North Sea for the production platforms and rigs of Shell. The amount of information that needs to be stored is great, there being numerous (sub)contractors involved, from the provision of the engines to the drilling mechanism itself. It has to be guaranteed to the Health and Safety Executive that the information is always kept up-to-date, and here we recall the Piper-Alpha disaster all too vividly. Now consider the similarity of this application to that of CALS or that of the civil airlines. There is thus no surprise that SGML is being used with CD-ROM as a storage medium, the information being full of hypermedia links for ready access to what is required, instantly. There is no need to search several portable cabins for the pertinent information — which may have been superseded.

9.2.3 Telecommunications

For the technical documentation that needs to be made available in the telecommunications industry, there is a DTD developed by the Telecommunications Industry Forum, known as the TCIF DTD.[7] Membership of the TCIF is large, including all the major telecommunications companies.

Ericsson Telecom had long been using generic coding, and it was easy for this company to have it conform to SGML. A policy decision was made to use SGML for structuring all technical documentation for delivery to its customers. SGML is being used in other ways too, one application being to develop a DTD to check for use of vendor's 'bells and whistles' with otherwise standard compilers. As a result of such checking, the software programs are portable, an important consideration.

9.2.4 Publishing

The first big application of SGML was by the Association of American Publishers (AAP) with its electronic manuscript project. This work culminated in the design of three DTDs (for books, articles, and serials), duly input to the American standards-makers. The result was ANSI/NISO Z.39.59-1988. This application of SGML is being taken up by many publishing houses around the world, and some of the SGML software in the marketplace knows about the AAP DTD. There are plans in ISO to fast-track the standard for it to become an international standard. Early work done on mathematics and tables was omitted from the standard, a committee now examining these topics for eventual input as amendments. An Electronic Publishing Special Interest Group (EPSIG) was formed, and although the group examines many of the wider issues of publishing in general and SGML in particular, at the core is ANSI/NISO Z.39.59-1988.

One of the first users of the AAP standard was Elsevier, for what it calls 'tops and tails', front matter and back matter of documents, exploiting the SGML methodology to result in secondary publications from the information base. Later the main body of articles will also be structured in accordance with SGML. It was for the Elsevier application that the Amsterdam parser was developed at the Vrije Universiteit Amsterdam.

As may have been expected, a number of publishing houses have been adopting the AAP standard. Some have been publishing books on SGML, for which the author has developed a DTD. Addison-Wesley and Kluwer come in this category.

Wolters Kluwer has been using SGML for legal publishing, where all the existing files are being converted to SGML, including the database of all the statutes of The Netherlands and files containing all the loose-leaf publications. In fact SGML seems to be used extensively for legal publishing on both sides of the Atlantic Ocean, use in the UK by Her Majesty's Stationery Office (HMSO) being described below.

Use of SGML is not confined to book publishing — it is also used by the American Chemical Society, for example, for a weekly magazine, *Chemical & Engineering News*. For this application the information in the weekly publication is organized to give rise to other publications, for example a cumulative index and *C&EN Concentrates*, short summaries of important business and scientific events.

Then there is the European Workgroup on SGML (EWS) concerned with the development of a DTD for structuring the bibliographic data for scientific, legal, and technical journal articles. That accomplished, the plan is to consider the main body of articles. This is based on the work of the AAP.

Perhaps the most prestigious publishing project in the UK where SGML is used is the *New Oxford English Dictionary*. The original edition was 1933, and it can readily be appreciated why a second edition was not forthcoming — that is until all the entries were in machine-readable form, duly marked up in accordance with SGML. For lexicographical work there is inevitably a wealth of markup, but indication of the structure in this way opens up many possibilities for database working in general and spin-off publications in particular. The really good news is that the dictionary can always be up-to-date, there being no need to wait a further fifty years before another edition is published. Work on the *New Oxford English Dictionary* was carried out not only at Oxford but also at the University of Waterloo in Canada. Special software was written for the project, including a structured editor at Oxford and a general extraction tool (PAT) at Waterloo.

Other lexicographical projects are using SGML at Oxford University Press in the English Language Teaching Dictionaries division. And Oxford University Press is also bringing out the complete works of Jane Austen, and other authors, with SGML tagging.

9.2.5 Patents documents

Whilst it is not affiliated to the CEC, the European Patent Office (EPO) seeks to avoid duplication of the procedures for the granting of patents for inventions, by giving the applicant patent protection in thirteen (European) countries. Thus it has, of necessity, to deal with many different languages.

There was early recognition that SGML would be ideal for the structure of these patent documents. As a first step, a generic encoding scheme called DATIMTEX was devised. In the fulness of time, the generic coding aspects gave way to SGML in accordance with DTDs.

This must be one of the largest on-going projects for the retroactive conversion of documents to SGML, there being just less than 2.5 million pages a year to scan and convert for 100,000 patent applications. The documents are not only in several languages, but can also contain many mathematical and other scientific symbols. The DATIMTEX character font contains 400 characters. And there are diagrams.

Applications are currently printed, with plans for use of CD-ROM in future.

9.2.6 Academic and research community

One of the first applications of SGML was in the DAPHNE project (Document Application Processing in a Heterogeneous Network Environment) at the Hahn-Meitner-Institut, Berlin. This was for all technical documentation, with DTDs for such document types as reports and slide sets — there could thus be a corporate image to presentations.

A great deal of useful work has been done at CERN, the European Laboratory for Particle Physics, where there is a suite of DTDs relating to the very technical work carried out at CERN as well as the not so technical. It was because of the experience gained here that such useful input could be made to part 13, in particular, of ISO/IEC TR 9573 Techniques for Using SGML, this part dealing with Public Entity Sets for Mathematics and Science.

In the US at Ohio State University there is the Chameleon project for the SGML Software Development Consortium, with the objective of providing public-domain software for SGML. Specifically, there is what is termed the Integrated Chameleon Architecture, a toolset for generating 'data' translators. The first tool is described as an environment for creating SGML DTDs, the second for assisting in retagging existing formats for later translation to SGML. More tools are being developed.[8]

Another group in the US that has been actively involved in SGML and related standards is the Applied Information Technologies Research Center (AITRC). In addition to taking an active part in initiatives of other similar groups, AITRC expressed interest in working with existing vendor products that support SGML document markup, DSSSL layout and style specifications, and SPDL standard print formats.

The compilation of the bibliography on SGML by editors from Dallas Theological Seminary and Queen's University at Kingston has aroused a great deal of interest.[1] This work was not carried out for its own sake, but rather to supply a valuable contribution for researchers tracing the progress of SGML applications, and also serving as a reading list and an information resource for groups wishing to evaluate SGML for their information management needs. Far more than a bibliography usually implies, the document includes much valuable information on products and information sources as well as descriptions on some of the larger applications. And the bibliography has its own DTD.

SGML is used at the Dallas Theological Seminary itself for the SGML Bible project, to put English, Greek, and Hebrew versions of the Bible, complete with commentaries, on CD-ROM. Hypertext browsing and full-text searching is possible.

The Text Encoding Initiative (TEI) is a mammoth task being jointly undertaken by the Association for Computers and the Humanities (ACH), the Association for Computational Linguistics (ACL), and the Association for Literary and Linguistic Computing (ALLC). It is described as an initiative for text encoding guidelines and a common interchange format for literary and linguistic data. It will have to take account of all languages, dead and living, all scripts and different writing styles, with the capability to add sufficient structure for any literary or linguistic purpose, for textual computing and natural language processing, from stylistic analysis to machine-assisted translation. Guidelines have been drafted and will be progressively updated during the four-year project, the guidelines being tested on large corpora at various universities around the world. In addition to the use of SGML, the possibility of using HyTime is being studied.[9]

In the UK a workshop on Document Exchange was organized by the Advisory Group of Computer Graphics. The workshop was subtitled The Use of SGML in the UK Academic and Research Community. Among the recommendations of the workshop were:

- SGML should be widely adopted for document distribution;
- a set of DTDs should be established for the documents to be distributed, using a common set of tags;
- a one-day awareness course should be given several times in the UK at different locations.

As a direct result of the workshop, the University of Exeter received some funding for what is known as the SGML Project, to explore and encourage SGML use within the UK academic and research community. Evaluation copies of several packages are held, on which information will be given to interested persons. Parser materials for ARCSGML were released on the Janet network on behalf of the SGML Users' Group, with e-mail messages peaking at 40 per hour shortly afterwards. The SGML Project is commited to making all findings and reports available on-line. A number of documents will be produced to offer responses to frequently asked questions. Another task is to assemble a collection of public domain tools and DTDs to support activities of current and potential users.[10]

9.2.7 Government departments

It is not just departments of defence that have decided to adopt use of SGML, where these governments include Australia, Canada, France, Germany, Italy, Spain, Sweden, the UK, and the US. In Australia the Department of Administrative Services has adopted SGML, for example.

The Department of Energy (DoE) in the US has declared its policy to apply SGML for all its technical documentation. This application is calling for all SGML features, not just those in FIPS PUB 152. Maybe it will be the DoE that causes the FIPS PUB to be updated, and not the DoD as expected.

Her Majesty's Stationery Office (HMSO) in the UK was an early user of SGML. The first project was the application of SGML to statutory instruments (known as secondary legislation), which together with acts of parliament (primary legislation) form a database. (Bills are introduced to parliament, and if passed become acts.) The Lord Chancellor's Department examined the possibility of setting up and maintaining a database of UK law. It is planned that the government legal service will have access to this database, not only for use in retrieving relevant parts to ascertain the law on a specific subject, but also to assist in the drafting of new bills. And it is expected that SGML will be used for *Hansard* in the not-too-distant future.

9.2.8 Commission of the European Communities

It was the FORMEX project for the Formalized Exchange of electronic publications under the aegis of the Office for Official Publications of the European Communities in Luxembourg that led to the development of the first SGML parsing system. This work was carried out on behalf of the CEC by Sobemap SA, the company later marketing the resulting product as Mark-It, still the only commercially available full features parsing system. The application chosen was the *Official Journal*, where this had to be in all nine languages of the members of the European Community (English, Danish, Dutch, French, German, Greek, Italian, Portugese, and Spanish).

A later project was FAME, or FORMEX Applied to Multilingualism in Europe. Some of this experience was taken into the EUROTRA machine translation project, where it seems that SGML has a place, as well as its use in the SYSTRAN system (and applied by two software vendors).

There are other CEC projects, including the CELEX databases of European Commission law (one database for each of the nine languages). The principal sources of input for CELEX are the the Office for Official Publications with the *Official Journal*, the European Courts of Justice, the General Secretary's Office, and the European Parliament as well as local data entry and a database of historical information. There is retroactive tagging.

The CEC also funds projects based on SGML. First of these was DOCMANUSC, which led to the publication of a series of SGML Guidelines. Representation of mathematics is catered for in the EUROMATH project, for which SGML is to be used.

9.2.9 International Organization for Standardization

By virtue of publishing standards and technical reports, ISO is itself a publishing house in its own right. For this reason part 11 of ISO/IEC TR 9573 on the Application of SGML at ISO Central Secretariat was developed, as described in Chapter 7. Its use is not confined to ISO standards and technical reports. Some of the standards-making bodies are considering its use, albeit modified to cope with their needs, those interested in this work being ANSI, AFNOR, BSI, and DIN. Additionally, its modification for industry standards is being considered, for example for building regulations in Canada. Uses of the ISO CS system are explained to other potential users at a series of seminars.

Further work on the DTD with respect to hypermedia links is proposed, also the capture of the logical content of tables as opposed to geometric content. And the distribution by ISO of electronic products is planned.

It is also useful to consider the work of some of the ISO technical committees under this heading. Work is in progress in several of them to develop applications of ISO 8879 SGML. These include:

- JTC 1/SC 29 Coded Representation of Picture, Audio, and Multimedia/Hypermedia Information
  - HyTime is to be used as one of the coding methods for Audio Visual Interactive Scriptware (AVIS) by this newly formed subcommittee;
- TC 46 Information and Documentation

— SC 4/WG 6 is interested in the application of ISO 8879 by the AAP project, published as ANSI/NISO Z39.59-1988, recommending the fast-track approval process to speed its acceptance as an ISO standard (NISO being the National Information Standards Organization);

- TC 173 Technical Systems and Aids for Disabled or Handicapped Persons
  — the SGML application here is for blind people using Braille, as well as a special project for Braille mathematics.

Notes

(1) There are several ways of learning more about SGML applications. The most comprehensive document is the *Bibliography on SGML and Related Issues*, edited by Robin Cover, Nicholas Duncan, and David T Barnard, Technical Report 9-299, Department of Computing and Information Science, Queen's University at Kingston (February 1991), ISSN 0836-0227, 312 pp. Other sources are the *SGML Users' Group Newsletter* and the *Bulletin* and also the *<TAG>* newsletter; read the articles on applications in comp.text.SGML on Internet; and read press reports.

(2) For further information on CALS, see Joan M Smith, *An Introduction to CALS: The Strategy and the Standards*, Technology Appraisals (1990), ISBN 1-871802-04-0, 143 + xxi pp. It is obtainable directly from Technology Appraisals Limited, 82 Hampton Road, Twickenham, Middlesex TW2 5QS, United States (telephone +44 81 744 1155; telefax +44 81 744 1149).

(3) See Ruey Chen, *The Integration of the Air Force Content Data Model and MIL-STD-1388-2B*, DTRC-90/034 (October 1990), 202 pp.

(4) *A NATO Industry Advisory Group Report on the Applicability of CALS to the NATO Countries*, AC/301(SG/D)D/3 (31 October 1991).

(5) Information about the work of JPEG and MPEG is given in 8.6.2.

(6) See also the examples given in Chapter 10.

(7) There were plans to make the TCIF and other public domain DTDs available on Internet comp.text.sgml.

(8) The contact person for the Chameleon project is Sandra A Mamrak, Department of Computer and Information Science, 2036 Neil Avenue Mall, The Ohio State University, Columbus, OH 43210, United States (telephone +1 614 292 4903; e-mail mamrak@cis.ohio-state.edu on Internet).

(9) For detailed information on the TEI project or a copy of the guidelines contact either of the two editors: C Michael Sperburg-McQueen, Computer Center (M/C 135), University of Illinois at Chicago, IL 60680, United States (telephone +1 312 996 2477; e-mail u35395@uicvm on Bitnet, u35395@uicvm.uic.edu on Internet) or Lou Burnard, Oxford University Computing Service, 13 Banbury Road, Oxford OX2 6NN, United Kingdom (telephone +44 865 273238; telefax +44 865 273275; e-mail lou@vax.oxford.ac.uk on Bitnet or Earn, @ox.vax on Janet). There is TEI-L, an electronic mail discussion forum on Bitnet, listser@uicvm, or listserv@uicvm.uic.edu on Internet.

(10) For further information contact Michael G Popham, SGML Project, Computer Unit, North Park Road, University of Exeter, Exeter EX4 4QE, United Kingdom

(telephone +44 392 263946; telefax +44 392 211630; e-mail sgml@uk.ac.exeter on Janet, sgml1.ex.ac.uk or 144.173.6.61 on Internet).

10

A comparison of SGML and ODA

10.1 SOMETHING ABOUT THE STANDARDS

In addition to hearing about SGML and SDIF for the representation and interchange of documents in a standard way, many people have also heard about another ISO standard for document interchange:

- ISO 8613 Information Processing — Text and Office Systems — Office Document Architecture (ODA) and Interchange Format (1 September 1989).[1,2]

There are some remarkable similarities as well as differences between the SGML and ODA standards, more popularly referred to as SGML/SDIF and ODA/ODIF, or SGML and ODA. Both SGML and ODA were standardized by the same subcommittee within ISO.

ODA started life in working groups 3 and 5 of this ISO subcommittee as a means of enabling one word processor to communicate with another word processor supplied by a different manufacturer. People wanted to be able to interchange documents of the type found in many offices, the emphasis being that the receiving end should display the document as intended by the author (formatted form). Some graphics capabilities were added to those of text, for both raster graphics to give the ability to include scanned images in a document, and vector graphics for drawings. Editing capability was also added.

ODA is essentially about doing in an electronic way what had previously been done using typewriters and other office equipment. It makes it possible for there to be an electronic filing cabinet for the documents previously contained in a metal filing cabinet, allowing for filing and retrieval information, for example, to be included on the electronic filing card known as a document profile. There is a document profile for every ODA document, stating who the sender was, who has received copies, what document it may have superseded, and so on. And if someone wishes to look up the document, it can be got out of the (electronic) filing cabinet and seen on the screen.

On the standardization route, three things affected the development of ODA:

- the widespread use of facsimile machines, that permitted (formatted form) office documents to be transmitted from one company to another without resorting to the postal services;

- the advent of desktop publishing systems, where part 6 of the ODA standard dealing with character content architectures had to be changed since it had been drafted for character boxes with golf ball and daisy wheel printers in mind;
- the emergence of SGML.

ISO 8613 Office Document Architecture is a multi-part standard, the following parts being those published on 1 September 1989:

- Part 1 Introduction and General Principles;
- Part 2 Document Structures;
- Part 4 Document Profile;
- Part 5 Office Document Interchange Format;
- Part 6 Character Content Architectures;
- Part 7 Raster Graphics Content Architectures;
- Part 8 Geometric Graphics Content Architectures.

Part 10 Formal Specifications was published on 1 June 1991, followed by two amendments:

- Amendment 1 Formal Specification of the Document Profile;
- Amendment 2 Formal Specification of the Raster Graphics Content Architectures.

Although ODA originally stood for Office Document Architecture not only in ISO but also in CCITT where it was being developed as a recommendation, and in the European Computer Manufacturers Association (ECMA) where it was also being developed as a standard, the latter two organizations decided to call it Open Document Architecture instead of Office, as it was for use in an OSI environment. ISO at first refused to allow the name change, hence the publication of ISO 8613 as Office Document Architecture. However, in 1990 ISO agreed that there could be a name change, and the working group responsible for ODA decided to keep it as Office until the standard was republished, taking into account some of the amendments, when Open would be in its title. (There are currently many references to ISO 8613 (1989) with Office in the title, hence delaying the change until the publication of ISO 8613 (19xx). This is why some people now refer to ODA as Office/Open Document Architecture, or still by its correct ISO title of Office Document Architecture.)

As explained in Chapter 1, SGML started life in another ISO subcommittee, that dealing with programming languages. But SGML and its related standards were for documents, albeit with a methodology that had its roots in publishing and not in the office, and as part of a re-organization process the projects were moved to the same subcommittee as that for ODA, now called ISO/IEC JTC 1/SC 18.

Unlike ODA which is an architecture, SGML is a representation or description language, and can be used to represent any document, even the very complex. And unlike ODA, it is concerned mainly with the information content of the document, and not (usually) with how that information is to be imaged. There will be the two text composition standards (DSSSL and SPDL) to take care of that, which will require the fonts standards, also under the aegis of the working group responsible for SGML (WG 8).

ODA does not need DSSSL because it includes a relatively simple formatter, but it does require SPDL when the document has to be output, and it needs the fonts standards. The relationships of these standards are described in more detail below.

With SGML, it is possible to address the elements of information that the documents may contain. It is therefore ideally suited for the multiple re-use of elements of information, especially multimedia information base publishing, as an SGML document may include any type of content — graphics, audio, video, and so on. This is why it is possible to work with it for integrated information bases. And because elements have attributes that can be identifiers, for example, these can also be the means of specifying hypermedia links — and of course HyTime can be used with SGML. Such functionality is not present in ODA as published.

10.2 TECHNICAL ISSUES

10.2.1 Basic principles

ODA documents have four related structures:

- a generic logical structure;
- a specific logical structure;
- a generic layout structure;
- a specific layout structure.

The generic structures (logical and layout) are for classes of documents, whereas the specific structures are those associated with an example of that class.

There is also the concept of the document profile, as already noted, and that of a document application profile (DAP). It was decided that because there were effectively so many options open to users of ODA systems, the only way to ensure meaningful interchange of documents was to provide standardized subsets of the ODA standard, known as DAPs.

With SGML, there is the concept of a DTD, this containing the rules for all the documents of that type, the elements it may contain, their relationships, any attributes they may have, and so on. It is essentially a hierarchical structure. The markup that is added to a document instance (as an example of a document type is called), has to obey the rules laid down in the DTD. It is the markup that indicates the structure of the document.

10.2.2 Architecture

It is sometimes said that an architecture is essential for an overall model and that SGML cannot be considered as the basis for the model because it is a language. Although SGML is a (meta)language, a DTD can be considered as an architecture since it is a hierarchical structure, progressively defining the (usually logical) structure of a document from the document type down to its smallest elements in a rigorous manner.

10.2.3 Extensions to the standards

Since ODA is an architecture by its very nature, it is excellent for carrying out that which has been expressly built into the structure (of the standard). But whenever a new facility is required, it has to be built in expressly, hence there currently being many proposed extensions.[3]

There are many addenda and amendments, and one annex. Amendments will also have to be issued containing technical corrigenda relating to the reports submitted, as would have been expected in a standard of the complexity of ODA. In fact a second edition taking approved changes into account is planned for publication, none of the extensions or corrigenda to be published in the meantime.

Subjects of addenda, amendments, and an annex under development or awaiting publication are:

- document application profile proforma and notation;
- conformance testing methodology;
- recording of documents conforming to ISO 8613 on media;
- formal specification of ODA document structures;
- tiled raster graphics;
- colour;
- alternate representation;
- security;
- streams;
- styles.

Additionally, three more amendments are being balloted for part 10:

- Amendment 3 Formal Specification of ODA Character Content Architectures;
- Amendment 4 Formal Specification of ODA Geometric Graphics Content Architectures;
- Amendment 5 Formal Specification of the Defaulting Mechanism for Defaultable Attributes.

Then there is the proposal for further parts, two currently being at the stage of working draft:

- Part 3 Abstract Interface for Manipulation of ODA Documents;
- Part 9 Audio Content Architecture.

In contrast, SGML is basically a representation language, and can be used to describe a facility without alteration to the standard.

Whereas it is necessary to extend ISO 8613 ODA to cater for spreadsheets and business graphics, for example, with SGML suitable DTDs would be written for this purpose. (A DTD for a spreadsheet is included in ISO/IEC TR 9573 Techniques for Using SGML.) Because tables may be described in SGML and there is the possibility of accessing individual cells, this information may be presented in the form of business graphics, if required, for example.

With ODA, any added functionality could then be incorporated in new DAPs, and vendors could start to implement the agreed DAPs, perhaps after they had been accepted by ISO as ISPs, as suggested below.

Greater functionality will be progressively added to the ODA standard. However, it can never achieve the flexibility of SGML (a (meta)language) and be able to represent all the structure present in complex technical documents or linguistic texts, for example, as can SGML.

It is also worth mentioning that some vendors have expressed concern about progressive enhancements to the ODA standard. This is because they will have to enhance their products progressively, and it could therefore be said that the standard and products are unstable. But this is inevitable if additional functionality is required within ODA, rather than transferring the ODA documents to the SGML environment to achieve the functionality that way.

Since the publication of amendment 1 to ISO 8879 SGML on 1 July 1988, there have been no alterations to the standard of any description. But it is now undergoing its five-year review, when re-organization of content is proposed, among other things. Also proposed is SGML-B, and of course there is HyTime for hypermedia working, this being a separate standard, scheduled for publication shortly.

To complete the picture for ODA, a technical report is being developed:

- ISO/IEC DTR 10183 Information Processing — Text and Office Systems — Office Document Architecture and Interchange Format — Testing Methodology and Abstract Test Cases — Implementation Testing Methodology
  - — Part 1 Framework,
  - — Part 2 Abstract Test Suites.

10.2.4 Application requirements for ODA and SGML

There are remarkable similarities between ODA and SGML with regard to application requirements. Table 10.1 shows one of several possible views.

Table 10.1. Application requirements of ODA and SGML

ODA	SGML
document application profile (DAP)	SGML declaration
document classes* (generic structures)	document type definition (DTD)
specific structures	marked up documents
document profile	related documents (eg a document profile) allowed for in SDIF*

*not mandatory

10.2.5 DAPs and SGML declarations

In ODA, a DAP is necessary to state what features of ISO 8613 may be used, and what interchange format class is selected. Since it is highly unlikely that any vendor would implement the whole of ISO 8613, the DAP is necessary to subset out the required facilities. And in common with SGML, there is provision for non-standard content architectures/content types (for example video).

In SGML, there is the SGML declaration to give notification of the features used, the content notations, the character sets used, etc.

10.2.6 Document classes and document types

DTDs in SGML have their analogy in ODA with the concept of document classes. A document class in ODA would have a generic logical structure associated with it, and this is analogous to the 'input' DTD in SGML. It would also have a generic layout structure to state how the documents of that class would be presented (one layout structure only allowable in ODA). This is analogous to 'output' DTDs in SGML in which the style requirements would be specified for a formatter. (When published, DSSSL will take over this role for SGML.)

The generic logical and layout structures for a class of ODA documents may be known at the receiving end; thus they do not have to be transmitted with the document itself. However, there is currently no formal mechanism for doing this.

In the case of SGML, the SGML declaration and DTD may exist at the receiving end, and may be referred to uniquely, immediately before the document instance, thus reducing transmission overheads.

Each ODA document in a class also has a specific logical structure, that may be derived from the generic logical structure for that class. In addition, a document in a class also has a specific layout structure, that may be derived from the generic layout structure. The specific logical structure is analogous to markup for an SGML document, and the specific layout structure will be dealt with by DSSSL.

In ODA, provision is made for three forms of interchange:

- formatted form — allowing presentation of the document
  - — generic layout structure,
  - — specific layout structure,
  - — specific layout structure only is required to accompany the document;
- processable form — allowing processing of the document
  - — generic logical structure,
  - — specific logical structure,
  - — the specific logical structure would accompany the interchanged document but the generic logical structure could be known at the receiving end where there could also be a generic layout structure — the specific layout structure would not accompany the document;
- formatted processable form — allowing both presentation and processing
  - — generic logical structure,
  - — generic layout structure,
  - — specific logical structure,
  - — specific layout structure,
  - — the generic structures could be known at the receiving end.

Note that with processable documents, the generic logical structure must be present.

10.2.7 Encoding the structures

The generic logical and layout structures are written by a programmer or equivalent in ASN.1 statements for a class of documents (for example letter or report).

The specific logical structure can be generated from the generic logical structure.

The specific layout structure can be generated from the generic layout structure.

Thus it is the generic structure(s) that must be present for a document class.

It could then be said that the generic logical structure for an ODA document is equivalent (in some respects) to an SGML DTD. In SGML terms, the specific logical structure would be the markup that was present in the document instance, in accordance with the DTD (the generic logical structure).

In ODA, generic logical and layout structures for a class of documents could be stored at the receiving end, and referred to in the document profile.

The specific structure(s) (logical and/or layout) would necessarily be interspersed among the content of a document, much as an SGML document includes markup. The basic difference is that ASN.1 encoding is only intended to be machine-readable, whereas the SGML markup is intended to be both human-readable and machine-readable. (Specific logical structure would be embedded during the editing phase; specific layout structure would be embedded during the formatting phase.)

10.2.8 Developing DTDs and generic structures

ISO 8613 does not define any particular generic structures or object classes. However, it allows the definition of a potentially infinite variety of document classes. Similarly, SGML allows the definition of a potentially infinite variety of document types.

It is recognized that the writing of DTDs for SGML is a painstaking task for anything other than a 'simple' document. It is undertaken by experts, who could teach the art to applications programmers or document designers. Whilst there can be editing software to assist the process of DTD writing, such software was not readily available after the publication of the standard.

Already it is known that the equivalent generic logical and layout structures for ODA document classes will be even more lengthy than the equivalent DTD, owing to the method used. It is not expected that editing software will be available for this purpose for some time.

ISO 8613 ODA part 2, B.3, gives an example of a class of documents called letter, the letter consisting of a logo, a date, the name of the addressee, a statement of the subject, a summary, paragraph(s), figure(s), a formal ending, the signature, and the name of originator. The actual letter (the specific document) contains four paragraphs and one figure with a caption. Text for the summary, the paragraphs, the caption, and the ending is shown symbolically. Several pages of encodings are given.

SGML equivalents, using the Office Document Language (ODL), are also given, these being somewhat shorter than their ODA counterparts.

10.2.9 Over-riding structures

In ODA, the specific structure (logical or layout) may over-ride the generic structure, to result in a document that does not conform to a document class. In SGML, it is possible to over-ride a stored DTD by declarations contained in a declaration subset. There is also the notion, in SGML, of inclusions and exclusions in a DTD, but these usually pertain to a content model that differs from others of a similar type; if inclusions and exclusions are used to modify an existing DTD, then another DTD results, retaining the concept of 'type'.

It is considered to be a strength of SGML that all documents must conform to the DTD. It is this that imposes the rigour on the system, and ensures data integrity.

10.2.10 The document profile

There is the notion of a document profile in ODA, that provides information about the handling of the document. The document profile contains information about the generic and specific logical and layout structures, the DAP used, file references, and so on. It has already been referred to above, when other information it may contain was indicated. Every ODA document must be accompanied by its associated document profile.

There is no mandatory equivalent in SGML. However, there is provision for the inclusion of a document profile in SDIF as a related document.

A document profile is illustrated in ISO 8613 part 5, both ASN.1 and SGML (ODL) encodings being given. Again, the encoding for ODL is shorter than the ODIF equivalent.

10.2.11 Interchange of documents

In ODA, the document profile may be interchanged separately, the purpose of separate interchange being to test the capability of the recipient; for example was the particular DAP supported, were the generic structures for the particular document class already stored? If the receiving end does not support the same DAP (or a superset thereof) as the sending end, there can be no (meaningful) interchange.

In SGML, the features and other functionality as specified in the SGML declaration must be supported at the receiving end, otherwise there can be no (meaningful) interchange.

There is therefore no such thing as 'blind' interchange for either ODA or SGML for much the same reasons.

GOSIP can be used for the interchange of ODA and SGML documents. There are three methods of interchanging documents using GOSIP or indeed any other OSI profile: SGML/SDIF, ODA/ODL/SDIF, and ODA/ODIF.

Documents can be structured in accordance with ODA, and both represented and interchanged in accordance with ODIF. Or they can be structured in accordance with ODA, represented in accordance with ODL and then interchanged in accordance with SDIF (since ODL is an application of SGML). The latter method is specified in ISO 8613 but not in the current versions of the equivalent CCITT recommendation or the ECMA standard.

There are several reasons why it could be useful to have an ODA document enter an SGML environment:

- if the functionality of the ODA formatter was insufficient for the requirements for imaging;
- if the document was not ephemeral in nature, and was to enter the integrated information system;
- and when it entered the information system, it could be split into elements of information, which could be reflected in the indexing capabilities and thus gain greater usefulness for the document, parts of which could now be included in other output documents.

10.2.12 DAPs and ISPs

Three DAPS have been agreed by the European Workshop for Open Systems (EWOS) for the interchange of documents structured in accordance with ODA. These are also known as Q profiles:

- Q/111 Processable and Formatted Documents
  — basic character content;
- Q/112 Processable and Formatted Documents
  — extended mixed mode;
- Q/121 Processable and Layout-Independent Documents
  — simple messaging profile.

Later there was Q/113 for what was termed enhanced mixed mode documents.

All refer to interchange using ODIF. However, EWOS then instigated work to extend these to take ODL/SDIF into account as an alternative method of interchange. This was because there is an 'urgent need to identify requirements to ensure interworking between ODA systems using ASN.1 encoded data streams and the publishing and databases environment using SGML'.[4] So EWOS recognizes that SGML is the standard to use for publishing and database working.

In addition to work done on profiles by EWOS, several other organizations were also developing DAPs: CCITT Study Group VIII, the Asia-Oceania Workshop, and the NIST OSI Implementors Workshop in the US. So the next stage was to develop a set of internationally aligned DAPs for ODA, the work for this being carried out by the Profile Alignment Group for ODA (PAGODA). The output from PAGODA was then submitted to ISO for processing as proposed draft International Standardized Profiles (ISPs).

The draft ISPs for ODA are:

- FOD11 Office Document Format Profile for the Interchange of Basic Function Character Content Documents in Processable and Formatted Forms
  — level 1;
- FOD26 Office Document Format Profile for the Interchange of Enhanced Function Mixed Content Documents in Processable and Formatted Forms
  — level 2;
- FOD36 Office Document Format Profile for the Interchange of Extended Function Mixed Content Documents in Processable and Formatted Forms
  — level 3.

Whilst level 1 allows for character content only, levels 2 and 3 also allow for raster graphics and geometric graphics. (FODs are Functional ODA profiles.)

It is interesting that all three draft ISPs contain two DAPS: one to allow interchange by ODIF and the other to allow interchange by ODL/SDIF. Conformance to an ISP could be to either one or the other DAP, or both.

The three profiles are members of a series of hierarchically related profiles, thus FOD26 is a superset of FOD11 and a subset of FOD36. Incidentally, as part of the alignment process Q/121 effectively disappeared, its functionality being subsumed in FOD11. There were, of course, several changes to the Q profiles to result in the drafts for the FOD ISPs. The draft ISPs are to be re-balloted — several years after the publication of ISO 8613.

Remember that ISPs may contain extra functionality not part of ISO 8613. However, it could then be said to be standardized since ISPs are ISO 'standardized' profiles.

Vendors of ODA systems will probably wait for the ISPs to be published before making ODA products generally available in the marketplace. In the meantime, the EWOS profiles are being copied into version 4.0 of UK GOSIP, and deleted by EWOS from its own list. Conversely, it is proposed that the ODA profiles are deleted from US GOSIP, which will reference the appropriate FIPS publications instead. (There may well be a FIPS PUB for SDIF as it is not currently covered.)

Before leaving the discussion on ISPs, note that ISO also allows for there to be ISPs for SGML, these to be known as FSGs, or Functional SGML profiles. Whilst no such profiles are currently under development, the possibility exists should a need be identified.

10.2.13 Presentation of documents

An ODA document can have one layout structure associated with it, for which purpose ISO 8613 includes a relatively simple formatter. SPDL will then be used as the final form for imaging. Until such time that SPDL is available in vendors' products, PostScript may be used, for example.

To take advantage of publishing facilities, an ODA document may be transferred to an SGML environment when DSSSL may be used to indicate the required style to a formatter. The output of the formatter could be encoded using SPDL, as above.

With SGML a DTD is not normally used to express the layout structure(s) of a document, although it can in the case of ODA documents as illustrated in ISO 8613 part 5, which shows the generic layout structure for the example letter. Instead, it is advocated that the logical and layout structures be strictly separated in an SGML environment, where the various styles of presentation required are specified using DSSSL, and imaging requirements are specified using SPDL. Any number of layout styles may be associated with one logical structure.

Both ODA and SGML standards need SPDL for imaging in a standard way. SGML also requires DSSSL, whereas ODA incorporates a (relatively simple) formatter, although DSSSL may be used.

The possible uses of the text composition standards are represented in Figure 10.1.

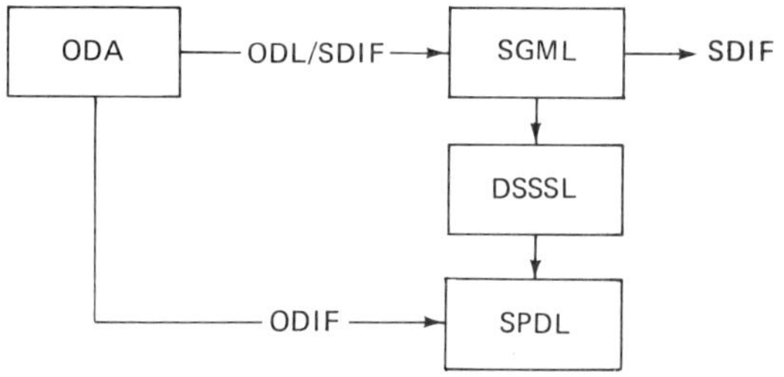

Figure 10.1. Possible uses of the text composition standards

10.2.14 Working with both standards

As described above, documents structured in accordance with ODA may be represented in ODIF and interchanged using ODIF, or they may be represented in ODL (an application of SGML) and interchanged using SDIF to enter an SGML environment. Thus an office document can enter a publishing environment, or an integrated information base governed by SGML for the re-use of the data. When it enters, it is possible that the structure will be enriched to take fuller advantage of such an environment.

Equally, SGML documents may be transferred to an ODA environment. However, as currently published, ISO 8613 ODA does not allow for many facilities considered desirable when dealing with electronic documents, for which there may be provision using SGML. These include:

- more than one layout style to be associated with a document (a screen and a paper representation, or draft and final forms, for example);
- spreadsheets or business graphics (histograms, etc);
- complex tables (and their manipulation);
- computed data (the ability to take elements of tables and represent them in business graphics, for example);
- mathematics (allowing for 'splitting' of equations and other presentation requirements, and also computation), including in-line mathematics;
- change bars (to denote revised text);
- the inclusion of text stored elsewhere;
- the keying of Greek and other special characters using an ASCII keyboard (as required for mathematics, for example);
- implicit numbering of (sub)sections, lists, etc (necessary for revisions);
- the means of having system resolution of cross-references (necessary for revisions);
- system compilation of tables of contents, figures, indexes;
- hypermedia links;
- 'living' documents;

- the ability to deal at an element level (identification of elements of information for their retrieval or manipulation);
- audit trail;
- security at an element level.

The above examples illustrate some of the things that may be done using SGML.

As already stated, it is proposed that ODA be extended to include facilities such as some of the above, but standards-making can be a lengthy process. When appropriate extensions have been standardized, it is likely that they will be incorporated in DAPs (which is itself a 'standardized' process so cannot be an instant decision), then ISPs, after which it is expected that vendors will provide products. Until that time, additional functionality present in SGML documents would necessarily have to be stripped out of the documents before they could enter an ODA environment. In effect, this would mean reducing the functionality of complex technical documents to that of office documents. In some cases, SGML-coded text could have to be represented as raster images to enter the office environment (mathematical equations, for example).

10.2.15 EDI documents

SGML allows for the (interchange and) subsequent use of elements of information comprising EDI documents (thus allowing for selected retrieval of parts of many documents, for example). (A DTD would be developed for each type of EDI document, for example as has been done for the United Nations trade data invoice in accordance with ISO 9735 EDIFACT.)

It is advocated that EDI documents enter the integrated information base governed by SGML. This would mean that all technical and commercial information could be (conceptually) in one system.

The possible inclusion of EDI documents in an ODA environment is currently being considered.

10.2.16 Some overheads

With ODA, although there is nominally provision for reference to be made to generic structures stored at the receiving end, this facility is not currently being used since there is no standard means of referring to them.

With SGML, a document instance (including markup) need only be prefaced by the document type declaration which may refer to a known SGML declaration and DTD, thus reducing overheads. There is the concept of what is termed 'public text'.

A document profile is mandatory with ODA but not with SGML.

More overheads are detailed in the section below.

10.3 BUSINESS ISSUES

10.3.1 Two case studies

Figures given by the director of the EXPRES project in the US for one thirty-page ODA document are:

- in final form — 1,600 blocks (820k);
- work space — 5,000 blocks (2.5M);
- almost one hour to print each test version of the document (using PostScript);
- 18 minutes to transmit the document on a network (87 trial runs).

Against this there is the figure of 2 to 3k per page for SGML with TEX; provided by ACSE, Belgium. However, page description figures have to be added to that. But note that with SGML, the interchange would not include text composition overheads; rather the text composition would be done at the receiving end, on demand. This is what SGML is about!

The EXPRES project was funded by the National Science Foundation (NSF), Carnegie-Mellon and Michigan Universities being awarded $3 million. More information available on the first overhead of the presentation on EXPRES made by the project director, Dr Kathleen Hennessay, was that to support the sixty faculty members who prepare NSF proposals, Texas Tech would use all the available VAX file space and all the available PostScript printer facilities. The last line of the first overhead read

Project abandoned: a cautionary tale for ODA.

Let us consider another project, this time the Automated Logistics Publishing System (ALPS) undertaken by the US Navy. Some of the statistics are:

- saved $1,600,000 with $400,000 investment in one year
  — costs cut by 70 per cent in less than 6 months;
- worktime reduction of 80 per cent in less than 6 months
  — work that took 6 months now takes 6 days,
  — work that took 6 weeks now takes 24 hours (3 shifts);
- 4,500 pages produced previously, now 12,500 pages
  — over a 9 month period.

Technical manuals were input in three ways:

- from scanned printed paper;
- by converting floppy diskettes from various word processing systems;
- by keying in data.

Reduced weight was referred to (23.5 tons for the Vincennes), and information retrieval was thus facilitated. The US Navy has been spending $4,000,000,000 a year on publishing, the number of pages changed a year being estimated at 22,500,000.

These figures were taken from the *CALS Report* (March 1990). The base standard used was SGML (with other standards for illustrations). What stands out is that cost savings were achieved in the first year of operation. Most companies work to an annual budget, being apprehensive of adopting new methods that may not show savings for a few years. Thus the experience of the ALPS project will hearten many companies.

10.3.2 When to format a document

Taking up the point about text composition overheads, it is useful to ask when a document should be formatted. Should it be formatted before or after transmission? Should a document be stored in formatted form, or with its logical structure only?

Unlike ODA documents where the emphasis is on the formatted form of a document, as is usual in an office environment, with SGML the emphasis is on the neutral form to allow for many different styles of format. Thus with SGML it is the neutral (SGML) form that is interchanged (using SDIF). One very great advantage is that storage and transmission overheads are kept to a minimum, as it is the text composition process that causes a significant increase in overheads. With SGML documents, formatting is done on-the-fly, as required.

For example, consider the case of a CD-ROM application, with hypermedia links, for screen viewing only. The user has the ability to view graphics at any time, and request split screen imaging. The text is then formatted on-the-fly to fill the available space on the screen, whether partial or full width.

Thus there are great benefits to storing information in SGML form, as 'living' documents. *It is good practice to format locally, as viewed, and not before.* Alternatively, composition can be done as a background job for paper publication, but only when actually required.

10.3.3 Which standard to use when

To a large extent, the decision of ODA or SGML will be self-evident in that they were designed with different needs in mind. 'Horses for courses' is an expression often used in this context.

If a company has many of the familiar four-drawer filing cabinets, and the company wants to get rid of them and have an electronic filing system, then ODA is the standard to use.

On the other hand, if a company has many technical manuals, SGML is the standard to use. SGML is also the standard to use if a company wishes to have all its information in one integrated information base.

It is possible that a company will need to take some of its ODA documents into an SGML environment to take advantage of advanced printing capabilities. And if a company wants to start using ODA for its office documents, and then migrates to an integrated information system, this too is possible.

But it is not necessarily wise to support the use of both ODA and SGML. Such a decision must be questioned closely.

- How much extra would this cost?
- What additional overheads would be incurred?

The company has to take into account not only the cost of another system, but also additional training costs (and time), multiplied by the number of systems. And then it comes to overheads that will be incurred simply because of working with two systems, starting with storage and transmission overheads.

There are three important reasons why the manufacturing industry could wish to work in SGML for all types of information, commercial as well as technical, and all the documents which could be said to fall into either category, or even outside both.

It is argued that notes passed among engineering development staff could well be in ODA, where these notes possibly relate to the design of a nut and bolt, and its possible composition. But such seemingly small points could be of major importance were there to be a disaster which resulted in an enquiry.

Consider the case of a few years ago when an aircraft flown by United Airlines shed a door when over Hawaii. How much easier it would have been to have responded to the enquiry had all the information relating to the aircraft been (conceptually) in one system. It is suspected that many companies can see the reasons why even memoranda, letters, and notes should be in SGML. Of course, its use would be transparent to the user, who would merely follow a house style for such simple documents. But additional structure would be indicated so that it was known that this note related to a nut and bolt for this specific airframe, for example, and all that would be included in the indexing system.

The second case is that of concurrent engineering. Here there is a multi-discipline team working on design considerations, in which cost is also an important factor. So there is the chief designer sharing his ideas with the man in charge of the production line, the chief maintenance engineer, the chief logistics engineer, and so on. And the finance director is also involved because he can be costing the proposed design as it progresses, monitoring what potential effect such a feature has on the price, which also must govern the business issues.

There is all the engineering and other technical information, which may be stored in the integrated information system governed by SGML (so everything is structured from day 1), and there are many tables of information that are used and re-used by the financial director. These tables can be very complex, and contain many different types of information related to the design, extrapolating information for production, and so on. Elements of information may be changed on a daily basis at this stage, where totals and cross-totals also change constantly, and are reflected in final costs. If the timescales change, then interest rates will change, and if parts come from abroad, exchange rates may fluctuate, and so on *ad infinitum*.

But if the tables are described in SGML, so the elements of the cells may be addressed uniquely (much as it is possible to refer to an element of a matrix), then computations may be performed on these elements so identified. Rows or columns may be supressed on output. Or information may be included in spreadsheets, or output in the form of histograms or pie charts or any other type of business graphic that will readily show the effect of changed data. This is possible now with SGML (given the appropriate vendor software, of course!).

And given that concurrent engineering is all about speeding up the process, it is an essential ingredient that all the information is present in one system.

Business issues must inevitably enter the argument. It is obviously much easier for industry to continue to work with a known system with known capabilities. The overheads of bringing a second system into the equation are very high, plus the overheads of interoperability. These information systems are going to be huge, much bigger than anyone at present can imagine, and anything that might add to overheads of storage, transmission, or retrieval times must be avoided. The business issues must be all important when the manufacturing industry is reducing its staff and even closing some of its sites in order to survive. And these arguments could apply equally well to other industries.

10.3.4 Availability of products

If the availability of products is a key factor in the choice of one standard or the other, then the choice has to be SGML at the present time. It will be remembered that ODA products are not expected to become generally available until after the FOD ISPs have been published (following approval). In the meantime, vendors will continue to gain valuable experience by demonstrating interchange in a closed environment (at the Hanover Fair, for example), and making beta-test versions available to potential customers. There is no point in one vendor jumping the gun, as it were, and guessing which characteristics will be brought into general use before the ISPs are approved, as the whole point of ODA is that of interchange among systems of different vendors.

Several vendors have formed the Open Document Architecture Consortium to develop an ODA toolkit and thus assist in getting products into the marketplace. It is stated in a brochure published that the ODA standard can be interpreted in a variety of ways, and a common model must be selected — hence the need for a consortium. But it is planned that the ODA toolkit may be licensed by anyone wanting to develop products that use the ODA standard.

SGML software is widely available, as can be intimated from the list of products in several publications as well as the information provided in Chapter 11. It ranges from word processors and PCs via workstations to minis and mainframes. Although the prices are often omitted, since the pricing structure can often be complex and subject to change, there are known to be some low-priced products. One such product is MacroTag, available from Allen Creek Software Incorporated at $49.95, using Microsoft Word and WordPerfect. (The company is prepared to increase its repertoire of DTDs.) Another low-priced product is the XGML Validator™, available from Software Exoterica Corporation for $195. And bureaux are prepared to undertake work if required.

10.3.5 Concluding remarks

SGML was designed to take account of all (technical) publishing requirements and is ideally suited to the multiple re-use of information. It is ideally suited for integrated information bases, with hypermedia links to assist retrieval of the required elements of information. It is ideally suited for the multiple re-use of elements of information of any type.

ODA was originally designed to allow word processors of different manufacturers to inter-communicate, so that an office document created on one word processor could be imaged as intended by the author on the word processor of the receiver. It is ideally suited to make electronic that which was previously done using typewriters, word processors, and other office equipment, with some extensions. It is ideally suited for the creation of an electronic filing system from which complete documents are extracted. It is inadequate for the specification of an integrated information system or indeed for complex technical documentation, but then it was never intended for that purpose.

Initially, ODA seemed to have many supporters in the US, notably in the National Bureau of Standards (NBS), now NIST. In 1990, NIST held a one-day workshop on Document Processing, at which two of the papers were on SGML. Over 400 people attended, but when they were asked how many were considering ODA for their own use, only half a dozen raised their hands. The rest were there to learn more about SGML. This was reported in the *Seybold Report on Desktop Publishing*,[5] two subheadings of the article being:

- Interest in SGML is high;
- Interest in ODA is low.

ODA from a Publishing Perspective is the title of an article that appeared in the *Seybold Report on Publishing Systems*,[6] and this too could provide useful background information to anyone considering the use of ODA.

Only time will tell what use is actually made of ODA. It is predicted, however, that once ODA products are generally available, such use will almost exclusively be for office documents for many years to come. In the meantime, SGML seems set to be used more extensively, with the building of integrated information bases governed by SGML, full of hypermedia links.

Notes

(1) This chapter is based on Joan M Smith, 'SGML and ODA: Technical Publications in a Defence Environment', *EuroCALS Newsletter*, number 7 (January 1991), pp 27-38.

(2) For the purposes of comparison of SGML with ODA, some of the information already given about SGML is repeated in this chapter.

(3) Further details are in ISO/IEC JTC 1/SC 18 N 2417 where 45 proposed extensions are listed.

(4) This statement comes from EWOS/TA/90/21 Rev 2.

(5) See 'Lessons in Document Interchange at NIST: A Look at Current Options', *The Seybold Report on Desktop Publishing* (13 August 1990), pp 38-40.

(6) See 'ODA from a Publishing Perspective', *Seybold Report on Publishing Systems*, volume 19 number 7 (18 December 1989), pp 3-20.

11

SGML product guidance

11.1 LICENSING A PRODUCT

11.1.1 General questions to ask a vendor

Choosing a system is not an easy task. Remember that you are likely to get only what you pay for. Equally, there is no need to go for an all-singing all-dancing system if your needs are relatively simple initially. There is time enough to go for a big system later, when the costs can be justified. The good news is that because you are working with a standard, all the SGML documents produced by one system can be input to the next. Do remember, however, to store the SGML marked-up documents (the living documents), and *not* formatted form.

It is also important to bear in mind your own requirements with respect to ISO 8879 SGML, and not to be bound by the SGML offerings that are currently available in the marketplace. Draw up your own specification and then ask vendors what they can offer that meets your specification. If they consider that getting your business would be to their advantage, they may well offer you software that meets your specification, even though some of the features and/or functionality was not available in their listed products. Certainly this is the case for large applications where government ministries, for example, go out to tender for SGML systems.

Remember also that there is not just SGML — there is also HyTime if you need hypermedia working, and preferably an object-oriented database system, as well as SDIF for transfer. Then there will be the text composition standards, DSSSL and SPDL with the fonts standard. There is much to consider.

Whatever your needs, you still have to choose an SGML system. How to go about this task?

Seeing a set demonstration of a product is not always a rewarding experience, and in itself can be insufficient to judge an SGML product. All too often the demonstrator is trained only to talk about what the system is doing, and knows little about SGML. I recall seeing one demonstration and later commenting (not to the demonstrator) that I liked what I saw, but I did not like what I did not see. In other words, the product so far as it went was very good, but it did not go very far! You may well want as much functionality as you can get within a certain type of system. Do ask searching questions, otherwise there could be disappointments later.

There are many questions that can be asked of a vendor. Have a list of questions ready. It could include some of the following.

Has the software been tested for conformance against ISO 8879?

Can the SGML declaration be examined?

Can a different SGML declaration be specified?

Can a variant concrete syntax be specified?

Can the character sets be amended?

How are character sets for other European languages handled?

How are multiple character sets handled?

How are Eastern languages/scripts dealt with?

What SGML features are available?

When are the remaining SGML features to be added?

Does the system offer any help in writing a DTD?

What content notations are supported?

How are these content notations dealt with?

Can other content notations be added?

What public entity sets are supported?

Can other entities be added to the document type declaration?

How are entity references dealt with?

Can a user declare entities in the declaration subset prior to the document instance?

How are these (document-specific) entities handled?

What happens if a DTD/document instance is parsed that includes use of unsupported features?

How are complex tables dealt with?

How is mathematics dealt with?

How are comments dealt with if I choose to insert them in the document instance?

The standard allows for application information to be present in the SGML declaration. How is this dealt with?

Not all of the above questions will be appropriate — it depends on the type of system required. And not all of the questions need be asked, for example whether or not a supplementary question is asked could depend on the response to the previous question.

Consider now some more specific questions. Some will be a repeat of the above, but this time some of the reasons for putting the questions will be explained.

11.1.2 Parser/parsing system

There may be more to a parser than strictly 'necessary' in that the vendor may offer what I call a parsing system as opposed to just a parser or software for checking the correctness. This additional software can either be available with the parser (bundled) or as an extra (unbundled). There may be translators for various character sets, an application language, and other facilities to assist in the application of the parser.

An SGML parser is software that checks the data stream for conformance with what is allowed by ISO 8879. Remember that the features are optional, so the parser may not be able to deal with all the features.

What SGML features are supported?

Since all of them have a use, and since most/all of them are in use in France, Belgium, and Japan, in particular, do be careful if the answer is a list as opposed to 'all of them'. If some of the features are not supported, ask about this.

Which SGML features are not supported?

There are supplementary questions that may be put.

Is it the intention to add the capability to deal with these other features in the parser, and if so, when?

Having dealt with the availablity of features, come onto diagnostics.

What error messages are given to the user in the event of failure?

Is a list of error messages available?

A word about the amount of markup added to a document. As you are aware, the amount of markup added to a document may be minimized in many ways. This has the effect of reducing not only the markup that needs to be entered, but also the amount present when storing the document or transmitting it. However, some parsing systems supply omitted markup, so the minimization benefits can be lost. Whilst some systems need the full form for database working, do use the minimized form as long as possible to gain the full benefits from minimization.

When is the markup expanded to its full form?

Is it possible to choose whether or not the markup will be expanded, and if so, at what stages?

Does the parser have the ability to strip out supplied markup to ensure a fully minimized document, as permitted by the SGML declaration and DTD, and if so, to what extent?

11.1.3 Editing software

In addition to providing assistance in the preparation or editing of SGML document instances, software could also be provided to assist in the editing of an SGML declaration and a document type declaration (which includes the DTD). It is doubtful if the editing system will provide assistance with the SGML declaration, alas, but it may well include the capability to edit the DTD, which can be most useful.

Does the editor assist in the preparation/editing of an SGML declaration?

Does the editor assist in the preparation/editing of a DTD?

If the answer to one or both of the above questions is 'no', a supplementary question can be put.

Is it likely that the editor will be extended to provide these additional facilities, and if so, when?

An SGML editor may or may not be what is termed context-sensitive. To be of maximum use to the person responsible for preparing the document instance, the editor should be context-sensitive. That is, the editor knows what elements are permitted in the context in which the user is currently working, perhaps displaying the possible list from which selection may be made. To do this properly, the system should work from the DTD, in what is known as 'native' SGML — the system *works* in SGML, there being no translation to/from the vendor's own code.

Is the editor context-sensitive?

Is it a native SGML editor?

With a context-sensitive editor, there is still the question as to how the permitted elements (and attributes) are listed. They may be displayed on a menu, perhaps with a point-and-click system using a mouse, or along the top or bottom of the screen.

Most people appreciate that it is not always a good thing to see the generic identifiers for the elements, for example in the CALS application. Instead, the system could show a reduced form or the full form. In the menu showing what elements were permitted, the list could show the full name of the element as well as the actual markup that will be added. There is thus no mistake that n stands for note, or w for a warning, for example.

Is there a menu showing what elements are permitted?

Does the menu show the full name of the elements?

If there is no menu, how are the permitted tags listed?

Some people like to see the actual markup being added to a document to indicate its structure, whilst others prefer to work in WYSIWYG mode, seeing no markup at all, merely its effect on the way in which the text is presented on the screen. But there can be hidden markup for references, for example, or someone looking at a document that has failed to be parsed may wish to see all the markup. So both modes of working can be useful.

Find out how the markup is shown. It can be colour if there is colour capability, or maybe using the angled brackets, or maybe an icon. Beware, as what may look interesting during a demonstration could be infuriating to use all day every day. Remember to let the authors of documents see the system you propose supplying to them before taking out a licence.

What are the ways of working with the text?

How is the markup itself displayed?

11.1.4 Publishing software

Beware of a publishing system that is merely application-specific. Some of these applications are subject to change, for example the CALS application. If the solution is tied to a specific SGML declaration and document type declaration, it may not be updatable easily — plus the fact that you may not be able to use the product for another application. The publishing system should be able to handle general SGML applications, and be based on a general SGML product rather than merely offering a specific SGML solution. It should then be possible to fall back on the general SGML capabilities if an application changes, before the vendor is able to bring out an updated solution.

Is the publishing software based on a general SGML product?

What application-specific solutions are available?

SGML offers seemingly unlimited facilities, from implicit numbering schemes to the handling of hypermedia links. The system can provide the information for lists of contents, including figures. And it could provide an index, not just a computer-generated one but one where the user has also marked up certain words and phrases to be indexed or linked with indexed words and phrases (the *see also* entries).

What facilities are available for numbering sections and lists, for example?

Are contents and other such lists system-supplied?

Are indexing facilities available whereby the information may be marked up in SGML?

Since tables may be described in terms of SGML by rows and columns, not only may they be imaged in different ways by omitting specified rows and/or columns on output, but also computations may be performed on values in the table, and the information even presented in the form of business graphics.

How does the system handle tables?

Are there facilities for taking information from tables and displaying it in business graphics?

A vendor could make facilities available for office documents, such as memoranda, letters, and reports.

Are any facilities available for general office documents, and if so, what?

Information for forms and spreadsheet information may be represented in SGML.

Does the system handle forms, and if so, how?

Is a spreadsheet capability included?

Mathematics can also be described in terms of SGML. This is very useful for splitting a long equation in a 'correct' way if it occupies more than one line. The notion could also be extended to input values to the equation and have computations carried out — although it is doubted very much if a vendor can offer such a facility today.

How does the system handle mathematics?

What about in-line mathematics?

Having dealt with text, think about graphics and other kinds of information (raster graphics, vector graphics, audio, video, interactive video, and so on).

What different kinds of content may be included in the SGML document?

Will other types of content be catered for, and if so, when?

Consider what facilities might be needed if you are interested in having an information base, containing different kinds of documents.

Can the SGML documents be considered as input to an information base, and if so, how?

Can it be used not only as a publishing system but also as a management information system, and if so, how?

What about audit trail?

There are many more questions that could be asked, but most of these are no longer to do with SGML *per se* but more to do with the system offered. However, they could be very pertinent.

Can the system support hypermedia facilities, and if so, how?

The response could be to the effect that this is through application of the HyTime standard.

It could well be that other facilities are offered. Find out what they are.

What other SGML facilities are offered?

There will surely be times when you wish to extend the capabilities offered, if only to deal with contract information. For this, you will need to have an application language supplied, so your own programmer can add the necessary code.

Is an application language provided to extend the facilities made available?

11.1.5 The software demonstration

When looking at the demonstration, one thing you are doing is assessing how easy it is to use, and how user-friendly the system is.

Is the system easy to use?

Is the system user-friendly?

You will probably be interested in how long it takes to parse/check a document, and perform other tasks that may not be directly associated with SGML. (This could be tested on a sample document you prepare as part of a benchmark, described below.)

How long does it take to parse a document of a certain length?

Ask to see the SGML declaration and also the document type declaration/DTD pertaining to the vendor's demonstration. You may not be able to see the SGML declaration, being told that it is one known to the system. In which case, beware, as it may mean that you cannot amend it or design your own.

Can I see the SGML declaration used in the demonstration?

Can I see the document type declaration/DTD used in the demonstration?

Can these be amended?

This is where some of the questions listed above can be asked, again if necessary.

11.1.6 Preparation of a benchmark

If you are still interested in the software described, and it copes with all the features of SGML that you are likely to need, ask to have your own benchmark or set of tests run. These could be on a floppy diskette.

In some respects, the benchmark could be thought of as being similar to the conformance tests that have been devised for SGML conforming systems. So some questions could be asked of a vendor about conformance of the product. Test suites are becoming available for different levels, in that optional features, for example, will not be tested in phase I although there are plans to extend the testing in phase II.

Has your software been run through a conformance test suite, and if so, which, and what were the results?

When devising your benchmark, remember that there are three parts to a complete SGML document:

- the SGML declaration;
- the document type declaration/DTD;
- the document instance.

In order to prepare tests for the SGML declaration and the DTD, you could always try amending one that is published, in ISO 8879 perhaps, or ISO/IEC TR 9753 Techniques for Using SGML, or published elsewhere. It is not necessary to start from scratch!

There are many combinations of what is possible that can reasonably be included in a few SGML declarations. For example in one of them, state YES to all the feature use, and SHORTREF SGMLREF (thus you have effectively stated that there is the possibility that all eleven features may be used subsequently). Add your own short reference list of codes. If the parser is acknowledged as not dealing with link features, how does it react if their use is called for in the SGML declaration? And if YES is put to SIMPLE, for example, without also giving the number of links, how does the parser react?

Come onto character set statements, quoting them correctly and incorrectly. And then do other alterations, as desired.

Now add some APPINFO. How does the system deal with this? Is it displayed for the operator to see? You will need APPINFO if you are also using HyTime for hypermedia working — this is where you tell the system that your application also conforms to HyTime. And after the system demonstrates that it can cope with your SGML declaration, change it.

Where the DTD is concerned, try specifying the use of OMITTAG with an SGML declaration that has said OMITTAG NO. And then try making errors with the different kinds of declarations. How does the system cope with public identifiers correctly and incorrectly stated? Add your own entity declarations. You know the idea!

In the document instance, it is possible to test many kinds of things, especially at the beginning where you are prefacing the document instance with the document type declaration subset. Some examples can apply to the use of SHORTREF at this point. Or there can be a DOCTYPE name that has no associated DTD. That should be easy, in that the parser should throw it off immediately. But how?

Try omitting quotation marks from attribute values with an SGML declaration that states SHORTTAG NO. And you can devise tests for other features as well as incorrect tags.

Put elements where they are not permitted; include content notation not declared; specify an end-tag incorrectly. Make a lot of errors in one of the document instances, to see how the parser deals with many. Include some marked sections in a document instance. Include some escape sequences.

Now assume that you wish to use the system for taking in a document already marked up in accordance with SGML, you wish to edit it on the system being assessed, and you wish to have it output, with SGML markup, for input to another system. One benefit of using a standard is that this sort of thing should be possible. However, the system may cause the markup to be altered in some way, but hopefully not so that it would cease to be a conforming SGML document. What does it do when other character sets or symbols are required? It may take in the requirements in one form (perhaps using the right-hand side of a code table) and output them for onwards transmission in another form (as entity references, say).

Above all, make the tests realistic for your applications. You know what you wish to do, why you need SGML, and the types of documents for which you need it. If you need the software for a defence application, for example CALS, prepare a document conforming to that application, but bear in mind that you may also need to have similar documents conforming to AECMA 1000D. They are not the same!

Remember, what you are judging is how the software being assessed deals with your set of tests. When you have tried the tests with the software from several vendors, you will be in a better position to assess the results than getting them from just one vendor, and certainly in a better position than if you just watched a demonstration.

11.2 AVAILABILITY OF PRODUCTS

11.2.1 Public domain software

The principal item of public-domain software is the SGML parser known as ARCSGML. This is available for down-loading from Internet comp.text.sgml, and is up and running on many different systems.[1] Also available on Internet is software developed from ARCSGML. This is sgmls, which outputs a simple, easily parsed, line-oriented, ASCII representation of an SGML document's Element Structure Information Set, intended for use as the front-end for structure-controlled SGML applications — according to the description. Charles Goldfarb is the developer of ARCSGML, and James Clark of sgmls.

An SGML toolset is under development by the Chameleon project, described in 9.2.6.

As other SGML software comes into the public domain, news will doubtless be posted to readers of the Internet SGML newsgroup in comp.text.sgml.

11.2.2 Commercially-available software

The list of commercial SGML software is ever expanding, and any document that provides detailed information on the availability of SGML software will necessarily be out-of-date before it is published, such is the speed with which new versions appear and new vendors bring out value-added software for retroactive conversions or similar functionality.[2]

Information given here is thus to be considered as a starting-point only. Moreover, it is limited to providing links to obtain further details. To keep up-to-date it is helpful to read the SGML publications, such as the *SGML Users' Group Newsletter*, the

<*TAG*> newsletter, and the Internet SGML newsgroup contributions in comp.text. sgml, the last one in particular for details of software in the public domain. The *Bibliography on SGML and Related Issues* also includes some information on products.[3]

Note that not all large computer companies have SGML products, but for the sake of large contracts they are often prepared to enter into third party agreements with developers of SGML editing systems, for example. Note also that some vendors concentrate on offering CALS solutions of which SGML is a part.

No value judgement is placed on any product or service listed. All details should be checked with the supplier, who will be able to provide the latest information and product prices. In particular, a check should be made that the software does what is required before a licence is signed. Be aware that not all software is based on the rigour of an SGML parser; indeed, this is considered to be unnecessary for some products.

In general, the address of the original vendor is given, although in some cases several distributors have been appointed throughout the world. Note also that many vendors and distributors are prepared to offer consultancy and training in addition to such services being offered by independent consultants (who are not listed below).

ACSE (Associated Consultants and Software Engineers), 29 Boulevard General Wahis, B-1030 Brussels, Belgium (telephone +32 2 242 22 21)

Consultancy and value-added services available, in particular for the use of SGML in complex database applications; distributor of the FORMEX parsing system developed for the CEC, which supports all the SGML optional features.

Agfa CAPS, 200 Ballardvale Street, Wilmington, MA 01887, United States (telephone +1 508 658 5600; telefax +1 508 658 2648)

Offers the CAPS publishing system that includes SGML capabilities, and the Shared Document Management System based on SGML.

AIS Berger-Levrault, 34 Avenue du Roule, 92200 Neuilly-sur-Seine, France (telephone +33 1 46 40 10 60; telefax +33 1 46 40 18 44)

Provides consultancy and value-added services; distributor of several SGML products, including PAT and Lector (see the entry for Open Text Systems Incorporated). SGML/Search is also available, this being an AIS SGML extension of PAT and Lector that automatically turns SGML files into searchable databases, offering a high-level SGML-based query language and hypertext interface.

Allen Creek Software Incorporated, 1209 West Huron, Ann Arbor, MI 48103, United States (telephone +1 313 663 4248)

Vendor of MacroTag software, a product for automatic tagging that supports SGML markup for documents created using Microsoft Word and WordPerfect.

ArborText Incorporated, 535 West William Street, Suite 300, Ann Arbor, MI 48103, United States (telephone +1 313 996 3566; telefax +1 313 996 3573)

Developed The Publisher, an SGML-based document processing system; capabilities for editing tables and working with hypertext; incorporated with

Sybase for database working. Also offers SGML Editor, which includes hypermedia capabilities, and Document Architect for customizing your own application for use with the SGML Editor. Licensed Sema Group's Mark-It parsing system.

Avalanche Development, 947 Walnut Street, Boulder, CO 80302, United States (telephone +1 303 449 5032; telefax +1 303 449 3246)

Developer of FastTAG software, that automatically enhances text and word processing files with the structural markup tags for composition systems and electronic publishing applications; IMSYS.CALS is for automatic tagging of the CALS SGML application.

Compugraphic (see Agfa CAPS)

Context (see Mentor Graphics)

Database Publishing Systems Limited, 608 Delta Business Park, Great Western Way, Swindon, Wiltshire SN5 7XF, United Kingdom (telephone +44 793 512515; telefax +44 793 512516)

Distributor for Datalogics and other SGML software; offers training and consultancy.

Datalogics Incorporated, 441 West Huron Street, Chicago, IL 60610-3674, United States (telephone +1 312 266 4444; telefax +1 312 266 4473)

Developer of DL Pager™, a high volume batch pagination and composition system that works with SGML; WriterStation®, a PC-based SGML editor; and ParseStation™, and an SGML parser. Also markets GEPR™, a general expression/pattern replacement program for file and data conversion, and TPE™, described as a complete system for production and management of loose-leaf technical publications that includes an SGML editor. Customized systems have also been developed. Offers tutorials and consultancy.

Datapage Technologies, 510 S Service Road West, O'Fallon, MO 63366-0568, United States (telephone +1 314 272 7820; telefax +1 314 272 7823)

Developed <data>CLIPS™, a collection of SGML support services for information management and electronic publication. Consultancy offered.

Data Retrieval Corporation, 8989 North Deerwood Drive, Milwaukee, WI 532235, United States (telephone +1 414 355 5900)

Markets TextDBMS/SGML text management tools.

DocuPro Incorporated, 620 Clyde Avenue, Building B, Mountain View, CA 94043-2214, United States (telephone +1 415 960 1214)

Licensed Software Exoterica XGML Engine™, to be incorporated in software.

Electronic Book Technologies, 1 Richmond Square, Providence, RI 02906, United States (telephone +1 401 421 9550; telefax +1 401 421 9551)

Markets *Dyna* Text™, described as an electronic book browser, but in fact examples are technical manuals, complete with illustrations; it accepts SGML files. Also offers the Instant Stylesheet Editor for use with the *Dyna*Text system.

Frame Technology Corporation, 2911 Zanker Road, San Jose, CA 95134, United States (telephone +1 408 433 3311)

Licensed Software Exoterica XGML Engine™, incorporated in FrameMaker for CALS SGML applications.

GMD-FOKUS, Hardenbergplaz 2, 1000 Berlin 12, Germany (telephone +49 30 25499214; telefax +49 25499202)

Developed DAPHNE, a document processing system that incorporates SGML and CGM, also LAUREL, a means of describing context-sensitive formatting instructions.

Grif SA, 2 Boulevard Vauban, BP 266, 78053 St Quentin en Yvelines, Cedex, France (telephone +33 1 30 60 75 10; telefax +33 1 30 60 75 27)

Developed Grif, a WYSIWYG editor for SGML documents, allowing editing of text, tables, graphics, pictures, and mathematics. Also markets DTD Builder.

Grumman Data Systems, 1111 Stewart Avenue, Bethpage, NY 11714-3584, United States (telephone +1 516 346 3855)

Offers value-added services, including an SGML-governed object-oriented database system.

IBM (contact local office)

Offers TextWrite for the creation and modification of SGML documents; TextWrite tools for the creation and modification of DTDs; TextTagger for the analysis and tagging of existing word processor or print files, or scanned documents; ProcessMaster with a CALS application feature; and SGML Translator for validation of SGML documents and translation to/from DCF GML.

ICPC Limited, Greencastle Parade, Coolock, Dublin 17, Ireland (telephone +353 1 474711; telefax +353 1 474546)

Offers processing and typesetting of SGML documents.

Information Dimensions Incorporated, 655 Metro Place South, Dublin, OH 43017-1396, United States (telephone +1 614 761 8083)

Developed BasicPlus, database software that supports SGML.

Intergraph Corporation, One Madison Industrial Park, Huntsville, AL 35807, United States (telephone +1 205 464 8050)

Offers CALS-SGML editing and publishing system.

Interleaf Incorporated, Ten Canal Park, Cambridge, MA 02141, United States (telephone +1 617 494 4826)

Markets LeafTag for CALS SGML application, and CALS Preparedness Package. Licensed Sema Group's Mark-It parsing system.

International Network Services, INS House, Station Road, Sunbury-on-Thames, Middlesex TW16 6SB, United Kingdom (telephone +44 932 761020)

Offers Design Express for paperless communication of design data, with support for SGML.

KnowledgeSet Corporation, 888 Villa Street, Suite 500, Mountain View, CA 94041, United States (telephone +1 415 968 9888)

Offers indexing and full retrieval software based on SGML for structuring data for CD-ROM applications.

MEC Information Systems Limited, 43A Cheval Place, London SW7 1EW, United Kingdom (telephone +44 71 823 9797; telefax +44 71 584 9493)

Markets MASS-11 system, the module for CALS Submission System including SGML capability.

Mentor Graphics (UK) Limited, Mentor House, Western Centre, Western Road, Bracknell, Berkshire RG12 1RS, United Kingdom (telephone +44 344 482828; telefax +44 71 344 483368)

Offers DOC SGML editor, an SGML editing system that supports CALS and other applications.

MID/Information Logistics Group GmbH, Ringstrasse 15, 6900 Heidelberg, Germany (telephone +49 6221 166 091; telefax +49 6221 23921)

Distributor for Datalogics products; offers consultancy and other services.

Naggum Software, Forskningsparken, Gaustadalléen 21, 0371 Oslo 3, Norway (telephone +47 2 95 86 22; telefax +47 2 60 44 27)

Offers SGML database and software development support.

Officesmiths Incorporated, 331 Cooper Street, Ottawa, Ontario K2P 0G5, Canada (telephone +1 613 235 6749)

Markets The Officesmith, a database management system designed to handle text with SGML import/export.

Office Workstations Limited (OWL), Rosebank House, 144 Broughton Road, Edinburgh EH7 4LE, United Kingdom (telephone +44 31 557 5720; telefax +44 31 557 5721)

Developed IDEX, a multi-user hypertext-based document management system with SGML capability; supports CD-ROM on PCs.

Open Text Systems Incorporated, Unit 622, Waterloo Town Square, Waterloo, Ontario N2J 1P2, Canada (telephone +1 519 746 8288; telefax +1 519 746 3255)

Offers SGML-based software developed for the New Oxford English Dictionary project, including PAT, a text search system for SGML marked-up databases; Lector, a text browser and screen formatter; and GOEDEL, a database management system.

Publishing Solutions, 205 East 78th Street, Suite 17-T, New York, NY 10021, United States (telephone +1 212 288 2470)

Markets dataTag, a database tagging utility; includes SGML capability.

Rank Xerox (see Xerox)

Sema Group (Belgium) SA, DTRD(B), AG Building, Place du Champ de Mars 5, B-1050 Brussels, Belgium (telephone +32 2 508 5323; telefax +32 2 512 1499)

Developer of Mark-It, a full features SGML parsing system, also Write-It, an SGML editor. Licences available to end-users and commercial developers. Offers training and consultancy.

Sema Software Technology, Sema Group Systems Limited, Avonbridge House, Bath Road, Chippenham, Wiltshire SN15 2BB, United Kingdom (telephone +44 249 656194; telefax +44 249 655723)

Distributor for Mark-It and Write-It as part of the Sema Group; offers training and consultancy.

Shaffstall Corporation, 7901 East 88th Street, Indianapolis, IN 46256, United States (telephone +1 317 842 2077)

Offers several SGML products based on Shaffstall 6000, a data and document conversion system. Shaffstall Translator 6000 is for commercial and general SGML applications; Shaffstall 6000 SW is a software only version of the 6000 system; and there is an SGML/CALS Translator for CALS applications.

SoftQuad Incorporated, 56 Aberfoyle Crescent, Suite 810, Toronto, Ontario M8X 2W4, Canada (telephone +1 416 239 4801; telefax +1 416 239 7105)

Developer of Author/Editor, SGML editing software, and also Rules Builder which allows a DTD subset to be created for use with Author/Editor; tables are supported. Application Builder is also available.

Software Exoterica, 383 Parkdale Avenue, Suite 406, Ottawa, Ontario K1Y 4R4, Canada (telephone +1 613 722 1700; telefax +1 613 722 5706)

Developer of XGML CheckMark™, an interactive editor; XGML Engine™ an interactive validating parser (being replaced by XGML Kernel); XGML Normalizer™, a validation and debugging tool; XGML OmniMark™, a scripting language facility; XGML Translator™, a combined parser and application generator; and XGML Validator™, a parser/validation tool. Licences software to end-users, corporate developers, and commercial developers. Offers training and consultancy.

Taunton Engineering Incorporated, 505 Middlesex Turnpike, Suite 11, Billerica, MA 01821, United States (telephone +1 617 663 3667)

Offers Silversmith, a full text retrieval system with SGML capability.

Telub Inforum AB, Ljungadalsgatan 2, SE-351 80 Växjö, Sweden (telephone +46 470 420 00; telefax +46 470 154 28)

Use of SGML for value-added services.

TeXcel AS, Gaustadalléen 21, 0371 Oslo 3, Norway (telephone +47 2 95 85 22; telefax +47 2 60 44 27)

Distributor for ArborText products; offers value-added services.

The Turing Institute, George House, 36 North Hanover Street, Glasgow G1 2AD, United Kingdom (telephone +44 41 552 6400)

Developer of Tolk, a program consisting of an SGML parser and an imperative interpreted language for translation of SGML documents into other formats.

The Unifilt Company, 6 Cody Street, 1st Floor, Fords, NJ 08863, United States (telephone +44 908 225 2243; telefax +44 908 225 2248)

Offers TABLE *TAG* ™, a software utility that automatically converts Lotus 1-2-3® and compatible spreadsheets to tagged tables for CALS and AAP applications, using the SoftQuad Author/Editor.

US Lynx, 853 Broadway, New York, NY 10003, United States (telephone +1 212 673 3210; telefax +1 212 673 5261)

Markets Instant Imager, a CALS to Ventura product for SGML marked-up text.

Vrije Universiteit, Department of Mathematics and Computer Science, Postbus 7161, 1007 MC Amsterdam, The Netherlands (telephone +31 20 548 8080)

Markets the Amsterdam parser, developed for the AAP and other SGML applications.

Xerox (contact local office)

Markets DocuBuild, an SGML publishing system, and also CALS solutions. Bureau services offered in some countries.

Xyvision Incorporated, 101 Edgewater Drive, Wakefield, MA 01880-1291, United States (telephone +1 617 245 4100)

Offers CALS Document Exchange, an integrated publishing system; and the Advanced Compliance Package, again for CALS, with capability of editing the CALS DTD.

Zandar Corporation, Box 480, Newfane, VT 05345, United States (telephone +1 800 662 9667; telefax +1 802 254 3399)

Developed TagWrite, a text conversion utility for text publishing.

Notes

(1) Additional details are given in 12.1.

(2) There are two publications that give information on SGML products and services. Firstly there is the GCA publication *The SGML Source Guide*. The other publication is *SGML Products and Services*, European Edition, edited by Joan M Smith (November 1990).

(3) Further details about these are given in Chapter 12.

12

Further information

12.1 SGML USERS' GROUP

It was in 1984 during the Oxford MarkUp conference that I made a proposal for there to be an SGML Users' Group, which would have international membership. The following year, at the 1985 MarkUp conference, the group was formerly inaugurated, since when it has been going strong. Its annual general meetings are held in conjunction with the yearly MarkUp conferences. The group does not itself organize a conference, preferring to sponsor and support the successful GCA MarkUp events.

Several chapters and special interest groups (SIGs) have been set up, the former enabling people in a region or country to get together, the latter being for those who are interested in a specific aspect of SGML.

Chapters have been started in Canada, Germany, Japan, Norway, The Netherlands, and the US (New York), there being plans at an advanced stage for chapters in the UK and the US (Washington, DC). (Although many of the early meetings of the SGML Users' Group were held in the UK, a chapter was never formally constituted; this omission will soon be remedied.) Others are proposed for France, Switzerland, and the US (Arizona). An independent group exists in Australia, where this will be approached with an invitation for it to become a chapter of the international SGML Users' Group.

Where special interest groups are concerned there is the Database SIG, the European Workgroup on SGML (EWS), and SIGhyper, the last mentioned dealing specifically with HyTime. There is one in the offing for the ATA (Air Transport Association), SGML being used for its technical manuals. The CALS in Europe SIG was also a special interest group of the SGML Users' Group initially, the relationship now being by way of an Information Exchange Agreement between the two organizations.

The international SGML Users' Group publishes a *Bulletin* and a *Newsletter*. Its *Bulletin* contains papers, articles, and reports, the *Newsletter* consisting of short articles, news of chapters and SIGs, summaries of documents, reports of meetings, product announcements, a diary, and any other news considered to be of interest to members.

A video on SGML was co-sponsored by the SGML Users' Group and the GCA, this now being marketed by the GCA under the terms of an agreement with the SGML Users' Group.

More recently the SGML Users' Group agreed to make available to anyone interested a copy of the SGML parser developed by Charles Goldfarb. This can be had on a 3.5 inch floppy diskette for the sum of $10 or £6 to cover the cost of handling, materials, and second class mail. Contact Gaynor West, SGML Users' Group, c/o Database Publishing Systems Limited, 608 Delta Business Park, Great Western Way, Swindon, Wiltshire SN5 7XF, United Kingdom (telephone +44 793 512515; telefax +44 793 512516). Alternatively, for an electronic version the contact person is Paul A Ellison, Computer Unit, University of Exeter, Mathematics and Geology Building, North Park Road, Exeter EX4 4QE, United Kingdom (telephone +44 392 263951; telefax +44 392 263108; e-mail net ellison@uk.ac.exeter). He has agreed for the SGML Project at the university to handle the source code and act as a clearing-house for information. The code is unsupported and there is a disclaimer, but there are no restrictions on use.

Pamela Gennusa took over as president from me in 1990. To get more information about the SGML Users' Group, and to join, contact the secretary, Stephen G Downie, SoftQuad Incorporated, 56 Aberfoyle Crescent, Suite 810, Toronto, Ontario M8X 2W4, Canada (telephone +1 416 239 4801; telefax +1 416 239 7105). The annual subscription is $75 or £40, which includes receipt of the publications, discount on SGML books, preferential rates for ISO standards and technical reports, and a discounted rate at the GCA MarkUp conference.

12.2 GRAPHIC COMMUNICATIONS ASSOCIATION

The Graphic Communications Association (GCA) has been foremost in promoting SGML from the outset. It has been organizing international MarkUp conferences, tutorials on the language, and selling publications in addition to having its own GenCode committee. The Tekkie award 'for meritorious achievement in the technical documentation industry' is a GCA award, many of the recipients being well known for their work with SGML. Another award recently given by the GCA is the International SGML Award.

The first GCA conference on markup in Europe took place at Amsterdam, The Netherlands, in December 1982. This was followed by MarkUp '84 at Oxford, United Kingdom, in April 1984. Thereafter they were held annually at Heidelberg, Germany (June 1985), Luxembourg (July 1986), and Torremolinos, Spain (May 1987). Then it was decided to hold the conferences on either side of the Atlantic Ocean in alternate years. This led to Ottawa, Canada (May 1988), Gmunden, Austria (April 1989), Charleston, United States (June 1990), Lugano, Switzerland (May 1991), but back again in Europe for 1992 at Amsterdam, The Netherlands (May 1992).

In early years the conferences were preceded by a one-day tutorial on SGML. And starting with the Heidelberg event when the SGML Users' Group had an inaugural meeting, it has had its annual general meeting during the conference. Charles Goldfarb, the editor of ISO 8879 SGML, is usually a keynote speaker at the conference, to share his latest thoughts on SGML with participants from different countries. The emphasis of the conference is usually on the more technical issues. The 1992 event will be coupled with a new GCA venture, Documentation Europe '92, at the same venue and following on from the MarkUp conference.

For many years there has been the regular series of twice-yearly TechDoc conferences at various venues in the United States. These have increasingly homed in on SGML, defence applications, and more recently the upcoming text composition standards. One is held during the summer months, the other being known as TechDoc Winter.

Then in 1989 a new series of SGML conferences was started under the chairmanship of Yuri Rubinsky of SoftQuad, one of the leading lights in the SGML world. These focus on applications of the language, SGML '89 with the subtitle of Interesting Things Start to Appear, SGML '90 subtitled Building Architectures of Information for the Future and the Past, and SGML '91 subtitled Practicality, Strategy, Vision + Technique. They are billed as being 'the conference for anyone who has written a DTD, contributed to a DTD, or may have to write a DTD soon'. So far they have been held in October or November in different States.

Tutorials on SGML are held every few months in different locations in the United States. Four days are usually offered, the first two by way of introduction followed by a two-day hands-on workshop. It is necessary to have attended an introductory session before participating in the hands-on workshop. The format has been subject to change, however, and the programme expanded to include tutorials on SGML management. It is necessary to check on the events offered.

The GCA GenCode committee has been going for a number of years. It was responsible for GenCode™, a forerunner of SGML. The committee is now chaired by Sharon Adler, editor of the DSSSL standard. GenCode itself has given way to SGML, the committee concerning itself more with conformance issues these days, and ways of promoting the work.

GCA joins with SGML Associates Incorporated to publish the *<TAG>* newsletter bi-monthly. It contains articles, implementation case studies, product news, interviews, and news of events and conferences as well as news of a more general nature. Also published by the GCA is the *SGML Source Guide*, a directory including contact points for vendors, users' groups, consultants, publications, and conferences pertaining to SGML. This is available on a subscription basis, with updating mailings every quarter.

Books on SGML are available from the GCA, as are copies of the international standards documents, often at a discount. A video on SGML is also available from the GCA, *SGML: The Movie*. The video 'presents SGML in a simplified, entertaining approach to generate and maintain interest in the topic matter'.

To receive information about conferences and tutorials as well as a list of publications available, and the video, contact Marion Elledge, Graphic Communications Association (GCA), 100 Daingerfield Road, Alexandria, VA 22314-2804, United States (telephone +1 703 519 8169; telefax +1 703 548 2867).

12.3 ELECTRONIC PUBLISHING SPECIAL INTEREST GROUP

The Electronic Publishing Special Interest Group (EPSIG) was founded to take over responsibility for the work carried out by the Association of American Publishers (AAP) on what was originally known as the Electronic Manuscript Project. This had resulted in the adoption of SGML for the preparation of books, articles, and serials, eventually leading to the publication of ANSI/NISO Z39.59-1988 American National

Standard for Electronic Preparation and Markup (1991), an application of ISO 8879 SGML. Some changes to the original version were necessitated as a result of comments received during the balloting process, and these are reflected in the DTDs as well as the accompanying information.

EPSIG sells copies of the standard, diskettes containing the DTDs, and the set of guides that had been prepared:

- *Author's Guide to Electronic Manuscript Preparation and Markup*, version 2.0 (1989);
- *Reference Manual on Electronic Manuscript Preparation and Markup*, version 2.0 (1989);
- *Markup of Tabular Material*, version 2.0 (1989);
- *Markup of Mathematical Formulas*, version 2.0 (1989).

Tutorials are arranged periodically on the use of the standard, which is supported by products from several vendors, and has been adopted by publishing houses and other organizations.

Work continues on the markup for mathematics and tables, not considered as part of the standard. A committee has been set up by EPSIG to revise the markup described in the two publications, the results to be input to ANSI for ballot as amendments to ANSI/NISO Z39.59-1988.

EPSIG is a membership organization, the annual subscription being $50. This includes receipt of *EPSIG News*, a quarterly publication. Other classes of membership are available. For details of these and additional information contact Betsy Kiser, EPSIG Manager, c/o OCLC, 6565 Frantz Road, Dublin, Ohio 43017-3395, United States (telephone +1 614 764 6017).

12.4 PUBLISHED STANDARDS AND TECHNICAL REPORTS

The published SGML and related standards and technical reports are obtainable at discount prices from the SGML Users' Group and from the GCA. Alternatively, they may be purchased from your national standards body. In case of difficulty, contact ISO Central Secretariat, 1 Rue de Varemb, CH-1211 Geneva 20, Switzerland (telephone +41 22 749 01 11; telefax +41 22 733 34 30). In any case, it may be beneficial to do some price comparisons before making a purchase.

Always request the latest edition, complete with any published amendments. Remember also that many of the WG 8 standards described as being at CD or DIS status are due for publication within a year, as are technical reports at PDTR and DTR status. Do keep abreast of developments.

Those obtainable at the time of writing are:

- ISO 8879 Information Processing — Text and Office Systems — Standard Generalized Markup Language (SGML), 15 October 1986,
  — Amendment 1, 1 July 1988;
- ISO 9069 Information Processing — SGML Support Facilities — SGML Document Interchange Format (SDIF), 15 September 1988;

- ISO/IEC 9070 Information Processing — SGML Support Facilities — Registration Pro- cedures for Public Text Owner Identifiers, second edition, 15 April 1991;
- ISO/IEC 9541 Information Technology — Font Information Interchange
  - — Part 1 Architecture, 15 September 1991,
  - — Part 2 Interchange Format, 15 September 1991;
- ISO/TR 9544 Information Processing — Computer-Assisted Publishing — Vocabu- lary, 15 July 1988;
- ISO/IEC TR 9573 Information Processing — SGML Support Facilities — Techniques for Using SGML, 1 December 1988,
  - — Part 13 Public Entity Sets for Mathematics and Science, 1 July 1991;
- ISO/IEC TR 10037 Information Technology — SGML and Text-Entry Systems — Guidelines for SGML Syntax-Directed Editing Systems, 15 March 1991.

French text is available for:

- ISO 8879 Traitement de l'information — Systèmes bureautiques — Langage normalisé de balisage généralisé (SGML), 1986;
- ISO 9069 Traitement de l'information — Facilités de support SGML — Format d'échange de documents SGML (SDIF), 1988.

It is not by chance that they were all published either on the first or on the fifteenth of a month — it is ISO practice to use just these two publication dates each month.

12.5 BOOKS ON SGML

If your company intends to use SGML, the advice is to get all the books on the subject, for they are complementary, no two books covering the identical area. And where there is some overlap, two different descriptions of the same thing can often be helpful. Sometimes a gentle introduction is required, and at other times a query needs to be resolved — the standard itself is not always helpful in this respect.

Martin Bryan, *An Author's Guide to the Standard Generalized Markup Language*, Addison Wesley (1988), ISBN 0-201-17535-5, 364 pp

The book contains a wealth of information about using SGML, illustrated with many examples. It goes into technical detail, showing how to use the facilities and features of the standard. More than an author's guide, it is the only book that covers the application of SGML in depth. Appendices address multilingual SGML documents, useful publicly declared entities, and a sample DTD (the one used for the publication of the book). Anyone designing SGML applications is well advised to keep this book handy.

Charles F Goldfarb, *The SGML Handbook*, Clarendon Press (1990), ISBN 0-19-853737-9, 664 pp, edited and with a foreword by Yuri Rubinsky

The editor of ISO 8879 has taken the published standard, and reproduced it in the pages of this book together with invaluable explanations. Part one is devoted to tutorials, part 2 gives a structured overview of SGML, part 3 is ISO 8879 annotated (including amendment 1), and part 4 contains ISO 8879 annexes. Appendices contain historical information and look to the revision of ISO 8879. Designed as a hypertext document, icons crop up pointing to further information. Implementors of the standard will need this book.

Joan M Smith and Robert Stutely, *SGML: The User's Guide to ISO 8879*, Ellis Horwood (1988), ISBN 0-7458-0221-4 (Ellis Horwood Limited), ISBN 0-470-21126-1 (Halstead Press), 172 pp

This is a reference book to the published ISO standard. It contains the SGML syntax productions by numerical and alphabetical sequence as well as giving an index to them; a combined list of the abbreviations; lists of all the character entities complete with graphic representations and indexes by entity reference name and by description; a complete index to ISO 8879; and a list of SGML keywords and reserved names. This book is essential for anyone who has to work with ISO 8879 or who needs to use the characters described in the standard.

Eric van Herwijnen, *Practical SGML*, Kluwer Academic Publishers (1990), ISBN 0-7923-0635-X, 200 pp

This book is for those starting to use SGML with emphasis on practical issues. It consists of three sections: an introductory section for authors and managers; one for those who are applying and managing SGML in the solution of document management problems; the last for application programmers who need to know what can be done with SGML and how to do it. Chapters end with questions to test understanding. The DTD used for the publication of the book is provided. This book gives a good introduction to SGML as well as sound practical advice.

12.6 OTHER USEFUL DOCUMENTS

Several guides have been written about SGML, some by the vendors of SGML products who are able to draw on their considerable experience for this work. A selection is listed below.

The SGML Primer, second edition, SoftQuad (May 1991), 36 pp

This is a very readable booklet for anyone who wishes to know about DTDs. It is billed as the quick reference guide to the essentials of the standard — 'the SGML needed for reading a DTD and marked-up documents and discussing them reasonably'. The primer is obtainable from SoftQuad Incorporated, 56 Aberfoyle Crescent, Suite 810, Toronto, Ontario M8X 2W4, Canada (telephone +1 416 239 4801; telefax +1 416 239 7105).

Understanding the SGML Declaration, second edition, Software Exoterica Corporation (February 1991), 34 pp

Exoterica Complex Tables, second edition, Software Exoterica Corporation (February 1991), 28 pp

The titles of these two booklets are self-explanatory, the booklets being obtainable from Software Exoterica Corporation, 383 Parkdale Avenue, Suite 406, Ottawa, Ontario K1Y 4R4, Canada (telephone +1 613 722 1700; telefax +1 613 722 5706).

Joan M Smith, *The Standard Generalized Markup Language and Related Issues*, British National Bibliography Research Fund Report 22, British Library (1987), ISBN 0-7123-3082-8, ISSN 0264-2972, 63 pp

Joan M Smith, *The Standard Generalized Markup Language (SGML): Guidelines for Editors and Publishers*, British National Bibliography Research Fund Report 26, British Library (1987), ISBN 0-7123-3112-5, ISSN 0264-2972, 49 pp

Joan M Smith, *The Standard Generalized Markup Language (SGML): Guidelines for Authors*, British National Bibliography Research Fund Report 27, British Library (1987), ISBN 0-7123-3112-3, ISSN 0264-2972, 64 pp

This series of three reports was written for the British Library when SGML was first published to encourage its use. They are obtainable from the British Library Publications Sales Unit, Boston Spa, Wetherby, West Yorkshire LS23 7BQ, United Kingdom, and the American Library Association, 50 East Huron Street, Chicago, IL 60611, United States.

Bibliography on SGML and Related Issues, edited by Robin Cover, Nicholas Duncan, and David T Barnard, Technical Report 91-299, Department of Computing and Information Science, Queen's University at Kingston (February 1991), ISSN 0836-0227, 312 pp

The main part of this very comprehensive bibliography contains over 1,500 entries, and five appendices. Not restricted to providing bibliographic information, it also gives useful information on SGML projects and other matters of interest to the SGML community, including contact addresses. It is available for $21 (Canadian) from Doug Hamilton, Department of Computing and Information Science, Goodwin Hall, Queen's University, Kingston, Ontario K7L 3N6, Canada (telephone +1 613 545 6056; e-mail Internet barnard@qucis,queensu.ca). There are plans to have the bibliography available on a network, an announcement concerning this to be given on the TEI-L forum (Bitnet) and on Newsgroup comp.text.sgml (Usenet/uucp).

Guidelines for the Encoding and Interchange of Machine-Readable Texts, edited by C M Sperberg-McQueen and Lou Burnard, TEI P1, version 1.1, Text Encoding Initiative (16 July 1990)

Draft guidelines only can be issued at this stage of the TEI project, since the development work continues with this four-year project. However, the guidelines contain a wealth of information and are commended to anyone dealing with texts for literary and linguistic computing, in any language. Comments on the drafts of the guidelines are welcomed by the editors. To obtain a copy of the document contact C Michael Sperberg-McQueen, Computer Center (M/C 135), University of Illinois at Chicago, Box 6998, Chicago, IL 60680, United States (telephone +1 312 996 2477; e-mail Bitnet u35395@uicvm, Internet @uicvm.uic.edu), or Lou Burnard, Oxford University Computing Service, 13 Banbury Road, Oxford OX2 6NN, United Kingdom (telephone +44 865 273238; telefax +44 865 273275; e-mail Bitnet or Earn lou@vax.ox.ac.uk, Janet ox.vax).

SGML Briefing Notes :

- No 1 An Introduction to the Standard Generalized Markup Language;

- No 2 SGML and Document Structure;
- No 3 SGML and Standardization in Publishing;
- No 4 Using SGML with Existing Publishing Systems;
- No 5 Choosing an SGML System;
- No 6 SGML and the Publishing Process;
- No 7 SGML and Electronic Document Interchange;
- No 8 Public Registration of SGML Text;
- No 9 SGML and Other Standards;
- No 10 Recognizing SGML Applications;
- No 11 Current SGML Applications;
- No 12 SGML Conformance Testing;
- No 13 SGML and Multilingual Text;
- No 14 Applying SGML to Complex Documents;
- No 15 The Terminology of SGML;
- No 16 SGML and ODA: Competitive or Complementary?

Technical Information, Commission of the European Communities, Directorate-General XIII-B

A series of one-page briefing notes on SGML was prepared for the CEC, copies being obtainable free of charge from SGML, Commission of the European Communities, Directorate-General XIII-B, B4/45, L-2920 Luxembourg.

SGML Products (European Edition), edited by Joan M Smith, CALS in Europe Special Interest Group (November 1990)

SGML products and services available in Europe are listed in this document, which provides a good starting point when assessing what is available. Updating information is included in the appropriate sections of the *SGML Users' Group Newsletter* and the *EuroCALS Newsletter*. The document is available for £20 from David Ardron, Secretary, CALS in Europe SIG, Ferranti International plc, Western Road. Bracknell, Berkshire RG12 1RA, United Kingdom (telephone +44 344 483232 extension 3605).

Dominique Vignaud, *L'édition structure des documents: SGML Application à l'édition française*, Paris: Editions du Cercle de la librairie (Janvier 1989)

There are three parts to this French publication: the SGML standard, document analysis, and the application of the SNE/Cercle. Two diskettes are included, one being 5.25 inches and the other 3.5 inches. These contain the DTDs for SNE/Cercle and tables, and the text of the booklet itself, coded in SGML in accordance with the SNE/Cercle DTD. It is obtainable from Editions du Cercle de la librairie, 35 Rue Grégoire-de-Tours, 75006 Paris, France.

AAP guides, which could also be considered in this category, are listed above.

12.7 THE LAST WORD

Very lively messages on SGML are passed around electronically, especially after Charles Goldfarb's (ARCSGML) parser was made available. The SGML newsgroup has been gathering momentum since it was set up towards the end of 1990. Articles and correspondence may be read by accessing comp.text.sgml on Usenet. Questions are asked and answered, thoughts shared, and advice given. Above all it is used to impart information, where this could be news of another system on which the ARCSGML is working or of other software in the public domain. And there are plans to make public domain DTDs available on the network.

These messages are not only interesting to read, but also give a very good indication that SGML is alive and well, and likely to be so for many years to come, being used for applications of which the standards-makers never dreamed when developing ISO 8879 SGML.

Appendix 1:
A brief history of the development of SGML

SGML, in its present form, is the result of the efforts of many people, channelled into four major activities that occurred over the past twenty years: generic coding, the GML and SGML languages, the SGML standard, and major SGML applications.

1 THE GENERIC CODING CONCEPT

Historically, electronic manuscripts contained control codes or macros that caused the document to be formatted in a particular way ('specific coding'). In contrast, generic coding, which began in the late 1960s, uses descriptive tags (for example 'heading' rather than 'format-17'). Many credit the start of the genric coding movement to a presentation made by William Tunnicliffe, chairman of the Graphic Communications Association (GCA) Composition Committee, during a meeting at the Canadian Government Printing Office in September 1967: his topic — the separation of the information content of documents from their format.

Also in the late 1960s, a New York book designer named Stanley Rice proposed the idea of a universal catalogue of parameterized 'editorial structure' tags. Norman Scharpf, director of the GCA, recognized the significance of these trends, and established a generic coding project in the Composition Committee.

The committee developed the 'GenCode® concept', recognizing that different generic codes were needed for different kinds of documents, and that smaller documents could be incorporated as elements of larger ones. The project evolved into the GenCode Committee, which later played an instrumental role in the development of the SGML standard.

2 GML AND SGML: LANGUAGES FOR GENERIC CODING

In 1969, Charles Goldfarb was leading an IBM research project in integrated law office information systems. Together with Edward Mosher and Raymond Lorie he invented the Generalized Markup Language (GML) as a means of allowing the text editing, formatting, and information retrieval subsystems to share documents.

GML (which, not coincidentally, comprises the initials of its three inventors) was based on the generic coding ideas of Rice and Tunnicliffe. Instead of a simple tagging scheme, however, GML introduced the concept of a formally-defined document type with an explicit nested element structure.

Major portions of GML were implemented in mainframe 'industrial strength' publishing systems by IBM and others and achieved substantial industry acceptance. IBM itself, reckoned to be the world's second largest publisher, adopted GML and now produces over 90 per cent of its documents with it.

After the completion of GML, Goldfarb continued his research on document structures, creating additional concepts, such as short references, link processes, and concurrent document types, that were not part of GML but were later to be developed as part of SGML.

3 DEVELOPMENT OF SGML AS AN INTERNATIONAL STANDARD

In 1978, the American National Standards Institute (ANSI) committee on Information Processing established the Computer Languages for the Processing of Text committee, chaired by Charles Card, then of Univac, with Norman Scharpf as a member. Goldfarb was asked to join the committee and eventually to lead a project for a text description language standard based on GML. The GCA GenCode Committee supported the effort and provided a nucleus of dedicated people for the task of developing Goldfarb's basic language design for SGML into a standard.

The first working draft of the SGML standard was published in 1980. By 1983, the GCA was able to recommend its sixth working draft as an industry standard (GCA 101-1983). Major adopters included the US Internal Revenue Service (IRS) and the US Department of Defense.

In 1984, with feedback from the GCA standard in hand, three more working drafts were produced. The project, which had been authorized by the International Organization for Standardization (ISO) as well as ANSI, re-organized. It began regular international meetings as what is now called ISO/IEC JTC 1/SC 18/WG 8, chaired by James Mason of the US Oak Ridge National Laboratory. Work also continued in the ANSI committee, now called X3V1.8, chaired by William Davis of SGML Associates, and supported by the GCA GenCode Committee, chaired by Sharon Adler of IBM. Alignment between ISO and ANSI was maintained by Goldfarb continuing as technical leader, serving as project editor for both groups.

In 1985, a draft proposal for an international standard was published and the international SGML Users' Group was founded in the UK by Joan Smith, who is its president. Together with the GCA in North America, it played a vital role in educating the public about SGML and communicating user reactions and comments back to the development project.

A draft international standard was published in October 1985, and was adopted by the Office for Official Publications of the European Community. Another year of review and comment resulted in the final text, which — using an SGML system developed by Anders Berglund, then of the European Particle Physics Laboratory (CERN) — was published in record time after approval (ISO 8879:1986).

4 IMPORTANT EARLY APPLICATIONS OF SGML

SGML applications are frequently developed for use by a single organization or a small community of users. Two early applications were developed with much broader participation: The Electronic Manuscript Project of the Association of American Publishers (AAP), and the documentation component of the Computer-aided Acquisition and Logistic Support (CALS) initiative of the US Department of Defense.

4.1 Electronic Manuscript Project

From 1983 to 1987, an AAP committee, chaired by Nicholas Alter of University Microfilms, developed an initial SGML application for book, journal, and article creation. The application is intended for manuscript interchange between authors and their publishers, among other uses, and includes optional element definitions for complex tables and scientific formulas.

The technical work was led by Joan Knoerdel of Aspen Systems, with participation by over thirty information processing organizations, including the IEEE, Council on Library Resources, American Society of Indexers, US Library of Congress, American Chemical Society, American Institute of Physics, Council of Biology Editors, and American Mathematical Society.

The AAP industry application standard has achieved significant acceptance, and has particularly been embraced by the emerging CD-ROM publishing industry. It has been adopted as a formal ANSI application standard (Z39.59) and a corresponding ISO standard is under development.

4.2 Computer-aided Acquisition and Logistic Support (CALS)

The SGML portion of CALS was initiated in February 1987 when Bruce Lepisto of the Department of Defense organized a committee to address the subject. The committee consisted of John Bean of Northrop, Pam Gennusa of Datalogics, Ed Herl of the US Army, and Mary McCarthy and Dave Plimier of the US Navy. They were subsequently joined by hundreds of representatives of military contractors and military commands, who participated in additional development and review. Their efforts led to the publication of a military specification (MIL-M-28001) in February 1988.

Similar SGML projects are underway in the defence departments of Canada, Sweden, and Australia, and are under consideration by other countries.

Appendix 2: Glossary

abstract syntax Rules for defining how markup is added to the content of a document, without regard to the specific characters used to represent the markup.

Abstract Syntax Notation One (ASN.1) An ISO standard defining a machine-interpretable way of representing structure, used extensively by the OSI standards.

application (of SGML) The use of an SGML product (conforming to ISO 8879) for the design of SGML documents.

attribute A string that gives supplementary information about an element. An attribute name and its value are positioned within the start-tag of an element.

comment declaration A markup declaration that contains only comments, perhaps documenting a DTD. It provides a method for the insertion of remarks in any of the three components of an SGML document.

concrete syntax Association of the abstract syntax with specific delimiter characters, quantities, markup declaration names, etc.

conforming SGML document An SGML document that complies with the provisions of the ISO 8879 standard.

document A collection of information that may comprise any form of digitized content, including text, audio, vector and raster graphics, coloured photographs, and video.

document instance The content and markup of an example of a class of documents defined by a DTD.

Document Style Semantics and Specification Language (DSSSL) An ISO standard defining how to pass information about the presentation of an SGML document to a formatter, associating style sheet information with a document instance. Additional functionality is to be incorporated to cater for database working, etc.

document type A class of documents having similar characteristics, for example memorandum, minutes, or technical manual.

document type definition (DTD) Rules that define the structure of a class of documents; it includes the vocabulary of generic identifiers, attribute names, entity names, and data content notations that can be used in the markup of the document instance of that class. It is here that the semantics are defined for a specific application.

element A logical part of a document, delimited by a start-tag and an end-tag; an object of information. Elements of a document form a hierarchical structure at the top of which is the document element.

entity A virtual file that is considered as a separate unit of information. It may be a symbol that is referred to by a character string, an expansion of a short string, part of a document, an illustration, etc.

entity reference A request for the information stored in a virtual file (the entity) to be embedded in the document at the point of reference.

feature An optional facility that can be employed by the application to minimize the amount of markup that needs be present, or link the document instance to layout structures, etc. There are effectively eleven features if SHORTREF is included.

generic identifer A string identifying a type of element, found in the start-tag and the end-tag that delimit the element; it is defined in the DTD.

hypermedia Applied to non-sequential searching of elements of information in related documents composed of more than one medium.

implementation (of SGML) The application of the rules expressed in ISO 8879 (usually by a vendor) to result in an SGML product.

layout structure The expression of the way in which the elements of a document are to be presented, for example the fonts to be used, the measure of column(s), etc. Layout of an SGML document is the province of DSSSL.

logical structure The expression of the roles associated with elements of information, for example paragraph, warning, section, or procedure, without regard to the style of presentation.

marked section A portion of a document that has been identified for a special purpose, such as its inclusion or exclusion for a particular recipient of the document.

markup minimization Techniques employed whereby the amount of markup that need be present to indicate the structure of the document is reduced. This applies to the amount of markup that needs not only to be input but also to be stored and transmitted.

notation The coding method employed by a type of content, for example CGM for vector graphics.

Open Systems Interconnection (OSI) A set of ISO standards to enable systems of different vendors to communicate with each other in a neutral way.

parser Software that checks the SGML document conforms to ISO 8879.

reference concrete syntax Specific values associated with the abstract syntax that are given in the standard. It also serves as a model from which other (variant) concrete syntaxes are formed.

SGML declaration The specification of the character sets, concrete syntax, feature use, and capacity requirements of the application.

SGML document The three components of an SGML document are the SGML declaration, the DTD, and the document instance.

SGML Document Interchange Format (SDIF) An ISO standard defining a method of transfer of SGML documents, particularly in an open systems environment.

Standard Generalized Markup Language (SGML) An ISO standard defining a metalanguage (syntax but not semantics) for the neutral representation of the structure of documents. The presentation/imaging of SGML documents is the subject of the text composition standards, DSSSL and SPDL. The semantics for an SGML application are defined in the DTD.

Standard Page Description Language (SPDL) An ISO standard defining a method of imaging a document on a presentation medium, for example on a screen or a piece of paper; SPDL input is the output of the formatting process.

variant concrete syntax Specific values associated with the abstract syntax where these differ from the reference concrete syntax in some way.

Notes

(1) For the complete set of definitions associated with ISO 8879, see clause 4 of the standard.

(2) The definitions given here are expressed in terms perhaps more readily understood than those of the standard itself, in which process some precision of meaning may have been sacrificed; in case of doubt, turn to the standard.

Index

AAP, 94, 96, 101, 133, 136, 137, 141, 145
AECMA, 54, 89, **91–93**, 127
AFII, 64, 65, 84
ANSI, 1, 2, 5, 10, 64, 68, 74, 83, 90, 100, 137, 144, 145
application(s) (of SGML), 5, 8, 9, 13, 22, 57, 58, 67, 74, **89–102**, 117, 124, 127, 128, 131, 133, 136, 138, 141, 143, 145, **146**, 147, 148; *see also* AAP, AECMA, CALS, defence (application(s)), DoD, ISO CS application, ODL
application considerations, 6, 7, 14, 15, 17, 18, 19, 21, 25, 26, 30, 31, 32, 33, 36, 39, 40, 41, 44, **45–54**, 55, 62, 64, 70, 75, 77, 78, 79, 80, 81, 82, 84, 120, 123, 132
ARCSGML, 99, 127, 135, 141, 142
ASCII, 1, 13, 14, 19, 25, 76, 84, 113, 127
ASN.1, 59, 63, 66, 68, 81, 82, 109, 110, 111, **146**
automatic tagging, 49, 128, 129, 133

benefit(s), 35, 46, **51–52**, 53, 115, 122
BSI, 2, 6, 74, 100

CALS, 67, 68, 77, **89–91**, 92, 93, 94, 96, 101, 123, 127, 128, 130, 131, 132, 133, 134, 145
CCITT, 10, 67, 90, 92, 104, 110, 111
CEC, 6, 97, **100**, 141
CEN/CENELEC, 6, 91
communication(s), 10, 12, 14, 46, 48, 52, 66, 67; *see also* interchange
composition, 36, 59, 60, 70, 71, 72, 115, 116, 129
Computer-aided Acquisition and Logistic Support, *see* CALS
concurrent document types (feature), 20, **21**, 144

conformance, 2, 3, 5, **83–84**, 106, 109, 112, 121, 122, 126, 127, 141, 146; *see also* parser(s)/parsing system, validation
context–sensitive editor(s), 48, 69, 74, 75, 123
conversion, see retroactive conversion
creation process, 69, 70, 71, 72

DAP(s), 105, 106, 107, 110, **111–112**
database(s), 5, 7, 45, 48, 50, 52, 53, 56, 57, 69, 70, 75, 87, 92, 93, 97, 99, 100, 111, 122, 128, 129, 130, 131, 146; *see also* information base(s) (integrated)
data tag(s) (feature), 20, **21**, 33, 75
defence (application(s)), 31, 35, 42, 43, 58, 67, 85, **89–93**, 94, 99, 119, 127; *see also* CALS, DoD
device(s), 6, 12, 14, 15, 20, 58, 59, 60, 62, 63, 69, 71, 72; *see also* hardware
document analysis, 28, 29, 30, 72
document designer(s), 13, 14, 24, 27, 28, 39, 40, 57, 71, 72, 109
document profile, 66, 103, 105, 107, 109, **110**, 114
Document Style Semantics and Specification Language, *see* DSSSL
DoD, 6, 32, 57, 67, 77, 79, 144, 145
DSSSL, 4, **55–58**, 61, 62, 70, 71, 91, 93, 98, 104, 105, 108, 112, 113, 120, 136, **146**, 147, 148; *see also* ISO/IEC DIS 10179

EDI, 50, 51, 52, 114
EDIFACT, 10, 50, 114
editing, 37, 38, 39, 45, 47, 59, **68–70**, 71, 72, 76, 103, 122, 127, 130
editor/editing system(s), 31, 69, 70, 81, 97, 109, **122–123**, 128, 129, 130, 131, 132, 143
electronic data interchange, *see* EDI
feature(s), 13, **20–22**, 24, **26**, 32, 33, 40, 51, 83, 89, 91, 99, 100, 120, 121, 122, 125, 126, 128, 132, 138, **147**, 148; *see also* concurrent document types (feature), formal (feature), link features, markup minimization (feature(s)), subdocument(s) (feature)

font(s)/font information, 15, 58, 60, **61–65**, 72, 84, 147
font resource(s), 60, 61, 62, 63, 64, 65, 66, 71
font service(s), 3, 5, 71, 72
fonts standard(s), 3, 4, 55, **61–65**, 70, 104, 105, 120; *see also* ISO/IEC DIS 10036, ISO/IEC 9541
formal (feature), 20, **22**, 67, 68, 90
formatter, 131, 146

GCA, 1, 84, 133, 134, **135–136**, 137, 143, 144
generic identifier(s), 13, 14, 17, 20, 21, 28, 31, 32, 33, 39, 40, 51, 74, 92, 123, **147**
glyph(s), 4, 56, 58, 61, 63, 64, 65, 72; *see also* font(s)/font information, fonts standard(s), ISO/IEC DIS 10036, ISO/IEC 9541
GOSIP, 10, 67, 110, 112
Government Open Systems Interconnection Profile, *see* GOSIP

hardware, 6, 35, 53, 69
hypermedia, 8, 25, **41–42**, 51, 53, **77–79**, 80, 81, 85, 86, 93, 100, 107, 120, 125, 126, 129, **147**
hypertext, 41, 77, 128, 131
HyTime, 3, 5, 27, 42, 53, 57, 58, 70, **77–79**, 86, 87, 91, 93, 99, 100, 105, 107, 120, 125, 126, 134; *see also* ISO/IEC DIS 10744, links(s) (hypermedia)

implementation, 27, 70, **147**
implementor(s), 6, 55, 139
information base(s) (integrated), 9, 10, 15, 22, 30, 32, 35, 36, 37, 41, 42, 43, **45–54**, 78, 79, 81, 87, 91, 93, 94, 96, 105, 111, 117, 118, 119, 124, 125; *see also* object–oriented information base
interchange, 1, 4, 7, 26, 32, 50, 58, 59, 61, 62, 63, 64, 65, **66–67**, 79, 81, 83, 86, 90, 98, 103, 105, 107, 108, **110–111**, 113, 115, 116, 118, 120, 141, 145, 148; *see also* ISO/IEC 9541, ISO 9069
International Organization for Standardization, *see* ISO
ISO, 1, 2, 5, 6, 10, 18, 22, 25, 44, 50, 61, 62, 66, 67, 68, 79, 82, 83, 84, 96, **100–101**, 103, 111, 135, 137, 138, 139, 144, 145, 146, 147, 148
ISO CS application, 5, **74–75**, 100; *see also* ISO/IEC TR 9573
ISO/IEC CD 10743, 5, **79–81**
ISO/IEC DIS 10036, 4, 61, 62, 65
ISO/IEC DIS 10179, 4, **55–58**
ISO/IEC DIS 10180, 4, **58–61**
ISO/IEC DIS 10646, 84, 85
ISO/IEC DIS 10744, 5, **77–79**
ISO/IEC TR 9573, 3, 4–5, 29, 33, 40, 44, **72–76**, 82, 84, 98, 100, 106, 126, 138
ISO/IEC TR 10037, 3, 34, **68–70**, 138
ISO/IEC 9070, 3, 23, 60, 63, **67–68**, 138
ISO/IEC 9541, 3, 4, 58, 60, **61–65**, 138
ISO/TR 9544, 3, **76**, 138
ISO 646, 24, 25, 33, 84
ISO 2022, 11, 33, 84
ISO 8613, 58, **103–119**
ISO 8879, 2, 3, 4, 6, 11, 20, 22, 26, 29, 33, 34, 35, 39, 45, 58, 67, 68, 72, 73, 74, 75, 77, 81, 82, 83, 84, 90, 91, 93, 100, 101, 120, 121, 122, 126, 135, 137, 142, 144, 146, 147, 148; amendment 1, 2, 3, 82, 107, 137
ISO 9069, 3, 4, 6, 63, **66–67**, 91, 137
ISP(s), 106, **111–112**

language(s) (natural), 1, 7, 9, 13, 25, 32, 64, 65, 72, 73, 75, 84, 97, 98, 99, 100, 121
layout, 40, 98
layout process, 56, 59, 60, 70, 71, 72
link features, 16, 20, **21**, 22, 89, 126
explicit, 20, **21**, 32
implicit, 20, **21**
simple, 20, **21**
link(s) (hypermedia), 25, **41–42**, 46, 77, 78, 79, 91, 93, 95, 96, 100, 105, 113, 116, 118, 119, 124
linking, 15, 16, 21, 32, 46, 126, 147
living document(s)/information, 7, 35, 52, 113, 116, 120

management information system, 9, 47, 53, 125; *see also* information base(s) (integrated)
markup minimization (features), 13, **20–21**, 22, **31–33**, 34, 35, 39, 48, 51, 75, 82, 91, 122, **147**; *see also* data tag(s) (feature), omitted tag(s) (feature), rank (feature), short reference(s) (feature), short tag(s) (feature)
minimization, *see* markup minimization (features)
multilingual (text), 58, 64, 72, 100, 138, 141
multimedia, 7, 41, 45, 57, 79, 80, 85, 86, 100, 105
music, 55, 58, 69, 77, 78, **79–81**

NATO, 92, **93**, 101

object–oriented information base, 46, 91, 120, 130
ODA, 5, 10, 16, 22, 66, **103–119**, 141; *see also* ISO 8613
ODIF, 103, 110, 111, 112, 113
ODL, 109, 110, 111, 112, 113
Office/Open Document Architecture, *see* ODA
omitted tag(s) (feature), 20, **21**, 22, 28, 32, 90, 126
Open Systems Interconnection, *see* OSI
operational model (WG 8 projects), 3, 4, **70–72**
OSI, 10, 58, 59, 66, 67, 68, 83, 86, 91, 104, 110, 111, 146, **147**, 148
overheads, 21, **31–33**, 35, 40, 51, 52, 67, 108, 114, 115, 116, 118

parser(s)/parsing system, 20, 26, 51, 74, 81, 96, 99, 100, **121–122**, 126, 127, 128, 129, 130, 132, 133, 135, **148**

parsing, 9, 17, 28, 72, 81, 83, 125
presentation, 15, 16, 21, 35, **36–37**, 40, 46, 53, **55–65**, 69, 70, 71, 72, 93, 112, 113, 146, 147, 148; *see also* layout
product(s), 52, 67, 68, 69, 75, 76, 83, 98, 99, 100, 107, 112, 114, 118, 119, **120–133**, 134, 139, 141, 146, 147
publishing system(s), **123–125**, 129, 133, 141, 144

rank (feature), 20, **21**, 31, 32
reference concrete syntax, 13, 14, 16, 17, 19, 21, 22, 24, 25, 26, 27, 28, 31, 70, 90, **148**
registration
  glyph and glyph collection identifiers, 62; *see also* ISO/IEC DIS 10036
  public text owner identifers, **67–68**; *see also* ISO/IEC 9070
retroactive conversion, 7, 48, 49, 50, 53, 75, 97, 98, 100, 127, 130

SDIF, 3, 4, 6, 10, 50, **66–67**, 76, 79, 83, 93, 103, 107, 110, 111, 112, 113, 116, 120, **148**; *see also* ISO 9069
SGML
  background, **1–2**
  concepts, 10, **12–13**
  definition, **148**
  development, 1–2, 10
  five–year review, 2, 4, 81, **82–83**, 107, 138
  history, 10, 138, **143–145**
  how it works, **15–20**
  objectives, **6–7**
  provisions, **17–20**
  publication, 2
  standardization aspects, **2–6**, **14**
  uses, **7–10**
  what it includes, **16–17**
  what it is, **14–15**
  see also ISO 8879
SGML–B, 3, 5, 42, **81–82**, 107
SGML Document Interchange Format, *see* SDIF
SGML Users' Group, 2, 11, 87, 99, 101, 127, **134–135**, 137, 141, 144, 145

short reference(s) (feature), 4, 5, 20, **21**, 22, 26, 32, 40, 48, 49, 50, 73, **75–76**, 126, 144, 147
short tag(s) (feature), **20**, 22, 32, 39, 40, 126
smart editor(s), *see* context–sensitive editor(s)
SMDL, 3, 5, 77, **79–81**; *see also* ISO/IEC CD 10743
SPDL, 4, 55, **58–61**, 62, 70, 71, 72, 91, 93, 98, 104, 105, 112, 113, 120, **148**; *see also* ISO/IEC DIS 10180
Standard Generalized Markup Language, *see* SGML
Standard Music Description Language, *see* SMDL
Standard Page Description Language, *see* SPDL
subdocument(s) (feature), 20, **22**, 70
supplier(s), *see* vendor(s)
system(s) (SGML), 3, 6, 8, 9, 13, 14, 17, 18, 20, 24, 25, 26, 27, 29, 30, 31, 32, 33, 34, 35, 37, 38, 41, 42, 43, 44, 47, 48, 49, 50, 51, 52, 53, 54, 62, 66, 68, 69, 70, 75, 76, 87, 93, 94, 95, 116, 117, **120–133**, 141

techniques for using SGML, 3, **72–76**; *see also* ISO/IEC TR 9573
tool(s), 48, 49, 98, 99, 118, 127
transmission, 21, 33, 51, 67, 68, 80, 108, 116, 118, 122, 127, 147

user(s), 6, 10, 30, 31, 33, 40, 43, 47, 49, 55, 57, 69, 75, 82, 83, 84, 116, 123, 124, 131, 132, 134, 135, 136, 139, 144
user interface, 30, 35, 51, 52
user requirements
  DSSSL, 55–56
  HyTime, 78
  SGML–B, 81–82
  SMDL, 79–80
  SPDL, 58–59

validation, 70, 130, 132
vendor(s), 1, 6, 13, 26, 27, 34, 40, 48, 68, 69, 75, 82, 83, 91, 96, 98, 100, 106, 107, 112, 114, 117, 118, **120–133**, 136, 139, 147

ELLIS HORWOOD SERIES IN COMPUTERS AND THEIR APPLICATIONS

Series Editor: IAN CHIVERS, Senior Analyst, The Computer Centre, King's College, London, and formerly Senior Programmer and Analyst, Imperial College of Science and Technology, University of London

Koopman, P.	**STACK COMPUTERS**
Kenning, M.-M. & Kenning, M.J.	**COMPUTERS AND LANGUAGE LEARNING: Current Theory and Practice**
Koskimies, K. & Paakki, J.	**AUTOMATING LANGUAGE IMPLEMENTATION**
Koster, C.H.A.	**TOP-DOWN PROGRAMMING WITH ELAN**
Last, R.	**ARTIFICIAL INTELLIGENCE TECHNIQUES IN LANGUAGE LEARNING**
Lester, C.	**A PRACTICAL APPROACH TO DATA STRUCTURES**
Lucas, R.	**DATABASE APPLICATIONS USING PROLOG**
Lucas, A.	**DESKTOP PUBLISHING**
Maddix, F.	**HUMAN–COMPUTER INTERACTION: Theory and Practice**
Maddix, F. & Morgan, G.	**SYSTEMS SOFTWARE**
Matthews, J.J.	**FORTH**
Michalewicz, Z.	**STATISTICAL AND SCIENTIFIC DATABASES**
Millington, D.	**SYSTEMS ANALYSIS AND DESIGN FOR COMPUTER APPLICATIONS**
Moseley, L.G., Sharp, J.A. & Salenieks, P.	**PASCAL IN PRACTICE**
Moylan, P.	**ASSEMBLY LANGUAGE FOR ENGINEERS**
Narayanan, A. & Sharkey, N.E.	**AN INTRODUCTION TO LISP**
Parrington, N. & Roper, M.	**UNDERSTANDING SOFTWARE TESTING**
Paterson, A.	**OFFICE SYSTEMS**
Phillips, C. & Cornelius, B.J.	**COMPUTATIONAL NUMERICAL METHODS**
Rahtz, S.P.Q.	**INFORMATION TECHNOLOGY IN THE HUMANITIES**
Ramsden, E.	**MICROCOMPUTERS IN EDUCATION 2**
Rubin, T.	**USER INTERFACE DESIGN FOR COMPUTER SYSTEMS**
Rudd, A.S.	**PRACTICAL USAGE OF ISPF DIALOG MANAGER**
Rudd, A.S.	**PRACTICAL USAGE OF REXX**
Rudd, A.S.	**IMPLEMENTING PRACTICAL DB2 APPLICATIONS**
Rudd, A.S.	**IMPLEMENTING PRACTICAL DATABASE MANAGER APPLICATIONS**
Salomon, D.	**ASSEMBLERS AND LOADERS**
de Saram, H.	**PROGRAMMING IN MICRO-PROLOG**
Savic, D.	**OBJECT-ORIENTED PROGRAMMING WITH SMALLTALK/V**
Schirmer, C.	**PROGRAMMING IN C FOR UNIX**
Schofield, C.F.	**OPTIMIZING FORTRAN PROGRAMS**
Semmens, L. & Allen, P.	**Z FOR SOFTWARE ENGINEERS**
Sharp, J.A.	**DATA FLOW COMPUTING**
Sherif, M.A.	**DATABASE PROJECTS**
Smith, J.M. & Stutely, R.	**SGML**
Späth, H.	**CLUSTER DISSECTION AND ANALYSIS**
Stein, R.	**REAL-TIME MULTICOMPUTER SOFTWARE SYSTEMS**
Teunissen, W.J. & van den Bos, J.	**3D INTERACTIVE COMPUTER GRAPHICS**
Tizzard, K.	**C FOR PROFESSIONAL PROGRAMMERS, 2nd Edition**
Tsuji, T.	**OPTIMIZING SCHEMES FOR STRUCTURED PROGRAMMING LANGUAGE PROCESSORS**
Wexler, J.	**CONCURRENT PROGRAMMING IN OCCAM 2**
Whiddett, R.J.	**CONCURRENT PROGRAMMING FOR SOFTWARE ENGINEERS**
Whiddett, R.J., Berry, R.E., Blair, G.S., Hurley, P.N., Nicol, P.J. & Muir, S.J.	**UNIX**
Xu, Duan-Zheng	**COMPUTER ANALYSIS OF SEQUENTIAL MEDICAL TRIALS**
Yannakoudakis, E.J. & Hutton, P.J.	**SPEECH SYNTHESIS AND RECOGNITION SYSTEMS**
Zech, R.	**FORTH FOR THE PROFESSIONAL**

ELLIS HORWOOD SERIES IN COMPUTER COMMUNICATIONS AND NETWORKING

Series Editor: R.J. DEASINGTON, Principal Consultant, PA Consulting Group, Edinburgh, UK

Currie, W.S.	**LANS EXPLAINED**
Chiu, Dah Ming & Sudama, Ram	**NETWORK MONITORING EXPLAINED**
Deasington, R.J.	**A PRACTICAL GUIDE TO COMPUTER COMMUNICATIONS AND NETWORKING, 2nd Edition**
Deasington, R.J.	**X.25 EXPLAINED, 2nd Edition**
Henshall, J. & Shaw, S.	**OSI EXPLAINED, 2nd Edition**
Kauffels, F.-J.	**PRACTICAL LANS ANALYSED**
Kauffels, F.-J.	**PRACTICAL NETWORKS ANALYSED**
Kauffels, F.-J.	**UNDERSTANDING DATA COMMUNICATIONS**
Muftic, S.	**SECURITY MECHANISMS FOR COMPUTER NETWORKS**